From GREECE —with— LOVE

S.L. JAMES

To order additional copies of this book, contact:
Bookwhip
1-855-339-3589
https://www.bookwhip.com

CONTENTS

Chapter 1

OPERATION SHADOW CURTAIN

The late summer sandstorm in Ankara made driving almost impossible to handle at early dawn just an hour before daylight. And the road to the isolated 2 story compound in Baglum was treacherous on the jeep's tires. Commander Christen drove in route to this seemly desolate area in an effort to meet some of his fellow agents. He had heard of a rumor going around the intelligence community of massive shipments of opium in this region of Turkey. Those rumors he thought could turn out to be valid and if by chance they were, then this operation had to be shut down quick, fast and in a hurry. From the distance he could see the compound just scarcely through the storm. He estimated that he was only about 10 minutes or less from it's outer perimeter.

And sure enough he pulls right up to the spot where he thinks he notices the door slightly open. The jeep is now within 12 feet of the back entrance.

Christen stops and parks, preparing to approach the compound with extreme caution but before he dismounts from the jeep he grabs his new P438 short assault rifle with a 4-inch silencer. And a few Mines packed with 2.5 lbs. of concentrated plastic explosives or C-4 the size of pie tarts strapped to his back vest. This P438 short assault rifle is just the type of weapon he may need for this incase something goes wrong. Also he slips around his head a pair of infrared glasses courtesy of P- department with 60MM scope built in, also the scope takes on eight times the magnification.

He'll need it for what he might discover and he gently shuts the driver side door so not to make any noise, or be heard. Walking toward the compound he takes a quick glance around area and it appears to be secluded. But the knob on the door had been tampered with. As matter of fact someone blew a hole through it. It gave him enough to be suspicious about, especially knowing he was to meet a few of his fellow agents.

Pointing directly at the inside he slowly pushed the door open to find the place been ravaged. And shockingly there laid before him three bodies riddled with bullet holes drenched in their own blood. He recognized one of the agents as SASS operative Carl Pratchett. He and Carl worked together several years before the terrorist accident at the UN Embassy in Sun City. Carl was put on disciplinary leave at one time by Admiral Manning for failing to execute target whom he fell in love with and Christen would later learn that Pratchett was bisexual. But he was still a damn good operative, and it pained him to see the guy laying there dead. He checked around the room where the others were to try and get some idea of what might have been left behind. And he struck pay dirt, under one of the slain agents body was a surveillance photo.

Christen bends down and pulls it out from under the nearest corpse, then quickly analyzed what looks like a business meeting that took place between three businessmen, but the third man in the far background was unidentifiable. What Christen will later find out is that this individual will become his newest nemesis. Sticking the photo inside his uniform he knew it was time he now leave this place and report everything he'd seen Admiral Manning. Once he returned to Pillisworth with the information regarding what, he witnessed his superiors would then take it from there. But before he even made it to the back door, there was a sound of some vehicles pulling up to the compound. He quickly glanced out the door to get clear view of who might be come in. The men dressed in commando fatigues exited their assault vehicles and rushed toward the rear entrance with weapons aimed ready to fire.

At that moment Christen races toward the front and hides himself down low behind a kitchen wall and out of sight. The assailants entered, two going straight up stairs and other checking out the bodies laying before him. Neither of them knew nor suspected that might have a intruder in their mist. After not finding whatever he came back for the first time Commando 1 joins his partners upstairs. That was the break Christen needed, with his right hand he reaches inside behind his vest compartment uniform and pulls out a explosive mine. It's has on its bottom sticking adhesive c overed by wax paper, so he tears the paper off sticking it hard to the wall behind him. Then sets the timer for 45 seconds. It would give him enough time to escape before they were aware of his presence. At that point the count down had already begun. 44, 43, 42, 41, 40.

He silently moves out the front door and races around the west side back to where he parked his jeep. 39, 38, 37, 36, 35, 34, 33, 32, 31, 30. He suddenly got the urge to sabotage their assault vehicles just in case but all he really wanted was to shot out the rear tires. 29, 28, 27, 26, 25, 24, 23, 22, 21, 20. Their transports were several yards away from his jeep, leaving him just enough time to shoot out the rear tires and get away to clear the blast. He aims and takes a few shots at the tire in high wind and it falls flat. Now he races back toward his jeep and prepares his gateway. 19, 18, 17, 16, 15, 14, 13, 12, 11, 10. Reaching the driver side door he opens it, quickly jumps in and shuts. Trying not make any noise he drives the jeep back in reverse, accelerating as fast as possible. The commandos realize that someone is attempting to escape and gave chase. 09, 08, 07, 06, 05, 04, 03, 02, 01, 00. The arrive at the base of the stairs too late approaching the back door in an effort to catch Christen.

As the first one hurries across the threshold unaware that a mine of plastic explosive was planted inside the kitchen wall, the mine detonates and it's all over at that point. The compound becomes a brief fire ball and with the storm around it feeding the fire it's instantly vaporized leaving no witnesses behind to report anything. Christen manages to get clear of the blast and heads back to his rendezvous base in Ankara, Turkey.

The photo he's found should be reported to P-Department and analyzed by the state of the art photo-scanograph and maybe those men in it will identified. Especially the one in the background too he maybe the brains behind at all. And if he is, then he Christen have a definite date with destiny. In the meantime all this excitement had him needing a much wanted vacation. He thought perhaps some place in Europe would suit him fine maybe even Geneva, Switzerland or Paris, France. Anyway he'd have to put in notice for leave of absence. Then he could make the trip over there provided no unforeseen international incident took place.

His first stop was to find the nearest foreign courier service, put the photo into a 8*11 manila envelope and address it Devarquis Exports the unofficial name for South African Intelligence or SASS (South African Secret Service). C/o P- Department and Winston Pinkheart, 4500 Mandela Pkwy, Pillisworth, South Africa. With the sand storm in Ankara dying down or he's driving out of it he notices just ¾ miles away a small out post with two vehicles parked out front of it. Surprisingly it's a courier service similar to the united postal service in the United States only this one does send parcels and packages around Eastern, Western Europe also the continent of Africa. As he approaches he observes it doesn't look too busy or business this time of day is very slow so getting in and sending off this photo shouldn't be a problem. He pulls in front of the small out post and allow the engine to idle while he grabs the surveillance photo and goes inside the office. As he suspects there are only two people working, two women dressed in traditional Islamic garb behind a counter sorting thru a pile of mail.

Christen looks around and sees to his right against the wall a variety of parcels, padded flat rates parcels and the 8*11 manila envelopes he needs. He grabs one off the wall and right away starts writing down the forwarding address in Pillisworth, South Africa. He then slips the photo into the envelope with a brief note for Winston in P-Department and Admiral Manning then seals it shut before paying the shipping fee. He hands it to one of the clerks who then weighs the parcel, stamps it express and he whips a out a charge card. She swipes his card while at the same time preparing the envelope for shipping in the receiving pile or basket and hands him his receipt. It's done! He figures it will take almost 15 days or less to reach the office while he's on Vacation or taking his leave of absence in Geneva, Switzerland. Christen now prepares for his trip to Switzerland and races back to the motel in midtown Ankara, Turkey where his luggage waits to be repacked and he's off to the airport to catch his flight. He uses the motels cordless phone to make his call for a local taxi company and fortunately for him there's one just a few street blocks away. After requesting a pickup and giving his location he grabs his case and luggage while making his way outside to the curb in front of the motel lobby and just waits till the car pulls up.

It doesn't take long before a greenish yellow taxi cab arrives in front of him and the driver pops the back trunk. Christen quickly places his luggage in the button and slams it in one motion. He races around to the right passenger door and jumps in the seat slamming it closed when the drivers pulls off. The driver gives him a look throw the rear view mirror then asks where to sir?

"Ankara International thank you, asap!" Christen replies reaching into his right suit pocket for his wallet pouch, he unzips it and pulls out 40 bills in euros handing it to the cab driver thru a glass window the size of a small bowl. And lucky for him the airport was just 13 and ¼ miles from his motel leaving him plenty of time to rest while his driver broke every traffic law getting him to his destination. A sense of survivor guilt came of Christen as he was just minutes, minutes from the massacre at the compound just before he arrived and no way of knowing who was responsible and why? He kept thinking to himself, telling himself it comes with the territory, occupational hazard but this time its personal, and the bastards who did this will pay dearly like those fools back at the compound.

The photo scanograph will extract that information digging thru every criminal retina scan or most wanted list on the planet. Every government agency has one even if they don't care to share, nonetheless Christen didn't care he needed some rest and relaxation and Geneva, Switzerland was the idea place to go getting off the grid for a while. The taxi cab pulled up to the outer parking lot of this airport with a red flag and white crescent waving, representing Islam he figured. The driver made a left turn at the intersection, the traffic light was yellow and took the arrow pointing toward Swiss-Air lines practically went all the way around the parking lot, Then stopped half a quarter mile to the run way. Christen really doesn't pay any attention to the direction or even how close he is to the boarding gate. But he figures the driver knows this route or this isn't the first or last time he's driven passengers to this Airport parking lot.

The car final pulls up to Swiss International Air lines terminal, pops the trunk, Christen opens the door and climbs out the back seat to the rear and without breaking stride he snatches the case by the handle and hoists it out the boot of the trunk and doesn't slam it. At this point he proceeds from the lobby curb to the inside of the airport and finds the boarding line and gate fast not wasting any time. To his surprise their aren't a lot of people waiting to board like most airlines and this has the women behind the counter wearing the funny Islamic garb around their shoulders and head. He places his luggage case on this revolving conveyor belt in between gates 15 and 16 boarding for Geneva, Switzerland.

And takes his place in the line only behind 7 other people just like he thought this isn't a busy airline or business travel was very slow this time of year. He looks to his left and right observing which side is moving the quickest, the fastest.

Who's getting these people processed and right away to board the plane? And to his surprise again he's only behind 2 people nice, they work very quick and very efficient here in Ankara Airport. Just one more person ahead of him and his opportunity finally comes he steps forward to the counter while reaching into his suit pocket for his case wallet and pulls out his master card, also his passport and engages the clerk.

"One way first class ticket if it's still available?" he asks her. "And where to sir?" she replies waiting for more details. "Oh my, pardon me, Geneva, Switzerland, one way, first class thank you!" again he says as she working the keys and mouse, he hears constant click, click. He places his credit card and passport on the counter as she grabs the card and passport to verify his identification he hears more clicks then she says,

"We have three seats available Mr. Christen in first class and each for $1875.50 with meals served in preflight." She replies again while this time the machine spits out the tickets one after the other and four together in all. She hands him the tickets and receipt while he watches his luggage taken to the cargo loading area where the plane is parked at terminal gate 17.

"We have three seats available Mr. Christen in first Class, sir here are your tickets, enjoy your flight." She replies while she folds the tickets, placing them in an Swiss airline envelope after she hands him back his passport and credit card. Both the card goes back into his wallet case and the passport inside his right suit pocket. He walks quickly over to the boarding line where the 3 people who were in front of him have already moved into the Jet bridge about to board the Boeing 747 bound for Geneva, Switzerland. The Jet bridge gate takes him directly into the

Boeing 757's aircraft cabin where to his left is the aviation galley or flight kitchen and next to that was first class or travel class seating area. So he moves past the flight kitchen and into the travel class cabin where its 12 seats in 3 rows left to right are vacant, and the one he has is row 2 next to the window. He takes his seat and pulls the seat belt strap around his waist, he attaches both and hear a 'click' sound, he can hear other people in the back ground boarding as well but none have joined him yet.

He closes his eyes calming himself until he finally feels a jerk from the plane as if the luggage and food was completely loaded and they are ready for takeoff. He hears a few more people coming in and he's joined by two more passengers before the pilots enter the planes business first class area going straight into the cock pit then shut the door.

The afternoon in downtown Geneva seemed to last so long and the merchants along Canton St, were having a block sell, all for all their merchandise went for 45% to 75% off retail. To residents of this district that was a plus also they'd been hoping for something like this for a long time. Up in a room on the second floor motel was James Christen dressed in a white muscle shirt with grey khaki shirts to match, seated by a window while surfing the internet, with a lap top notebook he borrowed from the motel general manager. Christen always did a little investigating of his own on the World wide web. He was requesting some information through Europol's online networks.

And nothing came up worth any use to him except a real unusually funny looking e-mail message, one he'd never seen like this before. It was of two people, man and woman dressed in wedding attire. Someone had sent him an invitation and at the bottom it was addressed Y. Tarken in Athens.

Chapter 2

THE WEDDING INVITE

He thought to himself this is very strange and he normally didn't get that type of e-mail at all from the Chief of Staff. Unless it was something important or just a memo passed from him via Admiral Manning. This most have been a major occasion he figured and so he typed in a message to reply back to the Chief of Staff that he would be honored to attend it. And that he'd get there as soon it was possible for him to do so. After sending that back to Tarken, he then went to the web site Swiss- air.com to book himself a online ticket so he could pick it up at the airport once he arrived there. He always buys the first class tickets, probably because he really wouldn't have it any other way. Besides chartering a private jet was too costly unless it was at the expense of the government of South Africa and the bean counters would never sign off on that. Also he wouldn't use one of those unless someone else invited him on a special flight somewhere exotic. On the web site he was given a choice of what to eat and drink on the flight to Athens, Greece. And his favorite beverage consisted of a Schnapps' Martini with Mint Cinnamon on the rocks, stirred not shaken, or peppermint Schnapps with a little cinnamon to take off the edge.

Theirs something about the taste of it that appealed to him so much and after specifying what he wanted to order on the menu to eat, he sent all the information over the internet to the computer terminal at the airport. It was now time to turn it off then with his index finger he stroked the arrow up to the icon that marked file and double tapped it. It showed a long list of options but an exit was what he was looking for. He tapped it and went back to the original start screen and hit the start icon he hit the shutdown sign, at that point the screen went totally black. He folded it closed and proceeded to pull out the

Ethernet and telephone cords and wires connected to the jack and USB connection. The notebook computer he was using happened to be a Intel Pentium 3 with MMX Technology 933 Mhz. he borrowed it, or actually it was given to him for personal use by the motel office manager. Christen packed the machine, its cords and wire connections in a case and took it all back down stairs to the first floor office which was the first door to his left. Afterward he'd have to call a taxi to take to the airport.

Before he entered, first he knew he had to knock.

But then the lady seated behind the office counter was talking on the phone, so might not have noticed him knocking. As he knocked three times, she signaled for him to come in. That was his hint to enter the office her glance at him was like a beam pierce straight through a wall. She was sexy brunette with short, very groomed hair. Her eyes were like a distinct turquoise, greenish color. He'd never seen a gorgeous woman with eyes like that before. Not to mention a European. He stopped at the desk placing the case in front of her.

"May I help you with something?" She asked him in deep, sexy Swiss voice.

"Yes, I'm here to return this to the Office Manager. Could you see to it that he gets this please?" His eyes met hers after he put the case on the counter.

"Well, if you'd care to wait, he'll be arriving soon, in fact he should be here any second now." And how right she was, the man just walked out of a jewelry shop next door to the motel office. Spotting Christen inside talking to his secretary. Before James could walk out the Office Manager met him at the door.

"Mr. Christen good afternoon. I hope the room was to your satisfaction?" he asked him with a smile.

"Yes, Peter thanks. I've brought you back your notebook computer over." Christen vaguely gestured at the case on the desk in front of his secretary.

"I'm leaving in the next 20 minutes so I thought id better bring down your notebook pc with me before I go."

"You're leaving, Mr. Christen?" Peter asked with a bewildered look on his face.

"Yes, something's come up so I have to fly to Athens, Greece. However, I'd like you to send one of your various Swiss souvenirs and here's my address in Pillisworth, Africa where you can send it." He writes the information down in front of him. The man picked up the note and analyzes the address very carefully.

"This is the address in which to send the package to you then?" he asks.

"Correct Pete. My upstairs neighbor will pick up the package for me until I return to Pillisworth." And after hearing this the man's face is now one of absolute amusement and perplexity.

"You have a nice neighbor Mr. Christen." Pete replied.

"Yeah well, I helped her out of a government jam so she owes me."

"It sounds like an interesting arrangement you have James!"

"Yes, indeed. Anyway I most bid you farewell, the time is rapidly ticking away, Pete thanks again." He walks toward the door and heads right back up stairs to the motel room. The door is slightly opened so pushed it and it swung open with just enough grace so that it didn't slam back. Sitting on the sofa next to a table was his long fold over his suit case, and all most everything was already packed so all he has to do is take off his suit strap on his shoulder holster with gun in it.

Which he does very quickly. All in one motion he grabs the case, and dashes back out door, and down the stairs to the outside lobby where the taxi pulls right up to the motel curb. The driver pops open the back trunk.

Christen walks around to the back and throws his luggage in the trunk as the driver observes his movement and prepares to begin sitting his fare meter. Christen enters the car's back behind the driver and closes the door.

"Where to sir?" the asked while peering through his hear view mirror on the windshield.

"Swiss International ASAP, thank you." Says Christen

The sped away from the curb and out into traffic in route to the airport. Christen noticed all the merchants seemed ready to close shop while the car drive by. He kind of hoped he could do a little shopping, but that would have to wait perhaps until he arrived in Athens. Besides the airport was just 15 minutes from the motel where is was staying.

He knew though he'd have to phone Tarken that he was on his way there or at least call him once he the plane reached a certain altitude. Christen peered out the window staring at all the buildings all lined up facing in the direction of Lake Geneva. As if they were all kind of just paying homage to it and he marveled at their architectural design, it must have taken years to construct them. Or more like decades!

Staring right up the street he could see the parking lot to the airport facing him. It wouldn't be long till we was boarding that plane to Athens, Greece. The driver made a left turn at the light proceeded around the front intersection just about 15 yards from the airport parking lot. When his plane first arrived in Geneva a few weeks ago, it was in the early morning at least 3:35am and dark. So he really ha no way of knowing where the taxi was going, but of course the driver knew though. While he kept trying to remember more about the route, the taxi driver pulled right up in front of the airport lobby. Christen reached in his suit pocket pulling out a money clip of $20 and $50 euros. He passes a bill of $20 over the seat to the driver as a tip. Then opens the back door to exit, while the driver popped the car trunk and after reaching in and snatching out his luggage he slams it shut and taxi drives off. Carrying his luggage, he continues through the front of the lobby and straight to the nearest check in counter.

Right above it is five screens displaying arrivals and departures also he quickly realized the reservation in which his flight to Athens was booked from the motel to be 10:45 am. I front of him were several people already getting their tickets.

So naturally he followed quickly behind the last person in line and lucky for him that individual was the fourth one. He figured he's get his ticket, and still have a little time to kill before he had to board the 737 for his flight. The woman behind the counter seemed efficient at checking every ticket that she handled. It wasn't long before Christen found himself in her presence. She had short sandy blonde hair cut just above the neck, it was styled to look wet, like as if before she came out to work she dipped her head in a sink full of water and then brushed it all back or something. Her eyes were a gleaming emerald green color like which he'd never seen in long time. As he walked forward to approach her, she gave him the most peculiar stare.

"I have a reservation in first class." He told her while taking out his wallet.

"Ok, sir, will that be cash or credit?" she asked. He pulled the master card from his wallet and handed it to her.

"Credit MasterCard!" He replied. She took it, typing in the numbers on her computers. Within seconds the machine next to her printed out several stubs of tickets. She then tore off the last one, folded all five and placed them neatly in an envelope for him. She handed it back to him with a smile.

"Thanks, very much." He told her. Walking away toward the boarding ramp he placed the envelope back in his suit pocket and his wallet in his right pants pocket but could almost feel the woman staring at him or maybe it was his imagination. The ramp walk way led him straight into the food compartment of the plane where he sharp left turn and wound up in the middle section. According to the ticket his reserved seat was B3. The section of the plane he was in happened to be C, so his seat was close. He counted every other third row before he finally reached the end and the second compartment started at the point with the first front row of seats marked B. Scanning closely from right to left, his reserved seat was right behind that of a business executive.

Christen made his way to the spot placing his suit atop the small open compartment right above his head. Sitting he took in a sigh of relief laying his head back against the head rest connected to the chair. A seat in front of him had a phone in its back and slot marked credit or debit. Obliviously it didn't matter whether he had a visa, Master Card, or America Express it would get charged anyway. He figured he'd have to wait until he was close to Athens, before he called Tarken about meeting him at the airport that way he could be introduced to his old college friend and possible his children as well. Christen looked up and saw the flight attendant from a far closing the planes slide door shut. That suggested to him the plane would be in the process of taking off, sure enough over the speaker was the voice one of the pilots giving off quite a thick euro accent.

"Good afternoon ladies and gentlemen. I'm your pilot Captain. Jurgoes Steed. Our destination is Athens, Greece and the scheduled arrival is precisely 3:45 pm. Uh, we have been cleared to taxi so if the flight attendants will take their seats, we'll be on our way and You will be instructed to remain in your seats until we have reached the appropriate altitude.

Your cooperation is most appreciated, thanks for flying Swiss airlines."

After the short preflight briefing from the pilot, Christen figured he'd only have 2 hours and 38 minutes to rest up before he reached his destination. Once he was sure the 737 jet was close to Athens he'd make the call then wait for them to meet him at the airport. It was all the time Tarken would need to prepare to meet Christen at the airport. Until that occasion James decided to order one of his favorite beverage a Schnapps Martini with mint cinnamon on the rocks. It had been awhile since he enjoyed that taste and right about now the urge for him was too great to ignore. He peeked down the aisle looking out for the flight attendant who just happened to be coming back down the aisle toward him. Christen gestured for her to approach him. She strode through the lanes with the grace of a fashion model on the runway. He was impressed with her body language, and her enthusiasm with the job. As she got closer to his seat, he felt the plane begin to move then she was standing right over him.

"Miss, I'd like to order a beverage now if I may?" He asked her.

"Sir we won't begin serving until after we've taken off, ok? She responded.

"Fair enough! Thank you." He told her with a gracious grin on his face.

Christen turned to look out the window and saw the 737 making its reverse turns backward until it was in the take off position. At that point the plane jolted forward and began to pick up speed and the feeling, sound of acceleration, the turbines getting louder came over him whenever the plane was in the process of taking off. He laid his head back while peering out the window to view the 737 ascend into the air, as it climbed higher and higher the ground below just seemed to disappear. Suddenly the plane soared into the clouds above Switzerland, vanishing in their thickness. It often amazed Christen how clouds could so effectively camouflage airplane as well. This was a phenomenon he would ponder a little more. Another airplane attendant came down the aisle once again, this time with all sorts of goodies. She stopped right next to Christen spot, he didn't even realize it until he turned and stared up at her. But this wasn't the one as before, she had red hair with beautiful emerald green eyes. The peach lip stick she wore matched the titillating freckles on her face. And the dimples in her cheeks made her bright smile look even more sexy.

She pushed the metal cart alongside Christens seat preparing to pour him a beverage. However only he knew what he enjoyed drinking and before she begin to take out glass and can of soda he hit her with his order.

"Excuse me!" He began to ask her.

"I'd like to order a Schnapps martini with mint cinnamon on the rocks please. Thank you." She nodded to him ok, so he could only guess that she would have it when she came back. That was good enough for him anyway, he waited until now so a few more minutes wouldn't hurt him. But surprisingly enough she had some of wanted anyway, that is as far as the schnapps go. The other stuff might take a little more time. He noticed the name tag on the airline attendant's shirt was Melanie, she looked like a Melanie. He started to wonder with just how many other Melanie's there were in the world with red hair. It was something about a gorgeous woman with red hair and sensuous curves that he found extremely sexy. She returned with glass of his favorite drink in it. As she handed to him. He felt the coolness of the glass. He used the straw to stir it several times before taking a sip.

The taste of it to him was like a cool sweet liquid breeze flowing down his throat. He was surprised the schnapps martini was served just right. Perhaps the airline attendant knew how to make the drink or had been shown sometime before. Christen was sure that the school of Bartending taught people how to make a wide range of alcoholic beverages. Maybe this woman was taught the art of mixing drinks during flight school. That's always a remote possibility he thought to himself. He started taking even more gulps of the alcohol to the point where it put him in a state of relaxation. He laid his head against the chair contemplating how soon or when they would arrive at the Athens airport. Maybe is he made a quick call using the number Tarken gave him on the e-mail message he sent him, he could be at the airport waiting once the plane landed. Feeling himself getting somewhat sleepy and little drowsy he took out his wallet with gold Euro American Express credit card in it.

Slipping the card in the slot marked debit/or credit, he then shut the shot closed snapping the phone out with left hand and begin to make the call. With dial tone normal the phone rang for a few seconds than someone with a sexy youthful voice answered.

"Hello, Mathias residence." The voice said. Noticing it and wondering who it might belong to Christen responded with utter curiosity.

"Yes, may I speak with Mr. Tarken please? Thank you." He Asked. The young lady on the other line seemed miffed at the request but than reality had set in and it had to be their guest this person was referring to. Christen waited patiently for his friend to answer the phone then finally that familiar voice came on.

"Yes, Tarken here." He answered.

"Yusaf, it's James." Christen replied.

"James, hey man where are you right now?" Yusaf asked him in fit of excitement.

"About an hour and twenty minutes from Athens airport terminal. We're supposed to arrive there very shortly. How far are you from the airport?" He asked gauging just how long it would take Tarken to get there.

"Not far all at all, as a matter of fact I'll call the airport to find out for sure when your ETA is, and we'll be there to greet you when you arrive." He told him.

"We?" Christen asked.

"Yes, of course. Myself and a old friend of mine the grooms father." Tarken replied almost wondering why he asked.

"All right, I'll see you once I've landed. Take care." Tarken hung up the phone and christen placed his back in the compartment then opened the slot to take his credit card out. He would have roughly a little time to rest up before the plane landed and he could prepare to meet Tarken and his friends. Christen had traveled to many places but never the opportunity to see up close and personal Athens, Greece. Also there was so much he'd read about it in South African Navel College during his leisure time and studies, the idea of walking the streets of Greece really freaked him out. As he peeked out the window their was nothing but some clouds and what looked like Serbia and Kosovo or what is known as the Balkans. He's recollection took him back to the Bosnian War in the early 90's. this was the route planes would travel to Greece.

Now just the thought of taking a nab was pointless considering once he got too comfortable the 737 would be pulling into the airport terminal for refueling and boarding new passengers. After half hour passed 3pm the Captain announces they are flying over Albania and into Greece airspace. Now it would be only a matter of time before they landed at the airport terminal and docked so he could prepare for his long awaited meeting with Tarken and his friend and old college class mate Gorgan Manolis Mathias. James closed his eyes and tried his best to rest his body or at least get a 15 to 20 minute nab while the Swiss International 737 continued to make its descent toward Athens International Airport.

He started day dreaming right away about all the stories and plays he'd read on Greek Mythology while attending the South African Navy Academy before his recruitment in South African Intelligence. He felt something or someone poking his arm to get his attention as he opened his eyes and low and behold the plane was in the airport terminal already 3/4 empty. It was the same flight attendant who served him.

"Sir excuse me but we have landed at the terminal and you must leave, please." She asks him.

"Omg! I must have dozed off, but thanks, thank you miss I'll get my things." He tells her.

He grabs his suit jacket after she leaves, stands up and quickly puts it on while he starts out the first class compartment of the plane and straight to the kitchen galley, where the plane exit to the terminal begins. As he walks through it's like the same scenario he'd gone thru before he walked into what appeared to be something like a white cocoon linking him straight into gate 09. The whole place was packed with tourist everywhere considering everyone's wearing or carrying fancy looking cameras of every sort. Christen rushed toward the luggage claim area which was just too his far right, it looked to be built around an arcade or something he thought the structure was very foreign to him. He'd never seen anything like it before especially in the middle of an airport this size.

Christen made his way through the crowd and toward the revolving conveyor belt to see a long line of luggage facing some forty to fifty people. A few of them began grabbing their things as they came around but he didn't yet notice whether his was in the same revolving pile. The closer he tried to get to the belt making his way through the crowd, from a short distance he saw his luggage among others revolving in his direction. Christen had his right hand poised, and ready to snatch the case off and when the opportunity presented itself he went for it. Another individual standing beside him also readied himself to do the same. Christen moved fast, his hands striking out like a cobra, he established a firm grip, then hoisted the case off conveyor belt. The man next to him didn't move fast enough and missed his turn. It was at that point Christen thought to himself, those self-defense classes sure came in handy right there.

Chapter 3

GORGAN AND TARKEN

He made his way back through the small crowd of people to look for the front lobby where he would meet Tarken and his Greek friends. Before he even got half way past the shops, bars, and the men's restrooms, they all appeared there right before him. Yusaf was dressed in his usual conservative fashion, Beige pleated trousers with cotton white button down shirt. The suit too was beige and his belt a had certain burgundy color to it and the shoes matched the Beige trousers. The people standing next to him however were unfamiliar to Christen, the much older gentleman and young lady at this his side were apparently related to each other. He approached them, Tarken gave him a smile, then began to gesture and introduce Christen to his friends.

"James Christen, allow me to introduce you to my old college friend, Gorgan Manolis Mathias." Gorgan resembled the typical millionaire recluse. He carried the aura of a man very charismatic, cagey and dangerous, yet witty in a dark morbid sense. He stood a little under 6 feet 2 inches tall and wasn't built or didn't present himself as a muscle bound alpha male but kind of just a nerdy account type or fancy dressing white collar executive. With a short man hair style for a guy in his late 50's.

"And this is his beautiful daughter Andromeda." She was exactly as he said, beautiful. But he would have preferred gorgeous as a better description. She had the most divine creamy dark butter complexion he'd never seen in a young woman. Her skin looked to be a smooth and delicate as a baby's bottom and while she was darker complexion than her father, Andromeda had his lips light blue eyes, hers were mixed with hazel. And she inherited his lips for sure. Andromeda appeared to be in her mid-twenties, but Christen wouldn't inquire about that until a more appropriate time. Christen glanced at Andromeda with a nod of the head saying, "how do you do?"

This was one of those rare occasions that anyone had ever addressed her that way. He made her feel somewhat like royalty, fore she almost was.

"I'm good, nice to meet you." She told him with a curious grin on her face. Tarken couldn't help but notice their was something happening there between Christen and Andromeda, Gorgan noticed it too, but tried to ignore it.

Mr. Christen, if you'd follow us please, the car is Waiting?" Gorgan asked.

"But of course, thank you." Christen replied. The four of them walked out toward the lobby entrance/exit where a limousine and driver sat there waiting for them. The moment Christen, Tarken, Gorgan and his daughter approached the limo the driver quickly pops the trunk. Christen makes his move around the back, placing his luggage in the back bottom of the trunk and he slams it shut in one motion. Afterward he proceeds to the to enter the left passenger side with the vacationing SASS Chief of Staff Tarken. As Andromeda quickly enters and Gorgan shut the right side passenger door behind him, the driver pulls away from the lobby curb and into traffic. Christen couldn't help but notice that inside of Gorgan limousine was immaculate. There was a wet bar just several inches from Gorgan left leg, and besides it appeared to be a small TV DVD with VCR built in. On the TV there looked like a presidential inaugural taking place somewhere in South Africa.

Christen would have to get the full details about that either from Currency, or Winston once he got settled in and relaxed. He knows they will use the covert channel scrambler on the office line to protect the call. So, he needn't worry about anyone eaves dropping on his conversations during his stay at Gorgans estate. The host began sensing the ride was turning uncomfortably quiet so Gorgan decided to get some dialogue going.

"So, Mr. Christen is this your first time in Athens, Greece?" Christen pondered the question before answering.

"Actually, I visited here before but I was a very young lad and I'm sure much has changed here since then." Gorgan studied his facial expression while he was answering the question almost as if hoping to catch him in a lie or something.

"I've live here since the mid-seventies, in fact I made Athens my home directly after graduating from college back in 73. I got a job working for a Greek businessman named Onassis." That name sent shock waves through Christen. "Your referring to Aristotle Onassis?" he wonders again.

"Yes, the shipping magnate, this was of course the same period he was involved with Jacqueline Kennedy, widow of the late JFK." Fascinating, Christen thought to himself.

"So, what have to you been doing since now? Christen asked out of pure curiosity.

"Now I make a good living selling art, in fact I own a gallery not far from my estate. Perhaps before you leave I will get the opportunity to show you around?" Gorgan asks him. This is something he can't possibly pass up, and he might even have a chance to buy some items and send them back to Pillisworth.

"I'd like that very much Mr. Mathais." Gorgan had taken a liking to Christen the moment they met back at the airport. So calling him by his last name was way too formal.

"Please, James call me Gorgan." He requested with a smile.

"Ok, sure." Christen replied nodding. Tarken quietly observes these two up till that point and decides it time for him to get some dialogue going with Gorgan.

"Gorgan and I spent summers here in the past before we split up and pursued our separate our careers, so being back here brings back a lot of memories for both of us. Yusaf and Gorgan both exchange smiles to one another, when they notice they very close to home. Just up the street ahead was a tall gate surrounding what looked like a mansion. This neighborhood in the Lycurgus District, yes named after the Late 1800 Greek American Businessman, resembled something out of the lifestyles of the Rich and Famous as far as wealth went. The limo pulled up to the entrance of Magnolis Estates and Magnolis Drive, before the car makes a right turn into the drive way the gate swings open full like it program for detection.

Just a across from the Mathias estate was the home of another Greek businessman and his mansion was about the same size as Gorgans or so it appeared. Before the limousine pulled up the entrance, a gate swung open and on the it was a round large oval shaped plate that read Mathias Manor.

The driver must have known just when to pull in because the gate started to close as he drove around the front water fountain. The drive way led them in front of the mansion where a butler stood at the entrance. The limousine pulled in under three columns and stopped directly in front of where the butler stood waiting. Gorgan exited the limo first, then Andromeda, Yusaf, and Christen followed after him. The trunk came open revealing his luggage to the butler who immediately approached the trunk to remove it.

"Mr. Christen, my butler Lupredo will take the luggage up to your sleeping quarters, for now if there's anything else you need my daughter will assist you." Gorgan told him with complete affirmation. But before he had chance to leave for his personal library Christen managed to get off a quick question concerning his son.

"Excuse me Gorgan, where's the groom?" Christen asks.

The question kind of threw Gorgan a little, fore he didn't usually disclose his children's personal business. But in this case Christen was a guest and most likely wanted to meet his son. So, the request was justified.

"He went out to do some last-minute shopping for his bride Mellisa. He should return shortly so you two will have plenty of time to meet and talk." With that, Gorgan quickly proceeds to his private study located just off to the west end of the estate.

The floors, ceiling, furniture, curtains, everything blends with Greek culture. Andromeda takes Christen up the stairs which leads up three floors then stop at the attic. They reach the first floor and make a sharp turn down the west corridor.

Facing four rooms on one side and four rooms on the other, she takes him to the second one on the right side.

"Here's your room Mr. Christen." She said as she opens the door and ever so curious Christen walks in and looks around.

The bed sat located right in the middle of the room, while to his right was a beige drawer sitting next to a mahogany table with a cream lamp on it. Also, hanging from the ceiling over the bed was beautiful cream chandelier and he noticed the closet happened to be walk in suited for a king. Its space had enough room for about 200 suits, 150 pants, 185 shirts, plus 8 dozen pairs of shoes. It was more than a closet for him a she stepped inside to take a peak, the moment he opened it, a fluorescent built in the ceiling to look like a disco light illuminated the closet. It also contained a six*five mirror, so he could watch himself dress in his suits and shoes at the same time. When he turned to back out the closet to inspect the bed he noticed a phone, just to over the right of its post. Once he got himself settled in and rested, he could phone the intelligence office using their channel scrambler. Plus, he had to report back there anyway and get that information regarding the surveillance photo he found in Ankara desert in Turkey.

"The room's perfect, and thank you for being most hospitable." He told Andromeda with a gracious smile.

"Your very welcome Mr. Christen, and I hope you'll enjoy your stay here. Well if you'll excuse me?" he quickly interrupted her before she could make the exit.

"You leaving so soon?" he asked her. She wanted to stay and chat more with him, however she knew her father wouldn't approve of it.

"Yes, I have many arrangements of my own to see before my brothers wedding, so perhaps we can talk again on another occasion?" That he thought to himself would suit him ok, sure all right.

"Till the next time then, Andromeda." He bid her good-bye with a nod of head and kind gesture with his right hand. She left out room and didn't even bother to close the behind her. still he'd wait until he knew she was gone before he made his call. He walked slowly toward the door cautiously peaking his head out to take a quick look. Peering down both sides of the corridor, it was apparent to him that she just disappeared.

However, Christen wasn't aware that all the rooms in the estate we're being monitored via digital camera. This Gorgan Manolis Mathias is a particularly paranoid individual.

But what would make such a man this damn peculiar and in any case Christen gently closed the door and rushed over to the phone to make his call. It was exactly 4:30 PM in the afternoon Athens time and he figured the SASS office was open. He picked up the phone and began pushing in the covert numbers. The line has a dial tone for a few seconds then click, some picked up. It was good old Nickel Currency.

"Hello, Darvarqius Exports Nickel Currency speaking." Darvarqius was proclaimed the new covert name for SASS by the ANC, giving it kind of a more corporate appeal to it's Intelligence allies.

"Currency, good afternoon it's Christen." He told her. Now every time she heard his voice over the phone she got animated and excited.

"James, how is it in Geneva?" She asked him almost anticipating explicit details.

"Actually, I'm in Athens right at this moment. Bye, the way Currency use the scrambler channel U9 I'm not calling from a secure line right now." While she switched the com line over to scrambler he knew it wouldn't take her long to figure out why he was there.

"Tarken invited you to his friend's son's wedding? How nice.

"So, what's the weather like there right now?" She asked.

"It's rather Luke warm and little windy." He replied with a smirk.

"I gather you didn't call to talk about the weather, did you?" She asked him.

"No, actually I managed to catch a glimpse of the Inauguration back in South Africa via satellite TV. When was Mbeki sworn in? he asked.

"Just a few hours ago, with hundreds of on lookers, and a half dozen heads of state observing. Including Muammar Gadhafi of Libya, PLO Chairman Arafat, UN Secretary General Annan." After that piece of information was disclosed it was time for more important stuff.

"Currency, I need an update on that photo I sent to P-Department and what information did Winston manage to extract from the Photo-scanograph?"

He wondered out loud, she wheeled her chair over to the digital filing cabinet system they have on computer. Scrolling down to the file marked P. She pushed a button on the key board to transfer it data to her pc at her desk. The file came up with a long list of everything on it including the dossiers of both men in the photo. She clicked the print icon on her screen and everything came out very quickly. Currency began checking out the file in front of her, it revealed the surveillance photo and the other documents provided via their Interpol sources.

"James, I'm looking at the picture now, the two men are identified as one Tisdale Minolta and the others is Mikhail Bahrain Khrichov." Those names meant nothing to him but he had to have information about the two men.

"Currently, what more do you have on this Minolta fellow?" He asked with a degree of concern and she began reading off the Intel on Menolta.

"James, he's in his mid to late fifties. He's a Danish arms dealer with numerous connections in France, Italy, and Austria. He's also wanted by the C.I.A., and S.V.R the new K.G.B in connection with the murders of at least a dozen or more double agents. James this guy's dossier reads almost like a novel." Christen processes all this information is his head.

"Ok, new what about this Khrichov character what's his story?" He wondered. She started to read off his dossier as well.

"All right, and here's Khrichhov another guy in his late Fifties, a former spook with the K.G.B. He served as a double agent back in Moscow up until the mid-late eighties. He turned into a freelance agent back in 1991 after leaving the K.G.B. He made millions trading in foreign currencies and founded some mining companies in Liberia and Sierra Leone. He invested his fortune in various off shore companies, oil, gambling enterprises, then he started a smuggling operation with another businessmen.

However our sources weren't able to provide us with information on who that individual is. As for the person in background Winston's still working on that one." Christen now has a mental picture of who he's up against and what he must do, or does he?

The real enemy hasn't been identified and remains anonymous. He has no choice now but just wait for an answer to present itself and he's sure it will.

"Thanks again, Currency, I'll get back in contact with you in a few days." Nickel closes the screen and begins updating the data memory for future reference.

"Your very welcome, James. Enjoy the wedding." She clicks off the channel scrambler and hangs up the phone, while Christen does the same in his end. He now has lot to mediate on. He climbs off the bed and walks over near the door to grab his luggage and starts to unpack his clothes.

He sets the case on the bed, opens it up, and begins to unzip it from one side to the other. Peeling off the cover he unpacks his suits, shirts, ties, socks, and three pairs of shoes. At the very button of luggage case is his personal folding toiletry bag. Containing all the usual hygienic stuff and other special effects including deodorants, toothpaste, mouthwash, and things of that nature.

Before preparing to move his bag of toiletry to the bathroom connected to the walk-in closet, he starts to hang all the clothes he packed for the trip in the walk-in closet. There was an abundance of clothes hangers so he didn't worry about not having brought enough, he grabbed the case off the bed to carry it into the closet, and began placing the ties, and last but least his suits. He only had three pairs of shoes and everything matched. Whenever he traveled abroad he liked to wear dark colors, sometimes light colors too, but shades of blue, navy blue and brown are his personal favorites. This time however, he packed several light blue suits, European style along with three Beige single breast Armoni suits all with slim lapels. Even the shoes he wore reflected his mood. On this trip however, he had a pair of black Stay Adams. While he continued to place the shoes under his hung clothes, someone knocked at the bedroom door. Christen walked out closet to meet whomever it was.

"Who is it?" He asked.

"Perseus, Mr. Christen. May I come in? Or are you not dressed? He wondered standing by the door. To Christen surprise it was the groom to be.

"Do come in, come in, Welcome." He told the young man.

Perseus opened the door, to reveal James Christen standing near the edge of the bed waiting to greet him with a grin. Leaving the door wide open he approached the unsuspecting spy to shake his hand for the first time.

"I'm Perseus Mathias, the groom to be, of which I'm sure you've already heard?" he said that with seemly reserved optimism.

"James Christen, South African Intelligence and a friend and colleague of Tarken." Christen replied while shaking hands with Perseus.

"And you've already met my father and sister?" he asked.

"Why yes, Gorgan and the lovely Andromeda. She seems like quite a spirited young woman?" Christen told him as he observed her demeanor and physical attributes.

"Yeah well, she gets that from her mother. We hmm, have different parents."

Christen wasn't expecting this kind of straight forward dialogue from Perseus, and he is kind of talking aback by it.

"Her mother was a Jamaican." Perseus tell him.

"Was?" Christen asked.

"Her name was Nona. She got sick and Doctor diagnosed her with having full blown cancer in her left breast when Andromeda was 3 years old. She died of the disease five years later when Andromeda was 8, and so my father raised her ever since." He told him.

That explains why she's kind of quiet around James, like she's waiting for something to happen or maybe he's just reading to much into it.

"Your sister's very an attractive young woman Perseus. She must be have got that from her mother?"

He asked the question baiting the young man to see what other information he might be willing to disclose. Perseus nodded his head cunningly with sly smirk.

"She certainly has her moments, that's for sure." He says. not confirming it, but not denying it either.

"So how's the bride doing right about now?" Christen wondered. Perseus didn't seem to be there mentally, in fact it was like he kind of drifted off into space then quite a toll on him, Christen thought.

"She's happy about it. I think she'll adjust to it better after the honeymoon." He tells him with a straight face.

"Look, I have to get back down stairs and see my father, it's been a pleasure meeting you Mr. Christen." He says to James. Gesturing with his right hand. Christen nodded his head in agreement with the young man.

"We will see each other again before, and after the wedding." James replies. Perseus turns to leave the room and out the door toward the stairs. Christen is left with a rather amused impression of Gorgans oldest and only son, least as far as he knows for sure. As Christen walked back over to the closet he remembers that he still hasn't taken off his shoulder holster with gun in it. He was surprised no one even noticed it, or maybe they did but, were too afraid or embarrassed to say anything. He took off his suit and hung it in the oldest, then unstrapped the holster from his shoulder with the gun and hide it in one of his other suits. He wouldn't need it there, at least he didn't think he would. He'd have to check the guns safety catch and clips later that evening before he went to bed. In any case the phone started to ring so without hesitation he answered it.

"Mathais, residence." He picking up the cordless phone.

"Mr. Christen, it's Gorgan. My house keeper has made us a late brunch, so if you're hungry come down and eat?" that was music to his ears, food!

"Excellent, I'll be down in a minute." Christen told him hanging up the phone. Gorgan was either calling him from the kitchen or his personal library, either way, he thought this mansion was so big, and had so many rooms and floors you had to have them all connected by phone line. In order to contact whom ever was staying there, without having to leave a particular room to see them for something. That's also very convenient, now he hoped the housekeeper was a good cook? Before he left the room, he thought back about the conversation he'd had with Currency a little earlier. He couldn't stop thinking about that unidentified image in the back ground of that surveillance photo.

Things just didn't feel right to him for some reason, he knew his minute was rapidly running out, so he closed the closet door gently so not to make a sound and proceeded for the other door to the hall.

The hall to both his left and right seemed to be endless, however to his left he was just a few paces from the stairs leading down to the first floor. Christen walked over to the stairs but, slowly strolled along the railing peering down at the living room floor area. The lavish marble cream columns seemly separating one side of the marble stairs from the other looked gorgeous. The interior designer must have taken weeks, if not months to perfect every little detail and specification

Gorgan wanted for the inside to look. Outside, though was a thing of beauty, the estates exterior echoed super wealth. After studying the insides interior Christen decided it was time he descended to the kitchen.

For the luscious smell of Greek cuisine made him even more hungry, moving down the stairs, there was a strong smell coming from the far left of the hall. He figured it had to be where the kitchen was, so he headed in that direction. All he had to was follow the aroma, once he reached the base of the stairs, he proceeded to look down the east and west end of the hall. The cream colored wall had six paintings on both sides and underneath each painting was brief paragraph summarizing what the artist expressed to the viewer. He didn't recognize any of them really, just one painting of a bearded man dressed in a toga feeding what looked like a beast with the body of a lion, the head and wings of eagle, and back covered with feathers. These Greeks were truly morbid, bizarre people he thought to himself. But then again, every European culture on earth out side of the west was considered a bit eccentric, before he managed to check out all the paintings he realized he was being watched.

The kitchen was directly to the back of him, as he caught the eyes of Gorgan, Perseus, Tarken and the very amused Andromeda.

"You have quite a collection here Gorgan." He said.

Feeling a bit taken aback.

"That's nothing, James. Wait till you see me gallery later on this evening. You will witness an abundance of art, I have clients from all over the world who come here to buy what I have to offer." He told him. Christen walked in the kitchen, and took his place at the table with Tarken seated directly across from him.

"So are we enjoying ourselves?" Tarken asked James. With the look of a man mutually impressed with that he's already seen.

"Immensely!" replied Christen exhibiting a slight grin on his face. The kitchen table was expensive mahogany measuring 7 feet in length by 5 feet in width. The kitchen was old world Greek design while the table was long enough to seat 8 to 10 people while covering it was several bowls of what appeared to be some eggplant with ground meat baked in a tangy sweet and sour sauce, and a platter of grilled goat's meat with vegetables and everything cooked in traditional Olive Oil, the other stuff was like cubes of lamb and more vegetables strung on a skewer that might have been roasted over a fire for 20 to 30 minutes. He was thinking to himself it was Shish kabob made to serve at least 6 to 8 people maybe more. He also noticed the plates or fine china had various designs on it of other famous Greek notables like Plato, Hades, Poseidon, and Apollo.

All the other plates also had these features as Gorgan started to dispense the food first, dipping a long spoon in the bowl of eggplant with ground meat. He applied a few helpings of that to his plate, then passed it over to

Tarken. Andromeda meanwhile, had already filled her plate with the lamb meat and cubes of vegetables strung on long needle. She was actually eating Greek shish kebab. Christen was finally given the platter of goat's meat with various vegetables garnished around it. It looked delicious, and the steam coming off it made his mouth water. He placed the platter in front of his plate, then grabbed a sharp knife and fork, he also carefully stuck the fork in the goats meat and began to slice into it.

Christen cut several deep slices through the meat before taking the fork and lifting the substance off, placing it on his plate. He then put the knife and fork back on the platter, using his spoon he scooped a few morsels of the vegetables onto his plate. At that point it was time to indulge his appetite. First he sliced a piece of grilled goat meat then took a bit of it. It taste like a across between filet mignon and chicken.

Although while he chewed he could sense the meat was superbly tenderized, the vegetables would have to wait until he fully devoured the meat first. But most people would eat a balance of meat and vegetables however this was one of those few occasions where he'd tasted grilled goat's meat. It wasn't like attending a western Barbeque or anything where the food or meat was traditionally pork ribs, or hot dogs and hamburgers this was Greece so why would they consume a diet in high fattening caloric intact? They wouldn't and they had a tradition of eating very healthy too! Everyone at the table had a full plate of food and some of the wines glasses also filled to the brim. For at least 15 minutes to a half hour the only sound in the kitchen is utensils being used by all four at the table feeding their faces. Christen took a liking to the kitchens design, the sink, cabinets, the stove, and in the middle hanging from the ceiling were all cooking and baking utensils were used.

While indirectly observing Tarken enjoying his meal, his brunch Gorgan finally breaks the silence in the kitchen.

"James, did Tarken ever tell you how we met in college?"

Gorgan inquired after taking a long sip of wine.

"No, Gorgan he never shared that story with me but you have more than peaked my curiosity." Christen responded with me anticipation.

"Yusaf and I met at the University of Cambridge in London, England where I was majoring in Economics and International Business Marketing, whereas Tarken was taking classes in Business Management and Public

Relations. Anyway, we had a semester together in International Finance as an elective. It was fun however the professor was a hard-core Marxist and as much as he tried to hide it from the students, well it was oozing out of his pores." Gorgan went on.

"I remember while in class one occasion Tarken was a bit aloof or kind of like bored out of his mind, but he kept himself occupied by drawing porn in one of the text books." Now Tarken looks embarrassed like I can't believe you went there.

"Porn in the text books?" an amused Christen asked.

"Oh yes, just imagine this. Your flipping through pages right and you come to one with drawings of a man performing oral sex on a woman right next to a picture of foreign currency, like what the hell is this doing here? I don't get the connection." Then having enough of this Tarken enters the discussion.

"Ok, ok, ok Gorgan, you like to tell half a story anyway, the class was excruciating to seat through that's for damn sure. This man Sergi Primokov or whatever the hell his name was, I digress but back then this universities hired these pinko commie bastards to teach and spread this the anti-capitalist bullshit. And if you wanted a descent grade and needed that course you swallowed whatever post-soviet garbage he feed you to graduate." With that exchange between Gorgan and Tarken, Perseus interjected himself in the conversation.

"Gentlemen, I really hate to break up this class reunion moment but I have wedding plans to finish so if you'll excuse me?" he says as he raises from his chair and the table, throwing his dinner cloth on the plate of left over veggies.

'"Son, excuse me I got carried away of course your more then welcome to leave." He says as Perseus gives his sister a kiss on the cheek before he exits the kitchen and bids Tarken and Christen a good bye!

"Gentlemen, Mr. Tarken, and Mr. Christen, till tomorrow." he says exiting the kitchen. Christen and Tarken yell out "till tomorrow Perse." Now Gorgan and Tarken finish their conversation while Christen and Andromeda look on in amusement.

"Tarken tried to be a teacher's pet and it didn't go over too well with Professor Primokov, in fact unless you read any of his favorite socialist authors he ignored you in class." Gorgan said to Christen regarding Tarken with a sarcastic grin. And once again not wanting to be out classed by Gorgan, Tarken fires back with a story of his own about Gorgan.

"James, Gorgan was known as quite the sinister prankster on campus, there's one incident I recall when Gorgan presented Professor Primokov with a fancy box in his faculty office wrapped in a bow. There was a rumor that Professor Primokov was a recovering addict and his poison of choice was hashish and the fancy box delivered to him contained deluxe brownies with hashish baked in them. Don't ask me who, what, or how the hell Gorgan found hash brownies on campus but the box was delivered with a 22 ounce bottle of goats milk. James there were 8 brownies in the box and Primokov devoured them with absolute delight." With this Gorgan sips his wine with a sinister smile on his face relishing the visual of Primokov while Tarken continues his story.

"Months, years later we heard he started having bizarre hallucinations and the university president sent him to their top psychiatrist to see if he was actually going insane or was it chemically induced. Now, according to his testimony while he was watching his favorite TV mystery the characters or actors would start speaking to him. In fact, they'd actually addressed him eye to eye from the TV screen, not that some powerful hashish." At this point Christen has heard enough and his body is screaming for rest, while he observes Andromeda taking all this in.

"Gentlemen, I'm stuffed and I'd hate to fall asleep here at the table in your presence so if you'll excuse me please the bed is calling?" he replies wanting to get back into his room and hit the mattress fast.

"No problem, get some rest James we'll have plenty of time later to talk and I have much to show you." Gorgan says as Christen raises from the table and almost stumbles backward, but catch himself regaining his balance.

"Wow, you must be tired? Yes go rest off the dinner wine and I'll collect you in a few hours." Gorgan tells him before his quickly exits the kitchen without even saying goodbye to Andromeda.

He didn't notice to his sharp left was a underground wine cellar connected to the kitchen patio by the back stairs. That would have to wait until he had time if he ever got it to really investigate the mansion. He proceeded back toward the base of stairs this time ignoring all those Murals and paintings on the walls, all he could think about was rest, and his back lying on that firm mattress, so the longer it took for him to get upstairs to the room, whatever was in that wine Gorgans housekeeper served, Christen couldn't handle it. As he reached the stairs base in the back of his mind he kept thinking no one step at a time no, no, no.

Like plotting to climb a 50-foot wall he begins his stride quickly taking two steps at a time and then reaching the first floor and back down the west corridor to his room. Just the way he left it, he pushes the door open and begins taking off everything shoes, socks, pants, shirts and boxers.

Then slides into the bed while just pulling the sheet over his chest to conceal his private's parts not reveal himself sleeping completely in the nude. He stares at the ceiling and chandelier right above him, feeling his eye lids growing heavier and heavier till they eventually close. The room almost starts to feel like it's spinning but then he figures he's feeling the effects of that wine and he has little tolerance for this vintage brand. Eventually he's out cold and starts snoring a little but not loud enough to be heard from outside and down the hall. Unaware that someone is standing at the door knocking Christen doesn't even notice that Tarken is staring at him, watching him with such amusement as his mouth is partially open from the mild snoring.

"James, …James, we really need to talk James." Tarken says before he steps into the room and pulls up a chair near the bed to take a seat near where Christen head is lying. Christen wakes up surprised but also a little groggy from sleeping off the dinner wine.

"Tarken what are you doing in here? I figured you were in Gorgan's personal library or something looking at the old college photos at the University of Cambridge or reminiscing about all the fun times you had together?" Christen asked. But Tarken wasn't interested in discussing the old college years he had with Gorgan oh no, this involves Christen surviving the blast in Ankara, Turkey and the mission going wrong.

"No Gorgan left for the gallery right after you departed from the kitchen Christen. Also I won't be attending the reception after the wedding either, it turns out I have to flight back to South Africa and give a deposition in Pillisworth to the General Council of South African Intelligence. They want an account of what happened, who was killed and how much those loses will cost the government." With all that said Christen observes

Tarkens facial expression and it occurs to him somehow this whole incident will result in major blow back on South African Intelligence.

"Also the moment I leave James, you are on your own and I can say this much to you, I know you are very capable man and can handle yourself. However, despite Gorgans charm and charisma knowing him the way I do he can be very ruthless and calculating when he wants also, when the questions come and they will, if he doesn't get the answers he's looking for things could get very ugly quick. So out of deep consternation my friend, my advice to you is be very careful and whatever you do, don't touch his daughter. She is his pride and joy, and like his most valuable possession if he suspects that you seduced her in anyway there will be hell to pay my friend." Tarken warns Christen with intensity.

He says this with great concern for his colleague's welfare and Christen takes heed of this warning but at the same time he's thinking she might prove to be notable ally.

"Tarken thanks for your concern however I will assure you here and now I won't disclose anything to Gorgan. I have a plan of my own, it's just a matter of time before I cease the opportunity and take it." Christen replies.

"James, Gorgan has partners, who have their own entourage or bodyguards and they don't take prisoners so again for the sake of being a hothead you should heed my advice and take it to heart. They have elaborate ways of getting information out of you and it doesn't have to include brutality. In fact, that's the more primal method, I would assume his business partners might use or carry some sort of psychedelic truth serum or chemical agent but if he wants answers and wants them urgent, he will get them James." Tarken warns him again.

"Yusef, my friend I'm tired and you disrupted my sleep with this, not that I don't appreciate it, don't get me wrong. However, I'm not running no matter what happens after you leave Athens." Christen reassures him again.

Watching him raise from the chair and back toward the door peeking down the hall left and right to make sure no one was eaves dropping on their conversation. Tarken looks back at Christen lying down across the mattress half nude with a satin sheet covering his body at the waist. He shakes his head knowing his friend is headed for a tense confrontation with a man who disguises his inner fury very well with extreme cunning. Under his breathe he says, "Damn you ….James be careful!" as Tarken disappears to his room down the hall a resting Christen senses another presence, in the door, and he can't imagine that it would be anyone else wanting more pointless conversation but of course he is very wrong.

It's the beautiful Andromeda dressed in a see thru lingerie fishnet gown which also looks like a jump suit that ends at the knees. As he's looking up the ceiling then at her he notices that she's sort of smiling at him kind of seductively. She looks like a weird cross between Delphine Seyrig and Sanaa Lathan only having dark beige tan skin like her mom was of Jamaican or Haitian descent. Also, her hair had a light brown color and was always in a puny tail only this time she had it styled with a short part in the middle and it looks wet.

And just when we was warned under no circumstances are you to touch her, and don't succumb to her beauty, the flesh is weak and she's hungrily staring him down like he's a fresh baked pizza with all the right toppings she can't wait to devour him.

"James… I had to see you. I can't stop thinking of you since my father greeted you at the airport this afternoon, it was difficult for me to disguise my attraction to you even then."

She tells him while she rubs her right fingers across his forehead.

"Andromeda, Andromeda, if your father catches us its over sweetie!" he warns her but she interrupts him with the same info that collaborates what Tarken said to him just two hours before she visits his room.

"My father left brunch for his business meeting right after you departed the kitchen for your nap and he's not coming back any time soon so you having nothing to worry about. I won't tell him anything James, and now I have you all to myself." She says as she works her way around the bed, then climbs on top of him with her beautiful beige tan feet and burgundy red colored toes.

She's planted her hips squarely on his groin moving back and forth getting him aroused at the feeling of his penis against her Virginia. She bend down to his face and plants a kiss on his lips like she trying to decide what to do with him next. Now he's staring at this beautiful young woman in her mid to late 20's and the temptation is just too much for him to withstand, in fact he can almost hear Tarken in his subconscious warning him, hands off her, she's off limits. And this woman's undressing slowly while she straddles on top of his waist, kissing him and removing her fishnet jump suit pajamas from her body and tossing them on the floor to the beds left side.

Christen now sees this nude, shapely, and voluptuous young woman seating on his lap and she guides him inside her, moving her hips around, back and forth so he can get deep penetration.

With the feel of his penis inside her vaginal walls it's like it gets longer and wider as she continues this rhythm while she's a top him. He doesn't move his body or try to maneuver it in any way, he just lays there in the center of the bed while she's now riding him like a horse in a rodeo only steady and gradually picking up rhythm and sometimes slowing down. Christen caresses her left hips and thighs with his left hand while and moving his right hand across her abdomen, then her breast and nipples. And judging her body language, she wants him to really get aggressive with her but at the same time he's very mindful of her youthfulness, and the fact that she has this hidden rebellious streak against her father. Christen rolls her over on her back and now he's on top of her with his waist planted just right between her thighs and he's still inside her. She wraps her legs, thighs around him tight, using her thighs and vaginal muscles to pull his penis inside her or at least squeeze when ever he motions his body to pull out.

And this continues until they get this unbelievable rhythm going between the two of them and he begins planting kisses on both her cheeks, her chin, her neck line to her shoulders, then traces the line of her lips with his tongue. She starts breathing hard and lets out soft moans with every thrust from

Christen, he then starts inhaling her breathe as if drawing some erotic sensation from the scent of it, combined with the intoxicating oils or perfume she was wearing all over her body. The sweet scent of her breathe drove him crazy, in fact the more he inhaled, the deeper he thrust himself inside her, she let out this moan crying "deeper James, I want it deeper please don't stop. My father doesn't have to know." And why did she say that?

Christen stops right at the point when she's about to explode, right at the point when she experiencing the height of her sexual peak and her body is crying out for him to thrust harder, to maintain his commanding rhythm over her. It suddenly hits him, he isn't wearing a condom and he doesn't know if or when her period came on or not. And if by chance he explodes in her and her dads finds out, becoming his adversary will be the least of his problems. And the damn cordless phone rings, talk about unbelievable timing for him especially as he rolls off her and she quickly get off the bed and races for the phone before it clicks off. She grabs it, hits the talk button and answers.

"Mathias residence," she says catching her breath with sweat pouring off his body from her brow to down to her thighs including sweat dripping from her nipples. It's her father in his office at the gallery checking in on his house guest as he prepares to send the limo to collect him after his meeting with his business partners.

"Andromeda, tell me Mr. Christen is awake and well rested?

I'm sending the car for him in a hour after my meeting, so be a dear and connect me to his room." At that point she doesn't panic but hits the hold button and hands the cordless to Christen.

"Gorgan hello," James replies staring back at Andromeda who give him this seductive glance with her right index finger on her bottom lip.

"James are you ready for the tour? I have much to show you and even more to talk about?" Gorgan asks him with absolute glee.

"Yes, Yes, I hardly wait Gorgan I'm picking out the clothes now. And I will be ready to leave within the hour."

"Splendid, splendid, very good my driver will collect you as soon as this meeting concludes." Gorgan says before clicking off.

"He doesn't suspect anything James, so you have nothing to worry about." Andromeda interjects after the brief conversation ends. But Christen knows better and will not underestimate Gorgan for a minute.

"Your father has keen intuition Andromeda and it would serve you well not to disobey him or make him unnecessarily upset." She hears him but at the same time her hidden lust and high sex drive keeps governing what she does, in other words her actions are controlled by her hormones and she's determined to get whatever she wants shades of her father. While Christen picks out the right attire for his gallery tour, some 6 miles from the manse away in the art-financial district of down town Athens, Gorgan puffs on a Cuban cigar in his posh office located in the center rear of his gallery.

He studies some specs on his flat screen monitor while he hears the vehicle approaching from down the street, perhaps his business partners and their deadly entourage. As he sends out emails and checks RSVPs for the wedding list he hears three olive green Range Rovers with foreign plates driving down Mesogeion Ave then turning into his parking area. There are double doors and the left door opens wide enough so he has a nice view of who's entering in the front gallery where the expensive statues and Greek rugs are placed also priced for the general public. Out the first Range Rover comes a man dressed in a peculiar light brown pinstripe suit with matching pants, socks and shoes also the shirts is white brown stripe bow to match. This man is a Russian arms dealer with receding red hair line standing at 6 feet, 2 inches with a modest build not too muscular, not too flabby with a slim waist line.

His name is Mikhail Bahrain Khrichkov and at age 52, and a native born of Kemerovo Oblast located in southwestern Siberia, he is one of the world's foremost arms dealers. Following close behind him are Roman and Gregory Gniewko, fraternal twins and specialists in the art of exotic tortures and other ungodly talents. As Mikhail makes his way to the open door with the twins staying behind he's finally followed by Tisdale Minolta, a man in his late 50's dressed like a Silicone Valley tech computer programmer wearing wired rimmed glasses and white tie shirt with gray sweater and charcoal suit and pants. Also sporting dark brown moccasins or fancy loafers to match. Minolta has a three henchman and one driver, his henchmen have the dubious distinction of being among the toughest shoot fighters in Russia's MMA underground. Although they all dress like wall street stock brokers and fuck the most beautiful eastern European women money can buy.

They have these very peculiar Euro Slavic names Anatoly Alexander, Vladimir "Crunchy" Bullnor, Krasimir Rostislav and former body guard to Russian Oligarch Boris Berezovsky, Natali Mochavic Radoslav. They stay behind with the Range Rovers listening to their weird euro rock music while the bosses enter the art gallery. Mikhail initiates the welcome committee shouting, in a deep former Soviet Siberian accent.

"Gorgan where are you, get your ass out here right now, And don't make me ask again." Feeling a bit agitated from what he's hearing Gorgan steps out from his office and pulls out a expensive cigar to light from his suit pocket. He pulls a fancy butane lighter out of his suit pocket, hits a button with his right thumb while holding the cigar up to the blue flame to light it till its cherry red and takes several hits before blowing rings of smoke at Mikhail. Interestingly Mikhail just stares at him with smirk then Gorgan enjoying the smell of his cigar begins to engage his Siberian business partner.

"Mikhail I invited you, Tisdale and your entourage here to my gallery, my place of business and you address me like I'm a little child? Not a good way to start a meeting but then again you were never the settle type no? You Siberians, Russians are very short on Social etiquette. And Tisdale you get to ride around with this raging ball of testosterone, that must get interesting for you?" he asks while observing Minoltas facial expressions.

"Why is it I always whined up the mediator between you two, why can't two grown men just have a civil conversation with out it turning into a dick measuring contest?" Minolta finally chimes in. And Mikhail congratulates Gorgans son while he begins his foreign policy briefing and Gorgan continues to puff on his cigar enjoying it's taste and listening intently.

"Ok, ok, ok alright Gorgan I stand corrected also give you're son my congrats on his wedding, getting married is such a major step in anyone's life, and I wish him much luck and much happiness. So with that said to business gentlemen, regarding the unfortunate incident in Turkey several months ago I have some interesting information to share with you Gorgan. There was a through investigation done in the aftermath of that blast at the compound we discovered was occupied by some South African spies, anyway their was a survivor of that blast.

We know this because a package was sent via courier less then a hour later and it contained photographs. These photos are of our meeting in Turkey days before the accident took place and now some unknown Intelligence agency has acquired them." after verbally completing his thought Mikhail pauses and studies Gorgan's expression or then continues his brief report with Minolta studying them trying to read or anticipate Gorgan's reply.

"Gentlemen I neglected to inform you I have guests from out of town attending this wedding and two of them are staying at my home at least until after the reception." Gorgan interjects knowing that soon suspicion will follow. After Mikhail's briefing or lecture depending on how one looks at it.

"Interesting? Tell me more about your guests and leave nothing out, I want to know everything about them including what type of food they like to the brand of beverage they enjoy drinking." Mikhail asks Gorgans looking forward to meeting these people and possible gaining more business contacts. Gorgan continues.

"One of them is a former college classmate of mine and the other his colleague works for South African Intelligence, in fact they both work for South African Intelligence." With this Gorgan takes another puff of his cigar while his partners digest what they've just heard from his lips, and he's still oblivious to the fact that Christen is the man responsible for killing his would be assassins.

"So let us understand this Gorgan, you have been entertaining house guests whom might have important info regarding the disruption of our Opium operation?" Mikhail continues, "Gorgan you are aware this new information is very vital to our continuing business relationship? We are awaiting a new shipment coming into Crete around the same time your son's wedding takes place? We are talking about shipment worth hundreds of millions if not billions of dollars in opium!" With that Mikhail stops as if he feels he's talking to himself just to hear himself talk and his partners are listening but they really aren't listening.

Indeed Gorgan is listening and continues puffing on his Cigar enjoying its aroma while he's walking around this enormous room surveying the art, murals and paintings around his gallery.

"Gentleman, I've kept nothing from you in fact you will get a copy of my RSVP guest list the day before the wedding and you will meet these men in person I guarantee it. Excuse my relax demeanor gents Greek wine can sometimes be a very powerful sedative." And as Gorgon closely examines a mural with exotic Greek designs Tisdale Minolta interjects his own opinion into this intense conversation.

"Gorgon I speak for myself not for Mikhail and I didn't come here to act as mediator, or referee although I'm concerned you've taken your eyes off this or allowed yourself to become distracted?" he asks.

"Distracted? Distracted you say? No not in the least Tisdale in fact I have never been more aware of certain events these past months. However, first things first for me gentlemen after the wedding and reception we will travel to Crete, inspect the vessels and the cargo for the opium processing.

Now if there's nothing else you'd like to discuss gentlemen, I have a tour to conduct with my house guest and more preparation to make with this wedding. Due see yourselves out I'm sure your entourage is getting terribly bored outside with you inhere conducting a informal interrogation." Gorgon tells them and out of frustration they leave the gallery signaling to their entourage start up the Range Rovers and go.

Chapter 4

LET'S TOUR THE GALLERY

Gorgon remains in the same spot, continues to puff on his cigar and watches the group from inside until they all enter the vehicles and drive off. He turns around and heads back to his office, grabs the cordless phone and makes two calls, one to his driver to pick up Christen and the other to Mathias Manor. He hits speed dial, it rings twice, then three times before the line is picked up by Andromeda still in her almost see though jump suite.

"Mathias residence," she answers.

"Annie, connect me to Christens room ASAP." He orders her while he's waiting for James to pick up phone. James steps out of the closet as he finishes buttoning up his shirt and puts on his suit when the cordless phone rings in his room, he takes it off the charge and hits transfer button line 1.

"Yes," he answers.

"James, its Gorgon I'm sending a driver to collect you now my meeting has concluded, so he should be pulling up to the estate any moment for you." Gorgon assures him.

"I'm ready and very anxious to see this gallery you have Gorgon and once I see your limo I'll meet him in the drive way." Christen replies.

"Excellent, he's just minutes from the manor James, once your in the limo page me and I'll greet you in front of my gallery lobby." With that Gorgon clicks off the cordless phone. Christen hears a limo pulling up to the manse and takes a quick peep outside his window and as scheduled the dark black Mercedes limousine parks right in front of the mansion lobby, and the horn goes off three times. That's his hint Get your ass out here now the ride is waiting, Christen doesn't miss a beat as he races out the room, doesn't close the door, and down the hall to the stairs, skipping two steps at a time until he reaches the base.

He finds Andromeda standing in the doorway with her arms folded giving him a look of sheer concern as if she suspects this tour is really something else entirely.

"I'm off beautiful," he tells her. "You two have fun, and don't let him con you into buying anything James." She replies.

He looks back at her as he enters the rear passenger door and takes a seat when the driver shuts it closed, then races around to the his driver side and pulls off in a hurry away from the mansion. Maneuvering the limo around the almost oval drive way and toward the open gate into the street, the limo heads back in the same direction with James Christen comfortably seated, observing this upper class neighborhood of Athens he never thought existed. Not very many mansions or big estate homes near Gorgons estate and from what he noticed in his ride to the Gallery were very expansive lofts and pricey condos, he'd guessed where white collar Greek politicians and city officials lived? Just a few blocks around the corner from one of the most wealthiest men living in this ancient Mediterranean country.

It was unreal to Christen who had always heard in his travels of the superrich in their secluded neighborhoods, with the private security firms patrolling these ultra private districts and their expensive private home security. But to actually see it for himself and experience it was like nothing he'd ever seen up close and personal. However being a secret agent/assassin Christen always maintained an particular indifference to rich and poor especially when the well to do pay so damn well. Even his posh apartment in the exclusive community of Botha Parkway in Pillisworth, South Africa named after P.W. Botha, State President of South Africa and nicked name Die Groot Krokodil (Afrikaans for "The Big Crocodile) its prime minister in the late seventies to early eighties and the first executive state president from early to late eighties. This exclusive district has had its share of some famous, some infamous but private upper class Tenants.

He figured to himself as the limo got several blocks closer to Gorgan's Originals Art Gallery, that this man must have a net worth of at least a quarter of a billion dollars if not more or possible close to or over three quarters of a billion. And no telling what else he owned and how many other investments he must have scattered around the world? To Christens surprise and excitement the gallery was just two blocks away and its sign could be seen from a quarter mile in bold neon letters designed in ancient Greek font characters. Now the limo was making a turn from Mesogeion Ave into the Parking lot of Gorgons art gallery ironically the same spots as Gorgons partners Entourage just a half hour before. As the limo comes to a complete stop just in from of the gallery lobby Christen is met by Gorgon with a smile of his face. Christen exits the limos rear admiring what he's seeing just from the outside.

"Gorgon this is very nice indeed, I'm enjoying this already and I just arrived." Christen says with amusement.

"Oh no.. no.. this is just the outside Mr. Christen I have yet to show you the entire gallery, it doesn't look as expansive from outside but once you go in and get a look around you'll notice space you never thought was possible." Gorgon replies. They enter through one of the dual front doors and Christen gets a full 180 degree view of almost everything around him. On one side or to the east he sees what looks rows of columns from floor to ceiling separating dozens, and dozens, if not hundreds of murals, statues, paintings, and forms of ancient Greek art for sale or display. From his observation the columns seemed to measure 16 feet to the ceiling by 27 inches in circumference at the base floor and separating his art from east to west or left to right he counted approximately over 50 columns in the gallery in rows of 5 front to back.

Also Gorgon had everything chronicled in periods of Greek history and mythology going back at least 1000 years BCE or more to 1 A.D. and the present. Directly in front of him was the middle gallery row 25 with a mural of the Trojan War (1250-1210) 1250 BCE.

Surprisingly in a fantastic hologram almost like a live action Japanese anime cartoon depicting the actually ancient conflict. And while Christen seemed like a kid in candy store or visiting a new museum for the first time an enthused Gorgon looks on while also counting his inventory of art and preparing to schedule a date of that clandestine opium shipment arriving in Crete within a few days. The columns had signs or charts depicting each period in ancient Greece timeline from Archaic Period, and Classical Greece to the Hellenistic Period dating 800 BC to 146 BC, his murals also had holograms for Greek Dark Ages, Aegean Civilians, Mycenaean Greece. The Greek Bronze Age, Ancient Greece, Medieval Greece, and Modern Greece all Chronicled from beginning to end.

Christen also notices a different mural with another insane live action hologram depicting The Battle of Marathon, Athenians defeat Darius and his Persian army 490 BCE. And so many others like it in such exquisite detail with the exact historical time lines and amazing craftsmanship all around. Finally Gorgon approaches Christen and decides its time for gradual Q and A session but not before he notices that James has some questions of his own.

"This collection of yours is like nothing I have ever seen before, what does all this go for on the international/global market? I'm sure you must find that somewhat amateurish of me to ask?" Christen wonders out loud.

"Hell no, if you didn't have any inquiry at all then I'd consider this a weird and awkward tour however, to answer your question, as you've observed in this Gallery the Greek Historic timeline goes back to 1000 BCE and yes these items are extremely pricey for the global market. 4 to 5 figures and more ranging from 6 to 7 figures when you add in international shipping fees, or taxes, trade tariffs, etc." Gorgon adds.

Now Christen thinks back when he was in the South African Naval Academy reading books on historic world conflicts, he took some interest in Greek history and mythology, the ancient battles chronicled in Greek and Roman history going all the way back to the Emperors themselves. Now he was recalling everything he'd read right here in this amazing gallery in the heart of downtown Athens, Greece. The other half of gallery were displays of numerous statues and paintings but one really caught Christen and stuck out among all the others. This one particular painting was of a old man dressed in a weird looking toga feeding this multi headed beast with the body of a hound or k- nine.

"Ok Gorgon, this one really has my attention, I'm not sure actually what I'm looking at so educate me?" he asks and Gorgon's is more anxious to obligate him.

"That my friend is called a "Cerberus" or in Greek and Roman mythology the guardian of the underworld! I particularly like this one, it represents my organization or at least the people I work with." He replies in kind.

"And here I'm thinking you're just a lone gallery owner, a wealthy independent businessman operating in Athens, Greece?" Christen inquires deeper.

"No Mr. Christen, I represent a small group of businessmen, a shadow empire stretching through out various parts of Eurasia and beyond. You will meet them at my sons wedding, I'll give you a formal introduction to my business partners James." Gorgon informs him.

"Gorgon have you heard of an organization called Excalibur?" Christen asks wondering if maybe he's crossed paths with Durant Lucern Craven.

"No that name doesn't sound remotely familiar too me James, there are so many competing syndicates around the world including the rather unsophisticated." He answers in a very condescending manner while Christen continues moving through out the gallery surveying the statues, and paintings depicting ancient Greek wars such as The Archaic Period from

(800 BC to 480 BC), The late Archaic Period (561 BC to 484 BC)

Classical Greece from (500 BC to 323 BC) Hellenistic Greece (323 BC to 146 BC) all these historic battles displayed on statues and paintings, each one in such intricate detail one after the other. Someone actually took out the time to write and paint these fantastic ancient battles and to think of all the research they needed. Christen unfolds his arms and places his hands in his pockets as Gorgon studies his guest with a arrogant smirk of absolute satisfaction. He really gets off when people visit his gallery locally and from around the world, the feeling that he has what everyone seems to want and will pay top dollar to posses.

Most be nice to find that special niche in the art market that only you can command not everyone else? But, Christen also suspects that somehow this is only a front for his real enterprise, the one he keeps very well hidden from the public and law enforcement. It's at this point during the tour Christen has seen as much as he can tolerate, not that he hates art galleries but he isn't a diehard art connoisseur or professional collector. And he knows he's tour guide is watching his every step, his every move, observing his physical posterior, his facial expressions toward every painting, mural and sculpture he comes across.

"Gorgon I'd be lying to myself if I said I wasn't impressed with everything you've shown me here, and just for the record, now I'm looking forward to the wedding." Christen tells him. And with that admission Gorgan prepares to call his driver back to the gallery and escort James back to the manse where he'll catch up on his rest.

"In that case James it was a indeed a pleasure opening my gallery to you and as you can see now my collection is top notch! Also should you have any new questions later on for any reason don't hesitate to ask me anything, anything! Nothings off limits my friend, you and Tarken are my quests, I want your stay in Athens to be most hospitable." Gorgon says almost guaranteeing him that no harm will come to him or perhaps Christen is just hearing things? Gorgon rushes into his office and grabs the cordless phone off the charge and hits speed dial straight to the phone inside the front seat of his other black Mercedes limousine.

"Yes, this is Lupredo." His driver answers! "Lupredo Mr. Christen is ready, our personal tour has concluded and he's waiting for you." Gorgon orders him.

"Very good sir, just give me 10 minutes and I'm there." Lupredo assures him. He clicks off the cordless from inside the limo and places it back in its arm rest compartment, hits the ignition, and the engines roars alive, then slips the gear into drive and looks around to make sure there's no cars approaching him from the rear and pulls away from the curb before making a complete u turn toward the gallery. And luckily for him the Mercedes limo made the complete u in the street without him having to maneuver it backwards.

Gorgon quickly approaches a switch board for all the ceiling lights in the Gallery next to the door if his private office and starts hitting switches once Christen moves closer to the lobby entrance and finally steps outside the door. The Mercedes limo driver is just two blocks away when he notices James Christen standing out in from of the gallery with arms folded across his chest, and sporting a pair of matrix like dark brown shades. Gorgon decides against asking Christen any specific questions about his past missions or if he was involved in the most recent incident just months ago in Turkey. But Gorgons suspects his partners will not hold back and when push comes to shove they will get very rough with Christen when the time arrives.

He observes the Mercedes limo pull up to the gallery and the driver steps out, races around to the rear passenger side of the car and opens the door for Christen, not that christen could do it himself but its custom that chauffeurs to open and close the doors for one passenger, and possibly two or more. Christen quickly steps in and takes a seat with a similar mini rack of magazines and books between the left and right seat arm rest. And just like before the driver gets back in, slams the door shut and slips the gear back into drive, then hits the accelerator making another u in the street back in the direction of Mathias manor in midtown Athens, Greece.

It always the same distance for Gorgons drivers going and coming from the mansion to the gallery just under 25 minutes depending on traffic sometimes even longer than that. This time while riding Christen begins thinking about Perseus beautiful brunette fiancé Melissa and no mention of how many out of town guests were coming in on her behalf? It was strange to him and very peculiar that Perseus fiancé Melissa seemed like a introvert? Not very sociable considering her soon to be father in law owns a very public and very popular art gallery in downtown Athens. Also Perseus didn't seem very excited when talking about his bride or was Christen just reading too much into it? Nope his instinct was telling him that this woman was more than just a overly cautious lover for Perseus, she may in fact be a undercover mole or double agent with Greek Intelligence? Maybe, or maybe not? But Christen is convinced that something is off about this so called loving relationship between Perseus and his estranged fiancé Melissa.

The limo pulls into the drive way of Mathias manor and around to the front lobby when Christen is surprised and greeted by Perseus, Melissa, Tarken, and Andromeda all standing out front. The car comes to a stop but this time the driver doesn't get out as Christen signals to him don't even bother, I have this bro! Before Christen has a chance to grab the inner handle and open the rear passenger door Andromeda quickly steps to the door and grabs the outer latch. The door whips open and Christen steps out in total surprise of this most unexpected greeting and Tarken is the one who does the initiating.

"James Christen, allow me to introduce the bride to be Melissa Youngmire Godfrey, and Miss Godfrey, my coworker and intelligence colleague, James Christen." Tarken greets and introduces Christen with a boyish smile like he's about to except a gold star or merit reward of some type. Christen gives him an awkward look like wow, you really set this up all by yourself Yusaf, I'm impressed, in fact I wasn't aware of how much a superstar show off you are? But he never verbalizes that in front of Perseus, Melissa, and Andromeda only gives Tarken a weird look like can we go inside now and discuss the guest list?

Oh yeah! And let's talk about the catering, the band, the presiding Greek minister or Rev. who will talk about the wedding vows between Perseus and Melissa. They all proceed toward the lobby door into the library living room quarters of Gorgons manse in the west wing where Melissa continues the greeting of dialogue with James Christen. While Perseus, Tarken and his sister Andromeda take another close look at the rather small guest list and items for the expensive catering.

"Mr. Christen it very nice to meet you and I understand you were given the rare honor of a personal tour by Mr. Mathias, in his famous Gallery?" she asks him. "Yes his collection is most impressive, I take it you've already seen it Miss Godfrey?" Christen replies with his own question.

"Only small advertisements in magazines and trade Journals, Mr. Mathias is very clever he figured out a way to get heavy exposure while keeping his advertising costs relatively low. Very smart!" she says with a convincing smile.

"He's shrewd as a businessman and I admire that about him Christen also people seem to think he's ruthless and cut throat. But you don't become successful being a push over in this world and Gorgon represents that, he's an inspiration for all of us." She replies again.

But Christen isn't convinced and like a real good poker player he will not show his hand or give away his tell. Also this cat and mouse game continues and he wondering when, just when will they finally approach him about what he knows even though he's a house guest but he's on borrowed time and he knows it. Christen and Melissa continue their conversation going into depth about she and Perseus met one weekend at a shopping mall outside Athens, Greece two summers ago.

"So Miss Godfrey tell me how you and Mr. Mathias met and how long have you been seeing each other?" Christen asks her? While Perseus looks on like he wants to eagerly interject himself into their conversation Melissa gives him this look like don't you dare open your mouth, I will answer whatever questions he asks me, Perse just worry about who's showing up for the VIP list your sister sent out.

"I was in town visiting a college friend in Agioi Theodori, it's a suburb outside of Athens and their family operates an eatery in town, anyway they make the most delicious beef, vegetables gyros in all of Corinthia. As it turns out Mr. Mathias knows the owner, and his son and Perseus attended the University of Athens during undergrad so anyway, we were introduced, he looked like this retro Hollywood producer with blue Ralph Lauren pants and white brooks brothers button down shirt and his belt matched his loafers, oh yeah he had on these nerdy navy blue argyle socks. I remember he was sort of nervous or he seemed like he wasn't used to meeting single women or introducing himself in public but I he overcame his fear and we had an interesting conversation. We talked about how we both like the same foreign films, pop music, that sort of thing after 2 weeks we went out again, and really started spending time Together. We eventually fall in love and so it's been over 2 years now and he finally proposed to me on his father's 215ft luxury yacht "The Kraken," it was very romantic. Every day he continues to surprise me with gifts and he treats me like a queen Mr. Christen." She finishes almost like she was out of breathe.

Andromeda's heard enough of this so she gets Perseus attention by grabbing his shoulder with her left hand while directing his attention to the monitor they both notice something rather peculiar with the RSVP list like someone has taken off certain guests.

"Exactly how many quests did father invite for the wedding Saturday? And why aren't they on the RSVP list?" she asked her brother. But Perseus is also in the dark about these details, and as much as he respects his father he too understands Gorgon operates almost everything so clandestine like he has to be in control no matter what the circumstance. Or he doesn't expect a lot of people to attend, meaning this wedding will be very private, and he doesn't like a lot of attention anyway with people asking questions about anything not having to deal with his business and his partners entourage being present.

"Annie you will have to pose that question to dad when he returns from the gallery, which should be anytime now." He replies as if he had nothing more to add or he never second guesses his father. And while all this is happening around him Tarken helps himself to the manse library and Gorgons vast collection of 10,000 foreign DVDs and a interactive library of some classical e-books and mostly hard copies and paperbacks. All including every type of literary genre you can imagine and most of the DVDs were cataloged from the History channel,

Biography, Arts and Entertainment, and an encyclopedia collection that put most public and private libraries to shame.

Tarken figured this whole collection most have cost Gorgon at least $60,000 or more and couldn't imagine him paying that much for it.

It was one of those private study libraries in the living room with couches and sofa in the middle surrounding a table, a 72 inch screen with surround speakers and top that off the DVDs and books were on shelves covering all three sides of the room including a sliding ladder incase you weren't tall enough to reach the top shelve. Tarken figured at this point why guess the price when all he had to do was just ask the man's children and with skipping a beat he did. "Excuse me", he yells. "Can anyone tell me how much Gorgon spend on this vast library, I mean really someone give an approximate figure?" he asks just waiting for either Perseus, Andromeda or perhaps even Melissa knows? And wouldn't you guess, Andromeda raises from her seat from studying the RSVP wedding list to voluntarily entertain Tarkens question.

"If recollection serves me correct Mr. Tarken, my father Invested some $600,000 in this library almost 15 years ago. In fact it's a major upgrade from before and it was much smaller as I recall." She answers him. $600,000 his thinking to himself? Wow now that's seems like a lot to invest for such a vast private library however there are others owned by small group of eccentric and other wise reclusive millionaires and billionaires worth double if not quadruple in value.

"Your father never ceases to amaze me Annie, I understand he's very wealthy and I have no problem with that at all. I'm a firm believer of the capitalist system even it's excesses and the vast sums that are spend on toys and recreation. Hell, I need to get some advice from him on how to better handle my 401k investments with DiVarquest Exports!" he replies out of inquiry.

"Divarguest Exports?" She asks him. "Why yes, the name of my governments intelligence agency, they allow us the option of investing in Futures, Foreign exchange, and Energy. I'm more interested in oil, natural gas and alternative fuels myself or what you might call biofuels?" he asks her as if she might know what the hell he's talking about. And before she can respond she notices Christen approaching the library as well so maybe he got bored with Melissa's love story of her meeting Perseus? While Tarken works the east side of the library Christen makes his way to the west studying all the foreign DVDs. Now here we go again he says to himself under his breathe, first the gallery and now this? Wow! A library of over 10,000 DVDs? Maybe or maybe not he keeps thinking. And he can feel Tarkens gaze on him and then comes the commentary, "So James you must be enjoying yourself here first you visit the Gallery and now Gorgons private library? What must be going through your mind?" he asks Christen. James turns his head slightly at Tarken with a smirk on his face, "Yes Tarken, you're correct money can buy just about anything, including a very expensive library!" he replies with a grin and shrug of the shoulders.

"Ladies and gentleman if you will excuse me I'm going upstairs to retire oh and by the way when the man of the house returns, well he knows where to find me. Miss Godfrey it was very nice to meeting you finally," he tells her before walking out of the library.

"And you too Mr. Christen the pleasure was all mine. Annie, Perseus, Tarken." He bids them all good bye before hearing in unison, "Ok bye James." He then makes his way to the entrance then the stairs to his direct left, taking them as he did before two at a time very fast until he reaches the top base floor. He walks down the hall to his left and notices the door to his room exactly as he left it slightly open, he pushes it open half way and kicks off his shoes first. Then takes off the suit and shoulder holster with his gun in it and clips and places both in the chair near the left side of the bed. He crawls on it on it, rolls over and lays down with his face pointed at the ceiling. He then closes his eyes and allows his body to enjoy the firm hardness of the mattress. Down stairs in the library The brother and sister Mathias and Miss Godfrey grill Tarken on his relationship with James Christen.

"So how long have you and Christen known each other Mr. Tarken?" Melissa asks while Perseus and Andromeda look on studying his facial expression.

"Well we meet 12 years ago at a global anti-terrorism conference in London, I was working briefly at Mi6 collecting intelligence data on terrorist groups in Irag and Afghanistan. We were monitoring The Mujahadeen, this is before they become known as the Taliban, Muslim Brotherhood, al-Qaeda, among other Muslim groups who we thought were sponsors of global terrorism. I was working long hours, and it effected my home life, the wife was cheating on me so I put in for a transfer during Christmas holidays to South African Secret Service. Christen was recruited by SASS thru The Dutch naval corps, and how he wound up a reservist with them I don't know how? You can pose that question to him! Anyway, we have had a good working relationship ever since." Tarken explains. And they continue to give him this look like there must be more you aren't telling us so spill it Tarken.

"Christens is a very determined agent and he's always, always being underestimated by very powerful people who view him as somehow inferior. Which is always to their detriment, and remarkably he finds a way to come out on top every, single time, despite the incredible odds against him." Tarken adds with a very confident smile of his face. Like yes motherfucker, yes, fuck with Christen and find out just how resourceful he really is! And so now they are wondering why he never mentioned any of this before he sent the invite to Christen in Geneva, Switzerland? But they don't press him about like this story was satisfactory enough for them.

And soon they all hear a sound coming from outside like Mercedes limo pulling up to the manse and Perseus scrambles to The nearest window, pulls the curtain back to get a peek and yes, its father returning home from the Gallery. The wedding is one day away then Tarken fly back to Pillisworth, South Africa soon afterward leaving Christen all alone to fend for himself. Before the three have a chance to react Gorgon is already exited The limo and coming through their front door with a warm greeting of a hug and kiss from his daughter and angel Andromeda.

"Hello, hello my little angel, my lovely, beautiful princess Andromeda. And where's my son and future daughter in law?" He says with almost watery eyes.

She grabs his left arm and leans into him as he gives her a kiss on the head and cheek and both walk into his private library where Perseus continues studying the RSVP list, while Tarken and Melissa have fun with Gorgons interactive library.

"Ah, there you are! Entertaining our house guests in the private library, yes? Tarken I don't see James, where is he?" Gorgon asks.

"He excused himself and rushed up stairs to his room for a nap, also he left word that you'd know where to find him when you returned." Tarken replies.

"I see and soon you will be leaving Athens, Yusaf and going back to Pillisworth, South Africa yes? It's a shame you can't stay for the reception, I have some surprises in store for everyone!" Gorgon counters while a smirk. With that Annie throws in her 50 cents worth.

"Father speaking of surprises, some ones altered the RSVP List and the VIPs are missing why?" she asks.

"Sweetie, I didn't want to disappoint everyone but some people just won't make it, they have prior engagements, work and family emergencies etc. I feel better if it's a private affair anyway, beside who needs hundreds of guests coming in from all over world expecting something for nothing? Free booze, food and some lonely women hoping to find their next sugar daddy or serial monogamists, listen I hate to sound cynical but that's a wedding in a nutshell. Traditionally the brides father usual pays for the wedding but in this case yours truly will gladly foot the bill." He shouts with much animation.

But Perseus has heard enough and before he has a chance to make his case Melissa rushes to his side to hug and console him before he can defend his honor he's cut off quick. "But dad please!"

"No no, son this is an important occasion for you, for both of you, you're getting married my boy, and to a beautiful and might I say very sexy woman, shit I'm jealous." With that he coughs, balling his right hand to a fist and raising it to his lips to stop himself from laughing.

"No, Melissa explained to me her situation and I told her with absolute certainty I understood and hold no reservations at all. You two will have a glorious wedding, I've called Greek Arch Bishop Augustine Sinilos to officiate also the band and catering arrangements have all already been made." He ends with a very confident smile and nod of his head. The bride and groom to be Perseus and Melissa stare at each other with smiles and exchange a passionate kiss while Tarken and Andromeda are observing. Gorgon moves over to where Tarken is standing in front of this shelf case which is part of his immense private library and handling this graphic novel on the Battle at Thermopylae.

This is the story of 300 Spartans warriors led by King Leonidas and their bloody war against Persian God King Xerxes the second son of King Darius of the Persian Empire.

"This is one of my all-time favorite stories Gorgon, you know I'm keen on historic military conflicts even ancient military wars? And this one stands out among them all my friend." He tells Gorgon flipping through the pages.

"Tarken we've had some good times man, but as the old saying goes 'all good things must come to an end'. It's a pity you can't stay after the reception, I had some urgent business I wanted discuss with you and Mr. Christen." He tells Tarken almost studying his face to see if he will give anything away.

"I can always come back Gorgon, hell you have my number on speed dial on your digital rolodex. I know you have it, and that nice Golf Stream 500 private jet you never talk about. You can contact me whenever you want! And you know this?" Tarken says with a look of caution in his face.

"So James is taking a nap? I'm debating whether I should go upstairs and just say hello or wait for him to come down?" he says with his arms folded across his chest and his right fingers stroking his chin. No he thinks better of it while watching Tarken indulge himself with his vast collection of dvds, and books. In his subconscious Christen can over hear a conversation going on between Gorgon and Tarken like its creeping into his sleep, then without warning he sees one of Khrichov henchmen rushing at him with a 9.mm pistol Beretta with

Silencer and puts the muzzle to his head before his has a chance to react. It's over with three quick shots blam, blam, blam but Christen wakes up in a cold sweat and a slight head ach and beads of sweat pouring down his face and unto his neck and chest. Even though it's just a dream he's wondering if this is some sort of premonition even though he's never even seen or met any of Gorgons partners henchmen or entourage. Christen raises from the mattress bed in a seating position wiping the sweat from his face and realizing the gravity of his situation, however he has to stay cool and keep his calm demeanor. He doesn't realize it but again there's someone standing in the door watching him and this time it's Gorgon. From the door he steps into the room where he spots a chair next to the left side of the bed, pulls it to him, then takes a seat facing Christen.

"Mr. Christen hello again? Is that sweat I see on your face?" he asks catching Christen by surprise. "Ah, yeah I have a lot on my mind Gorgon and I don't much like surprises however

I'm the guest on your home." Christen replies.

"I do hope you're feeling better the weddings in 2 days and my son, daughter and future daughter in law are reorganizing the RSVP list. You see I made some revisions to the list that my daughter didn't approve of in fact some guests won't arrive on time because of other engagements, business etc. and others simply can't make the trip. So we could have a very private wedding of under 30 attendees, possible 20." Gorgon says with another smirk as he folds his arms across his cheat.

And now Christens wondering about the brides' parents but no mentioned them at all not even a hint that they might show, very weird if not peculiar he's thinking to himself.

"And the brides family will attended I would assume? Or coming from out of town or perhaps somewhere in Europe?" He asks Gorgon. But Gorgon being the cagey, cunning man that he is will not divulge any real information regarding his future daughter in law.

"Special arrangements have been made between myself and Melissa, James nothing more, nothing less." Gorgon replies again with an expression of unless she volunteers that information, I will not. And with that Christen just gives him a look of so be it Gorgon, I will play your game of hidden agendas.

"So be it then, in two days you'll be a very proud father in law and maybe in the following months a grand dad?" Christen replies again throwing that into the discussion knowing it plays well to Gorgons ego the very thought of becoming a grandfather and corrupting his grandson.

"Yes, yes this is an absolute possibly Mr. Christen should my son Perseus decide to give his father a grandchild, a new extension to the Mathias family. It would make me very proud yes, yes indeed!" Gorgon responds in kind to that idea. After this exchange the cordless phone rings load on a table across the right of Christen and Gorgon raises up to answer it clicking line 1.

"Yes, Gorgon Mathias." He answers and his daughter Andromeda's on the line in the private library. "Dad I have Mikhail Khrichov on line 2 transferring now." She says clicking over. "Yes, yes patch him thru Annie, Mikhail, Gorgon here. What can I do for you my friend?" Gorgon asks. Mikhail's voices sounds very urgent over the phone and Gorgon is sensing he and Tisdale are looking to invade his mansion despite the fact he still has house guest.

"Gorgon, I know you have guests staying at your estate however we have an urgent matter that's needs discussion now." Mikhail demands of Gorgon.

"Mikhail, after the wedding all of this business will be dealt with and you will have that other opportunity you been planning for." Gorgon replies with certainty but before he clicks off the cordless he contacts his on call driver once again and knowing he'll race back to the manse to pick him up, then clicks off the cordless phone. But he didn't take it outside to the hall and allowed Christen to hear everything word verbatim, not even attempting to hide it from him. As if he wants his guest to imagine what's coming and prepare himself only his isn't any ordinary guest. "So your partners are arriving now yes, no Gorgon?" Christen asks.

"No, no, they have a brutish, unsophisticated entourage and I value my manse dearly. My partners have henchmen who shoot first and ask questions later or to put it other terms they are specialized fighters/ Brawlers. MMA or shall I say Mixed Martial Arts experts, such men I don't often deal with." Gorgon explains. And Christen begins to ponder this, the idea strikes him that could he could end up in room with one of these grapplers or god forbid, he tries not to think about it but Gorgons phone conversation has peaked his curiosity.

"Interesting, MMA you say, mixed martial arts? Sounds like some kind of underground fighting competition in Russia or Eastern Europe?" Christen asks.

But again Gorgon won't divulge any more information on these guys, maybe in some twisted form of loyalty in his business partners? Christen continues to play this game even though it's getting real tired and boring. But Gorgon continues.

"Very soon Mr. Christen, you'll meet my other guests and their entourage, and whatever questions or curiosity you have will be answered by them." Gorgon replies with a stern grin on his face as if he fully anticipates what's coming like a excited fight promoter.

"Excuse me Mr. Christen I have to cut this discussion short, I have an appointment with my partners in downtown Athens. You rest up and I'm certain my children have more to discuss with you." Gorgon says as he raises from the chair and quickly leaves the room, down the hall and to the stairs until he reaches the base but doesn't enter the private library this time. No he's going back to the gallery to meet Mikhail this time, and before he reaches the door he hears that limo coming into the gate and racing around the drive way right to the front door with a screech!

Yes, it's faithful Lepredo again seating, waiting, patiently watching and he doesn't exit limo at all, as Gorgan storms out the door and swings it closed all in one motion. He quickly opens the rear limo door jumps in the back seat and shut, the limo speeds off whipping around the drive way and doesn't miss a beat. With the gate wide open the car accelerates throw it and hits the curb turn at break neck as if this isn't the first time Plato has performed this routine drive with his boss. Gorgan quickly fastens the belt buckle and crosses his legs, folding his arms across his chest thinking dammit, dammit, these vessels can't arrive fast enough in Crete.

The ancient island of Crete where so many tourists would travel from around the world to visit Kissamos, Chania, Georioupolis, and Paleochora. Gorgan used his political connections to bribe the Mayor of Crete and allow his partners Tisdale, and Mikhail to dock their giant luxury ships there. All to be used as smuggling containers for massive opium shipment covered with strong ground pepper to throw off the scent should any customs agents send trained dogs in to sniff out any illegal contraband, the oldest trick in the book. And it never failed, it seemed to work every time. This was one of their largest shipments to date with a street value of well over $2.3 billion in raw opium.

Gorgon understood how important this shipment is but something else was going on behind the scenes and he figures once he arrives at the Gallery all those blanks answers would be filled. The limo is just several blocks away from his Gallery as Gorgon notices the peculiar olive green colored Range Rovers parked in the Lot outside his building. The limo doesn't even pull into the parking lot it just stops directly outside the door leaving Gorgan enough room or space to exit the rear passenger door and races toward the lobby entrance. He ignores Krichkovs middle henchmen fraternal twins Roman and Gregory Giewko seated inside the Range Rover on the driver and passenger side. He doesn't lose a step as he strides through the double doors observing Mikhail standing in the middle row near murals reading off a plate.

"This couldn't wait till after the reception, tell me what the urgency is Mikhail?" He yells out of frustration. But Mikhail is very cool and calm, he continues to study all this exquisite art in front of him. Then turns slowly to acknowledge his seemly distracted business partner with his thick Russian accent.

"Gorgon, I have demonstrated remarkable patience with you and I understand you have house quests, I'm so looking forward to this wedding and meeting your children again. However we have a responsibility to our clients who have paid a considerable amount of money for this shipment so your immediate attention is required!" Mikhail replies, barely giving Gorgon a glance as if he's talking to a teenager.

"I would appreciate it if you address me directly and not The murals, Mikhail, when you're talking to me, address me eye to eye!" Gorgon fires back, offensively. So Mikhail turns to Face him and flashes a smile for good will saying.

"Yes your correct Gorgon, let's stop acting like Adolescents and conduct ourselves like competent businessmen and adults." Mikhail replies again like he's testing Gorgan's resolve but why?

And then there's a hard knock on the outside door and its one of the fraternal twins Roman Giewko the oldest of the two brothers by two minutes, standing in the doorway and Motioning or waving to his boss Mikhail with his right hand come here quickly. Both men Gorgon and Mikhail turn to acknowledge Roman but Mikhail nods his head and turns to toward Gorgon saying.

"Gorgan give me a moment thank you this won't take long." Mikhail says, walking away from Gorgan and toward his 5ft, 10in Muscular but slim and stocky euro Slavic bodyguard. Before Mikhail gets within 5 feet of Roman, the former middle weight MMA grappler motions to his boss let's take this outside for a minute. Mikhail follows Roman to his Range

Ranger driver side door where his brother has a portable phone and hands it to Mikhail, saying in thick euro Slavic accent.

"Boss, it's Minolta!"

"Yes, Tisdale." Mikhail answers as he grabs the phone from Gregory's left hand. Tisdale Minolta seats by a table in a posh hotel room sipping a expensive glass of Chardonnay wine and eating a plate of stuffed veal with pasta and baked Italian garlic bread.

"Mikhail the shipment will arrive a day early this week Friday on the Isle of Crete docked at Ano Vouves, it's in a very wide Cargo tug boat used to haul tons of waste disposal via water route. We have over 30 men transporting the opium from Ano Vouves across Crete to ports in Kissamos and Chania were the 3 Private luxury yachts name after the titans Hyperion, Cronos, and Oceanus are being docked also. The hulls of these Private luxury vessels designed to hold 3 1/2 tons of raw opium. The arrangements have already been coordinated by Gorgon and Crete's mayor." Tisdale reports to Mikhail while taking another sip of his Chardonnay wine then wipes his lips with a diner clothe. Staring at Greek news report translated in Russian he continues.

"These luxury yachts are larger then the usual we've had in recent years, ranging from 225 feet in length down to 170 feet. As far as customs is concerned these private luxury yachts pose no threats of holding any bio-nuclear materials or hazardous substances so their haven't been any through inspections. That's just a preliminary report for now the rest will come during the reception, give Gorgon my regards Mikhail." And he clicks off.

Mikhail almost seems disappointed as if he were left out of the loop but then he deduces that Gorgon had all this arranged months in advance and felt no need discuss it while his guest were at the manse. But he isn't satisfied, not one bit, and hands the phone back to Gregory before reentering the gallery to confront Gorgon about what he just heard.

"So you weren't going to tell me about this Gorgon, this arrangement you made with the mayor of Crete? Are we now keeping important secrets from each other, details that should be shared openly?" He yells at Gorgon.

But as always Gorgon keeps his cool, remains calm and gives his impatient Russian partner another puzzled look, then he speaks crossing his arms over his chest.

"Why did you call me here for a meet? Why? We had an agreement Mikhail that during the reception we would discuss everything in full detail, everything, and yet you act as if

I've keep information from you? And nothing could be further from the truth." He replies again.

But Mikhail isn't satisfied with that answer and as he's about to go into another lecture Gorgon throws his hands in the air, turns toward the entrance and strolls quickly through lobby door again ignoring his partners body guards while yelling back, "turn out the lights and lock up when you leave." He reenters the back rear passenger door of his limo slamming it in one motion while ordering his driver, "Take me home now"! the limo pulls out into the street and accelerates back in the direction of Gorgons mansion.

Gorgons cross his legs and shakes his head in utter disgust wondering in the back of his mind this wedding, the reception and this damn shipment couldn't come fast enough for him. It was never this complicated in the past his dealings with Mikhail and Tisdale but this time with his old college friend Yusaf Tarken visiting and this man James Christen also his house Guest he was just bidding his time before he'd have to confront Christen. Something happened those months before in Turkey and his instinct, his gut keeps telling him Christen might know something about it. Or have information regarding the unfortunate blast and those untimely deaths of Mikhail's would be assassins.

Before Gorgons limo makes its trip half way across town back at the gallery Mikhail just had his comeuppances with Gorgon and turns the lights out at the front doors, whiling closing both. He holds back his embarrassment even in the face of his henchmen Roman and Gregory Gniewko, enters the passenger door as Roman also enters behind Gregory in his personalized Range Rover, slams the door and orders Gregory to take him back to Athens Radisson Hotel. Mikhail straps in his seat belt then hits a button on the middle dash board for the Range Rovers modern high tech radio, but Gregory won't allow that and the questions come. And again, in a thick Euro Slavic accent almost like listening to Former Soviet President Mikhail Gorbachov being interviewed.

"Boss what happened with Gorgon, I don't like when he gets the best of you?" he asks with a frown. But Mikhail isn't in the mood for any conversation and especially coming from his former Neanderthal middleweight MMA competitor henchmen from Kiev, Ukraine. And without a glance or even a look he responds,

"Just take me back to Athens Hotel Radisson, I want no conversation please, it gives me headache." Mikhail replies rubbing his fingers across right temple with his eyes closed. Roman puts the gear in reverse quickly pulling out the parking lot and into the street. Turns and straightens the wheel and into drive with acceleration all in one motion, while his brother Gregory continues his gaze on Mikhail who looks very frustrated and beaten.

"Boss it's not good when you are like this, so please relax and breathe inhale, exhale." Roman says while the Range Rover picks up speed running lights and thankfully there are no Pedestrians crossing the street. The brothers Giewko exchange comments with each other in their native Ukrainian tongue and are interrupted by Mikhail who understands every word they utter.

"I will not tell you again, I want silence from both of you, I need to focus and concentrate." He orders as the Range Rover pulls up to the Radisson Hotel Athens lobby where a valet is waiting dressed in black silk pants, matching shoes and suit covering a white silk with black bow tie. The Range Rover comes to a stop and Roman puts the gear in neutral, then grabs the emergency brake while Mikhail and Gregory exit the vehicle.

Roman follows from the driver's side leaving the keys in ignition as he watches the handsome looking valet climb in, shut the door and drive off to an underground parking lot just around the corner. The three of them enter the lobby and don't even bother checking in with the receptionist at the counter, they move straight for the lobby elevators to they're left and right.

On the left the even number floors and the right the odd number floors. The building itself is over 26 stories tall or 26 floors also with penthouses too!

Roman is the first to reach the elevator with odd numbers on the right and hits the button pointing up, watching the numbers descend or count down from 25 all the way down to lobby floor. When the doors slide open he steps aside allowing Mikhail first entry then his brother Gregory, now stepping in behind him he punches the button for 17 floor they hear a ring sound and the doors slide close and they begin to ascend again. This time not fast or slow just a steady speed up the shaft to the 17 floor. They all stand silently staring at the elevator doors as the floor numbers hit 12, 13, 14, 15, 16, and then finally 17. The doors slide open and this time Gregory steps out first followed by Roman and Mikhail afterwards, he moves very causally to his left down the hall just 6 doors from the elevator. Before he reaches Mikhail's room he and pulls out a 9mm Beretta with 4inch silencer or suppressor attached as does Roman. R1706 is the room number and exclusive executive suite reserved by Mikhail days before arriving in Athens, Greece over a week ago. He reaches into his suit pocket taking out his special card key for the hotel room door, placing it in a slot like a ATM card, the light on the slot reads green and they hear a pop.

The door is open and in one motion Mikhail twists the door handle while snatching the card out the slot placing it back in his suit pocket. He pulls the door open and his guys rush in one with his gun drawn and the other ready for anything and they find nothing. No sign of any forced entry, or break in. Mikhail takes off his suit placing it on the chair. The room is quit spacious for Mikhail and almost resembled a penthouse fit for a millionaire with expensive taste. Unlike most hotel executive suites this one didn't have a swimming pool or Jacuzzi outside but it did contain a very well stocked wet bar. With almost every possible spirit and brand of wine you could imagine for a room costing $3500.75 a night to stay.

Just 11 feet from Mikhail's bed was a table design to seat 5 people and when he lays down to rest, his henchmen take their seats, beginning a strategy of their own. Mikhail doesn't even bother to take off his shoes, in fact he kicks them off at the heel one after the other while he's laying on his back.

Fortunately for him there are slip on shoes and require no laces to untie very quick, very convenient. He orders Roman to make himself useful and pour Mikhail a drink from the bar, while Gregory stares at his brother, then Mikhail and shakes his head in disgust. Roman walks over to the wet bar and grabs a class out of the cabinet while opening the freezer in one motion and grabs several cubes of ice. He drops them into the class, while looking for a bottle of Kamchatka Vodka to pour. He finds it seating next to several different bottles of gin and whiskey.

So now like a pro he handles the bottle left hand first, unscrews the cap with his right fingers then twists it off with his thumb as it spins off and hits the counter. He pours it into the glass just before it reaches half full then snatches the cap from the counter, twisting it back on the bottle. All while

Mikhail is consoling with confused and frustrated Gregory Gniewko.

"Gregory I know I told you in the car to keep silent however when I'm dealing with Mr. Mathias things tend to get intense and overly heated. He always gets the better of me and I have a hard time dealing with that, so when you witness this it's embarrassing to me personal." Mikhail explains to him like he's giving the young man a lecture on nuclear physics. Watching all this Roman walks over to Mikhails' bed when Mikhail directs him to place the class of vodka on the rocks to his left night stand, and place a napkin over the glass and under it. Afterward he seats back down across the table from his brother and the rooms cordless phone rings, this time it's Alexandr Anatoly sharing a room with Vladimir "Big Crunchy" Bulnor. And where he got this infamous nickname will be explained later on in the story. Mikhail grabs the cordless phone and hits a green button for open line and begins his conversation with Mr. Anatoly.

"Mikhail my boss has informed me that after this wedding reception we're having a Q and A session with one of Gorgons house guests? Do you know anything about this?" he asks Mikhail while plays with his hand grips.

"Yes, this man could be very dangerous and he's South African Intelligence, meaning he could have some valuable Information on that unfortunately incident in Ankara, Turkey some weeks ago." Mikhail responds in kind. But he's well aware that Tisdale has henchmen of his own or shall we say his personal guards and he won't order them around without absolute approval from Minolta. Now Alexandr takes all this in as his roommate Vladimir "Big Crunchy" Bulnor watches his favorite gothic TV show The Buchanans in Greek subtitles. Alexandr continues his conversation with Mikhail while also lying down watching the same program as Vladimir.

"Now I most also bring Krasimir and Natali up to date on this new development, they also travel with us here from Ukraine and Moscow. Anyway, for recap the wedding is less than two days from now then Q and

A during reception and finally the shipment comes in to Island of Crete from Afghanistan? Do I have this correct Mikhail?" he asks before he's about to click off his cordless phone and continue watching the Buchanans.

"Da, you are correct Alexandr" Mikhail replies meaning yes in Russian.

"Very good so now I give Krasimir and Natali a call informing them of this conversation and they make prep for information extraction." Alexandr replies again this time clicks the cordless off and hits the room number of Krasimir Rostislav and Natali Mochavic Radoslav the specialists. Krasimir Rostislav holds the unique distinction of being bodyguard to former Russian Oligarch and business magnate Boris Berezovsky who was close advisor to former Russian President Boris Yeltson before he sought exile Great Britain to escape the new regime of Vladimir Putin Yeltsons' successor. The cordless phone rings several times before Krasimir picks up, it seems he and Natali are heavy in a game of Chess. They also sport the same close crop hair cuts as Roman and Gregory and have very weird looking tattoos one both arms and chest to back, one suspects they did belong to the Russian or European mafia syndicates before defecting to Mikhail and Tisdale for more money and finer living standards.

Krasimir grabs the nearby cordless and hits the green button for open line. "Alexandr, you lucky bastard you and Vladimir get executive suites? It must be nice huh? A view of beautiful skyline?" he asks with envy in his voice.

"By the way I want to have talk with "Big Crunchy" in fact why don't you just put me on speaker, this concerns you too?" He asks. And with that request Alexandr hits the button for speaker and Krasimir begins repeating the same conversation he had with Mikhail.

"I was on the phone with Mikhail just minutes before I called you and it seems we have a situation, after this wedding their will be Q and A session during the wedding reception. Those are the only details I care to disclose at this moment also you two maybe called for other extra curricular activities of the torture variety but I'll allow him the honor of explaining that." He says before he attempts to click off speaker and he's interrupted. "So if I understand this, Mikhail wants information extracted from this person during the reception? Is that what this is about?" he asks.

"I never mentioned anything about any person it's just a Q and A session." Krasimir replies. But Alexandrs not buying into it and he already has the inside scope from his boss Tisdale.

"Whatever, so consider myself and "Big Crunchy" informed! We will deal with it when the moment arrives in the mean time thanks for the call and enjoy the suite." Alexandr responds before clicking off the cordless and continuing his chess game with "Big Crunchy" Bulnor. The aftermath of this conversation begins to aggravate Krasimir while in the back of his mind he's thinking that phone call was for nothing it would seem as if they already know what Mikhail and Tisdale have planned or it was on a need to know basis? Either way all this damn secrecy made doing business with Tisdale and Gorgon very irritating and had their boss Mikhail constantly feeling like he's out of the loop. Krasimir continues thinking to himself business partners, close business partners are required to share everything at least when it comes to matters concerning money and commerce but their was something else happening. On the surface it only seemed like everyone's functioning on the same page however, the recent rumors swirling about an explosion in Ankara, Turkey just weeks if not months ago has everyone on edge and wondering when the Perpetrator is caught, who will dish out the retribution.

After taking several long sips of his vodka on the rocks Mikhail asks for another reload or refill but this time Roman has had and seen enough, he gives a look to Gregory then takes a seat. So then Gregory get up from his seat and rushes over to the wet bar to grab a glass from the same cabinet and pitcher of ice from the freezer. He uses the same method as he's brother when he reaches for the bottle of Kamchatka Vodka, twists the cap with his left fingers and uses his left thumb too spin the cap off. He grabs several cubes of ice with his fingers dropping them into the glass before pouring it almost half full the way Mikhail likes it. He sticks the ice pitcher back in the freezer and quickly rushes the glass back over to Mikhail being very careful not drop or spill any of it on himself or the floor. He places the new vodka filled glass next to the one Mikhail finishes off and watches his boss snatch it and toss it back with one long gulp. He gently seats it down and leans back against his pillows and finally he begins to fade off, yep that strong 15% proof alcohol is taking effect. Its sleepy time!

They just watch him nod off with his mouth slightly open and as always happens when he drinks he starts snoring but not loud or too annoying that they can't bare the sound of it. They glance at each other shaking their heads and smiling, then Roman grabs a remote control and hits the power button for the 45 inch screen TV in their suite. Lucky for him it's already preprogramed so he doesn't have to scan or look for channels to watch just hit up or down arrows and the channels give him the usual satellite content in Greece. Gregory makes himself comfortable on a sofa across the room directly from the bed Mikhail sleeping in. Takes his suit and shoes off and gets into a lazy slouching position on the sofa with his right leg crossed over the left concentrating on whatever his brothers watching on TV.

Another unexpected call comes in on the cordless and this time it's bad ass "Big Crunchy" Bolnor Vladimir wanting to talk strategy with Mikhail's henchman Roman and Gregory. Before Roman has a chance to tear himself away from the TV screen his brother jumps up from the sofa and races for the cordless phone. The caller ID reads Athens Hilton Hotel, Gregory snatches the cordless off the charger and hits the green talk button. "Yes, who's calling" he asks in Ukrainian. "It's Vladimir Bolnor, I need to speak with Mikhail." He replies also in Ukrainian.

"He's asleep at the moment may I take a message for him?" Gregory asks? "I have a better idea is this Gregory, you can meet me outside the hotel lobby so we can talk business yes?" Gregory eagerly agrees to this, "No problem just give me 10 minutes to get dressed." Gregory answers then clicks off the cordless phone, placing it back on the charge he slips his shoes back on then singles to his brother Roman that's he's about to step out for a moment. Roman barely acknowledges his twin brother well his attention is on the TV program and Gregory just quickly slips out the door and gently closes it, hearing it lock behind him. He races for the elevator down the hall to his right after passing six room suites before finally reaching the elevator and hits the arrow button pointing down.

The elevators at the third floor then begins to ascend to 4 and 5, 6, 7, 8, 9, 10, 11, 12, 13, 14, 15, 16, then finally 17th floor. As the doors slid open there's a buzz sound then the infamous elevator music and he steps in hitting the lobby button as it begins its descent to the lobby floor. He patiently watches the numbers till it goes down to 1 then stops and the doors slid open again. And without losing stride he darts out the elevator and directly toward the lobby door where "Big Crunchy" Vladimir stands outside waiting for him while smoking one of his Expensive designer European cigarettes. Gregory pushes his way through the revolving class door to finds "Big Crunchy" Vladimir standing leaned up against a street light with arms folded across his chest and taking hits of his cigarette at the same time. Gregory stands just 4 feet from

"Big Crunchy" looking around as if he suspects he might get jumped from behind or surprised by someone while at the same time observing this man's intimidating build. He stands 6 foot 3 inches tall with a lanky but very solid build and dresses very casually. "Big Crunchy" had him sizes up the moment he came through the revolving class doors but he maintains his composure while smoking his cigarette. His face has a slight smirk as if he in his mind he likes the balls on this 5 foot 9 inch Ukraine Gregory.

"So you want to talk? Well I'm here, let's talk!" he says as Vladimir nods his head and offers him a smoke. "You wanna hit of this?" Vladimir asks.

"I don't smoke but your welcome to continue and I'm waiting to hear what you have to say." He replies again already growing impatient with "Big Crunchy".

"See it's like this my boss tells my me and my partners we could have a situation tomorrow afternoon after this wedding with some guy who's a agent with South African Intelligence. He may be dangerous and they want to ask him some questions so if he resists then that's where we come in." he explains.

Now Gregory already knows this but he listens and nods his head in agreement anyway thinking this guy looks like he has a lot of brawn but no brains to go with it.

"Yes I was informed of the same intel also he has a collogue and fellow house quest of Mr. Mathais. Its seems this man has history with Gorgon if my information is correct?" Gregory asks. But Vladimir just ignores that question and continues like he's more concerned with the information extraction and possible some torture if it comes down to it. Things might get ugly and physical if Tisdale and Mikhail orders this guys to soften Christen up a bit.

"I need to know that when the shit gets intense and I suspect it will that you and your brother won't punk out on us?" "Big Crunchy" Vladimir asks Gregory in a very subtle tone. And Gregory looks away trying to hide his emotion and not allow Vladimir the opportunity to his expression. He gives him a calm, cool, indirect stare eye to eye and fires back confidently,

"When the moment comes my brother and I will are well prepared to handle this situation, just don't you underestimate us, I've heard stories and rumors of Russian arrogance, hubris.

You should learn to separate your ego from such matters Vladimir. Oh, by the way, where did your acquire that nick name anyway "Big Crunchy?" Gregory asks before he begins to reenter the hotel lobby and get back to his room for rest.

Vladimir smiles with a slight chuckle finishing off his cigarette and touches it to the side walk.

"So your curious to know how I got the nick name "Big Crunchy no? I used to compete in MMA let's say several years ago light heavy division in Moscow, anyway one of my finishing holds was a what I called dragon swipe slam. I would hoist my opponent in the air while he had his legs wrapped around my neck and shoulders then slam him hard to the mat several times." Vladimir "Big Crunchy" answers with glee just thinking of the pain and punishment he dealt out to his opponents inside the UFC octagon. And he continues!

"Then I'd get in real close quarters snatch him by the waist and twirl his body in midair dropping him directly across my right knee or sometimes left knee until I heard crunch sound of his lower back or vertebrate listening to the sound of his spine upon impact. That beautiful crunch sound of my knee connecting with the lower spinal cord." Vladimir replies and Gregory has heard enough. So Vladimir continues, "So fans start to chant "Big Crunchy", "Big Crunchy", and it just stuck also my former trainer and manager started to call me "Crunchy" also and that's been my nick name ever since." He finishes. At this moment Gregory signals or motions he returning to his room and Vladimir remarks "ok".

"Interesting "Big Crunchy" well I'm tired and it's time for me retire so if you'll excuse me Vladimir till next time." He says entering the hotel lobby glass doors again. "Big Crunchy" returns to his hotel suite also just around the corner with his partners sound as asleep. Gregory returns into the hotel lobby and straight to the elevator door when this time its on the 1st floor he just hits the button and it slides open. He steps in and pushes

17 on the panel when it begins to ascend same as before. Now he's tired from the trip and flight from Ukraine and all the other bullshit he and his brother have dealt with since arriving in Athens 4 days ago. Going from 1, 2, 3, 4, 5, 6, 7, 8, 9, 10, 11, 12, 13, 14, 15, 15, 16, then finally 17th floor again he steps out then back to his left again, six rooms down. Back to the private suite, he knocks three times on the door and Roman answers after under a minute and 25 seconds.

Gregory grabs the handle of the door and slowly closes it so not to disrupt Mikhail from his sleep and he snores kinda loud too! Roman takes his seat by the big screen TV but then decides he wants to know what was discussed between Gregory and Vladimir. Or "Big Crunchy." And before Gregory has a chance to seat down his brother gives him a look of 'so what did he have to say?' Gregory takes a seat at the table directly across from Mikhail's bed and the two of them begin their conversation even though their bosses snoring only seems to get louder by the minute. Gregory gently folds his arms across his chest while beginning to share his thoughts.

"Vladimir seems to think we don't have the stones, you or I no wait let me rephrase that … the balls to follow through so I had to reassure him there's no punk in either of us." Gregory tells his brother while studying his expression after this encounter and Roman chimes in with his two sense. "So this arrogant Russian fuck basically thinks we won't follow through? You know I figured something was off at that gallery with Mr. Minolta and that guy Gorgan." He replies with a frown on his face. "These guys still think the fuckin cold war is still happening, motherfucker you lost the arms race to the west, get over it." he says throwing his hands in the air in disgust. With that said Gregory takes a seat on a couch directly across from the sofa from where Roman was lying down and he does the same.

The moment he gets comfortable he quickly nods off asleep at the same kicking off his slip on shoes getting comfortable again. Now it's three of them finally seating down or lying down resting, preserving their strength for this wedding reception coming up. After several hours into the morning just before dust the cordless phone ranging in Mikhail's suite and its Gorgan this time calling from Tisdales executive suite and helping himself to a nice continental breakfast of Bran muffins,

Blueberry muffins, and margarine with pitchers of cold apple juice, Tomato juice and gourmet coffee smelling like French Vanilla accompanied by three plates 1 a mountain heap of Scrambled eggs with turkey sausage and bacon, soy margarine hell yes and gluten free spread over 18 hot bagels with grape and strawberry jam.

Also cinnamon oatmeal with dates and walnuts swirls in a bowl steaming hot with glasses, china plates, forks, and spoons with napkins set for 2 to 8 people, only this time it's just Gorgan and Tisdale until there's another knock on the door. Surprise, surprise Tisdale's crew arrives just in time for breakfast, Alexandr Anatoly, Vladimir "Big Crunchy" Bulnor, Krasimir Rostislav, and Natali Mochavic Radoslav. Tisdale opens the door while Gorgan has already taken his seat at the table while his guys make their way into the suite and over to the table also. With no reserved seats they all seat down without missing a beat and start passing around the food, hell without even saying grace. Lending credibility to the universal rumor that Russians are indeed atheists, don't believe in god or the sight of this buffet has them very hungry indeed.

Observing this Gorgan has already prepared his cup with cream and no sugar he grabs himself a few bagels and pours a cup of coffee ¾ full before he tears the one bagel apart and takes a bite. The other five keep talking turns passing around the plates and bowls of scrambled eggs, oatmeal, turkey bacon and sausage until all their plates are full. Surprisingly though Tisdale doesn't touch the coffee but fills His glass with tomato juice with his plate of turkey bacon and Scrambled eggs and two Bran muffins. He breaks pieces of his muffin in half then begins to eat biting off chunks of this bran muffin and washing it down with a few sips of the tomato juice. This intrigues Gorgon who's never seen anyone drink Tomato juice with a bran muffin before but Tisdale noticing Gorgon's rather amused expression quickly gives an explanation. "Incase your wondering about my unusual diet? My personal physician ordered me to try this at least for a while, until my symptoms improve." He responds to Gorgon. But that brief explanation doesn't satisfy Gorgon at all and before he has a chance to inquire, Tisdale continues but Gorgon interrupts anyway?

"I wasn't aware you had an illness my friend and here all these years I thought I we knew each other very well?" Gorgon interjects. So now Tisdale figures may as well explain in full detail as oppose to later on.

"During a routine physical 2 years ago my Doctor discovered I have rare form of Knugobpic cancer." With this Gorgon gives him a real funny look like 'what the fuck is that'?

"They found several polyps the size of grape seeds outside my large intestine walls interfering with my digestive system so it was recommended that I change my diet just slightly with Tomato juice and Bran muffins". He continues taking another bite of his muffin and this time a much larger gulp of his tomato juice. What's really interesting is while these two are having this back and forth discussion Tisdale's henchmen continue to feed their faces. However no one touches the blueberry muffins then all of sudden the fellows decide to leave the table and hit the gym three floors below.

"Wait, wait your leaving now but you haven't finished your breakfast." Tisdale orders, but Gorgon nods his head and singles to the guys, "Gentlemen go work it off, your boss and I have some important business to discuss." And they file out the room one after the other leaving their plates half full and the last man gently closes the door behind him.

"So I need to know that we are on the same page here Tisdale on 2 issues, starting with #1. your men will not engage my house quest until after the wedding reception and #2 the shipment will arrive this week hours after the wedding reception. Also a small team will help with the loading process we have a unique loading mechanism set up so time wont be a major factor?" And with that said Tisdale studies Gorgons face a moment, after taking another gulp of his tomato juice and the last bite of his gluten free bran muffin.

"Let me understand this Gorgon you have already made arrangements with the authorities in Crete correct? On standby will be 3 luxury ships, yachts whatever correct? Each ship well over 250 feet long with deep hull capacity, including the product wrapped or shipped in ground peppers and coffee grounds also? And there will be no problems at all with customs?" he questions then takes a deep breathe and sighs.

"You will excuse me if I don't share your optimism my friend, it simply seems too convenient Gorgon." He fires back and Gorgon counters as if he saw this question coming from a mile away.

"I can't believe we're going over this again, how many times must I keep reassuring you time and time again for the love of Zeus and Apollo it's been weeks, months now, I own the Mayor of Crete. I'm the reason he's Mayor, he will do whatever I say!" replies Gorgon, while Tisdale takes the last gulp of his Tomato juice. And just stares into space kind of studying Gorgons plans for this special transfer mechanism then grabs a napkin and wipes his lips, chin and crumbles it up in a ball gently tossing it on his plate.

"So tell me about this transfer contraption, this device that you have prepared for our shipment this weekend? I may have an idea of what your speaking of?" Tisdale asks. And Gorgon pulls out of his suite pocket what appears to be a folded diagram of the machine with connecting conveyor belt built for transporting very large quantities of narcotics from point to another. This machine named after a very popular car manufacture the Chrysler model 1800 is mobile and connects to 16 wheel tractor trailer and will hold and or carry 40 to 75 blocks of product on the belt per 8 to 10 feet of space. The conveyor belt is 100% cow leather 1 inch thick and measures 35 inches in width.

"It's very tough, extremely sturdy and it's designed to handle whatever amount weight we deem necessary to transport from the trailers to the bow of the luxury vessels." Gorgon answers with absolute confidence and observes Tisdale studying the 4 page diagram like a 15 year teenager combing through his favorite comic book but then Tisdale interjects, "This looks like something I might see in an industrial warehouse or perhaps the shipping and receiving centers of Macys or JC Penny?" he finishes. Turning to the fourth and last page before folding it and sliding it back across the table to Gorgon, who grabs it, and sticks it back into his suite pocket. While the two bosses are discussing shipping and transport strategy before visiting the Isle of Crete, the henchmen are making use of the hotel weight room and quest gym.

The guys spread out in the hotel gym and weight room Roman and Gregory take off their shirts exposing the many tattoos they have covering abs, chests, shoulders, arms, hands, fingers, and other body parts not shown in public. They wear an identical tattoo of a pig nailed to cross with eights stars on its body and fire at its feet like its being burned at the stake. With strange foreign symbols or writing around the cross or crucifix. An anti-Ukrainian tattoo from Russian nationalist. Ukrainian text reads 'Long live red Ukraine. Gregory turns pounding and kicking a Ever last punching bag, so Roman holds it firm while his brother Gregory throws in solid combinations of punches and jabs, while Vladimir "Big Crunchy" Bulnor works on his pectoral muscles with the bench press machine his too has an interesting 'lyrical tattoo', containing an extract from the words of a criminals' song.

The woman, the black panther and skulls are symbols of devotion, fearlessness and cruelty. The wearer was twice convicted of theft under article 144 of the Criminal Code the USSR. The dates 1959-1962 refer to time spent in the Omsk Corrective Labour Colony. Now he's too young to have spent any time in this Soviet Labour Colony but he wears this and many other tattoos for emotional connection. On Vladimir's back near his left shoulder is another bold tattoo, a 'nationalist' from an 'Old Believer' convict. This is an example of an extreme nationalist tattoo that expresses the bloodthirsty attitude of devotees of the 'Great Russian Idea' towards all non-Russians. typical for warriors', 'hitmen' and 'wet-jobbers'. He wears another tattoo next to that of a smiling tiger holding a gun in one hand and army knife in another.

A 'warrior's grin'. This means 'Take out bitches, stool- pigeons and traiters!' The acroym 'MIR spells the word peace and stands for 'Stood will reform me'. He carries yet another tattoo under this meaning 'Don't touch me if you want to live!' This menacing tattoo depicting a two-face like werewolf is usually applied to so-called 'satanists' or 'dunces'-inveterate transgressors of the prison regime. He also wears under this a tattoo of two poker cards with a rose in the middle and syringe on top worn by Alexandr Anatoly, Krasimir Rostislav and Natali Mochavic also.

Besides Vladimir they all wear very weird and elaborate tattoos covering their neck, shoulders, waist, fingers, back, only to be hidden by their pants from the waist down. Alexandr and Krasimir take turns spotting each other on the triceps extension machine with 75 and 85 pound weights as a warm up, also last but not least Natali works out on the triceps pull down doing 5 sets of 10 then, builds up to 8 sets of 12 and so on. With each pull he stops in mid stride then pulls straight down, and continues this very difficult regimen not breaking a bead of sweat. Alexandr and Krasimir didn't look like your typical hard bodies in fact they are deceptively powerful and amazingly agile for guys their size and height.

But underestimating SAI agent James Christen will prove to be their ultimate downfall. The two continue to take turns spotting each other and placing more biscuits or 45 pound weights on the bar bell. This time its hit 345 pounds and Alexandr goes first breathing a certain way so as to preparing his body for the shock of pressing weight into the air and off his chest. His Pushes it up the bar bell letting his chest muscles do all the Work and not his arms but they're screaming or he can feel them crying out this shit is so heavy. But he know the other guys are watching him and so strains but pushes that bar straight over his head and holds it there for under 4 seconds then drops it to back to the bar.

They clap hands and encourage him push a few more but his Arm muscles are burning from the pain and he can barely left them above his waist let alone his shoulders. He seats up and takes a rest then grabs a towel and throws it over his shoulders before leaving the hotel gym for a vending machine. The others continue their work out while Alexandr walks the hotel hall for a can of Seltzer water just around the corner to the left of the gym. He finds the vending machine is nearly empty but his luck has changed, theirs a can and its flavor is lemon lime. He reaches into his pockets and pulls out a dollar worth of euro coins. He feeds the coins into the vending machine and hits the button designated for his can, the machine pushes it out and he snatches it.

Pulls the flap open on the top and tosses the can back toward his open mouth and doesn't even swallow, just lets it flow down his throat till its half gone then he finally swallows. He takes a look down the hall as if he hears something and gulps down the last of the seltzer water before throwing it into a trash bin next to the vending machine. Now he feels refreshed it time to get back to the gym and lay back while his partners wear themselves out with the dead weights. Before he gets back down the hall to the gym he's met by them turning the corner and heading straight for the elevator back up to the executive suite. Vladimir is the first to comment while the others wait for the elevator to ascend from the lobby floor.

"Alexandr you left gym for vending machine and didn't offer us refreshments? That very selfish of you no?" Vladimir asks as the elevator gets closer to the 15th floor.

"Did you not wolf down a plate of eggs, turkey sausage and muffins with two tall glasses of apple juice and your bitchin? That rep of yours is over rated Vlad, over rated!" replies Alexandr. Finally they hear a ring or bell it's the elevator stopping at the 15th floor then it opens and within a few seconds they quickly enter and this time Gregory hits 17 button. Roman and Gregory wipe the sweat from their faces while the Elevator closes and begins its ascent back up to the 17 fl, the Others just stand quietly sometimes murmuring to themselves as the elevator finally ascends and stops at the 17 fl. And they can't wait for it to open in a matter of seconds the doors separate from each other and they race out toward the suite with Gregory reaching the door first. He pulls out his key card and drops it in the digital slit, the light turns green and the hear that pop sound again, the door is unlocked. The guys find Tisdale and Gorgan right where they left them as one after the other they enter the executive suite and the last man in is Vladimir shutting the door behind him.

Being the very observant man he is Gorgan quickly notices the beads of sweat pouring off the brows and necks of Roman and Gregory.

"So gents I gather your workout was satisfactory, your boss and I were just discussing the shipping details for this weekend. And time is money in my business so if you all will excuse I most return home, Tisdale!" Says Gorgon raising from his seat and grabbing his suit from around the chair, he makes his way around Tisdale and Mikhails henchmen until he's within mere a few feet of the door and Tisdale wishes he wouldn't go.

"You don't have to leave Gorgon, stick around for a few more minutes come on?" Tisdale asks. But Gorgon will have none of it and responds before his hand hits the door knob.

"I've already neglected my house guests' gentlemen, Tisdale we will continue this very soon, fellas it's been fun.

Oh yes there's plenty of left overs so help yourselves." He says before leaving the room and makes his stride back to the elevator on his right all in one motion swings the door closed behind him. He wondering to himself are they back there discussing his shipping plans or wondering why he was so quick to leave? And the truth is Gorgon isn't comfortable around thugs, hoodlums, as weird as it sounds be it Russian, Ukrainian, Western, Asian, U.S. thugs, they are all the same in his eyes But at the same time they are a means to an end.

They serve a specific purpose, they have the skills he needs to get information or send a brutal message don't cross him or suffer the consequences.

Also Natali and Krasimir have a well-known reputation For being kleptomaniacs or they have very sticky fingers and For them Gorgons estate is off limits. Unlike their follow henchmen these gentlemen never miss an opportunity to find something of great value they can steal or fence for quick profit.

While Gorgon tries to shake the very thought of these brutes stealing from him he finally approaches the elevator and presses the arrow-button going down. He pulls out his cell phone from his suit pocket and calls his driver who's parking the limo in the parking garage next door to the hotel, he hits speed dial as the elevator stops and the doors slide open. He steps in, hits 1st floor lobby button and stands back against the wall while it descends to the lobby floor. "I'm in the elevator now coming down, so I will meet you out front near lobby." He orders his driver as the elevator nears 8th and 9th floors gradually descending.

"Very good sir, give me a few minutes to collect you." He driver replies. Gorgon whips out his platinum Rolex watch and times the elevator once it finally hits 3, 2, and then 1st floor lobby. The sound of a bell rings and the doors slide open. He bursts out the elevator never losing stride, nor does he look to his left or right just straight forward. He pushes through the revolving doors to the side walk and curb where other bell hop men are helping pedestrians load and unload their luggage. His driver must be aware his being timed and before Gorgon has another chance to glance at his watch, he finds his driver making a sharp u turn and pulling directly in front of him. He quickly opens the back door and slips inside as his driver pulls off into the street. His driver decides to open the drive with some conversation about the meet and breakfast. "Sir I hope your meeting went well this morning?" he asks. And Gorgon crosses his legs, giving his driver a look but he answers.

"Yes it went fairly well Lupredo, theirs some concern about the shipment and cargo however that problem has already being resolved." Gorgon answers. It's like a routine for him the driver always takes the same route back to Gorgons estate and it's the quickest route from downtown, Gorgons estate connects between Mt. Lycabettus and the Attica basin. He was fortunate to find and purchase the most exclusive private real estate centered in Greece just after the cold war in Europe. Now he play devils advocate with his house quests James Christen and his old college classmate

Yusef Tarken who are suspecting something's coming but unware of the sinister plans being hatched.

Gorgon stares out the passenger window where he can see Just several blocks away his gate leading to the drive way of his manse. It's nearly dusk and the morning sky shows the sun raising from the east, while Gorgon knows in a few hours his son's wedding will draw many out of town guests. Some Gorgon has seen in recent years others not for well over a decade and everything must be on schedule including the catering, band and the Greek Orthodox Priest preforming the ceremony. The limo approaches the gate and it opens without fail so the driver makes a sharp right turn guiding the limo through and around the driveway to the front lobby. There's no one to greet him and he presumes everyone's asleep after all its close to 6am in the morning.

As usual he exits the limo right rear passenger side without his driver assistants, he also instructs his driver to get some rest and he call him when he needs him, without missing a beat he strolls thru lobby, into the manse straight to his private study directly across from his private library to his right. It has a glass office desk with pc tower on the floor and flat screen monitor with mouse and key board on the desk. Two couches surrounding a table and 52 inch satellite screen TV facing him. His private study also has 5 HD dynamic surround sound speakers Each one placed in the room giving it a cinematic theater appeal.

With a room adjacent to it housing a king size bed with drawers, mirrors, shower and coat rack with his pajama robe hanging from it. No walk in closet though. Entering the room his quickly undresses, pulling off his shoes, pants, suit, and tie placing every then on a chair placed 3 feet from the bed then crawls in the peeling back the covers and blankets until he's found a comfortable position then closes his eyes. Upstairs Yusaf Tarken starts packing his luggage, all his shoes, suits, pants, shirts, ties and he didn't bring any fire arms with him on his trip. Perhaps in the back of his mind he knew he wouldn't need a gun while visiting Gorgon anyway. Theirs was a very cordial relationship of two former college classmates who maintained a semi competitive streak between them. But Tarken knows his former college mate has a very hidden dark side and for the sake of keeping the peace or maintaining his love/hate relationship with Tarken he will engage Christen after his plane takes off. Tarken hasn't lost his faith in Christen and he knows his sudden departure won't stop Gorgon from pressing Christen for answers.

The wedding is just hours away and Tarken like Christen has been left in the dark about who these out of town guests are and what relationship they have with the bride and groom. Then there's the issue or question of Gorgons business partners showing with wedding gifts for Perseus and his future bride Melissa. There's so much mystery in the air for this occasion it almost seems like a dress rehearsal for an assassination or something more sinister. Keep positive thoughts, positive thoughts, Tarken says to himself repeatedly as he continues folding his cloth items as the scent of breakfast coffee and eggs comes from the kitchen below. He still worries about Christen knowing he already has a valid escape plan or he won't Have the opportunity to back up his coworker, oh what a dilemma. Tarken leaves his cloths for a minute or more and goes down stairs to the kitchen where Andromeda's making breakfast. Before he enters he observes her working the stove and cooking counter, with bowls, cartoons of eggs, packs of turkey bacon and sausage, bagels and fruit jelly, grape and strawberry, with pitchers of water, orange juice, apple juice, and gourmet coffee French vanilla with amaretto on the table.

She notices someone watching her from behind and strikes a Smile then begins her dialogue or conversation with Tarken.

"Have a seat breakfast is almost ready Mr. Tarken," she tells before a he slowly seats down. And can't resist the urge to critique her culinary abilities. "I had no idea you were so talented in the kitchen Miss. Andromeda, the food smells good and looks delicious." He comments fixing himself a cup of coffee while adding the sugar and creamer first then pouring the French vanilla almost to the rim of the cup. He inhales the vapors from the hot French vanilla when she answers him, "My talents extends beyond mere cloths and fashion Mr. Tarken so have you know, a few years ago father hired a chef to teach me Culinary arts and the proper way to prepare food. Thinking it might become my vocation in life, I turn into a major disappointment for him." She replies with a slight frown as she whips the eggs in one Skillet, they scramble and tends to the turkey bacon and turkey sausages in another. Multi-tasking all while having a conversation with him and she continues "My father is very old school and old fashion man, taught that a woman's place is in the kitchen, I reject that thinking,

I like to conduct trading online, investing and he takes exception to that. So we reach an impasse and we don't talk like we used too anymore thus the tension between us." She replies all while Tarken is sipping his coffee and listening very intently to her then adds his two cents again.

"Annie your dad just wants the best for you sweetie also he's trying to prepare you for when you become a future wife, you and you hubby wont starve or eat out every other night. Those culinary skills come in handy when money gets tight or financial times get hard." Tarken adds before pouring himself another cup of French vanilla coffee. And they hear a knock at the kitchen door its, James Christen visiting the kitchen and drawn by the strong smell of breakfast seasoned eggs with turkey sausage and Bacon. Annie takes the skillet combined with both heaping's bacon and sausage carrying It over to the table and pours it into a bowl in front of Tarken. Who's also chewing a bagel with strawberry jelly while drinking his coffee.

"Well, well look who's cooking breakfast this morning the beautiful Andromeda." He says before taking his seat indirectly across from Tarken. Who offers him a cup of fresh brewed gourmet

French vanilla coffee with amaretto mixed in and a small plate of bagels with grape jelly spread over. Before Christen has a chance to ask any questions or make any comments Tarken interjects quickly, "Annie was explaining to me the tension between her father and regarding her career choices and yes she knows her way around the kitchen." He says. But Christen doesn't comfortable discussing Annies relationship with her father. And he's already on edge considering the wedding is just 11 hours away and his still suspects that moment is coming for him very soon.

But for the sake of socializing he offers his own advice in the matter. "I'm confident whatever disagreement they have will be resolved between them in time, it sounds like a mere misunderstanding is all. I'm I correct? Andromeda? Yes, no?" he asks her bluntly and she gives him a look of what the hell do you know about it but doesn't verbalize that out loud. "Sort of, slightly on target." She says with a smirk on her face afterward. Taking the skillet back to the stove and quickly grabbing the other with a pile of seasoned scrambled eggs, carefully taking it over to the table and with a spatula unloading it into a 8*18 plastic cookware pan. At that point she walks back to the stove as Christen and Tarken take turns scoping portions into their plates.

Both men eat the delicious turkey bacon and sausage with seasoned eggs while Annie cleans up everything, all skillets, including other utensils, spatula, long folks and knives. Thank god for portable dish washers, she loads all the cookware into it with the utensils, and pours in the machine wash liquid detergent and shuts the door. Hits a button, the machine does all the work and finally she seats down with the guys and takes a cup of French vanilla coffee herself with a little sugar no cream, then without missing a beat she answers christen question.

"Only have correct Mr. Christen, I'm what you would call the problem child, or black sheep of the family?" she laughs then continues. "No, no, no gentleman, I must confess a little secret and Tarken I presume already knows or maybe he's doesn't. Perseus and I have different mothers, yes it's true." She replies, while Tarken nods his head in agreement but can't talk with mouth full of seasoned eggs and turkeys sausage. He takes a sip of apple juice to wash it down then offers he's own commentary.

"Yes I'm aware of this Andromeda, there's nothing about you and your brother I don't know! In fact I met your mom very briefly many years ago at a business conference your dad was attending, yes it's a small world." He tells her. Now Christen is even more intrigued at the strange but cordial relationship between Tarken and Gorgon while he doesn't interrupt their conversation.

"Mr. Christen in case you aren't aware by now my mum was born on the island of Jamaica, a Caribbean woman, yes father also liked dark skin women too." She says while laughing.

"Did he also tell you my mum wanted me to follow her into Culinary arts?" she asks again?

"I have nothing against cooking however my true talent is was and is finance, investing. That's my passion but my parents didn't think that was a worthwhile occupation for a young Euro-Caribbean woman. I had to obey my parents, then my mum was diagnosed with Breast cancer when I was 18, by that time it was too late the doctors didn't catch it in time before it spread half way across her body. We watched her grow weaker and weaker everyday until she just wasted away. My dad couldn't handle it. He rededicated himself to his Art Gallery and building it up as a distraction.

After her funeral he never remarried again, the Gallery has become his wife." She finishes and Christen and Tarken cleaned their plates but there's still so much more food left, bagels, sausage, and jelly, fruit juice and water. So now Christen is ready for some entertainment of any kind and Tarken has other items to pack before his plane leaves late in the evening.

She continues drinking her gourmet French vanilla coffee with amaretto flavor when Christen raises up from the table and attempts to excuse himself. But before he gets out the door Tarken gives him a look like where are you going man? And of course Christen can read his expression, "I have a some unfinished business waiting for me I upstairs ladies and gentlemen to be continued. Annie the breakfast was delicious, thanks again." He replies and this time he makes it out the kitchen and back down the hall to the stairs at his right. He starts from the base up two at a time then one step once he reaches the top thinking he must check in with Currency for his update. He turns directly to his left just down the hall where his room seats until he leaves Athens either in a box or first class flight back to Pillisworth, South Africa.

He enters the room closing the door behind him this time and applies the clock. He reaches for the cordless phone seating on the bed room counter top to his right already fully charged. As grabs it with his left hand, he uses his right index and middle fingers to punch in the numbers to the channel scrambler

U10 this time. Waits for a dial tone and within 45 seconds she picks up.

"Davarqius Exports, Nickle Currency speaking." She says every time she gets a call or off business hours you will get her voice message or the office voice message. He loves the sound of her seductive voice.

"Currency, Its Christen checking in from Athens also transfer me to Channel Scrambler U10 this time darling. You should have that information by now, hell it's been almost 2 weeks." He charges her over the phone but her cool demeanor brings him down.

"James, enjoying your stay in Athens? I want photos of the bride, groom, parents, everything, Including the wedding cake and band leave nothing out." She says smiling with her phone on speaker.

"Currency, I need more intel on that photo I sent back to Headquarters almost two weeks ago, or I will talk to Manning directly. This is very urgent like a matter of life and death?" He demands trying not to lose his patience and temper with her.

"James your no fun, alright, based on the picture you send back we fed it into the photo-scanograph linked to our international criminal database. And what came back is very interesting on that mystery man in the background, in fact Interpol identifies him as Atreus Pavlos Damianos." She says with absolute certainty. Now Christen thinking to himself Atreus Damianos? Atreus Damianos?

"He's wanted in South America, Latin America, and Australia. Was there anything else James you need regarding Intel on this man?" she asks scrolling down the screen.

"Yes, South America, does anything come up?" he asks while staring at the base of the door wondering who might be listening outside in the hall or not?

"Damianos was indirectly instrumental in destabilizing the governments of Columbia, Ecuador, Brazil, El Salvador, and Chili. He was financing opposition gorilla soldiers and propping up the poppet presidents and governors of these countries using tens of millions in opium profits. And he supported coups on both sides left and right creating chaos everywhere, riots, public executions. All for the sake of gaining control indirectly." She says before closing down the site and the screensaver comes back up.

"That photo extracted a lot of deep data from those facial Ids James also they have accomplices or an entourage and I'm sure you want names? I'm I correct?" she asks with a smirk.

"Why not, I need to know who I'm dealing with so I can prepare, also my instinct tells me these men are in town and partners of Gorgons or whatever he calls his entourage. Maybe even associated with his business partners." He replies again waiting for the other names to drop.

"I have 6 in total so here goes the first two for you, Roman and Gregory Gniewko from Kiev, Ukraine. Fraternal twins, born about 2 to 3 minutes apart and former MMA underground fighters, basically Ukrainian mob muscle for Tisdale Minolta. And here's the final four names- Alexandr Anatoly, Vladimir Bulnor, Krasimir Rostislav, and Natali Mochavic Radoslav all muscle for heavyweight Russian Oligarch Mikhail Bahrain Khrichov. He was at one point body guard to Oligarch Russian Boris

Berezovsky former advisor to Russian President Boris Yeltson. Anyway there you are James thread carefully and give my regards to Tarken, enjoy." She hangs up or clicks off the scrambler.

Christen seats back in the chair near the bed and ponders what he's just been told by Nickel Currency, it's all on the line now. But he's enemies still have this advantage at the moment while Christen tries to formulate a plan of action in his mind that will give him a counter advantage. First this entourage for his partners and they have to have an entourage or bodyguards, henchmen, its sounds really cliché but it's just reality. At this point he isn't really nervous or scared just anxious to get it over with and if it means dealing pain, or getting bruised and banged up, then so what, with pain comes the final resolution to this conflict for him.

And the damn wedding, something about it is so off to him, like the arrangements, no mention of the guests, catering, the band if there is one, so he's guessing everything will be sent to the manse on time and in order as planned by the grooms father. He glances at his watch and it reads 7:30 am and like some weird omen of something the cordless phone rings, he reaches for the cordless phone to his right, grabs it and hits the talk button with his finger. "Yes, James Christen here," he answers. The voice on the other end is Perseus sounding very excited and a bit agitated at the same time and trying not to give off any negativity.

"Mr. Christen your needed down stairs to meet the wedding planner, and we have some things to discuss with you." Perseus orders over the phone.

"Very good, give me a few minutes and I'll be down." Replies Christen clicking off the cordless and placing it on the counter before he rushes into the bathroom to relief himself. All in one motion walks the bathroom while unzipping his pants, Loosens his belt, he lifts the top off the toilet bowl and completely drops his pants, taking a seat and before he can relax himself the black/brown feces falls out and plops into the bowl of water, more coming out and smelling like sulfur, yes rotten eggs courtesy of that breakfast he just had almost 2 hours ago. Still mindful the time he waits another 45 to 72 seconds which is over of minute, and grabs a piece of tissue from a roll, next pulling about 3 feet of tissue or 40 plus inches, wrapped around his right fingers and very carefully wipes his rear end.

He drops it into the toilet, and flushes, pulling the lid down on top then pulls the pants up to his waist, zips his pants and fastens his belt. He walks over to the sink, turns in both cold and hot water and wets his hands and fingers thoroughly then applies some orange scented liquid soap to his right hand palm. And begins rubbing both until they are completely lathered in orange scented soap, next he places his hands under the warm water letting do it do all the work, rinsing the soap from his waist to his fingers. Turns off the cold and hot water, after his hands and fingers are completely clean he grabs a short towel, rubs them dry, places it back on a wall rack next to the sink. And without missing a beat he strolls through the bedroom and out the door to his left down the hall till he reaches the top stairs again. He finds them at the very base waiting for him to come down. He sees Perseus, Melissa, Annie and two another unfamiliar women standing next to them with purses and note books.

"Uh, Mr. Christen there you are finally, allow me to Introduce our wedding planners Miss. Bathzatha Damali Berenike and her assistant Monica Eleni." Says Perseus making the informal introduction while they both give Christen a look of total indifference. Like who the hell is he and why is he here? Is he the owner and if not where's the owner? But Christen notices Tarkens absent also and making it clear he really has interest in sticking around for the reception. Or even meeting the wedding planners for that matter.

"Good morning to you ladies and nice to meet you." He says extending his right hand for a shake once he makes it to the button stair and they both oblige him. The assistant Miss. Eleni starts first walking around the lobby followed by Andromeda and Melissa as Perseus gives her the lay out of the mansion.

"Miss Eleni, through here is the living room," he tells her and she amazed not realizing just how enormous the mansion really is.

He continues, "It's actually 3 stories with 18 bedrooms, 7.5 bathrooms, 9 on the 2nd floor, and 9 on the 3rd floor with a private home theater and screening room adjacent to the west wing of the manse. On the left wing is our private library or shall I say my father's private library with an archive of close to 25,000 books in print and digital including dvds, audio books." He stops to watch her take notes as she looks around getting a sense of where the wedding photos will take place or possibly the gallery?

"I'm really not interested in seeing the rest of the mansion but take me someplace around here where the actually wedding will be or where we can hold it and plan space for the guests?" She asks. But upon hearing this he reveals to her that this will a very small wedding and not a lot guests coming.

"Well we decided to keep this fairly small, so there won't be a very big wedding, not like dozens of quests or even over a hundred for that matter." He confesses. And she looks somewhat disappointed but at the same time she understands, they want it private, so then it's a private wedding. She also figures she's being paid to help plan it no matter what the out come, or how big it is so what the hell does she care one way or another?

"So, so take me someplace you think it should be or Somewhere very close to you and the bride to be where you like to exchange the vows?" she asks again. And with that Perseus, Andromeda and Melissa escort the wedding planners to the Mathias Gardens a plot of 2 acres directly outside the kitchen.

"Omg, omg, omg this is beautiful and you want to hold the wedding here?" she asks with sudden excitement!

"The garden actually starts some 5 yards from the kitchen door and Its large enough to house up to 200 people but sense this will be a private wedding and very small we decided that this is the ideal spot to hold it." Perseus tells her, with everyone standing by including Christen. He also explains to her as she continues taking notes and her boss observes her with arms folded over her chest.

"To the west of the garden is the multicar garage able to house up to 20 cars." He says but she just retorts with, "Umm, hmm, very nice." And they settle on Mathias Gardens for the wedding and now where to hold the reception? This is where the food will be served or catering held and the classical Greek music for the Bride and Groom.

"Ok, ok so now that we have settled or agreed on where the wedding will be held next lets decide or have you decided about the reception area yet?" she asks again. With this Perseus thinks hard about it with his sister looking on as if she waiting for him to make a decision but doesn't want to embarrass him in front of his fiancée Melissa or the wedding planners or Mr. Christen for that matter. And just when it appear he's about to make up his mind, she sees some doubt in his eyes, like what if father disproves of his decision to where the wedding should take place? Although it's in the mansion, Gorgon can be very guarded at times with visiting strangers only this occasion he's invited his business partners and their entourage only these guys aren't attending to enjoy the music or festivities. They are hired bone breakers or for information extraction. So before Andromeda has a chance to intervene, Perseus makes up his mind and suggests the wedding take place in the Mathias private library.

There's more than enough room for 100 people however since this is private their won't be that many chairs used if any at all for seating. "We will exchange vows in the private library and as awkward as that might seem, it just makes sense." He says studying Melissa's face when she pulls him to her and plants kiss on his left cheek. He's blushing in the presence of his sister, the wedding planners and Christen who himself smiles out of happiness for the soon to be bride and groom.

"Ok, ok, so it's the private library then were you will hold the wedding. Now the clothes, its custom that the groom not see what the bride is wearing before the ceremony so Perseus we will go up to Andromedas room with Melissa and look at some dresses she's already rented for his occasion." Says the wedding planner while Christen and Perseus stand by in the east wing hall and takes seats in waiting. As they leave the men behind and rush upstairs, the guys finally have a moment to themselves to reconnect since the very first time the met just days before.

"Wow, time flies," says Christen. Indirectly facing Perseus.

"Yes, it does. Yes indeed it does." Perseus responds in kind with a light chuckle, but at the same time feels very cautious in the presence of this South African spy.

"Cherish every moment, every second, every hour, every day the two of you have to together Perse, and listen to your bride in whatever you discuss don't argue, even when and if your correct you will lose." Replies Christen with a smirk. And the two of them share that laugh together. With that Perse feels a little comfortable with James to ask him, "Have you ever been married Mr. Christen?" and as if he was expecting this question finally he responds, "Yes but It was a long time ago. And let's just say my job came between us. Can't have a happy marriage with a list of enemies and foes on the side the two don't go together." He ends with Perse studying his words and face but not really passing judgment only observing what he just heard.

"So what about the ring Perse?" Christen asks. And Perseus pulls out a platinum diamond engagement ring with a smile and hands it to James, who analyze its brilliant sparkle and shine.

"Very, nice, so how much did this set you back?" he asks again but Perse almost anticipates the question replying.

"My dad has connections up the ass. This baby came with a $25,000 price tag." He says taking the right from Christen and placing it back in it's box then his right pocket.

"She completes me Mr. Christen, I knew from the moment we met almost 8 years ago she was the one. I believe in love at first sight Mr. Christen." Perseus explains again then there's another moment of silence between the two of them as if their still thinking of what else to say to each other and then Christen makes another inquiry.

"Any plans for the honeymoon?" Christen asks while Perseus seems again preoccupied or a little dejected.

"Umm yeah, we've been talking about visiting Jamaica for a week or two then possibly the Bahamas for another week then last but not least take a sail or rent a sail boat for a month and or just disappear." Perseus responds with a smile and closes his eyes as if to imagine himself and Melissa laying on hot sands with shades covering their eyes and their bodies baking in the hot Caribbean sun.

"Now that's a nice image I must say so, clear, blue Waters, fresh fruit and juice every morning and the woman you love laying next to you, very nice." Replies Christen.

"And you mentioned renting a sail boat?" Christen asks. And Perseus is happy to answer this one.

"Yes my father knows a businessman who owns a company outside Athens that builds Yachts and Sail boats. So I can get a discount on a 60 to 80 foot yacht or sail boat." Perseus replies again.

Christen starts thinking to himself, yachts huh? He can't imagine the last he actually went sailing or at least traveled on a luxury liner, no wait, wait there's the Peter Botha ferries that travel cross Johannesburg canal between Cape town and Murys port. A 78 mile stretch of water traveled mostly high speed by the well to do or white collar, movers and shakers of Pillisworth, South Africa. But that could be an ideal investment for him when he ever retires or if he gets the chance to retire? In his business death is always creeping around the corner just waiting to surprise you at any moment then its lights out. And his enemies list just gets longer as time goes by! Still pondering the ideal he thinks he should check this broker himself and find a vessel that best fits his own style and personality. They start hearing footsteps from upstairs coming downstairs, this being the wedding planner, her assistant with Andromeda, and Melissa. As the women reach the base of the stairs the wedding planner admits everything seems to be in order and the only issue he has is the quest list, catering, the Minister, Bishop or Rev performing the wedding?

"Ok so we have established the wedding will be held in library and we have agreed the reception will take place between the kitchen and your father's garden. Now the caters, the band and the Bishop presiding over the wedding arrive sometime this afternoon or that's my understanding from Miss Andromeda and Melissa? She's asks them. They don't even look at each just nod their heads yes, this afternoon sometime after 1 pm my brother jumps the broom. The big moment will come finally! But Annie, answers, "yes, yes, that's the plan, my father has arranged everything." And with that the wedding planner inquirers about Gorgon whereabouts, they've met the son and daughter, the Fiancé and house guest but the man paying for all this is absent from the scene.

"So where's our benefactor, the man with a very large check book or bank account, bank rolling all of this? Shouldn't he be here to sign off on all of this? It seems weird that we have gone over all this and he's nowhere to be seen?" the wedding planner asks again! But Annie, knows her father has business partners in town for this wedding but doesn't reveal too much.

"My father will see you in due time long before the Wedding starts at the moment he's resting in his private study." Annie replies.

"Fair enough, I have to review my notes, makes some calls and check my Calendar schedule, we have other appointments to make this afternoon before 5pm." She reminds her assistant Eleni. Now the two of them briefly step away from Melissa and Andromeda and go back into the private library.

"Pardon me, excuse me again but there is a phone in the private library yes?" she asks and this time Melissa gives her a look of agitation.

"Yes, directly to your right on the dresser next to the lamp." Melissa answers again!

"Thank you sooo much Hun! Eleni this way ok?" she says motioning with her left thumb. Melissa and Andromeda join Perseus and James in the foyer area of the manse, the opposite west side of the kitchen. Melissa gives Perse a hug while James follows Andromeda to the Garden where the reception will be held just outside the kitchen.

"So James when are you planning to take the plunge again?" she asks him before they enter the Garden from the west side of the foyer area.

"Honestly, Annie remarrying is the last thing on my mind at this point, but I understand the question. Your brother's finally making it official and love is in the air, but in reality it will sink in after weeks and some months into it when the honeymoon is over. Oops! I'm sorry to kill the moment, it's just something I've seen over the years again and again." He answers her with a look of certainty.

"I want to marry one day James, if I ever meet my man, my future soul mate? I sometimes wonder who he is, or where he is? What he's doing, or is he happy or sad?" She says trying to read Christens expression.

"Well if you will excuse me James, I must get dressed for My brothers wedding, omg, time just flies by so fast." She says before leaving him in the garden to reflect on what she said, as she races past Perse and Melissa still in the foyer area and reminds them to get dressed but the groom can't see the bride until she given away. Perse agrees with his sister when he turns to Mellisa, "She's correct you know, Missy you go up to your room and change cloths and I'll be downstairs in the library dressed, ready and waiting for you." He tells her before she leaves him.

Meanwhile in the private library the wedding planners are actually undercover agents with Greek Intelligence. The two undercover operatives take a seat near the entrance, one making the call from the cell phone and the other looking through notes or maybe intel data on the mansion.

And in sweet irony neither of them hears Gorgon awake from his slumber, slowly tip toeing around in his slippers so not to be over heard. Berenike Bathzatha Damali and Monica Eleni aren't aware that their host or the financial benefactor is actually A Opium Smuggler/Gallery owner. He continues to listen while Berenike Damalis call connects to her supervisors or bosses and Gorgon continues to listen and looks around ensuring he isn't he spying isn't disrupted. He over hears Damali tell her supervisor that 'she saw no evidence of anything illegal in the mansion.

Only exotic paintings and murals on the walls in the ground floor of the manse with Greek art and family pictures nothing more, unless his Gallery holds the hidden contraband?' she continues conversation having no idea that just outside in the hall is Gorgon listening to every word and after a few minutes have past he decides it's time to walk in on them.

"Good morning ladies, the lovely wedding planners!" he says with a shy smirk and smile.

"I see your still here, calculating the cost for me? Ha, ha, ha, ha, ha, ha, hmmm. I'm sure my kids give you a through tour of the house?" he asks?

While Berenike is totally caught off guard or surprised But she doesn't let it show in fact she just plays along almost suspecting he overheard everything but won't say anything. And her assistant Monica keeps her eyes on the paperwork like she's studying for an exam.

"Yes, we have agreed on two areas, and or places around The mansion where the wedding and reception will take place. The Wedding shall be held here in the private library, while the reception is just outside the kitchen." She explains. This pleases Gorgon as he walks around the two women almost forming a circle then stops to analyze the exact spot where his son and future daughter in law will exchange vows.

"I'm curious Miss Berenike, exactly where in here will this take place?" he asks unknowingly that he standing just 8 feet from his far left between a desk and coat rack.

"Your actually very close Mr. Mathias. I was told this will be a very private wedding?" she inquires again.

"You are correct we expect at most, or at least 15 quests, but you still haven't answered my question? He says giving them both a look of well?

"Sir, your actually standing 7 and 9 feet from the spot to your left, and just enough space for the minister or Bishop conducting the ceremony along with bride, groom, maid of honor, and groomsmen, if there are any?" she asks again. But he doesn't even acknowledge that question just tells her.

"We're working out the details on that, right now that issue isn't up for discussion." He replies before preparing to making his exit then one last question.

"Have you seen my children by any chance?" he asks. And Berenike is very happy to oblige him so long as he leaves the damn library.

"Yes I think Andromeda and Mr. Christen? Your house guest are in the kitchen or maybe the garden outback. And your son Perseus with his fiancé Melissa are still in the west foyer we think?" She replies.

"Think you ladies both, I need to shower and get dressed for this afternoon, oh yes I will leave a check and cash in manila envelope before you go." He tells them before exiting and she has to get in the last word.

"Mr. Mathias we are leaving right away sir so if its any inconvenience we'd like to get the cash now?" she asks him not sure if he'd cooperate.

"NO, no not at all, this won't even take a minute in fact I have the checks and cash already prepared." He says, racing Into his private study and closing the door behind him in one Shift motion.

He reaches into his drawer and pulls out a 2, 3 by 7 Inch manila envelopes, then where a mirror is located on his wall behind it is a small digital combination safe. He punches in the numbers or code, and hears a beep sound, then grabs the latch turning it down 15 degrees to open it. Inside he has a few stacks of cash in euros 50 and 100s in denominations, so he grabs 20 thousand or 20k in 100 euros and puts them in the two separate manila envelopes also with a personal checks made out to both women, he then write on them Berenike and Monica in bold black marker. He closes the digital combination safe shut at the same time closing the mirror too, then takes the thick envelopes out to his library where the ladies stand waiting patiently. He hands them out one after the other.

"Ladies here you are, one for you Berenike, and this one for you Monica, I won't disclose the contents of these envelopes ladies but you won't be disappointed." He tells them before he rushes to the lobby door to open it, and ushers them out, with smiles on their faces ear to ear.

He waits and watches them both enter Berenikes convertible red 2 door ford mustang parked just 3 to 4 foot in front of his personal limo. They both wave him goodbye at the same time the engine rpm roars when she turns the ignition, then throws the gear into D and pulls off very fast around the drive way to the open gate. Gorgon watches them leave and returns inside his manse closing the lobby door behind him. He now has time to take that shower and get dressed before the caters, band, guests, and minister show up for the big event in just under 2 hours. But in one spilt second he's remembering Tarken as if he totally forgot he's must important house guest. Making wedding plans, meeting with out of town business partners and their deadly MMA entourage will take distract anyone from house guests.

And in Gorgons case he still has to supervise the bulk shipment of Opium coming into the Isle of Crete just 24 hours after his partners have their much anticipated Q and A session with James Christen. Gorgon reenters his private study with a walk in stall shower equipped with cordless phone on the wall and mini bathroom directly behind it and he's own personal sauna. Oh the privilege of being wealthy and access to vast resources, the amenities of luxury how nice?

Gorgon takes off his pajamas and slippers but keeps his rope on while he enters the mini bathroom and reaches into the walk in shower stall with height adjustable nozzle. He adjusts the water quickly for Luke warm then just over 75 degrees, nice and warm steamy water shooting out in a steady stream to the floor. He hangs his rope up on a rack in the mini bathroom before he steps into the walk in shower nude right under the stream of hot water running over his face and through his curly straight silvery gray hair and scalp. Seconds, and minutes go by in the shower and Gorgon hears the cell ringing as he's lathering his body down with strong cologne scented body wash. Fortunate for him the phone is water proof also on the other line is his favorite house guest Tarken.

"Yes, this is Gorgon," he answers when he reaches for the cordless phone.

"Gorgon, the wedding is today, this afternoon correct?" he asks seating his room working on that critical deposition he has to give.

"Tarken, where have you been all this time, I figured you were either sleeping or I don't know, you just disappeared on us and yes it begins today at noon exactly." Gorgon replies while he has the cordless on speaker.

"No, no, no, Tarken chuckles. I'm working on legal papers right now before my flight back to Pillisworth this evening. And don't worry I have my clothes already prepared for the event." He says before clicking off his cordless phone.

Gorgon clicks off the cordless phone and continues rinsing the Expensive body wash off until his body is cleansed of all toxins and dead skin. He turns off the shower and grabs a towel around his neck and shoulder at the same time slipping on his rope, while he steps out the mini bathroom but not before he slides a window open to release the heavy steam and walks back into his private study. And before he changes into his white and black tuxedo with red bow tie or the pants are black and the tux white or cream color, he takes a seat and stares at a map and Calendar or plans for his massive shipment coming in from Afghanistan. That shipment of 2 and half tons of raw opium to be brought in reprocessed and reshipped all over South East Asia and some parts of Siberia, Eastern Europe.

He made a mental note about the transport machine Designed to transfer heavy blocks of Opium from the Tractor trailers to the lower bowels of the 3 luxury ships Gorgon will have docked at the Island of Crete early Sunday morning. And if everything went well one of those luxury ships will carry his newly wed son and daughter in-law Melissa. Before Gorgon has a chance apply some lotion to his calves, ankles and feet he gets a call on his cordless, and he figures it's the Caterers and the band he hired. He grabs the cordless phone and hits the talk button before he speaks, "Yes, Mathias residence." He says answering the call and there's a brief silence for a few seconds then he hears.

"Mr. Mathias, I presume?" the chef asks.

"Yes," Gorgon replies again.

"Very good sir, my teams in route to your estate for the set up which will be kind of small considering what you told me before this being a private wedding and not many quests no?" he asks again.

"We are expecting at the least maybe 15 people, if that Mr. Skarmoutsos so with that said you maybe cook small portions or use your own judgement." Gorgon responds again. As another call comes in and it's the band also.

"Mr. Skarmoutsos, a important call has come and I most take it, we'll continue this." He says. Gorgon clicks over and it's a semi famous middle age Greek pop singer Severon Christatos on the other line, this guy is like the Luther Vandross or Lionel Richie of Eastern Europe, he recorded 15 cd's, six of Which have been on the international billboard top 100 charts, also he's one of a few a recording artists in Eastern Europe to have multi-platinum and double platinum cds within a 10 year period. And always performs to sold out crowds in the tens of thousands whenever he's in Germany, France, the United Kingdom, Scotland, Denmark, Holland, and Belgium just to name a few countries in Europe.

"Gorgon? It's Christatos, Severon." he yells over the phone and Gorgon cracks a smile which he doesn't do very often.

"Yes, yes, Severon, how are you my friend"? Gorgon asks presuming in the back of his mind, this guy must be either in route or calling about the proper directions?

"Gorgon, I still have those directions you give me to your estate all those years ago." Severon replies.

"It hasn't changed Severon, I'm still here." Gorgon responds.

"Very good then, my band and I are in route with all equipment in tow, I trust you have the necessary space for us to perform?" he asks.

"Yes, yes, of course, more than enough Severon, I think you'll find it more than adequate for your use?" Gorgon responds again.

"Very good Gorgon, I will let you know when I'm close, my Band and I are traveling in 2 luxury Coaches." Severon replies again.

"Severon that's excellent, also for a side note there's a catering crew coming also or they might show up before you, in any case, show them every courtesy." Gorgon requests.

"I'm here dressed and ready, see you when you arrive." Gorgon replies again. And they both click off and at this point Gorgon remains in his private study. Still not completely dressed and finally applies the special lotion to his arms, legs calves and feet before grabbing his dark green socks to match his shoes. Now satisfied with his skin or parts of his body moisturized with his favorite lotion he slips on his pants with a brown belt already fitted in the loops, his creamy silk muscle shirt and designer Ralph Lauren cream white cuff link shirt. He buttons up the shirt quickly tucking it into his pants then applying the brown belt and last but not least his sliver cuff links. Now he pulls one of several brushes out of his drawer with hard black paddle brush and carefully applies it to his head first the left side. It's fairly straight like most European white men and slightly curly or wavy with a silvery grey color all around.

He doesn't apply any moose to it or gel and just quickly brushes both sides and the middle swept back. At one time his hair was shoulder length and he wore a double pony tail for a few years from his mid to late 40's into his early fifties, then decided it was time for a more mature look and had it cut almost completely bald. He gives himself a few more looks or poses in the mirror left side, then the right, yeah, yeah, ok he thinks to himself very nice indeed. And then, it starts the cordless rings and it's the caterers and the band one after the other. However there's one more important person he hasn't heard from, The Greek Arch-Bishop who will preside over the wedding.

Bishop Christov Giovanni Phlatos whom Gorgon has known for well over 15 years is a former assassin turned monk sort of. As fascinating as that sounds he murdered so many people, man, women and children, one day he got sick to the stomach of the killing and as it turns out some of his victims were innocent. At that point it occurred to him, he was just another a pawn or blunt instrument of faceless evil bureaucrats, doing their bidding. He decided no more and fled to Tibet in search of personal redemption and to escape the horrors of his past and cleanse his soul, people find god or whatever higher power in the most unusual places.

Turns out this will be his 13th wedding to officiate in the last 6 years also he likes to give a brief testimonial before every bride and groom. Meanwhile Gorgon finishes putting after shave his face in the mirror, one of his house quests stands outside the door, the ever brave and courageous James Christen. He knocks hard a few times before Gorgon finally responds in his direction and flashes a smile of where the hell have you been all this time?

"Mr. Christen? Well rested are we? And I can see your dressed and ready for the festivities?" Gorgon asks.

"Yes, I'm very much looking forward to this and the groom Seems jazzed as well. He has love coming out of his pores, and Excuse me for sounding cynical but I've been there, done that." James responds.

But Gorgon kind of ignores his house guest as he finally Hears a ringing at the door and yes it's one of the Caters at the door while the others pull their trucks around the back of the mansion just 15 to 25 feet from Gorgons Garden. He also hears again a ring from the Cordless yes, just around the corner is the Greek Pop sensation Severon Christatos. He and his band must be just minutes from the manse as the caters managed to arrive just before he did. Inside one of the trucks is a carefully stored and wrapped 3 tier Greek vanilla cake specially made for the bride and groom. Topped with thick vanilla icing all around and decorated in yellow candy or icing petals two on each side bottom, middle and top with two dolls the likeness for Perses and Mellisa.

Christen returns up stairs to his guest room to wait just a few more minutes when the lobby door rings, yes it's the caterers and Gorgon races to the door to greet them. As he opens the door, he quickly directs 3 of the 5 chefs to the kitchen on the west wing of the manse including their specialized cooking equipment and the many varieties of meats, fingers foods, hors d'oeuvres and or appetizers. The other two chefs carefully bring out the 4 foot, 3 tier Greek Vanilla cake from the truck, they have it on a table in box and wheel it out to the edge of a hydraulic lift. One of the caters hits a button and the lifts descents to the ground very quick and folds out straight. They then push and guide the table from the rear of the truck to the front lobby of the manse and into the same path the other chefs take to the kitchen.

Fortunately for them Gorgon has a walk in freezer directly across the hall from his kitchen and its climate controlled and digital. One of the many advantages of having money and wealth you can afford certain amenities like a walk in freezer or you own multi-powered generators for parties, private concerts or intimate business gatherings. The chefs maneuver the wedding cake box/table into the walk in freezer for the duration of the wedding for which they will take it out for the reception and the guests to enjoy. The last chef goes back outside to the lobby where the truck is parked in front, he steps up on the lift, hits the button again and the lift ascents up to its original position. Slides the door shut and walks from the rear to the front truck driver seat and also pulls it around to the rear of the manse where the other catering truck is parked.

Finally another ring comes in on the cordless phone and its Severon Christotos and his band just outside the gates of the manse waiting for the green light or ok to drive in and set up. Gorgon picks up the cordless phone and hits the green button again.

"Gorgon, Gorgon It's Severon I'm outside the gate with my band." He says with excitement.

"Yes, Yes, yes, I just activated the gate and your welcome to pull up to front of the lobby. I can see you here from the distance, welcome." He replies while opening the gate via remote. He sees two funny exotic brownish rust colored buses or Entertainer Coaches pulling into and around the driveway right up to the front lobby entrance again. The Entertainment Coaches have designs of lightening striking in the same place multiple times, maybe that's a metaphor of his success in the recording business? When the coaches pull up to the lobby of the manse the first to step are His lead drummer Bosman Bartholomew, his lead bass/electric guitar man Aristotle "Gimmie Some" Papalos, and backup guitar man Lois Manula also his key board players Arnie Tatoplaous and Jean "fast fingers" Phillini and Yes, pop band members have some stranger ass names.

Severons in the second coach and watched his guys disembark from the first coach with their roadies or handlers carrying their the instruments into the lobby and straight to the huge private library where they are directed by Gorgon what spot to set everything up where the ceremony will be held. Gorgon then is met by Severon in front hallway with a hand shake and friendly hug.

"Severon, Severon, it's been to long my friend. How have you been?" Gorgon asks him before they both walk into the library and observe the roadies setting up and staging the instruments for the reception.

"Gorgon it's been only 7 years since we last saw each other at the World Trade Conference concert benefit in Amsterdam, Holland. And that was a wild occasion, all those damn protestors came out, it made the performance very challenging to say the least." Severon replies!

"Yes, well you didn't have to deal with them I did and without the euro police armed in heavy riot gear and tear gas grenades launched at the vandals, who knows what would have happened?" Gorgon continues.

"I hate civil unrest Severon, there has to be other ways, other methods to resolve global economic conflicts?" Gorgon asks, but Severon won't entertain that at all.

"Gorgon, I'm a performer and musician period, I have no stomach for geo-political bullshit you know this, I make music bro, I entertain people. That's what I enjoy doing, all that other bullshit, I have no dog in that fight!" Severon replies again.

Ready to start practicing since his band has everything set up nice and neatly. The 11 piece drum set, the piano key- boards and wire amps for the microphones and guitars speakers. Gorgon begins catching the smell and aroma coming from the kitchen of traditional Greek cuisine and deserts. Wines, beers including Greek euro ale, brewed off the Isle of Crete, ironically close to where the shipment of opium will be transferred to the bowls of luxury ships. Now Gorgon's missing the Greek

Arch-Bishop Augustine Sinilos, his business partners, their entourage and the photographers Tisdale referred him too. But to his satisfaction the calls keep coming in and it's the Greek Arch-Bishop Sinilos just minutes from mansion and traveling from the opposite side of town.

Standing in the hallway just several feet from the lobby door Gorgon quickly grabs the cordless phone off the charger from his private library to his left and hits the green button. And yes it's the reformed former assassin turned holy man in his used black BMW holding his specialized cell phone trying to avoid running through stop signs and traffic lights.

"Gorgon, I'm 5 minutes from your estate rushing through stop signs and avoiding traffic lights." He says doing between 80 and 90 mph.

"Hello Augustine, as long as you remember the address we have no quarrel my friend? I'm expecting some more quests to arrive at any moment." Gorgon tells him before clicking the red button off.

From the kitchen he begins to smell the aroma of gourmet food being prepared, varies meats, fingers foods, and a wide variety of beverages including wines. Also last but not least the wedding cake stored in the specialized freezer directly across from the kitchen. He checks his platinum diamond Rolex watch and it reads 11:45am, so before he has a chance to visit the kitchen and supervise caters or at least sample the delicious smell of meat coming from his kitchen. Its smells like rack of lamb or possibly veal but he can't resist going around to get a peek into his kitchen.

He stands at the door dressed in his custom made white

Tuxedo and sleek black pants with a very pleasing smile on his face when one of the chefs notices him finally.

"Mr. Mathias, there you are, we have a few more entrees to prepare before everything goes into the trays for heating. As you can see, we have already prepared over 10 trays of different meats and salads, cheeses." He tells him and shows him.

"Gentlemen, everything smells delicious and I'm sure my family and guests will enjoy all of this." He replies with satisfaction.

Chapter 5

MEET THE TRIAD
OF CERBERUS

It is at that moment the lobby door rings and his business Partners and their entourage are waiting outside, along with Arch Bishop Sinilos in his official religious garb or custom Clothes and leather bag or case over his shoulder. Gorgon leaves the kitchen entrance and walks back toward the lobby door where he sees the crew outside all dressed up and waiting to enter his manse. He opens the door and is greeted by Arch Bishop Sinilos first with a hug and hand shake, along with entourage of Russian mobster Mikhail Khrichkov then his euro Slavic partner Tisdale Minolta with the same hug and hand shake followed by a Passionate congratulations in his native Czech language.

"Gratulujeme mym pritelem na vasi synove svatbu. Or Congratulations my friend on your sons wedding." He says with Genuine affection.

And Mikhail Bahrain Khrichov steps to Gorgon with a hand shake and hug speaking in his thick Russian Accent.

"Kello my friend and kongratulations on yur sons vedding." Mikhail greets him, then walks inside the lobby area followed By his personal bodyguards, fraternal twins Roman and Gregory Gniewko also from St. Petersburg, Russia and born just 4 minutes apart. And they both give the same greeting to Gorgon hands shakes and brief hugs, then enter the lobby entrance, followed by Minoltas personal henchmen the tall but slim and muscular Vladimir 'Big Crunchy' Bulnor, Alexandr Anatoly, Krasimir Rostislav, and Natali Mochavic Radoslav all dressed like wall Street bankers. Three of them wearing three piece suits of various colors like black on Vladimir, gray on Alexandr, and beige on Krasimir but the shirts are all silky white with matching neck ties.

Natali dresses causal wearing a Salmon colored long sleeve band collar linen/cotton shirt with dark gray vest and suit to match the vest. They each give Gorgon a hand shake but no hug and file into the lobby area when Gorgon closes the door behind them and gives them all a direct escort into his huge private library where they are seated and offered glasses of water instead of alcohol. Gorgon exits the library and races toward the kitchen where the chefs have nearly completed the food preparation and everything sets in various deep dish pans. Waiting to be served during the reception. Gorgon enters the Kitchen and in one motion snatches 2 tall ½ gallon pitchers from the middle his kitchen cabinets and takes a wide hand full of napkins, placing them on a 4 foot tall cart and 15 inches in width with top and bottom sections.

He also grabs 8 tall glasses and pulls open his custom refrigerator freezer and snatches a bag of ice cubes to fill the pitcher. He dumps 1/3 of the bag into one pitcher filling it over half way then empties the rest into the other pitcher before pushing the cart over to his sink in the middle of the kitchen, he places the tall pitchers full of ice cubes in the sink and hits the cold water handle, letting the water run for 3 to 4 minutes then placing one pitcher under it, then the other once the water almost reaches the near top.

He carefully places both pitchers on the cart and shuts off The cold water faucet while carefully pushing the cart through The kitchen with the chefs looking on in amusement and out the door. He gets back into the long hall to his right back towards his private library where his quests wait for the cold water to be served.

He yells down the hall, "gentleman your water is near don't get up!" he continues pushing the cart until he reaches the entrance of the library and makes a sharp right turn where he just pushes the cart directly in the middle where they are seated. And one by one they grab the glasses from the button section of the cart and start pouring like every man for himself, but there's enough for everyone. Mikhail fills his glass and grabs a napkin, folding it around the bottom of the glass followed by Tisdale and the other guys in the same pattern. It's just after 12 noon and the Arch Bishop Sinilos done setting up, he has his bible and his dressed in his custom Greek religious attire.

The caters or chefs are practically done whereas now Gorgon waits for his house quests and kids to finally come down stairs least we not forget the bride to be. But without warning Gorgon is met by Tarken also dressed up in white and black, Observing the quests in his private library and picking up the Aroma food coming from the kitchen of the east wing of the manse.

"There you are, I was just about to call up stairs Yusaf." Gorgon tells him on the spot.

"Well I just saved you the time and effort Gorgon, so care too introduce me to your business partners?" he asks in an annoying tone.

"Gentlemen, allow me to introduce Yusaf Tarken. An old college classmate of mine visiting from South Africa on unpaid leave." Gorgon replies expecting a quick retort from Tarken.

"Why thank you Gorgon, for divulging my personal business to your partners." Tarken continues with a smile with out losing a beat.

And before Gorgon has a chance to respond to that Mikhail chimes in on Tarken with his thick Russian accent studying Tarkens demeanor.

"Mr. Tarken, if I may ask?" but before he can continue Tarken interrupts him.

"No, no, no Mikhail. NO… let's not be so formal here on this occasion, please call me Yusaf, Gorgon does." Tarken replies again. All while the fraternal twins Roman and Gregory just zone out or ignore the conversation and everything else around them followed by Tisdale's personal body guards. With that Mikhail finishes gulping down his cold ice water and places the empty glass on the cart, then continues his dialogue with Tarken in that thick Russian accent.

"Again, if I may? What is it you do in South Africa? What's your occupation? Or Opjat'zhe esli ja mogu? Chto eto takoe, chto vy delaete v Juzhnoj Afrike? Kavoa vasha professija" Mikhail asks again only this time in a more inquisitive tone in Russain. But Tarken won't bite, not even for a moment fend offers a rather comical answer even as Gorgon looks on at both men. Now Tarken takes a deep breathe while folding his arms over his chest then begins his spin.

"Well, long story short Mikhail, I study climate detail for the South African Conservatory in Pilliworth and present my findings to the government for quarterly audits." He replies with a convincing straight face as Gorgon suddenly stares up at the ceiling to conceal his amused glance. Thinking that was the most brilliant piece of bullshit he'd ever heard coming from Tarken and he didn't contradict him nor did he want too considering their past relationship. But Mikhail isn't satisfied with what he's heard and continues to press the cagy and smart

Tarken again in that think Russian accent.

"Yusaf, you excuse me but I don't like having my intelligence publicly insulted and especially on an occasion such as this one so, please indulge me?" Mikhail asks again.

And this time Tarken isn't aware directly behind him stands James Christen and the groom Perseus dressed in his cream white tuxedo and black pants white shirt and red bow tie to match his red handkerchief in his left pocket in the left suit lapel. Christen however stands dressed in all grey suit with black vest and grey matching pants, also sporting a white shirt with black and white poka dot neck tie. Christen and Perse just happen to walk in the entrance of the private library at the moment when Mikhail hits Tarken with that question and James announces his presence.

"Gentleman, Gorgon, Tarken? The gangs all here?" Christen says with a smile when Tarken notices him and Gorgon finally has an opportunity to introduce Perse to his partners, and their entourage or body guards and for the moment Tarken has dodged the bullet. Perse moves toward his father as his introduces him to each man very meticulously, starting with Mikhail then Tisdale Minolta.

"Mikhail, Tisdale, my son the groom Perseus." He says as Perseus moves to shake hands with Mikhail and then Tisdale but doesn't ignore their bodyguards either.

"Perseus, congratulations are in order or Perseus, blahoprani jsou v poradku." Says Tisdale in his euro Slavic Czech accent, followed by Mikhail.

"Congratulations Perse, we brought you a few surprises for the reception, god bless you boy. Or Pozdravlijaem pers, my prinesli vam neskol'ko sjurprizov dlja priema, Bog blagosovit vas mal'chik." Says Mikhail in his Russian accent. And Perseus introduces himself to Roman and Gregory Gniewko first and then works his way to Vladimir Bulnor or "Big Crunchy" and Alexandr Anatoly. Followed by Krasimir Rostislav and Natali Mochavic Ratislav. All men giving him hand shakes but not much conversation or they are too wired up for their anticipated encounter with James Christen, who's chatting with Tarken about the delicious aroma of catered food coming out of the kitchen from the west wing of the manse.

"That food smells incredible, I can't wait to see the finish product and as for you Yusaf, your really leaving during the reception?" Christen asks him and Tarken gives him a blank stare while not ignoring Gorgon but he want James to read between the lines.

"Yes I'm leaving but as long as you have a plan of action you have nothing to worry about. And 2, almost everyone is dressed in black and white except you James." Tarken points out to him and continues.

"You never introduced yourself to Gorgons partners. Or their entourage!" Tarken retorts when Gorgon approaches Christen and offers to introduce him to the Triad of Cerberus but doesn't call them that by name. It's so ironic that now he comes face to face with the very men who have inquired about him for months and look to make him disappear.

"Gentlemen, allow me to introduce you to James Christen of South African Intelligence." Gorgan says.

But this time James doesn't shake any hands or give any hugs no, no, no just waves his right hand in acknowledgement to Mikhail, Tisdale, Roman and Gregory, also Alexandr, Vladimir, Natali, and Krasimir respectively. And now before the bride, Groom make an appearance, Perseus sister Andromeda comes down stairs while Christen is approached by Tisdale Minolta for the first time and its very awkward for him in that Gorgon kind of just steps away to give these men some space. Christen takes a glass and fills it with ice before he pours he's own water from the pitcher when Tisdale begins the conversation. But not before Annie informs her father that the bride Mellissa is ready and will come down in a few minutes just after Perseus fully dressed.

"Father, Mellissa's nearly ready to come down but not before Perseus. Its custom the groom can't see the bride before the wedding." She tells Gorgon and goes back up stairs. At that moment Tisdale creates his opportunity and approaches Christen.

"So, Mr. Christen you work for South African Intelligence? They must keep you very busy?" Tisdale asks him as if Prying for info or seeing if he will give anything away but no can do.

"Oh, you have no idea in fact gathering intel is always the easy part, it's the execution that I find very tedious for my occupation." Christen responds. But Minolta just continues his Q & A.

"The execution you say? And what does that mean exactly? You've peaked my curiosity Mr. Christen. If you don't mind due tell." He asks again, but Christen won't entertain his enquiries or divulge anything just continues his answers in misdirection. And takes a few long gulps of his ice water while Gorgon indirectly listens and becomes more and more agitated as he instructed Tisdale back in the hotel not to engage or ask any question till after the wedding reception and this guy has his own agenda or he just doesn't give a damn.

"Collecting intelligence, tracking down leads, trusting Informants, it can get boring at times but that's the nature of the beast I guess. Either way the job has to get done." Christen replies.

But Minolta isn't satisfied with this answer and Continues to press, continues this question and answer drill. Until Gorgon steps between them while holding his half empty glass of water and Either way Gorgon keeps his cool and feels a tap on his left shoulder from Tarken while he takes a sip of water.

"Wow, I'm picking up some intense vibes in here Gorgon, and oh yeah the bride should be ready by now it's almost 12:30 pm." Tarken scolds at him. But Gorgon doesn't loose his cool or get upset this occasion is about his son making one of the biggest decisions of his life. And once all this is over he can at last focus on the shipment coming in from Pakistan and Afghanistan. He gives Tarken another amusing smile then takes a sip of his water before he responds in kind.

"Not everything happens as quick or fast as we might like my friend so relax soon the food, wine and wedding cake will come out and after the bride and groom eat theirs and the pictures are taken, you are free to indulge yourself." Gorgon replies in kind.

Chapter 6

I TAKE THEE AS MY WIFE

He also feels the presence of his son standing behind him dressed in creamy white tuxedo with black pants and red bow tie on his custom white shirt to match and black slip shoes just like his old man. He turns and Perseus strikes a pose for Gorgon and does a 360 turn like a model with Gorgon smiling and laughing along with Tisdale, James, Tarken, Mikhail and the rest of the entourage giving him applause. And like clockwork again a call comes in on the cordless phone, but time it's the photographers pulling up to the street gate just as Gorgons guests are about admiring Perseus dress code.

"Son I'm so moved, so please with you right now, you make your father proud. Hold on again I must get this." He grabs the cordless off the charger and hits the green button and answers.

"Yes, yes I can see you in the distance from my library,

I'm opening the street gate now, just pull the car around the front where you see the 4 columns outside near the lobby." He says while he presses a remote button on the wall to his left above the cordless charger.

"Finally, gentlemen my photographers are here for the wedding pictures, now once the bride to be and my daughter comes downstairs we can finally get this thing done." He says watching the car pull into the gate as it closes behind him, and he drives around the front of the house.

While the car makes its way around the well manicured lawn and the weird looking cement statute of the multi headed beast Cerberus pointed directly facing the gate parallel to the street. The car finally comes to a stop just a 5 feet from the 3 column of gorgons lobby entrance when photographers Arrie Perraud Moraitos and Spyros Andreadis exit the vehicle. And they are some short men like 5 feet, 3 inches tall both of them and dress very casual each one carrying his own case with camera hanging from his neck like a neckless. The cases contain different grade of lenses for the camera angles and lighting to be used in any setting they deem appropriate. Before they have a chance to knock or even ring a door bell, they are met at the door by Gorgon each getting a firm hand shake and welcomed into the mansion.

"We got here as fast as we could Gorgon and almost forgot we had you scheduled for today, also you paid us in advance too so we couldn't disappoint." Arrie tells Gorgon.

"Gentlemen, you're here, you made it in the nick of time And I'm very grateful so your free to find any areas you want to shoot the bride and groom on the ground floor. Any place else in this estate we have to talk!" Gorgon replies.

"Fair enough Mr. Mathias, I will make the best of this occasion and pick my spots." Arrie responds again.

"Very good, You do that and I will see if my son and future daughter in law are ready to jump the broom?" Gorgons says before Arrie leaves and he grabs the cordless phone and calls up stairs to Annie's room where she and Melissa are preparing and comparing dresses.

Gorgon dials Andromedas room while his son looks on at the Band, The Entourage of Tisdale and Mikhail Krickrov, also Bishop Sinilos dressed in black with the white collar reading his bible. Gorgon reaches her room and she answers the call or he thinks she's answering but its Melissa.

"Andromeda? Annie, what going on up there?" he asks.

"No, no, Mr. Mathias, its Melissa and I'm ready, here Annie wants to talk to you." She hands Andromeda the phone.

"Dad, were leaving the room and coming down now." She tells him then clicks off the cordless placing it back on the charger next to her bed. She looks to Melissa with happy grin.

"Your going to make a beautiful bride, are you ready, my future sister in law?" she asks her.

"Let's do this, I'm ready to become Mrs. Perseus Mathias." She replies with an exciting smile. On that they exit the room one after the other from the west wing hall of the mansion making they way to the stairs where they see at the base Gorgon, Christen, Tarken and Perseus standing outside the library entrance when they notice the two coming down the stairs. She's dressed in a white gown with what looks like a white net tiara around her head coming down to her shoulders and white high heel shoes to match. When they reach the base of stairs Andromeda and Melissa are met by Gorgon, while James and Tarken give them some space observing Perseus staring at his bride then walks over to where the Greek Archbishop Sinilos was seating down but then stands ready to conduct the Wedding ceremony.

It remains an awkward situation being that Gorgon has to give her away whereas she has no family there at all. No parents, brothers, sisters, cousins nothing and Andromeda is the brides maid. Perseus stands directly to the left Archbishop Sinilos with his arms and hands at his side watching his father Gorgon slowly escorts Melissa dressed in her gorgeous white gown, past Tisdale, Mikhail, and the entourage or henchmen on both sides and straight to The right of Sinilos while the band plays "The Bridal Chorus" that traditional song played at most weddings around the world.

Even in different languages, and cultures one thing remains almost the same, "The Bridal Chorus" or "Wedding March" an universal tune for weddings. At this point photographer Spyros Andreadis positions himself directly to the right of Augustine and knells to one knee while he catches Gorgon escorting Melissa past their quests and he snaps photo after photo like a skilled cameraman panning with them until she reaches the Archbishop. Making a another move for a better position he quickly cross over to Perseus's left side, just 5 to 7 feet from him and snaps some more photos of Archbishop Sinilos handling his King James Bible then remains steady in that spot composed and still.

Archbishop Sinilos opens his bible and requests everyone in the library bows their heads including the Euro- Slavic Russian thugs for prayer. At this moment the band stops once These two stand directly across from each other and in front of The Archbishop. The band stops playing and its members also bow their heads for prayer when the Archbishops begins reading aloud verses from Genesis 2:18-24.

"Genesis 2:18-24 The LORD God said, 'It is not good for man to be alone. I will make a helper suitable for him." 19 Now the LORD God had formed out of the ground all the beasts of the field and All birds of the air. He brought them to man to see what he would name them; and whatever the man called each living creature, that was its name. 20 So the man gave names to all the livestock, the birds of the air and all the beasts of the field. But for Adam no suitable helper was found. 21. So the LORD God caused the man to fall into a deep sleep; and while he was sleeping, he took one of man's ribs and closed up the place with flesh. 22 Then the LORD God made a woman from the rib he had taken out of the man, and he brought her to the man. 23 The man said, "This is now bone of my bones and flesh of my flesh; she shall be called 'woman,' for she was taken out of man." 24 For this reason a man will leave his father and mother and be united to his wife, and they will become flesh." He stops to look at the wedding attendees before him and says, "Amen." And in unison they say it without looking at each other while having their heads bowed. Then he begins his all important wedding sermon and this time everyone pays attention…

"Friends and family, we are gathered here before the eyes of god to bare witness to the union of this man and this woman. It is by the grace of almighty god the most sacred of public ceremonies is observed by family and friends." He says while watching those in attendance and from his peripheral or away from his center view is Perse and Melissa staring at each other until he orders them to exchange rings. And he continues with another bible verse but this one coming from 1 Corinthians 13:4-13.

"My friends from the book of 1 Corinthians Chapter 13, Verse 4 to 13 reads, Love is patient, love is kind. It does not Envy, it does not boast, it is not proud. 5 It is not rude, it is not self-seeking, it is not easily angered, it keeps no record of wrongs. 6 Love does not delight in evil but rejoices with the truth. 7 It always protects, always trusts, always hopes, always perseveres. 8 Love never fails. But where there are prophecies, they will cease; where there are tongues, they will be stilled; where there is knowledge, it will pass away. 9

For we know in part and we prophesy in part, 10 but when perfection comes, the imperfect disappears. 11 When I was a child, I talked a child, I thought like a child, I reason like a child. When I became a man, I put childish ways behind me. 12 Now we see but a poor reflection as in a mirror; then we face to face. Now I know in part; then I shall know fully, even as I'm fully known." And he ends with those while the two star crossed lovers continue staring at each other then look at him for their cue. Now he looks to them and nods his head before instructing them step in closer front of him and recite their vows, also this isn't taking place at a church so they aren't taking traditional Greek vows which are nonverbal.

"I, Perseus Pavlos Mathias take thee, Melissa Youngmire Godfrey, to be my wedded Wife, to have and to hold, from this day forward, for better, for worse, for richer, for poorer, in sickness and in health, to love and to cherish, till death do us part, according to God's holy ordinance; and thereto I pledge thee my faith [or] myself to you." He says with a smile and looks back to his father Gorgon and sister Andromeda while also turning his attention back to Melissa. Now it's her turn!

"I, Melissa Youngmire Godfrey, take thee Perseus Pavlos Mathias, to be my wedded husband, to have and to hold, from this day forward, for better, for worse, for richer, for poorer, in sickness and in health, to love and to cherish, till death do us part, per God's holy ordinance; and thereto I pledge thee my faith [or] myself to you" she says to him with a happy smile. Now the moment comes when it time to pull out the wedding rings and at the same time both bride and groom are ready and very anxious. Perseus goes first… Spyros snaps some shoots motion for motion.

"With this ring I thee wed." he speaks the words while sliding the ring on her right second index finger, now it's her turn.

"With this ring I thee wed." she speaks the words while sliding the ring on his right second index finger. Again Spyros snaps continuing his stride shot after shot of vows being exchanged. Now the moment arrives when they are about to exchange a passionate kiss in front of the guests when Archbishop Augustine says, "With this holy union ordained and witnessed by almighty god, I now pronounce you both husband and wife…" Spyros snaps more shots of the newlyweds kissing.

And with that said there comes a thunderous applause from everyone in the private library, Mikhail, Tisdale, Gorgon, James Christen, and Mikhails Ukrainian henchman Roman and Gregory, also Tisdales body guards and last but not least the band led by Severon Christotos. They all watch Perseus and Melissa shakes hands with Archbishop Augustine then turn in their direction for the formal congratulations, when they are approached by Tisdales henchmen. First Vladimir approaches Perseus extending a hand shake then also Melissa, followed by Mikhail's Ukrainian body guards Roman and Gregory, then finally the newlywed couple are met again by Tisdales Minoltas Russian thugs Krasimir Rostislav, Natali Mochavic Radoslav, Alexandr Anatoly and shaking hands with the newly weds.

Before Perseus has a chance to embrace his father again the chefs bring out the 4 foot, 3 tier vanilla wedding cake just in time. The chefs roll it out at the entrance of the private library as Tarken and Christen turn and notice it directly in their rear.

"Very nice, that cake looks delicious Tarken." Christen comments… and Tarken offers a witty quip.

"Yeah too bad I won't be around to enjoy any of it James, you forget I'm already packed and ready to leave." Tarken replies shrugging his shoulders.

Gorgon over hears this but before he can address it he directs the chefs into the private library with a wedding cake in tow directly in the middle or center of the room. The top of it has two miniature dolls or what looks like the bride and groom all dressed up 5 inches tall. But before they about to cut the cake the other photographer Arrie Moriatos shows up from touring or finding areas around the east and west side of the Gorgons manse where he wants the bride and groom. He signals to Gorgon it's time for the family wedding portrait if that's what it's called? Perseus and Melissa stand at the large 8 to 9 foot library window with Gorgon standing to the Perseus' right and Andromeda to Melissa's left.

Arrie moves not directly in front but just slightly the left of their center and knells down on his right knee for group family wedding shot. Taking several more before moving to get yet another shot or angle this time to the right of them and keeps the shot very steady. Now it's just time for the bride and groom only, while Gorgon walks over to the cart carrying the wedding cake and finds a sharp 10 inch cutting knife laying underneath the cart with 2 stacks of twelve cake plates or desert saucers. He takes one plate and the knife, places both on the top cart with the cake and decides which angle he wants to start cutting into?

So he decides he'll start at the top with those little 4 inch candy dolls and starts making deep cuts into the thick vanilla icing until he has two deep slices, then turns the knife into an impromptu spatula, sticking it in the bottom or base of the cake and lifts it off to place on the cake saucer. At this point he steps back and away from the slice of cake looking at his son, like it's all on you now Perse baby. Perseus steps over to the cake followed by Melissa and grabs a piece with his right fingers while in one motion grabbing the plate, she opens her mouth for a bite and begins chewing, while everyone claps again in applause. And while this is happening no one notices that the chefs also brought in the champagne bottles and classes. Gorgon takes a bottle of Bollinger Grande Anne Brut, pops the cork and begins pouring 16 glasses of champagne one after the other, passing them out to everyone with the exception of the band and the Archbishop who only looks on in appreciation.

"Family and friends, I can't fully express my happiness, my eternal gratitude, right now as I watch and witness my son, my first and oldest child has jumped the broom. And so I raise my glass and propose a toast to you both." He says while everyone including Tarken and Christen holding their champagne glasses prepare for this toast.

"To Perseus and his beautiful wife Melissa Godfrey Mathias, may your marriage and life together be filling with much joy and happiness, to the bride and groom." He says again raising his glass and before taking a sip makes that classic gesture of gently taping Tarkens glass, Tisdales', Mikhails' glass, and Tarken, tapped Christens glasses, while the body guards tap their own then takes a sip followed by everyone else in unison.

"To the bride and groom." Echoed by everyone throughout the private library, with the sounds of sipping champagne from wine glasses everyone places them on the champagne cart one after the other. At this point photographers Arrie and his partner Spyros want more photos this time and suggest the newly weds including Gorgon and Andromeda move over to the west wing where the library connects directly to the west foyer. Gorgon motions to his business partners, "Tarken, Christen, gentlemen enjoy your selves my chefs are bring out the food and Hor- d'oeuvres and Caviar, the champagne bottles, glasses are there, drink and enjoy." He tells them following his son, Melissa, Andromeda and the photographers into the west wing foyer where Gorgon stands to Perseus right side and Andromeda to Mellissa's left side. Now Arrie and Spyros Chris cross each other taking photoshoots of the family while getting certain angles for the wedding album.

Yes, photographers like setting up or shooting from particular Angles for a certain effect or style depending the look they are going for or looking for? And finally the newly weds switch with Gorgon next to Andromeda this time its Melissa and Perseus standing next to one another with the last shoots taken. While in the still private library Tarken and Christen are discussing his trip back to Pillisworth for this so-called deposition he's giving before The South African Intelligence General Assembly overseen by UN and NATO officials.

"Your leaving when Tarken?" Christen asks, taking another sip of his champagne. Tarken looks at his watch knowing its almost 1pm and his private flight leaves at 2:15pm.

"I'm taking a 2:15 afternoon flight back to Pillisworth James, for this prescheduled deposition. And you my friend take heed in what I said days ago, be very careful James, everything seems cordial now with this wedding but it's coming James, the betrayal is around the corner so prepare for it." Tarken warns him. But James pretends to sip his champagne while pondering his friends grave advice.

"I'm not sure how to take that Tarken, you two are old College classmates and friends? I'm I missing something here?" Christen asks with concern.

"I don't control Gorgon, James, however his business partners Mikhail, Tisdale and their personal brutes? Well they will expect his full compliance whether he likes you or not, and the questions are coming my friend, so I can't protect you however I have faith in your ability to handle yourself." Tarken responds holding his glass of champagne then taking that final sip before pouring some more but this time just enough for under half full glass.

Then out the corner of his right eye, he notices the photographers Arrie and Spyros returning from the west wing foyer of the Manse with Gorgon, the newlyweds Perseus, Melissa and Andromeda smiling, laughing and joking amongst each other. At this point Gorgons heading back in his direction noticing Christen standing next to him but he's totally unfazed by it. This man wears an expression he's on a mission no matter what no one will get in his way, including house guests. He walks past Tarken motioning him to follow him in the outside hall of the private library knowing he has a flight to catch under 55 mins.

"So, have you enjoyed yourself old buddy? Wow, you'll have to excuse me for being so emotional right now, I'm a very proud father. Oh, yes, yes, the flight I presume your luggage is already packed?" He asks placing his left hand of Tarkens right shoulder.

While Tarken knows Gorgon all too well he's the type to avoid conflict, however Tarken knows the moment his plane ascends into the sky the betrayals coming with a vengeance. Tarken has this rolling around in his head and gives Christen a look of sorry my friend I have to leave now, you are on your own from this point on. And before he takes the first stairs he bids everyone good afternoon including the Archbishop and that Greek pop group.

"Ladies and gentlemen, it's been so much fun, it's been really entertaining and seeing my old college classmate brought back so many fun, interesting memories for me. Unfortunately I must bide you all farewell." He says before going back up stairs and briefly turns his head but doesn't give James a straight look.

"James hopefully I'll see you back at Head Quarters soon? And Gorgon I'll be ready to leave in 15 mins." He replies again This time continuing his stride up the stairs, while Christen almost has nothing to say, but Gorgon graciously invites him to take the ride with them.

"Mr. Christen your more then welcome to join us and see Tarken off?" Gorgon offers.

"Thank you Gorgon, I will." Christen responds surprised by the invite.

As Tarken reaches the top and turns toward the west side of the hall straight to his room Gorgon orders his guests to drink enjoy themselves eat there's plenty of food and champagne for everyone. Christen tries to maintain his discipline regarding the catered food and champagne while fully aware he's being watched indirectly by Minolta, Krichkov and their Ukraine and Russian thugs. Gorgon watches the newlyweds dancing to the pop music of euro star Severon Christotos and his band with Andromeda watching on then inviting a reluctant James Christen to dance with her.

"Mr. Christen will you have a dance with me?" she asks while her Father looks on with a smile giving his approval at least until Tarken comes down then they all leave.

"Why Annie, I'd be delighted to dance with you." Christen Replies and the clock is ticking down. The two of them embrace each other again which she's been wanting since the first time they secretly slept together unbeknownst to her father. Standing just several feet from Perseus and Mrs. Melissa Godfrey Yougmire Mathias. The two of them almost went into a waltz just for the sake of having fun, enjoying each others company and this goes on for under 9 mins until he hears Tarkens ready and emerges from his guest room with his specialized 2 tier luggage in tow. Carefully carrying it down stairs almost step by step till he reaches the bottom or base of the stairs again and notices Gorgon alerting his driver it's time to go. Tarken witness James dancing with Andromeda and whistles like lets go my friend, when Christen notices he's all packed and ready to leave.

"Oh Annie, sorry to disappoint but it's time for me to go however I will return, we can pick up where we left off?" he asks her when she smiles.

"Ok, I can't wait." She replies and looks for someone else to take his spot maybe Mikhail or Tisdale? Oh no the unthinkable happens its Vladimir "Big Crunchy" Bulnor volunteers or steps up.

"Oh, does anyone care to dance with me?" She asks again! And the tall slightly ripped Vladimir volunteers.

"I will dance with you Annie, and I have some unique skills." He says taking her hands when Christen grabs Tarkens 2 tier luggage and drags it outside to the lobby curb and gently places it in the back trunk when the driver pops it open.

Then shuts it closed, Tarken enters the right passenger side while Christen enters the left and Gorgons already in the car more then ready for this trip to the airport. The driver looks through the rear view mirror and Gorgon nods his head the valet pulls away from the curb at the usual speed and before he reaches the gate its opened already. Gorgon has it perfectly programed to open very quickly so before the limo crosses the threshold and into the street. In the back seat Christen grabs a magazine on men's fitness all translated in Greek featuring Greek and European body builders and experts of sports nutrition. Gorgon and Tarken continue their conversation about that crazy college professor they had who eat those brownies laced with a weird strain of cannabis or marijuana.

"Tarken I can't stop thinking about Professor Primokov and those damn chocolate cannabis laced brownies. My god! We had some much fun that semester in International Finance."

Admits Gorgon reminiscing about the past before he has to bide his college friend good bye.

"Gorgon I can't believe we're having this conversation, your son just got married, the most important day of his life and your bringing up some crazy former Marxist professor at Cambridge University in the UK?" he asks? And Gorgon admits Again.

"I know, I know, I know, but Tarken besides being just a little smashed or shall I say under the influence of expensive Champagne. You and I had some good times man, just admit it Tarken, you and I were the Butch Cassidy and Sundance of Cambridge University?" Gorgon insists but Tarken makes this amusing facial expression like really Butch and Sundance?

"Gorgon yes, yes we had some good times at Cambridge however that was in the past my friend and Mr. Christen your being quiet here you have nothing to add?" Tarken replies to Gorgon and tries to shake up things in the limo when they are getting very close the Greece International Airport parking lot and lobby just a few blocks away.

"Gentlemen I'm just here to enjoy the ride and speaking of which I isn't that the Airport parking lot ahead? Looks like a plane is landing Tarken a 747 maybe even your flight?" Christen says while glancing over the pages of the magazine.

The limo comes to the same intersection before but from a reverse direction to the airport parking lot, there aren't many cars parked or tourist visible when the car pulls around the east parking lot area right up to the street curb of the front lobby.

The driver pops the trunk open while all three exit both passengers sides including the driver who races to the back to grab Tarken 2 tier luggage before his has a chance to touch it.

The driver places it on the ground wheels first and he Grabs the hold latch and pulls it out now it's ready to pull. He steps away for the luggage and Tarkens takes it thanking him When the driver returns to his seat again taking the wheel Waiting for his boss and Christen. The three of them enter the Airport lobby where they encounter activity everywhere or crowds of people waiting to board there flights, while seating around patronizing the different shops and restaurants while the registering for flight tickets nearly at the very but set up in the middle. With various airline gates on both sides in odd and even numbers when they come to a registration counter in the middle of the inner lobby. There's already 18 people in line with luggage in tow waiting to get their prepaid flight tickets or they're picking them up the airport check in counter.

"Gentlemen you don't have to stay and baby set me, listen when I touch down back in Pillisworth James and Gorgon I'll call you both asap, James take care, Gorgon once again it was fun!" he says before giving Gorgon a firm hug also a handshake for James Christen.

Then steps in line after 15 people biding his time before he gets his flight ticket and has his luggage collected by the airline laborers to be loaded on board the plane while he waits to board it. Christen and Gorgon finally head back toward the front airport lobby where the limo driver seats idly reading a Greek newspaper. They pass again the same shops and different Airline carriers going out only this time the mood between them seems less cordial then when Tarken was around. It's as if Gorgons attitude, his whole personality has changed but the vibe between the two appears hospitable at least for now.

Christen observes the various advertisements for soda, beer, gaming clubs and western restaurants like McDonalds, Arby's, Wendy's, Subway, all in Greek characters. He indirectly continues to follow Gorgon half way thru the front of the airport until the parked limo can be seen just 30 feet away. Gorgon makes a friendly gesture with his left hand to Christen before asking? "if there's anything he'd like to get before they exit the airport?" at that point christen stops looks around and decides hell no.

"Not today Gorgon, not today, however I've worked up quite an appetite since the ride here, I'm thinking about the aroma of that sweet smelling beef and other meat hors'd'oeuvres your chefs cooked up." Christen replies. By this time they are practically at the airport revolving lobby door when Gorgon pushes through it and Christen right behind him when the driver quickly exits the car and grabs the rear passenger doors for Gorgon and Christen to enter. Gorgon slips in to the right passenger side Christen quickly goes around to the left, slides in the seat and they close both close the doors at the same time. The driver hurries back in the driver's seat closing his door car in one motion, while pulling off after putting the limo back in drive.

He takes the left parking lot loop toward the street intersection leading into the Greece International Airport, and exits out back in the direction toward the greater Athens suburb. Christen relaxes in his seat while grabbing another alpha magazine, this time its Hustler, yes Hustler magazine translated in Greek, yes after all why can't Greek businessmen read and watch centerfolds of sexy nude European women? Gorgon notices Christen reached into the slightly hidden slot in the door, grabbing the swanky nude magazine translated in Greek character. And he just can't resist the urge to inquire whether he even understands what he reading?

"Mr. Christen, I'm a little curious… right now! That's a 9 month old magazine translated in Greek and you understand it?" He asks James with an arrogant smirk on his face. And Christen doesn't even break his glance at the page but replies anyway without giving Gorgon a look.

"It's all relative to me Gorgon, whether in Hustler, Playboy, or GQ magazines, translated in any language the pictures of nude women interests' men or at least the look of smooth bare skin, nice curves, and well-manicured feet." Christen responds again giving him no eye contact but focusing on the pictures and articles instead.

At this point the driver keeps his eyes on the road and the rear view mirror watching Gorgon and Christen but never says anything, only observes and acts. They causally pass by the art gallery or at least the driver notices the outside banner In bold letters and maintains his speed anyway. They are just under 10 city blocks from his Mansion and Christen continues eyeing the nude women in this 8 month old edition of Hustler magazine.

Gorgon takes out his flip phone to call his newly wed son informing him he's just a few minutes from the estate and wants a update on his business guests, the Archbishop and the popular Greek recording artist Severon Christotos. He hits the speed dial, gets a dial tone and waits after several rings someone answers, and its Tisdale Minolta on the line.

"Gorgon what's your eta? And the opportunity we spoke about a few days before is near, my guys, Mikhails crew continue to feed their faces while drinking this expensive but tart champagne. The men are getting restless Gorgon and I can't promise any civility so long as your remaining house guest still here." He mildly depends and Gorgon can hear it in his voice.

"We're less than 4 mins from the manse and Mr. Christen returns with me looking very anxious to continue his dance with Andromeda. But yes, I understand completely Tisdale however you know my policy about such matters, so once the Arch Bishop Sinilos, Severon and his band leave, and I presume the photographers are still around Arrie and Spyros?" he asks.

"Yes, yes your weird western hippie looking Photographers are waiting to get paid Gorgon, you left so all of a sudden, almost everyone wondered where you were?" he replies. While this conversation persists Christen grows bored glaring at these nude European beauties be it, blondes, brunettes and redheads, relatively short or at least judging by the centerfolds 5 foot, 3 inches to 5 foot, 10 inches, the photographer looked for those particular type of woman. Very slender or petite but they don't look anorexic or malnourishes judging by the shapes of their body and apparent BMI or Body Max Index.

Christen looks up to see the limo making left turn at the same time the gate quickly opens, while the driver pulls up into Gorgons drive way and they observe his friend the Arch Bishop Augustine Sinilos standing, waiting patiently with bible in hand outside the lobby doors for Gorgon to step out of his limo. The driver circles around to the front stopping directly parallel to Arch Bishop Sinilos who gives Gorgon an amusing stare before he exits the rear passenger side.

"Gorgon? I think we have a break down in communication or, or, you didn't plan this in full detail, in any case I'm leaving but not before I'm compensated!" He demands! When Gorgon steps out, closes the door and moves directly to Sinilos right side folding his arms over his chest and slightly leaning in to speak indirectly face to face.

"Of course, of course haven't I taken care of you in the past…. Arch Bishop Sinilos? As I recall once upon a time you weren't always a man of the cloth?" he replies then follows up.

"We both know you weren't always a man of god, don't we? In fact…. truth be told, at one time you were a murdering, Psychopath, a cold blooded, sick, sadistic son of a bitch but who am I to judge father?" he tells Sinilos while reaching into his left suit pocket, and pulling out another thick manila envelope containing over 10 thousand euros and handing it to Augustine or placing it in his right suit pocket himself.

While Christen looks on at this exchange from the left rear passenger side door, shuts it and walks into the mansion without breaking any stride. Leaving Gorgon and Sinilos alone to finish their private discussion when Christen is met by a very eager Andromeda. Sinilos notices Christen entering the mansion and over hearing everything that was said between them but Gorgon doesn't give a damn about that, he already has plans for Mr. Christen that will remain hidden from everyone including his Daughter and the newlyweds.

"I think your house guest overheard or suspects something Gorgon and you never really introduced him to myself or anyone else for that matter?" he asks concerned.

"You don't have to worry about him father, he poses no threat to you or anyone for that matter, in any case our business has concluded so I wish you a safe trip to your next engagement farewell." He tells him.

They step away from each other as Sinilos quickly moves to his vehicle while Gorgon enters the lobby door and he's back in the mansion, he can hear the car door open from outside and Archbishop Sinilos pulls away from the mansion and to the gate which remains open and leaves finally. Gorgon is met by a very impatient and eager Minolta still holding a half glass of Bollinger Grand Anne Brute Champagne in one hand while watching Andromeda and James Christen engage each other in a rhythmic dance routine where it seems she's actually leading and he's following her.

All this in the bold presence of Mikhail and Tisdales Henchmen who don't register any emotion at all or that Champagnes finally have its effect on them now. The Photographers Arrie and his side kick Spyros Andreadis step to Gorgon when he pulls out more thick manila envelopes from his suit pockets, so they all get euros and personal checks but they don't count the cash before they leave and why? They know Gorgon has a reputation for being a semi big spender or he tips very well so no need to count it.

"Gentlemen, thank you, so much for the wedding photos, I'm in your debt again…. also how soon will I or they see the finished product?" he asks before they leave.

"Give me a few days to process them and I'll send the package to you within 9 days and you've already paid full price so no need to over charge."

Arrie says leaving out the door with his side kick following him and he leave it open slightly open.

While remaining are Severon and his band continue performing for the newlyweds Perseus and Melissa, followed by Christen and Andromeda doing something called Hasapiko or dancing in a straight line and is composed of 9 basic steps and a set of variations. Then all four of them line up side by side by their and begin this interesting improvised dance well once again Gorgon and his business partners look on in amusement. Before Gorgon has a chance to check the kitchen for a talk with his hired Chefs and catering crew he's approached by Mikhail and Tisdale regarding their private Q and A session with James Christen.

They all gather or congregate outside the library to The east wing of the hall where they can't be seen or heard by anyone except maybe the chefs and caters but they assume the chefs won't say anything. Tisdale and Mikhail seem to circle Gorgon as if attempting to rattle him or at least cause him to make a hasty decision right then and there. While Gorgon continues to maintain a cool, calm demeanor in the face of his partners, who have waited, and waited, and waited patiently for him to act. The timing remains very awkward for him and he refuses to move on Christen while his newly wed son and daughter in law are present with his daughter Andromeda.

The henchman notice their bosses have left or ducked around the corner outside the library and one of the twins Roman decide to ask Andromeda for dance after that Greek dance Hasapitko ends.

"My lady, Miss Andromeda might I have this dance?" he asks a stunned Andromeda.

"Yes, yes, sure why not,"

"James, do you mind?" she asks him before Roman moves in.

"No, no, of course not by all means." He says stepping away to set down in Romans chair next to his fraternal twin brother Gregory and the other Russian bone breakers. Roman firmly grabs around her waist and holds Andromedas' left hand while Vladimir, Natali, Krasimir, and Alexendr look on but don't engage until given absolute orders to do so. While Roman and Andromeda enjoy each others talents her father finally opens up to Mikhail and Tisdale about the best way to approach Christen without causing suspension among his daughter and newly wed son Perseus.

"So have you decide on the right course of action Gorgon? You had more than enough time to plan and plot this out, in fact you let him ride along with you to the airport, while you played host!" Tisdale demands.

While Mikhail pulls out one of his expensive Cuban cigars and a stainless steel flip lighter, holds it to his lips and puffs while he lights the tip and its bright cherry red. He than leans against the wall next to Gorgan and continues enjoying the smell of his Cuban Cigar, puff after puff and not a word from his mouth or even a grin or smile. He continues enjoying it, holding it with right fingers, staring into space or the weird looking Greek murals on the walls of this east hallway.

Gorgon has his arms folded across his chest, biding his time, staring down at the floor and considering what Tisdale has said but sticking to his own instinct, following his own intuition while he copes with the smell of his Russian partners cigar, then he opens up to both.

"I need the two of you to understand that I fully intend to execute this however, it will be done my way and not yours…. gentlemen you are in my home, enjoying my hospitality, drinking my Bollinger champagne, eating my caviar and Hors d'oeuvres and everything on my dime? So what I require from you is patience as difficult as that maybe right now, keep your thugs at bay and after Severon and his band are done entertaining everyone we will take a trip with Mr. Christen. Now are we on the same page or no?" he asks them without giving each man a look of acknowledgement.

Tisdale seems to want to argue or respond but Gorgon just muscles his way past him and back into his private library to dance with the bride, while Tisdale and Mikhail look stupid in the east hallway.

He then yells out, "it's my turn, it's my turn, I wanna dance with the bride."

He steps to Perseus and Melissa while they're in the middle of this popular Greek dance routine and just interrupts it and there's nothing young Perseus can do except step aside and watch his bride dance with Gorgon.

"Melissa, Melissa my darling daughter in law may I have this dance?" he asks with arms and hands opened wide? And she smiles back when Perseus who takes a seat next to Christen, the one once occupied by Roman who continues to dance with Andromeda.

"Yes I would be honored to dance with you Gorgon." She says with a smile pulling him into her space.

Who would have thought Gorgon can dance or at least he displays a little rhythm for a European Greek with low cut silvery gray hair. He holds her while they carefully move from one side of the floor to the next staying in front of Severon and his band. The two also perform an unfamiliar dance routine in front of Christen, Perseus, Gregory, Vladimir, Natali, Krasimir, and Alexandr. They stare at each other and engage in a slight conversation while these men look on then it turns into laughter as if he cracking an inside joke that no one aware of or isn't privy too. He continues holding her firmly, softly when they dance close to Roman and Andromeda, and without warning or notice Alexandr steps up to them for a cut in and Roman obligates.

"Annia, can I please have a dance with you?" he asks with both hands held out.

"Yes, yes why not, Alexandr!" she says while Roman steps away taking Alexandrs seat next to Christen and gives him a weird smirk or smile like it's only a matter of time, just a matter of time.

But this doesn't register with Christen while he's watching these people dance and he notices Gorgons partners remain in the east hall but finally reenter the private library. Tisdale steps to Krasimir and Vladimir signaling them to meet him in the east hall for a brief chat while Gorgon dances with Melissa and Alexandr has fun with Andromeda while still a little buzzed from the Champagne. The three discretely meet in the east hall and discuss or a begin a strategy of their own independent of Gorgons on how they will deal with Christen or at least grill him for information. Krasimir paces back and forth in the east hall out of frustration before he opens up to his boss Tisdale Minolta the money launder with Vladimir looking on about to Light one of his fancy cigarettes without any protest from Gorgon.

"So what are we doing boss? I've had expensive champagne, Three slices of wedding cake and those funny looking but very tasty beef Meatball Horderves/appetizers. I watch the bride and groom exchange vows and dance while this guy seems oblivious to what's about to happen? This Christen fellow? Talk to me? What the fuck is happening here?" he asks in his native Russian tongue.

Now Tisdale nods his head in agreement but Nonchalantly shrugs his shoulders expressing he's own frustration with the situation. "Lads I fully understand your disappointment however we must respect Mr. Mathias wishes, this is a special occasion he sons wedding, as corny as it sounds he's celebrating, so show some restraint or swallow your ego even if it means choking on it." Tisdale replies. Now Vladimir has sometime to add in his native Russian tongue after taking a few hits of his cigarette.

"We don't always agree on subject of business but In this case we are on same page myself and Krasimir. Second, theirs a matter of the important shipment tomorrow arriving in Isle of Crete. We have yet to discuss that with Mikhail or the manpower needed for transport? 3 tons of raw opium? That's a lot of product to move?" says Vladimir. And Tisdale interjects after Vlad kind of loudly brings up the issue of raw opium in the east Hall presuming he was hear by the caters and everyone in the private library. He steps up close to Vlad with his right index finger in his chest pressed hard.

"Don't, don't ever let me hear you mention that again, not in this environment, not at this time, do we understand each other?" he tells him in Russian.

When Vladimir raises both hands with the cigarette between his right index fingers almost embarrassing himself while Krasimir looks on nodding his head in agreement.

"Da or yes!" in Russian. Vlad replies.

"Now finish that cigarette outside near the curb I don't like the smell or stench of it." Tisdale orders Vlad to step out and again folds his arms over his chest when Krasimir tries a much different approach.

"Boss, what do you want to do? I agree with Vladimir however this is time for celebration not conflict in the face of someone else's happiness. So now what? What's our move?" he asks in Russian tongue.

And Tisdale remains in his spot with arms folded across his chest, staring into space or either he was listening to Krasimir or he's his mind is elsewhere? He finally refocuses and gives Krasimir on his left direct eye contact and with a smile he says, "For now enjoy the reception, and I want to see you dancing with the Bride, Krasimir and the lovely Andromeda. Don't be antisocial my friend, enjoy yourself, there will be plenty of time afterward for us to deal with Mr. Christen." And Krasimir throws up this hands with a gesture of Ok fine with me boss. He reenters the private library to see Andromeda getting bored with Alexandr and possibly looking for another dance partner when he makes his move. Except Mikhail has his own motives and attempts to cock block Alexandr only Andromeda won't have any of it and she politely stops Mikhail and invites Alexandr to dance with her instead.

"So, sorry Mikhail but I want to dance with Alexandr, Alexandr can dance real nice!" she says with a smile.

And Mikhail throws up his hands, shrugs and takes a seat between Christen and Vladimir. Alexandr and Andromeda have a slow dance and groove to Severons' band, they also request them to speed up the tempo or play one of his faster pop tunes. Gorgons having too much fun enjoying this Euro pop music while he wraps his left arm around his daughter in law Melissa and whispering into her ears also, while his son watches or looks on with a smile.

Gorgon takes a peek at his platinum Rolex watch and it reads just fifth teen minutes after 4 pm. He takes a glance at Severon and his band who looks hungry and thirsty after watching The guests eat horderves and drink expensive Bollinger champagne. Also one of the caters comes out of the kitchen for a talk with The boss about their payment and possibly a tip being that Gorgon is perceived as a big spender.

"Mr. Mathais we hope the food was to your liking and Satisfaction?" he asks.

"Yes, yes I couldn't be more pleased…oh by the way before you leave I'd like to give a discount on any items in my Gallery in downtown Athens?" he replies.

While at the same time waving and pointing to Severon and his band members to dig in and help themselves to the food and wedding cake. The other caters emerge from the kitchen ready to leave when Gorgon notices all three of them changed and ready to depart but not before they all paid.

"Gentlemen, just wait here momentarily while I grab your Money." He tells them before he quickly races into his private Din area and grabs a manila package envelope from his dresser And back into the hall where they patiently stand waiting. He pulls out a thick envelope from the package containing over $200,000 in cash all in euros and hands it to the head chef with a smile of his face.

"Gentleman again, thank you for your time and divide this among you." He says.

At this point they all grin at each other before leaving

Out one by one and the lead chef shakes his hand giving a Congratulations before following his fellow chefs out the door.

"Gorgon you've been such a wonderful host please give your Newly wed son my kindest regards thanks." He replies before finally leaving.

Now remaining behind are Severon and his band serving themselves food, cake and finishing off the last bottles of Bollinger Grand Anne Brute Champagne. Severon steps to Gorgon After washing down a mouth full of roast beef horderves and some Greek salad now holding a full glass of Champagne they pick up on the conversation they were having earlier.

"Gorgon, gorgon, you always have the best of everything and your fellow company excluded, I haven't seen you on the circuit lately since you reopened this Art Gallery of yours in downtown Athens?" he says sipping his champagne.

"Well business has picked up somewhat and my client Referrals have been steady so yes, I'm doing well for myself, Speaking of which, I heard your latest recording with Lionel Richie at the London Sound Observatory a few months ago, very nice Severon. Although I never pegged you for a R&B recording artists you really pull it off. But that voice of yours, wow, impressive, most impressive." Gorgon tell him with arms folded across his chest.

With that Severon just blurts out a haughty laugh and gives Gorgon this sudden look of what the fuck would you know about it but he doesn't verbalize it, just shrugs his shoulders as if to say when you have it, you have it.

"When I first got into this business 20 years ago Gorgon, I always wanted to make the kind of music I liked but also record with the best in the world, and I've been very fortunate and blessed to have had that opportunity. So getting the chance to record with Lionel Richie for me was a cherry on top, as sweet as it gets." He replies taking another sip of his champagne then continues while his band finishes eating and begins breaking down their instruments for packing.

"Lionel Richie's a legend among singers so anytime you get the chance to record with him or perform at his side it just raises your game up to another level, it makes you want to be better then what you are." He responds again.

While Gorgon seemly aware of everything going on around him asks the question almost every singer gets asks what next for you?

"So, you touring next, recording or what? What's next for you Severon?" Gorgon asks while the two of them watch his band members finish up breaking down the drums set, the key board, the amps for the speakers and guitars. Everything placed in cases, containers and neatly compartmentalized and ready to move.

"I'm scheduling a tour with my band in 3 weeks after we record our 12 album together, yes album number 12 Gorgon. Then afterwards maybe I go solo again, maybe, maybe not, with these things one never knows. I will talk it over with my follows band members and see what happens." He says after taking one last sip of his champagne and he's guys start carrying the equipment out the door to their luxury buses.

"Severon, judging by your performance today Severon I have no doubt you will do very well in the studio or on your next touring schedule." Gorgon says before Severon asks him another question before receiving his payment.

"Gorgon you ever thought about starting your own record label? I mean getting into the music business?" he asks an amused Gorgon.

"What are you serious? Ha Ha ha ha ha ha ha ha ha ha ha ha ha ha ha ha ha ha ha ha ha ha ha, ha ha ha ha ha no way Severon, me, a record mogul, me a record industry executive? That's beyond comical, no I'll leave the music for guys like you Severon, I'm afraid I don't have the patience for it or the right attitude either. Ooooooooh wow, I needed that! Thanks for that comedic bomb. No I sell and deal in art my friend that's my calling and anything else would be a major distraction for me." He says while pulling out an envelope from his right suit pocket to hand over to Severon watching him analyze it.

"This seems pretty light to be cash Gorgon? I'm getting a personal check and you've been handing out thick manila envelopes all afternoon?" Severon asks a little disappointed.

"Relax Severon, I ran out of euro cash but call me in a few days and I will wire the rest to you asap!" Gorgon tells him and Severon takes the envelope, nods his head and walks out the door waving Gorgon and everyone else goodbye, while at the same time Vladimir reenters as Severon is leaving and they don't even exchange a look. In the background we hear the sound of luxury buses cranking up or engines turning over also the caters truck are following behind too, when the 2 luxury buses parked outside beginning slowly moving after the band has everything fully packed on the bus.

The driver navigates around the drive way when the gate opens to the outside street, the driver pulls out does the left to right look to see when it's clear to pull out and hits the accelerator making a left turn toward their motel just 6 miles to the east of downtown Athens. Now they are gone! Gorgon has the gate programmed to close on its own with underground wiring and sensors for proximity entering and leaving.

Inside the manse and private library the newlyweds start opening up the wedding presents while everyone looks on or continues drinking Champagne. Perse begins opening his gifts first around Mikhail, Tisdale, Gorgon and the rest of the henchman while Melissa has another sister to sister girl talk with Andromeda. Perseus is given a very expensive platinum Omega watch by Mikhail while Tisdale smiles, nods his heads and

Waits for Perse to open his gift instead. These guys are always in competition.

"This must have set you back some thousands of dollars? Mr. Khrichkov?" Perse asks him. But he only laughs it off.

"No, no, no my good boy, for this occasion money is no Object. Marriage is big step and you are son of successful Businessman so you must look the part." Mikhail replies clapping his hands. At this point Tisdale points to his gift which looks a book or something wrapped in red and velvet paper with a card on top. Perse picks up the package, and analyses it before he tears the paper off from one side to the next and it's completely exposed. He opens the box inside to find a solar powered all purpose weather radio, and it whines up too! Perse gives Tisdale a look of ok?

"Oh, you really put a lot of thought into this one didn't You?" he asks shrugging his shoulders at Tisdale.

"Perse, your father informed me that you and your lovely bride were planning to vacation on the Kraken, one of Gorgons sail boats, so I started thinking wait, wait a minute I will get him, her an all purpose solar weather radio for the journey, and as you know the sea can be dangerous and treacherous at the same time?" Tisdale responds in kind. With that said Gorgon steps over between Mikhail and Tisdale and points out a surprise gift of his own, in what looks like dinner or kitchen ware with glasses and coffee cups on top with different size plates on the Bottom. All carefully packaged inside the neat and clean Styrofoam case painted beige and wrapped up like a wedding gift in red and velvet also. There are other gifts on the table but it doesn't seem like Perseus is interested in opening anything else and gives his attention to Melissa who was having a girl moment with Andromeda.

"Ladies, ladies, do you mind if I interrupt your woman bonding for a moment? Melissa, looks like you got most of the wedding gifts sweetie, but I'm happy that your happy. Annie, I can never thank you enough for being here for me and my wife, its means more to me then you will ever know Annie." He tells his sister as Melissa looks on than chimes in.

"As far is gifts go Perse, at least you got the watch and expensive shirts, I'm looking at a gift wrapped box of china ware with plates, saucers and cups." she says before Gorgon interjects with some gentle sarcasm.

"Now, now children, you never looked at the other presents on the table including cooking ware and a brand new set of cutlery/kitchen knives, flatware spoons, forks, butter knives, bake ware, yes bake ware for cakes, pies and making cookies. Oh, yeah Melissa for the record I will assume you have some skills on the kitchen?" he asks her while smiling and shrugging his shoulders.

At that point Perseus just stares up at the ceiling for a moment until Melissa fires back with a cute smile and retort of her own…..

"Why Mr. Mathias not only are my kitchen skills top notch but in case your son never told you or you haven't heard no one and I mean no one bakes a cheese cake like I do or whips up a delicious macaroni, shrimp and veggie casserole. So yes sir, Mr. Mathias I'm very skilled in the kitchen." She replies most confidently as Tisdale, Mikhail and their henchmen look on somewhat interested and a little indifferent considering Christen is also present.

"Well, Perse take notes son, when I'm not traveling or following up on client referrals I may decide to come and visit, Andromeda and I for Thanksgiving and or Christmas. So I'm anticipating you at your best and I'm bringing my appetite too Young man so you learn as much from her as possible, there's nothing worse than a man who can't cook or doesn't know how to feed his wife and family." Replies Gorgon.

Just about to ask them about plans for the honeymoon sending a definite signal to his partners that time is rapidly coming for that cruel Q&A session with James Christen.

"So newly weds have you decided when and where you plan to go for your honeymoon? Oh just so you know Melissa, Perseus has full use of my luxury yacht 'The Kraken'. One of several I own in fact." He says with a smile before she comments.

"Ok, now you can tell me what the hell a 'Kraken' is? Can you describe to me exactly why you name a luxury yacht The Kraken?" she Ask with her hands in the air. Gorgon laughs at that but indulges her question with humor and humility.

"As you know I'm very proud of my Greek heritage Melissa and growing up I would here these stories as a young boy from late my mother before she passed, god bless her right now, she's smiling down from heaven or Mt. Olympus right now, hmmm…. Anyway she would tell me stories about this sea god Poseidon and Greek fisherman battling this huge, ugly monster the 'Kraken'.

Over the ages or centuries its description has changed but it is a monster, depicted as a gargantuan octopus or sea beast. I'm a connoisseur of sail boats and yachts so when I found several to my liking, I name one after the 'Kraken' based on its size so there you go in a nut shell." He tells her at the same time his son nods his head in agreement with arms folded across chest.

"So newlyweds, Perse and Melissa indulge me, I'm curious about your honeymoon plans? You decided if I'm not mistaken or correct me, to take a sail for a few days, weeks, what? And then fly to the Caribbean or Hawaii? Which to me is a very good idea by the way so are we talking plan A does this or plan B try this later?" he asks when Perse offers his own views on the matter.

"We talked about this in private also I give her a tour of the 'Kraken' a week ago, yes dad from top to bottom. So we mutually decided on taking a sail the first couple weeks or month and plan the Caribbean trip while at sea." says Perseus while firmly holding his bride.

"Excellent, excellent, very good and more words of wisdom to the both of you, always talk to each other, keep the lines of communication open even when it's the most mundane topic or issue no matter what, no matter what confide in each other. Cherish each others opinion, even if it isn't your own." Gorgon tells them before they prepare to undress and pack for the trip.

"Well everyone I can't express enough my sincere gratitude that you all showed up for this occasion and thank you again Father, Annie, Mikhail, Tisdale, James, and gentlemen, time for Melissa and myself to depart so if you'll excuse us?" Perseus tells them while the two excuse themselves waving everyone goodbye including James Christen and make their way to the stairs.

Tisdale gives Gorgon and peculiar look almost like the two are reading each others minds while Christen raises from his seat. Before he has a chance to leave the library and follow the newlyweds upstairs he's approached by Gorgon.

"Ah, James I have some other important business to attend too outside Athens and id like your advice as a consultant?" he asks Christen with the Mikhail, Tisdale and entourage looking on.

"Interesting, yes, after I change clothes than we can discuss it, everything in detail on the road." Christen replies. Now leaving and turning the corner to his left straight up stairs to the second floor level where his room awaits on the wide side hall. Andromeda steps to her father, grabbing his left arm while pulling him to her and she has her head in his chest.

"My child, my beautiful Andromeda have you not enjoyed yourself? You seem somewhat buzzed sweetheart from the champagne? Gorgon asks her concerned she may have drank too much indeed.

"Father, I'm in need of a nap, I must sleep this off and

Yes, your daughter's slightly drunk but still very much in control father." She tells him literally leaning against her father, while her eyes and head looks like its spinning like a top.

"Oh my word, yes, yes daughter you get upstairs quick to your bed and Sleep this off sweetie a few hours. I have some business to discuss with my partners baby." He tells her when she walks away from him and out the private library before she says.

"You always do dad, you always do," she adds again before turning the corner.

"Gentlemen, the dance was fun, till next time if there is a next time?" she replies again laughing, giggling to herself after she makes the turn and hits the stairs to her room one at a time so she don't trip and fall back. She also grabs the stair rail working her way to the top.

The guys watch her leave along with Gorgon while Roman and Gregory decide give her an impromptu farewell.

"Goodbye Andromeda, and sleep off that champagne doll." They tell her in unison while the bosses watch shaking their heads in amusement.

"Fellas, Roman, Gregory if you would help me clear out the wedding cake, champagne, water glasses, pitchers and Horderves d'oeuvres please so we can discuss this Finally?" he asks and they respond and comply with question or resistant's. Gorgons positions himself behind the cart of the tall wedding cake and begins pushing it toward the entrance followed by Roman pushing the champagne cart with Horderves d'oeuvres entrees, plates, forks and Gregory with the cart of water pitchers and glasses. Gorgon reaches the hall and proceeds to the west wing walk in freezer directly across kitchen.

Gorgon stops within 3 feet of the freezer door, steps around the cart and quickly moves to open with Roman and Gregory looking on to make their move behind him. Gorgon swiftly opens the walk in freezer wide enough to make his entrance followed by the twins. The interior looks like your non typical walk in freezer/cooler by Kysor 11' 6" * 20' 10' 4" H. 6' tall Steele shelves on both sides stack with some can goods, ice cream, dairy products, stacks and stacks of frozen meat. He parks the cart inside the cooler inches from the wall followed by Roman and Gregory who park the remaining carts next to Gorgon and behind Roman. The two go back to the library while Gorgon wraps the wedding cake with light stretch wrap, and covers the meat horderves d'oeures completely in light foil while leaving the cart of champagne/pitcher water and glasses before closing the freezer. Gorgon leaves rubs his hands together for a little heat friction from the cold and its back to the library for some business discussion.

Gorgon makes a bee line for his private room and pulls out a mailing tube with the in depth shipping details before reentering the library for his presentation.

"Gentlemen, gentlemen, if you please just step over here?" He asks them while he opens the tube and pulls out his plans in 3 to 5 long pages, placing everything on the table near the window overlooking the outside.

"Take a look for yourselves, gents, please everyone gather around. The plan this time will be different from what we've done over years past. As you all know in order to maintain our success this operation must remain unpredictable but methodical at the same time." He says again this time as they all exam the shipment details.

Tisdale and Mikhail analyze pages 1 and 2 while Roman, Gregory, Vladimir, Anatoly, Krasimir, and Natali exam pages 3, 4, and 5.

"So fellas, pages 1 and 2 involve the details of those 3 luxury yachts and their hulls all design to carry over 4 tons of Opium combined or 8000 lbs. of product or 3628.7389kg with each ship measure at 170'3"ft to 200'2"ft in length." He continues while Tisdale and Mikhail nods their heads in agreement.

"And what about these red X marked in the middle on the ships at the bottom just below the windows? I presume that's where the hulls are or correct me if I'm wrong?" Tisdale asks while glancing at Mikhail or reading his expression.

"Yes, Gorgon these are compartments no? Or areas, rooms being used for compartments? Yes, no?" Mikhail asks while he squints his eyes at the varied details of plans he's viewing with Tisdale.

"Yes, yes, gentlemen you're correct the X means Specified compartments on each ship where the drugs are to be stored and how they will be loaded and unload using certain equipment and manpower." Gorgon replies to both men.

"The equipment and manpower? That's what I'm curious About Gorgon, I've been wondering about that for some time now." Acknowledges Roman while he brother nods his head in agreement.

"Gorgon you mention before something about the Mayor of Crete? You made arrangements with him yes? You don't foresee him being a problem no?" asks Mikhail shrugging his shoulders. At that question Gorgon lets out a slight chuckle and smiles at them all with a look of absolute certainty nothing will go wrong.

"Yes the cargo is scheduled to arrive sometime tomorrow morning via tractor trailers in Crete packed with Opium gents. And in regards to the Mayor… lets' just say he owes me big time and I'm cashing in my chips." Replies Gorgon who hears footsteps coming down stairs and it's the newlyweds with luggage in tow before reaching the bottom stairs Perse announces.

"We're all packed and ready dad." Says Perseus with Melissa close behind him smiling from ear to ear.

Gorgon turns his attention to the library entrance when he sees his son pulling his luggage to the door, that's the cue and not far behind is James Christen back in his casual dress code armed with gun in shoulder holster.

"Very good, well gentlemen time to escort the newlyweds to their private pleasure cruise, while you and I Mr. Christen have some special business to discuss." Gorgon tells his partners while Perse and Melissa proceed out the door to the Mercedes limo parked outside and the trunk popped open. Christen stops at the base of the stairs fully dressed and being watched Tisdale, Mikhail and the rest of the goon squid.

"Gorgon I'm ready so let's do this, oh are they coming with us or staying here?" Christen asks while they all give him a look of what do you think idiot? But Roman and Gregory volunteer to go along for the ride thinking maybe this is the opportunity they've been waiting for finally, a chance to finally get some answers and win brownie points from the big bosses.

"Mind if we tag along Mr. Mathias?" Asks Roman while his brother nods his head in agreement then adds his two cents.

"Yeah, it's getting kind of boring here anyway, a long ride would break the monotony." Gregory says while getting a silent nod of approval from Mikhail and Tisdale.

Gorgon concedes "Sure, sure why not fellas, as long as Tisdale and Mikhail don't mind I see no problem with you coming with us." With all this going on in the private library and front lobby entrance the newlyweds are waiting in the Mercedes limo for Gorgon and Christen to come out, unknowing they're about to have two more passengers. Christen continues outside toward the lobby curb and straight to the limo rear left door where the newlyweds are already seated and having an intimate conversation. Christen seats directly across from them and soon they are met by Gorgon, Roman and Gregory grinning from ear to ear.

"Don't mind me lovers, I'm just along for the ride, and for the record you two are truly blessed to be together." Christen tells them right before Roman takes his seat and adds his five cents.

"Well look at this, one big happy family huh? Man and woman mad, crazy, insane in love, and happily married. Perse you are one lucky guy." Says Roman in his thick Ukraine accent with his brother looking on nodding his head in agreement then adds.

"Yeah, in this life a guy's lucky, blessed to find that right one woman, that one lady who's ride or die for him only. Take that love, that respect, that honor you have for on another and hold on it forever." Gregory tells him extending his hand to Perseus who shakes it in full gratitude when Gorgon gives special orders to the driver about their destination.

"Lupredo, take us to Port of Piraeus ASAP! And try to avoid the midday traffic please and areas with tourist who don't know where the hell they are going?" Gorgon orders his driver.

"Very good sir, in route." He replies after Gorgon quickly closes the door and the Mercedes limo pulls off, away from the manse making the usual turn around the drive way toward the gate which opens once the limo comes within several feet of it. The gate opens wide again this time internally inside the Mathias compound while the driver pulls out into Lenorman street and toward downtown Athens. Gorgon pulls out a miniature copy of the luxury yachts docked at the Island of Crete and specific diagrams on the ships where the opium will be stored and already packed in ground pepper to throw off customs dogs.

"Perse my boy just a quick overview while we ride toward Port of Piraeus in downtown Athens where the Kraken is docked. The vessel is fully fueled, the kitchen compartments packed with plenty of food and beverages so you won't starve, bathroom and sleeping quarters very clean also last but not least you newly weds are traveling with Capt. Argyle Juden. He maintains the Kraken when I'm not using it, from here you will travel to Crete and stay there for a few hours then it's off to your honeymoon." He informs them with a smile. The limo comes within 9 city blocks of Port of Piraeus with the full view of tourist everywhere exiting buses and or taxis to board the ferries. As the buses and taxi pull off from unloading the passengers the limo gets closer and closer to Piraeus. Starting at Immitou, Ipiro, Mikalis, Alon, Retsina, Fokionos, Akti Kondili all streets within less than half a mile from port when finally, the limo pulls within 10 feet of the docking area.

The driver stops pop the trunk open while Perseus and Melissa exit the car quickly racing around to grab their luggage waving Gorgon, James and the twins good bye. Perseus and his bride board Gorgon's private Jade Yacht luxury vessel The 'Kraken' where they are met by the ships Captain Spiridon Petros who also gives his boss Gorgon and military salute before grabbing a thick rope to unwind and pull it on deck. The two take their luggage into one of the vessels private rooms down below while Captain Petros mans the Jade yacht wheel of this luxury vessel and pulls away from the dock. Gorgon watches the vessel pull off from the dock then start to accelerate into the Sea of Crete heading south east toward the Island of Crete. Gorgon then orders his driver to take them his other shipping and receiving warehouse in Vouliagmeni another port in Athens but further south of the city limits, in a more industrialized area.

"Lupredo, take us to my compound in Vouliagmeni please ASAP and again try to avoid the traffic lights I'm on a strict schedule." He says while indirectly glancing at Christen and the twins. James can still sense something is coming but doesn't let his emotions show or tried keeping himself composed just in case it seems he's showing fear or nervousness.

"Vouliagmeni Mr. Mathias, that's just 15 mins away sir in route." Says Lupredo willingly complying with his boss. While at the same time Christen notices all the tourists coming and going, boarding the ferries seemingly toward Crete or some other islands either in the Sea of Crete or the Mediterranean Sea.

"Now Mr. Christen about that business I was eluding too back at my mansion, I have a slight security problem." Gorgon tells a suddenly intrigued Christen.

"Really, do tell and please don't leave out any details just give me the full picture." Christen replies while gorgon continues and the twins don't make a sound or even interject, just enjoy the ride.

"I've had several break ins in the past few weeks in fact most recently the locks were blown off, but the fascinating thing is nothing was stolen or at least that's what the thieves want me to believe." Gorgon tells him in a very animated tone.

"So have you notified the local authorities, I mean Greek police about this matter?" Christen asks him while Gorgon just shrugs off the question.

"The police here conduct themselves like amateurs Mr. Christen, it's more like class warfare, because I'm a successful Businessman means I can take a loss? Hell no, these fucks don't understand I run legitimate business with my gallery and expect professional cooperation but it means nothing to them." Gorgon continues before Christen can respond.

"I need your expertise on this matter Christen, just take a look around and you may find something that the police didn't think to look for?" he asks him.

"So Number 1, what exactly do you think they were looking for and Number 2, why your place, why you? And finally Number 3, what enemies do you have that you aware of? Sounds like someone had your place steaked out or this being a small city where almost everyone knows everyone, you have enemies lurking in the shadows Gorgon, so what say you?" Christen asks him while its seems the limos pulling up outside the shipping/receiving warehouse at Vouliagmeni.

"We're here now? Lupredo knows all the quick city routes, so now you get to see firsthand exactly what I've been discussing before we arrived." He says opening his door and Christen exits closely behind followed by Roman and Gregory.

"And those three questions you asked are about to be answered hopefully, uh…. Roman and Gregory stay out front while I show Mr. Christen around and if I need you I'll call." He orders them and they comply. While Roman and Gregory stand outside the warehouse in front Gorgon, and Christen quickly move around to the east rear of the building where they come to this entrance so Gorgon pulls out a key for the pad lock and 13inch chain wrapped around a Scissor gate that's 6*8 feet in length. After Gorgon releases the pad locks, pulling the chain toward him and using some force yank the gate open then he now has access to the door when carefully Christen analyzes the knob and door lock where a key goes it. It clearly been tampered with like someone tried to pick the lock and that didn't work so they simply plugged it with cement or some other dense substance where a key no longer fits.

Chapter 7

THE BETRAYAL

S o he gives Christen a look of have you seen anything like this before and what would you do to open this damn door?

"You see someone has tampered with my security locks and filled this with concrete or something, my key won't fit."

Gorgon says still trying to open door when finally Christen intervenes.

"Gorgon I presume your insured?" he asks.

"Yes of course but!" Gorgon replies then..

"So you won't mind if I do this stand back oh cover your ears please." Says Christen pulling out his P227 Smith & Wesson, pointing it down at an angle where on impact after several shots it will sever the inner lock with holes. He pulls the trigger and Blaam, blaam, blaam, blaam, four shots and the door swings open from impact.

"Introducing my personal master key!" Christen says with a smile of satisfaction but Gorgon has a frown on his face while they both enter the building from the rear east side.

"I thought secret agents carried around a tiny pouch with an assortment Picks and whatever you use?" Gorgon asks again this time finding an opportunity to keep James preoccupied while his has the twins knock Christen unconscious.

"Sounds like you been watching way too many Spy TV shows or movies Gorgon, The Man from UNCLE perhaps or James Bond 007?

Hmmm… ha ha ha ha ha ha. Nothing beats a good pistol to do the job." Christen replies again.

While they move into the warehouse theirs a noise of footsteps from outside entering the east rear door, this time its Roman concerned about the sounds shots heard from outside.

"Gorgon, we heard shots fired out front, talk to me?" he shouts in the warehouse in that thick Ukraine accent.

"Relax, relax, relax, Roman there's no need for alarm just stay there till I need you." Gorgon tells him while he and Christen stand outside an empty office cubicle with chairs, desk and an old PC Monitor with a seemly untouched open briefcase and PC tower on the floor.

"I'm here just in case there's problem." Roman shouts back. Christen goes in and sits down at the desk with his back to the door, not a very good position while Gorgon begins instructing him on his problem with accessing some highly sensitive information.

"So, Gorgon it looks like the PC and everything else is plugged in so let's boot it up and see what's it tells us." Christen says while booting the PC and he has his attention on the monitor and off Gorgon who slips away and signals Roman your opportunity has finally come. The screen starts to boot up Windows 98 and blinks a few times then finally the screen comes up for ID, and password, but before he has a chance to ask or even reach for the case, Roman catches him from behind with his right arm firmly around his neck and the left hand over head.

Christen makes every attempt to resist and even put up a fight but the Ukrainian already has him subdued to point where he passes out, with Gorgon watching just several feet away.

Soon Gregory enters and joins them when Gorgon instructs the twins, they carry him in the chair outside the cubicle and in the middle of the warehouse. Strip him of his suit and shoulder holster with gun while Gorgon leaves the compound to get his special case from inside the limo trunk and returning with it placed in a chair next to Christen while he remains unconscious or subdued. The case has a specific numerical combination lock which 4 digit code just happens to be the month and year Gorgon was born February, 1942. The case has two four inch syringe 50ml with needles and three full vials of what's called truth serum or Sodium Pentothal, also in the case are a roll of sterile tissue, rubbing alcohol and scissors for cutting, along with other miscellaneous items. Gorgon briefly monitors or carefully analyzes Christen to make sure he's still breathing and has a pulse while Roman prepares the syringe and injects the needle into the top vial of truth serum.

Gregory rips off the left sleeve of Christens shirt exposing his arm while at the same time preparing it for the injection. Gorgon observes what he sees, nods his head in content that the twins may have done this before and are fully capable of handling this without him remaining present.

"Gents, you seem to have this situation under control? So I will leave you here to conduct the Q&A process while I return to the estate and if you need to reach me, next to the entrance is a phone and a jack at the base of the floor. You've already been instructed what to ask him also finally but most important don't kill him, soften him up but don't kill him." He orders both of them and they nod in compliance however Gregory has a question before Gorgon leaves.

"What about the shipment Mr. Mathias, and the manpower? And one last thing, not trying to second guess you but supposing just supposing he doesn't confess? You have a plan B?" Gregory asks shrugging his shoulders.

"Let the cocktail do all the work after you've injected him once he regains conscious, wait 15 mins, hell a half hour while the chemical circulates through his veins, he will tell everything he knows. Oh yes, just incase here's my card where you can contact me for updates on any information you get from him and I expect to hear from you both hours before midnight." Gorgon tells them before turning to leave and he's out the door quickly racing toward the front then he's in the limo and the driver pulls off.

"Lupredo, back to the estate asap!" he orders his driver.

"Yes very good sir." He says in reply. Taking the same route and streets as before seemly in the direction of Port of Piraeus while the twins were preparing to torture and interrogate James Christen under the influence of truth serum. Gregory moves in with the syringe filled with three/fourths a dose of the Sodium Pentothal and finds the spot on Christen left arm but decides to stick the needle directly into the deltoid muscle while pushing the plunger for full injection. It's in so now Gregory steps back and places the syringe back into the case and waits wrapping both arms across his chest.

They watch him from a few feet on both sides then start circling him like vultures studying his demeanor, watching for signs of convolutions, involuntary spasms, ticks, anything to give them an idea that serum is having its effect but there remains total silence. Then Roman moves in close and makes a motion as if he's about to execute with his left a back hand slap to Christens face but Gregory intervenes.

"Dude, what the fuck? Chill out bro, let the cocktail do its job." He tells his brother in a thick Ukraine accent.

"Fuck this truth serum shit, omg, I just want to kick his fucking ass. You better regain conscious quick you piece of shit." Says Roman with much venom and hidden prejudice for Christen a black South African.

"Roman, roman, settle down, take a deep breathe and relax Ok? We don't want to fuck this up on account of you being overly anxious, so just mellow out let the chemical do it's job. And when he comes through, we hit him with the questions." Gregory orders his brother while he too fights the urge to punch or slap Christen in the face.

This is something that doesn't happen to him very often, getting caught off guard for one thing and knocked unconscious, strapped to a chair, and the real kicker injected with truth serum by psycho Ukrainian rejects. Has he really lost his edge or just beginning to play this game of human chess? He starts having weird visions or perhaps horrid hallucinations of getting himself decapitated and walking around trying to find his head, then finally he becomes road kill and get struck, ran over by a tractor trailer or Mack truck.

And that's just the first hallucination when it seems like he's about to possibly come through his head jerks up for several seconds then slumps back down. He's walking down a hall of what appears to be an abandon building looking for a informant for information and the deeper he goes the hall gets darker and darker. But what he doesn't realize there are three major holes in the floor ahead where the drop is at least over a hundred feet down and he has no flash light for use. So as he continues to move he wonders should I go left or right against the wall or straight down the middle of the hallway? He decides to follow his instinct and moves very close to the right against the wall using his hands to feel his way while he progresses down the hall.

And as fate would have it he's two feet from a major hole in the floor and no way to avoid it even if he could so he labor on and finds himself dropping but he manages to grab what feels like wood slab sticking out, but he can't see he suffers a deep cut on his right hand and fingers but he can't recover. He's trying to hang on by one hand while the other is a bloody mess and his left hand also suffers crapping pain, while he struggles too hold his body up and the wood slab feels like it wants to crack and break not good. Then it suddenly hits him if it's now my time to go then it's my time to go, and he holds on as long as he till he feels the break coming, and he drops at that point his subconscious kicks in again, and his head does another jerk upward while his eyes do their rolling up into his head.

And for another several seconds then its slumps back down and he gives off this body spasm like something is shaking him and nothing still no response. They continue to study his demeanor waiting patiently for him to regain conscious until finally it seems like he's coming out of it, his eyes flicker right to left, left to right, up and down. And he begins to speak in mumbling gibberish or unintelligible sentences while they look on for that moment when he may drift again.

"What, what, what is happening, why, why, I'm I strapped to a chair? OMG!! The room is spinning." He says trying to shake off the effects of the Truth serum.

"Mr. Christen good to have you back with us and for your sake, don't even think of not cooperating." Roman says while smiling and without any warning Christen takes a punch to the left side of his jaw by Gregory. Showing just how tough he is he absorbs the blow while cracking a smile as if to say, is that your best? Gregory moves in for another strike and this time he's stopped by Roman from following through and in his thick Ukrainian accent.

"What did I tell you? No, no, back off Gregory, for Christ sake let the damn chemical do it's job." Roman orders his brother.

"Oh for fuck sake man, he's regained consciousness already, Gorgon said softened em up, remember? What's a few harmless shots to the face gonna hurt? Hell I haven't even started on his chest or kidneys yet." Says Gregory very anxious to do bodily harm to James despite the fact that his brother injected him with half a vail of Sodium Pentothal. Christen starts grunting in pain or he's trying to resist the chemical with all his will but it's just too potent and its racing through his veins and blood stream.

"What do you want from me?" he asks with a plea of pain and or frustration that he can feel his jaw swelling and side lip bleeding.

"Why are you doing this and for what reason?" he asks them both and then they both strike him in the face and chest but not very hard.

"We want answers Mr. Christen, plain and simple. So comes the game of Q & A and make please make your answers genuine

Sir." Roman demands from him.

"What were you doing in Ankara, Turkey some months ago, and what we're you looking for at that compound?" Roman asks again.

"Ankara, Turkey, Ankara, Ankara that name sounds very familiar, it's a Muslim country correct? Yes, no, maybe?" he answers the question with a question agitating them more as every second and minute goes by.

"A very reliable source informed us that a man fitting your description exactly and build was seen fleeing the compound just a few minutes before explosion?" Roman asks him again. And this time Gregory holds back his rage, keeping his composure with Roman continuing the interrogation.

"Mr. Christen or shall we just call you James? Truth serum or not you will tell us what we want, you will answer our questions, it's just a matter of time. And we have all the time we need so with that said, your cooperation will make this process so much easier or we take a more creative approach and beat the living shit out of you, that would be option B for us. So with that said back to the original question?" Roman asks again while Christen is still reeling from the blows and the effects of Sodium Pentothal coursing through his veins.

And it seems like he wants to talk but his will keeps him from giving up his mission directive and he knows eventually he can't hold out forever, if only one of them leaves him alone and he uses that opportunity to incapacitate the other he might have a chance to survive this and whip a brief antidote to the poison in his body. So far two hours have gone by he makes a mental guess, in the back of his mind he recalls a similar situation he found himself in almost three years ago. It was reported a fellow agent with South African Intelligence was at a bar in Eastern Europe possibly Bucharest, Romania while flirting with a beautiful brunette, someone slipped a rofie or drug into his glass of beer.

He woke up half nude hanging from a pole and had been doused with water, while his captors were preparing jumper cables attached to a sponge. They turn up the voltage from a battery contraption and apply it to his stomach with 100 volts shooting through his body. He shakes violently, screaming, yelling in pain while they ask him questions but he won't answer no matter what while they turn up the voltage to 350. Eventually he gives them gibbering bullshit having nothing to do with why he was on assignment in Romania and they buy into it after hitting him several times with electroshock treatment. Surprisingly this lasts two hours, talk about high pain threshold and he's left for dead.

No one ever found his body and luckily for him a sympathetic stranger or Samaritan witnesses his being tortured, waited for tormentors to leave and helped him escape to a save house for recovery, if only Christen had such fortune? He would have to create his own opportunity and make the best of it while he has a chance. His eyes close again but he can still hear the twins deciding on plan B against the orders of Gorgon, if only one of them would leave the damn room, all he needs is a few minutes, just a few minutes for that opportunity to make his move and turn this whole thing to his advantage. When Roman decides to call Gorgon for more instructions to the dismay of Gregory.

"I think it's time to consult Mr. Mathias again?" says Roman to a very aggravated Gregory.

"No, no, no, no, no… we can handle this Rom, he left us in charge, don't fuck this up." Orders Gregory very eager to inflict more punishment on Christen.

"I'm MAKING THE FUCKIN CALL, he left me in charge so just set tight and prepare another dose of serum shit." Says Roman leaving the room and going back to the rear entrance where the wall phone is stationed.

Gregory throws his hands in the air in pure disgust after this disagreement with his brother, while Christen listening to everything is thinking yes, yes, yes the opportunity I've been waiting has come. Now all he must do is just get close enough to me so I can bite his face off and get free of these bonds. Gregory starts pacing back and forth, back and forth, back and forth while Christen gradually opens his eyes, than Gregory steps to the table eyeing the open case with syringe and another full vail of Sodium Pentothal. He injects it into the vail again this time extracting all the fluid when it appears Christen has something to say but he can't hear him.

"What the hell are you trying to tell me, I can't fuckin hear you?" says Gregory putting his left ear to Christens lips attempting to understand him, then as he moves to listen with his right and James bites him in the nose tearing it clean from his face. Blood spews out heavy like a geyser and the poor guy sticks himself with the syringe, falls back hitting his head on the table legs. Christen lunges himself forward in the chair to get free with one arm when he hits the floor, and struggles briefly to free the other arm and bounded hands. Gregory is now blinded from blood squirting in his eyes when Christen catches him with a swift right handed chop to his throat and he's out. Roman makes the call outside the rear entrance unaware of his brothers sudden demise.

He hears a dial tone and it rings several times before someone finally answers and it's Tisdale with another full glass of Champagne in had standing next to Mikhail and Gorgon with the entourage in the back ground.

"Hello Mathias residence, Minolta speaking." He answers the phone half drunk.

"Put Mr. Mathias on now!" Roman orders him while he passes the phone to Gorgon in the private library.

"Roman, yes, yes what's the status with Mr. Christen? What has he told you?" Gorgon asks with much anticipation.

"Mr. Mathias, you said this truth serum, this Sodium Pentothal was potent enough to get him to talk and thus far he's shown some resistance to it, but we gave him a small dose from the start." He tells Gorgon.

"So hit him with another shot and this time you have my permission to employ whatever other methods you choose. The side effects will give him permanent brain damage so killing him defeats the purpose, anyway keep me posted more before midnight Roman." Gorgon says before clicking off. And gets a stern look from Tisdale and Mikhail on the progress of the twins at his Vouliagmeni warehouse in downtown Athens and north east Port of Piraeus.

"Before you two say anything the situation is under control at my warehouse at Vouliagmeni and I'm expecting a call from Crete any moment now." He tries to reassure them. Mikhail reluctantly nods his head while Tisdale just finishes off his last glass of Champagne and takes a seat next to Alexandr, Natali, Vladimir, and Krasimir looking on in amusement while his driver Lupredo seats outside the private library patiently waiting for an another escort trip. Gorgon clicks off the cordless phone and before he has a chance to place it on the table it rings again and this time it's a call from Crete.

"Yes Gorgon Mathias." He answers with much anticipation while the others look on.

"Gorgon, this is the Honorable Titus Timotheos, Governor of Crete, do you recall a conversation we had over a year ago while attending the Grecian Commerce Gala in Berat, Albania? You mentioned you were expecting several vessels to arrive here correct?" the Governor asks him from his office.

"Yes, yes Governor, I recall that conversation and presume you have my paperwork to sign?" Gorgon asks him.

"I do! So how soon can you get here Mr. Mathias?" the Governor asks waiting for his bribe or payoff.

"Governor give me about 7 hours, maybe less and I'll see you sometime after midnight." Gorgon replies before clicking off the cordless phone.

"The shipment has arrived yes, just as you said Gorgon?" Mikhail asks ribbing both hands together like an anxious kid who can't wait to see his Christmas present.

"And what about Roman and Gregory? They should be informed about this Gorgon, we can't keep them out of the loop." Mikhail suggests.

"Yes, I'll check in with them while we are in route to Crete in the meantime we leave now for the Trigonia Ferry, next to Port of Piraeus. It moves very fast unlike the other ferries and will cut 4 hours from our trip." Says Gorgon.

But Tisdale isn't satisfied with what he hears from Gorgon and insists they visit the Vouliagmeni warehouse just a half a mile blocks from this warehouse, however Gorgon has his one agenda.

"Gentlemen, I have an idea? Why don't we stop by the warehouse on the way to the ferry, and check on the progress of this interrogation?" replies Tisdale.

"I have no reason to doubt the twins and full confidence in them. They will not fail, my boys are competent and professional in this matter." Mikhail insists.

"I want to see for myself, unless you disagree Gorgon?" Tisdale asks almost knowing what the answer will be but asks Anyway.

"Looks like you've been outvoted Tisdale, I think they're more than capable of handling this themselves so with that said, its settled we leave ASAP! Gentlemen after you?" says Gorgon. Knowing his quo Lupredo has already left preparing the limo leaving the front door slightly open by Gorgon. And they all file out one after the other Tisdale, Mikhail, Alexandr, Natali, Vladimir, Krasimir and Gorgon the last one out the door when he pauses for a moment to think about his beloved Andromeda still upstairs in her room sleeping off the Champagne.

He finally closes the door, making his way to the Mercedes Limo with Mikhail, Vladimir and Krasimir while Tisdale is escorted by Alexandr and Natali entering their Range Rover waiting to follow close behind. Back at the warehouse Roman goes back inside to check on his brother and a very doped up James Christen. When he reenters the room near the office he hears nothing, not a sound only the sight of his twin lying on the ground with syringe his chest and what looks like his throat was violently chopped. He scans the room for any trace of Christen anything, but not even a shadow gives him a clue and in the back of his mind he's thinking where else could this guy go? The front door is jammed lock and the only way out is through the rear and I didn't see him so what the fuck?

But Christen very shrewdly hides behind the cubicle only 5 feet from where Roman is standing, just waiting, is mind and body trying to fight off the potent effects of that Sodium Pentothal. He studies Romans posture, making sure when he strikes or attempts to catch him off guard, he gains a sizable advantage or at least inflicts as much physical harm as possible on him where he won't recuperate as fast. He's also thinking this guy is 5 feet 10 inches and solid muscle for his size well guessing he weighs more than 190 possibly over 200 pounds.

And he knows if he's too anxious and moves in too quickly he could will lose the element of surprise allowing Roman an opportunity Christen doesn't want to give up. He steps out from behind cubicle in a somewhat stalking kung-Fu stance while

Romans attention is still elsewhere briefly grieving over the body of his dead brother when Christen catches him off guard with a headlock, and attempts to set him up with a chock hold.

But Roman isn't that easy a target and he counters Christen on practically every offensive and defensive tactic he tries, almost as if he can read or predict what he's gonna do before he does it. Roman and Gregory had extensive backgrounds in underground fighting while living in Ukraine before going to work for Mikhail Khrichov. Roman drives Christen backward against a wall with various elbows shots to his rips and mid section, however Christen blocks a few from getting in while attempting to reverse it, only to have it countered by Roman.

Well since that won't work Christen tries the frontal assault and close quarter combat with a few right and left jabs to the face and chest for which Roman mostly blocks. And Christen sees an opening when Roman throws a right upper cut that nicks Christens chin by mere inches, he ducks under to apply a side chock hold with his left arm cutting off air from Romans throat.

However Roman proves himself a very worthy grappler, he shifts his body in a downward maneuverer to throw Christen only to have James follow him while not giving up his chock hold. Now the two are on the floor, one struggling to break free and avenge his brother, while the other determined to either incapacitate this foe or kill him. Getting very frustrated Roman belts out a howling sound of a wounded animal fighting for his life when Christen suddenly switches his arms and applies a guillotine chock hold on Roman. He rocks back knowing this guy will never tap out and uses the last bit of energy he has applying it tight as possible, while he can feel Roman gasping for air, gagging, trying to breath but he in no position to counter or even punch or kick his way out of this.

He's at the mercy of Christen who manages to squeeze his neck with everything he's worth and finally there's sickening crunch sound and it's over. Roman is slumped now dead weight when Christen rolls him over to his side and struggles to get to his feet while fighting the effects of that Sodium Pentothal. He staggers around the room and stumbles to the ground mustering every ounce of his being to find that cordless phone and break disheartening the news to Gorgon, his partners and their entourage that things don't always work out as planned. He manages to pick himself back up, while carefully steading his body when he finds the phone on a wall next to the rear door and fully charged. But he soon realizes he can't make a call to Gorgons private number without that card he left with Roman, he turns around to reenter the room and staggers again back to Romans limp corpse and the card in his back pocket. Now he reaches down to grab the private business card from Romans left back pocket and hurries back to the rear entrance. This time he hopes he can catch Gorgon before he leaves the Mansion in suburban Athens.

He grabs the phone from the wall, hits the private numbers from the card and gets a dial tone for several seconds, then up to almost 18 seconds and Gorgon answers.

"Yes, Roman, Roman give me an update on your progress and what information were you able to extract from him?" Gorgon asks with absolute glee and then comes the letdown.

"So sorry to disappoint you but Roman and Gregory are Indisposed? No, incapacitated, yes, yeah that sounds about right or shall I just say dead?" he replies waiting for the retort from Gorgon.

"Mr. Christen, I must say I'm disappointed in them and extremely surprised you survived? Oh by the way, the chemical cocktail you were injected with? Sodium Pentothal! Has an unfortunate side effect, permanent brain damage and while you have any thoughts of trying to find me or us just keep in mind the poison coursing through your veins." Gorgon warns him while Mikhail looks on in disgust that the twins were unsuccessful while thinking about dispatching Natali and Alexandr to finally finish him off for good.

These guys seem to be on the same wave length when Tisdale calls Gorgon right afterward guessing he was on the phone with one of the twins and keeps observing him while following close behind and to be expected that car phone rings again.

"Gorgon I want an update, tell me the twins were successful and made him break? What did he tell them Gorgon I want full details?" he asks while Alexandr listens eves dropping on the conversation.

"They failed Tisdale, Christen lives." He replies reluctantly.

"Dammit, dammit, dammit, no more missteps." Tisdale demands over the phone.

"I'm sending Alexandr and Natali to finish this up, afterwards we will meet you at the Trigonia Ferry." Tisdale continues.

"Very well, we'll be waiting for your call when it's done. Gentlemen the Trigonia will take us to the Isle of Crete so transportation won't be a problem." Gorgon tells Mikhail before clicking off.

Alexandr reroutes the range rover and heads toward Vouliagmeni warehouse unaware that Christen is attempting to contact HQ in Pillisworth, South Africa and Winston from P Department regarding an antidote for this deadly Truth Serum. He punches in the numbers to Nickel Currencies office desk and to his absolute surprise she picks up.

"Devarquise Exports? Currency speaking?" she answers and lights up once she hears his voice on the line.

"James, James how did the wedding turn out? And don't leave out any details please." She asks him with an excited smile on her face.

"Currency is this a secure line?" he replies.

"This is urgent, so please connect me to P Department right away, I must speak with Winston." He tells her again.

"Hold on James!" she says pressing a button twice connecting him to P Department where Winstons in his office enjoying a Chicken Caesar salad with garlic dinner rolls.

"Winston, I have Christen on the line in Athens, Greece and he says its urgent." She tells Winston.

"So patch him through Currency." Winston tells her. And she hits those buttons again and they both connect.

"Pinkheart here, Christen what the hell is happening, are you coming back? What's so damn urgent?" Winston asks. And Christen knows or suspects his time is running out while he desperately tries to fight off the effects of the truth serum.

"Winston, Winston I need information on an antidote for Sodium Pentothal fast, anything you can tell me quick." Christen demands from him while Tisdale and his henchmen are getting ever closer merely half a mile away.

"Christen there really isn't an antidote for Sodium Pentothal or Truth Serum, however if you mix these herbs and roots together Ginger, Dandelions, and Nettle into a kettle and or pot cook for 35 mins allowing the heat to draw out the enzymes and strain it into a mug with no sugar or anything just drink it straight. Even though the taste maybe unbearable at first, it should dilute the potency of the Sodium and buy you some time to flush this poison out of your system." Winston explains with a sly smirk on his face.

"Oh that's just wonderful, wonderful, sounds like this will require some grocery shopping? Anyway, I should get off this line my times running out by minutes and seconds." Christen tells him sarcastically.

"Are you alright Christen?" Winston asks concerned.

"No, Winston not in the least but thanks for asking." Christen replies.

"Well, take care of yourself James!" Winston says calmly before clicking off.

"Thank you, talk to you soon." Christen tell him again before he clicks off and goes back in the warehouse looking for his gun and holster which are very close, in fact hanging from an old coat rack with the clips still in the gun and magazine pouches.

He keeps a 3inch silencer in a hidden compartment on his holster for those last resort kills when all other options have been exhausted, this occasion being one of them. He inspects the gun after placing the holster around his shoulder, pops out the clip, its full with the safety off and pulls out the silencer while screwing it on in one motion. He gently pulls back the slide now a bullets in the chamber and waits for the others to show up while he finds a spot to hide in the warehouse and there aren't many.

Listening intently he can hear street cars driving by every minute or so and then it gets really quiet, on the streets there's a dead calm, and yes the Range Rover pulls up just several doors down from the warehouse. Tisdale continues down the street toward the front while Alexandr and Natali cover the back hoping to catch Christen off guard gaining a definite advantage, now all three exit the Range Rover armed with Gluck's and sub machine guns. Again Christen positions himself in a dark area of the warehouse where he isn't spotted, noticed or heard and finally he hears footsteps approaching the front door which is jammed close and steps getting closer.

He crotches down on one knee pointing focusing his gun sights on the rear door, when he sees a shadow and what looks like Natali one on side and Alexandr approaching from the other.

Or maybe its Tisdale creeping up to the door very quietly attempting to catch Christen off guard and he call out to Gregory and Roman.

"Roman, roman, Gregory, what's your status? He shouts again approaching just 4 feet from the door when he's met by Alexandr first then Natali coming up from close behind.

"So what's the plan Boss? I suspect he's in there someplace near the door but it difficult to see from this angle." Natali says looking like he's about to make his move when he peeks in quick and nothing happens then ducks back.

"Alexandr will go in first and flush him out or at least send him back toward us, then we can end this and get back to business." Tisdale orders and signals with his fingers move.

And at the same time Alexandr makes a move toward the rear entrance and before he even has a chance to get inside he shot in the left side of his neck by Christen still crutched down on one knee. The shot spins Natali around, knocking him flat on his back while grabbing his neck as it spews blood everywhere.

Natali starts chocking on his own blood and dies with Alexandr and Tisdale looking on in total shock and disappointment. Now Tisdale weighs his options and decides the hell with this, he ducks inside and hits the floor before Christen can get off another shoot off and his followed close behind by Alexandr who spots what looks like Christen hiding the in shadows. Tisdale while laying perched on his side looks back at the Alexandr and signals with his fingers and eyes when to start shooting in Christens direction, but he too realizes that he's in their line of sight.

Before they get the chance to pin him down in what looks like a corner or blind spot, he makes a swift dash indirectly towards Alexandr, when they both start firing straight at what they think is Christen a stationary target. Blam, blam, blam, blam, blam, blam, blam, blam, blam, blam, blam, blam, blam, blam, blam from both directions of Tisdale and Alexandr each, at least 30 to 55 rounds shot and hitting nothing except a wall filling it with holes. Christen manages to avoid getting hit but when they reposition themselves toward the direction they think he ran, he manages to catch Alexandr off guard with a few shots from his silencer to the back of his head. Blip, blip, blip, blip and he's gone, eyes still open. Witnessing this from a safe distance Tisdale rethinks his strategy while he slowly pulls himself up against a wall opposite or directly across where Christen was hiding.

Tisdale knows or suspects that Christen is still suffering from the effects of the Truth Serum but did he get lucky or is this guy really a trained secret agent from South Africa he's thinking to himself.

"Let's talk about this James or shall I refer to you as Christen?" he asks holding his mini-sub machine gun while looking for a decent angle for his shot.

"Really? You want to converse with me? You and your partners murdered several of my fellow agents in Ankara, Turkey months ago." Christen replies back enraged. Now Tisdale makes a move inching closer to Christens position while at the same time trying not to give away his own.

"So you were in Turkey? Mikhail suspicions turned out to be accurate." Tisdale says while looking for a point of attack.

"And your so called hit squad left a surveillance photo behind…. and when they return to finish the job I closed their eyes forever." Christen says in absolute defiance but keeping his attention on Tisdale who looks like he's making a move.

"We heard rumors of international intelligence seeking to disrupt our business and terminate this lucrative pipeline we worked so hard to establish, and yes some people showed up, sticking their noses into a very profitable enterprise. It's the nature of the beast Mr. Christen, like the law of the jungle, kill or be killed, eat or be eaten, or as the Japanese say Di Kuritzu, 'business is war.' counters Tisdale with his semi- auto machine gun and silencer pointed at Christen and he lets off several rounds but they don't hit anything, not even within several inches of range.

"A set of companies interlocking with business relationships and shareholdings, grouping of enterprises. So what the hell does that have to do with the Opium business?" Christen asks while Tisdale moves again and this time to a empty room adjacent to the cubical where Gregory put Christen to sleep in a headlock.

This is it now, he sees Christen stumbling around, struggling to hold himself and regain his bearings. The effects of that Sodium Pentothal are wearing him down but he's putting up quite a valiant fight of resistance. Tisdale let off some more rounds and its seems like he scored a hit but it's only a faint shadow of Christen but no clear shot or hit. He moves in closer making every attempt to not to make any noise, step by step tip toeing unaware of Christen indirectly behind him and fires blam, blam, blam, blam, and its finally over for Tisdale taking three in the back and one in the head. Christen slumps down against a wall to his knees with beads of sweat trickling down both sides of his fudge brown head. It's amazing how after all this he's still functioning, or his will is still very strong however his body keeps sending signals where the hell is that damn solution or antidote?

And after all this he doesn't even bother to clean up the mess or even move the corpses, considering the fact he barely survived, his need for transportation now exists outside courtesy of the deceased. He carefully checks all the slain bodies for car keys, first Tisdale he goes through his suit pockets inside and out no luck, then he checks his pants pockets and finds nothing only a wallet with a few hundred dollars in euros, then with Alexandr the same thing his suit and pants pockets empty with nothing but a wallet filled with small bills in Euros.

But this time he hits pay dirt with Natali who has the keys to the Range Rover in his left pocket, Christen quickly snatches the keys out while he steps over the body of Natali looking both left and right, to his front and back almost expecting more surprises or more Russian goons to show up but nothing, it's quiet. In the narrow side walk Christen makes his way back to the front of the warehouse peering down the street to his left where he finds Tisdale's Land Rover parked just two blocks down. He starts moving toward the Land Rover steading himself, walking quickly but carefully while he struggles with the poison in his body, Sodium Pentothal and it won't ware off. Judging by the clouds and the sun starting to set it has to be close to 7 pm in the evening he figures, at the same time Gorgon must be in route to Crete with Mikhail and his chief bone crushers.

Christen keeps thinking to himself once they find out he successfully eliminated Tisdale, Alexandr and Natali, the big guns will come his way this time, that being Vladimir 'Big Crunchy' Bulnor, and Krasimir Rostislav. But he's unaware in the very back compartment of that Range Rover is a small arsenal of semiautomatic weapons, some C4 explosive and grenades. He had one more block to go when he found himself within

10 feet of Tisdale's Land Rover and while his body was screaming for an antidote, he continues to will himself, keep moving, keep moving, keep moving, don't you dare give up, don't you dare throw in the towel dammit. And half of him wants to drop to the ground and die but he knows he can't punk out no matter what pain his bodies enduring.

A few more feet and he finally makes it to the driver side door, luckily from him it wasn't locked and he crawls into the driver seat, and closes the door while he slips the key into the ignition.

The engine turns over and he quickly puts the gear in drive and takes off down the street, his mind racing, think, think, think, think, what's his next move? He must presume

Gorgon and his remaining partners boarded a private ferry in route to Crete for this special shipment of Opium coming in from Afghanistan and Pakistan. And he can't just show up back at the manse with Andromeda there wondering or suspecting what the hell happened and whither she should tip off her father or not, and he has to find a store or some place with the roots or herbs Winston told him about. Or maybe he could get creative and mix a salt and pepper solution with a glass of wine until he can find those herbs he needs so badly.

The ferry at Port of Piraeus would serve beverages to its riders and he could request that while he rode it across the Mediterranean Sea to the Isle of Crete. And they might even allow him to park the Range Rover on the ferry as well, he wouldn't have to concern himself about how to get around the Island and they never see him coming. He drives toward Marina Seas and doubles back in the direction of Piraeus Harbor but on The South Harbor side. It only takes him a few more minutes to reach while he looks out for traffic police on patrol itching to give someone a ticket for violating downtown Athens traffic laws. Now just a few more blocks to before he sees the Piraeus ferry dock, taking in passengers to its top level and vehicles on the bottom.

Christen gets closer and closer with each passing second, minute till finally he's within mere feet of the dock when suddenly a man appears on the massive boat in his line of sight waving him to drive in but gradually. He drives the SUV up to the top level in the middle left of the ferry after receiving those instructions from the ferries Captain, and it pulls away from the dock. Christen puts the vehicle park at the same time the ferry does a 180degree turn toward the Isle of Crete picking up speed at 10 to 25knots 29 mph, after two minutes the Captain takes the ferry up to 45knots 49 mph and higher at 55knots 56mph. Christen exits the Range Rover after turning the engine off and makes his way up stairs with his fellow passengers looking for a bar or café for refreshments and finds a mini bar on top floor with beverage menu posted above.

A nice brunette woman dressed a little conservatively behind mini bar studies his face while he glances over what they serve and notices salt and pepper shakers on the counter.

"I'd like a tall glass of French red wine and another empty glass if you don't mind?" he asks with a smile holding back the inner pain of that truth serum.

"Two tall glasses, one of red wine and one empty coming up!" she replies grabbing one empty glass while opening a bottle of red wine and filling another multitasking.

Christen briefly turns to catch a glance of the Piraeus Ferry racing toward The Isle of Crete and the other islands along the way. Thinking to himself the Mediterranean Sea is so beautiful, it's easy to understand why so many thousands of visitors and tourists to come here. He turns around and finds his two glasses waiting for him, one with the red wine and the other empty.

"That will be $11 euros Mr." the woman says. This time Christen digs into his right pocket and pulls out a $20 in euros handing it to the lady behind the counter.

"No change please, you keep it, thank you." He tells her while he grabs both salt and pepper shakers, fills the empty glass at the bottom about less than 1/3 then pours the red wine into it.

Then back and forth, back and forth, back and forth, till it's a full mixture in one glass. Finally he takes the glass to his lips, tipping it up and slowly allows it to flow down his throat while he takes long sips, one after another. Until the glass is finally empty he places it back on the counter and returns to the Range Rover parked outside. He approaches the driver side door for a moment then decides to stand in front of the vehicle, leaning against it while he plots he next move at the same time breathing in the air from the Ionian sea.

Ironically, he isn't being followed in fact his foes happened to have a head start on him in route to Crete or so he thinks. Gorgon, Mikhail, Vladimir and Krasimir seat at a table with 2 full pitchers of Russian Imperial Stout lounging inside the mini bar of the Trigonia ferry with a Greek flag waving in the breeze.

"I have this uneasy feeling Mikhail, my gut keeps telling me something happened to Tisdale and his guys, they haven't reported, no calls, nothing!" Gorgon says concerned while he and Mikhail study the blueprints of the private luxury vessels docked on the Island of Crete while Vladimir and Krasimir sip on tall cold glasses of Russian Imperial Stout, a very strong beer brewed in Eastern Europe.

"I'm thinking the same thing Gorgon, I will try and make contact with him and what about the Mayor of Crete? Should one of us call him?" asks Mikhail while Gorgon has already taken out his personal phone and hit the speed dial button.

"No, no, Mikhail I'll check in with Tisdale and allow me the responsibility of dealing with this Mayor of Crete thank you." Gorgon replies to Mikhail with a look of let me deal with the politics and technical shit and you handle the shipping and receiving end.

Meanwhile they continue to examine or look over blueprints shown back at his mansion in Athens of changes or modifications made to the hulls of these vessels, allowing them more space to conceal and smuggle huge quantities of opium.

The blueprints again pinpoint areas on these vessels in The ships hulls and the middle lower levels where the opium packs are to be stored and covered with strong smelling ground pepper. This should mask the scent of narcotics once the vessels cross through customs and the police dogs are sent in sniffing for hidden contraband. Now the unanswered question comes again and again from Mikhail, this important shipment arriving from Afghanistan and Pakistan, some 3 tons of product, what mechanism or how is it getting transported onto these luxury ships?

Along with the vessels blue prints Gorgon shows Mikhail, Vladimir and Krasimir a specific machine or mammoth device used for transporting items from one point to another fast and in record time for speed and efficiency. It's a diagram of a 1st generation portable Maxxreach Pocket

Telescopicconveyor system or MR3-25/80-24 designed for shipping and receiving materials and shows all the detailed specs, everything.

"This is ingenious Gorgon, absolutely ingenious, I totally underestimated you and I stand corrected, it won't happen again." Says Mikhail.

"No, no, no apology warranted Mikhail, I'm sharing this to educate you and your guys on the many methods of shipping and receiving materials in this case narcotics." replies Gorgon.

He keeps the blue print diagram laid out on the table so even Vladimir and Krasimir can get a good look at it and study it being that they will take turns supervising the delivery and transport of these packets from trucks to Vessels. Gorgon grabs his own full glass of Russian Imperial Stout and takes a long sip without gagging or choking, while at the same time staring out at the beautiful Ionian and Aegean Sea, waiting for a call from his son the newly wed and or the Mayor of Crete regarding the arrival of these Tractor Trailer trucks carrying his product. Gorgon finishes off his glass and attempts to pour another one but Mikhail snatches the pitcher and empties it into his own glass then quickly takes a sip while Gorgon just watches him thinking to himself really, you are such a selfish fucking lush but he's doesn't verbalize it.

Now from the distant horizon they can almost see the Island from dozens of miles away, and unaware not too close behind them the determined, tenacious, James Christen follows while struggling with the after effects of the Truth Serum/Sodium Pentothal. He rests himself against the grill of the Range Rover with arms folded across his chest staring up at the Aegean sky, plotting his next move again knowing this time he's gonna have to step up his game when confronting Vladimir and this time Krasimir the more formidable henchmen of Mikhail Khrichkov.

Gorgons impatience reaches it's peak and he pulls out his Private phone trying to contact Tisdale and his Lt's but all he gets are long dial tones and finally a dark menacing voice message from Christen vowing 'revenge and he won't be denied.' Mikhail studies Gorgons expression after he clicks off and doesn't react but waits for Gorgon to speak expecting some disappointing news.

Gorgon smiles to himself and shakes his head while at the same time staring at his empty glass then confesses his frustration over what he just heard.

"Gentlemen, looks like it's come down to us, I received a message from Mr. Christen. It seems Tisdale and company failed to eliminate him or they got careless and he's damn lucky, either way this changes nothing." He says with Mikhail, Vladimir and Krasimir looking on, whereas Vladimir and Krasimir are very eager to get this over with.

"So you have backup plan no? Presuming he has Tisdales' Range Rover and isn't aware of the arsenal hidden behind the back seat, we still have a slight advantage Gorgon." Mikhail replies offering his own game plan while Krasimir and Vladimir finish off their beers and decide whether to discuss their own game plan or whip out a deck of cards and start playing to kill time.

"Well I know this, he's aware we have Ferries traveling from Port of Piraeus toward the Isle of Crete among other islands so I'm betting he's gonna try to disrupt us somehow. Krasimir, you and Vlad, must be on point so the moment we start the transfer keep your eyes out for him no mistakes, no miscalculations, no second guessing, just kill him." He orders while they start playing with a deck of cards in Russian. And at that moment his private phone rings again but this isn't Christen barking any warnings it's the Mayor of Crete and Perseus calling at the same time.

"Hello Perseus, my boy hang on I've another call on another line, Yes, Mr. Mayor, yes, yes we are in route now and should arrive within the next hour and a half." Says Gorgon very excited.

"Excellent, Mr. Mathias your product has arrived ahead of schedule with the fleet of trucks waiting at Ano Vouves, and as soon I receive the fax concerning The International Commercial Invoices, the paperwork will be ready for your signature sir." Replies the Mayor holding what looks like a small booklet of five to eight pages.

Ano Vouves happens to have the oldest living Olive trees in the world and legendary for its popular Olive oil production. It's also northeast of Kolpos Kissamou where the Trigonia ferry carrying Gorgon, Mikhail, Vlad and Krasimir will dock.

"That's wonderful, Mr. Mayor and I'm bring some able hands to assist me with transfer, I'll call you once we officially dock." Gorgon tells him clicking off than starts his conversation with Perseus.

"Perse, my boy, talk to me, talk to me son, how's the Honeymoon going and are you close by chance?" Gorgon asks him with a smile in his face.

"Interesting you ask that dad in fact I'm already at the Island but on the opposite side. Well between Paleohora and Ayla Roumeli, we are stopped at Souyla South west of the White Mountains, Crete." Replies Perse.

"And how's the bride? Tell me she's enjoying herself Perseus, she must be having a blast on that luxury yacht?" asks Gorgon again looking at his own map of Crete.

"Actually she's resting dad and I think she may be a little sea sick but she refuses to say anything, I guess she doesn't want me worrying about her." Says Perseus making light of the situation.

"Hmmm, that's very interesting well we're 1 hour and 45 mins away from that location", when Gorgon instructs him again.

"Perseus stay where you are until I tell you otherwise, don't make a move unless I give the greenlight, understood?" Gorgon orders him.

"Sure, sure dad whatever you know best, I will pass that order on Capt. Juden don't move the Kraken until you say so. No problem dad, it's done." Says Perseus at the ships command center looking around for Capt. Argyle who's in his private quarters taking a short nap.

Perseus notices five monitors centered above the large steering wheel detailing all the islands in the area within a 50 to 100mile radius. He shakes his head and smiles realizing this luxury cruise ship has its own navigation system on board like most vessels this size larger or smaller. He continues studying the navigation when he's joined by Capt. Argyle Juden holding a cup of coffee in his right hand, while he has a newspaper or magazine tucked under his left armpit.

"Did I overhear you talking to your dad Perse? Sounds like he's meeting us soon?" Juden asks while taking sips of his coffee.

"Yes he wants us to stay put here for a while until he says otherwise, then he clicked off." Perseus tells him while he glances at the diagram of the engine room or system.

"I haven't seen or heard from the Mrs.'s. since the two of you checked into your private quarters? I hope she's feeling well?" Juden asks seeming concerned.

"She seemed ok but didn't unpack, I unpacked her clothes while she grabbed a remote, laid down and starts watching TV. After about two hours and 45 mins she's fast sleep so I don't know but I will talk to her later." Perseus answers his question.

At the same time a silent buzz goes off one of the phones at the ships Command Center but neither of them notices it. Melissa's making a secret call to her contact with Greek Intelligence while Perseus is preoccupied with the Capt.

"He doesn't suspect anything and my cover for now is solid, I can't stay on this line too long its being monitored." She tells her contact before she clicks off. She attempts to regain her position of comfort when she hears a series of knocks on the door but takes her time answering.

"Melissa, Melissa, your still resting? I hear the TV as well my love, tell me your feeling better?" Perseus asks very concerned.

Melissa peels herself off the bed, walks carefully to the door and makes a manipulation with the knob switch and its unlocked, Perseus doesn't force the door open but gently pushes it open revealing his newly wed wife in her purple velvet robe partially exposing her voluptuous breasts and clean shaven vagina. He grabs her hand and they both set on the side of the bed but then she climbs on his lap with her legs wrapped around his waist and arms around his neck, planting a passionate kiss on his cheek and lips. Their eyes meet each other and she opens up to him with a slight smirk on her face.

"Baby I feel like you've neglected me? This is our honeymoon aboard your father's luxury ship the 'Kraken' and when we get on board and unpack you disappear someplace with Capt. Juden?" she complains.

"Sweetie it's not like that at all, you feel asleep the moment I unpacked, you hit the mattress baby and dosed off so I give some time to rest hun, you seemed very tired anyway, so I give you your space while I study the ships navigation system along with my conversation with Capt. Juden." He explains to her.

"Perseus make love to me right here and right now, stick it in. I can feel your cock getting excited, stick it in right now." She begs him.

Perseus quickly pulls off beige Khaki trousers and tight boxer shorts while snatching his shirt off as well when he finally reaches down between her thighs and finds the spot, then she helps him slid it up into her vaginal walls. He has his left arm around his lower waist while his right hand and fingers fondle her breasts and nipples, now he switches up and grabs her hips with both hands pulling her in for deeper penetration. She lets out this super erotic moan as she can feel all of him deep inside her when she begins moving her hips back and forth, up and down, back and forth, up and down, until they have this wonderful rhythm going on between them.

Their lips meet each other's and simultaneously the tongues come out licking each other's lips, at this moment Melissa uses her lips to trace the surface of Perseus face, his cheek bones, both sides of his face, the tip of his nose, the bridge of it, and finally his eyes brows and they continue kissing again. Perseus picks her up with he's still inside and turns Melissa over on her back, now he has her in the missionary position, and he continues to thrust himself into her as deep as her body will allow and this continues until they both hear a knocking on the door and its Capt. Juden.

"Perseus, Perseus, I hate to disrupt your moment of intimacy but your fathers on the line again and says its urgent he speak with you." Juden tells him before going back to his Command Post.

And Melissa stares into his eyes and cracks a seductive grin while he still has her legs spread in a tee bone like position around his thighs.

"Yes, yes, yes, tell him I will call him back ASAP! ASAP Capt. Juden." Perseus replies.

"Ok, no problem I will rely the message to your dad and you'll find me upstairs at the command post." Capt. Juden says again turning right toward the stairs and walking away till he comes to the base and starts fast stepping up and around till he at the command post and take his seat.

Perseus pulls out of Melissa even though she tries to tighten up her thigh and vaginal muscles he manages to disengage from her lower body, while rushing to get his clothes back on.

"Baby, baby, baby can't this wait till later, I'm so hot and horny right now, I want you back inside me, let's go another hour then you and dad can talk?" she pleads with him.

And he gives her this look of are you serious right now? Really, really, you made me wait almost 6 months when we first met until I could sniff your panties and now your libido can't wait?

"Melissa, sweetie, beautiful when I return and I will I can assure and promise you, very long, steamy hot, and wet stokes, so keep the bed warm for me baby and I will return ok?" he says to her before slipping out the door, down the hall and up the revolving stairs to the command post.

While she rolls back over on her left side grabs the sheet to cover her half body to the waist, and picks up the remote control at the same time raising the volume back to midlevel so only she can hear her favorite program. Perseus takes a cordless phone from the command table and hits redial for his dad, there's a dial tone, several rings and Gorgon answers.

"Dad, I'm returning your call, Capt. Juden just reminded me to contact you so you must be close?" Perseus asks him.

"Perseus we are 4.8 kilometers from Ano Vouves now I need you to send a fax to Mayor Daisuke asking for 3 International Commercial Invoices documents regarding the luxury cruise ships, and don't worry about him making any inquires or asking questions, he won't." Gorgon orders him while the 4 of them leave the top café and start reentering Mikhail's Range Rover while it nears the docking area of Ano Vouves.

"Two, here's the fax number for that office phone, +30 639 3529 and make sure, make absolutely sure it's legible in black ink no pencil, are you writing this done or do you have it in your head Perseus? I need this done ASAP the moment we click off, I can see Ano Vouves from where I am and we're approaching the dock shortly." Gorgon orders him while climbing into the driver side seat closing the door.

"Yes, yes, no problem, no problem dad just take it easy,

I'll send it now, I'm the Command Center of the Kraken as we speak, consider it done." He tells his father to reassure him.

Gorgon clicks off, Perseus clicks off, Gorgon patiently waits for the ferry to dock before he drives off and Perseus follows his fathers instructions with Capt. Juden present directing him his office in the right corner of the Command Center with a desk, drawers and a few mini screens on the wall with just enough seating room for two people and the fax machine ready to transmit. Perseus takes a black Bic ink pen and writes out the info almost exactly as his father said word for word, 3 Invoices for International Commerce made out to Gorgon Manolis Mathias.

After writing it very neatly he feeds the sheet of paper into a thin slot on the fax machine until it stops, then carefully types in the Nine digit numbers and hits the dial enter button. He waits a few seconds while hearing more dial tones, and another few seconds goes by then the sheet descends into the top fax machine and comes out the button with time of deliver and date printed successfully. In Crete Mayor Diasuke patiently seats comfortably on his office couch while watching UK's version of Americas Got Talent when he hears a beeping sound coming from his fax machine, the request he's been waiting for all morning, afternoon and now seems like its arrived. He takes the sheet and gives it a quick look over before he starts preparing the International Commercial Invoices for an official stamp on all three pages.

Now he quickly grabs a brief case, flips it open while at the same time placing the paperwork inside a manila folder before he leaves the office. He makes another call arranging for 13, 16 tractor trailers carrying the opium to meet him at Ano Vouves for immediate transfer ASAP with 15 local men hired for labor reasons and races to out for his meeting with Gorgon.

Now following very close behind the Piraeus Ferry is James Christen seating in the driver seat of Tisdales Gray Range Rover with both hands on the wheel and his head Racing while leaned against the seats head rest. The side effects of the truth serum starting to wear off and feeling a sense of intense anxiety for what's he anticipates, a brutal confrontation.

The ferry maintains its speed on the same route taken by the Piraeus Ferry which has already docked at Ano Vouves, while from a distance Christen can almost see that Range Rover carrying Gorgon and company drive off into the Crete Country side. Christen continues going over in his head, wait until they fully load all three vessels, then make my move and don't let them force his hand. Christen ferry moves closer and closer to Ano Sfiniari on the northwest section of Grete just 6 miles from Ano Vouves a good enough distance that may give him the element of surprise. Christen pulls out his pistol and reexams it, ejecting the clip and pushing back the slide bar watching the bullet pop out the chamber while in one motion he catches it in his right hand, sticking the bullet back into the top clip.

He slides the clip back into his modified P229 Smith & Wesson while pulling back the slide, and keeping the safety off now its armed again. He looks up to find the ferry just 10 feet from the dock of Port Ano Sfiniari at that moment he suddenly get the urge to exit the driver side, and races around to the back trunk were the hidden semi auto weapons are stored. A nine gauge shoot gun, a few semiautomatic weapons including 2 Bushmaker AR-47 Assault Rifles, a small case of specialized c-4 explosive packs containing (6) 3 * 5inch cubes with string stick fuses for detonation, 1 Spectre, 3 Uzi, 2 AR-15 semi- Automatic Assault Rifles with munitions and ammo up the ass and he now has access to all of this.

The only thing that remotely looks worth using the Bush Maker AR-47 Assault Rifle with 4 matching clips already locked and loaded. But he doesn't find any grenades or m18 claymore mines so it looks like that's all he'll need if he can take out Gorgon, Mikhail, and his muscle bound Russian thugs with the assault. Now he feels a sudden jolt or the ferry stops moving then looks up and its already docked. He quickly shuts the trunk closed and races back into the driver seat to pull off shutting the door behind him, he puts the gear in drive and hits the gas pedal carefully watching the ferry porter signal with his hands its ok to leave now waving come on let's go mate, let's go.

Christen nods his head and waves back ok, ok I'm off alright thanks driving pass the guy till he hits the port dock and is safely back on dry land. He realizes they have a head start on him so he maintains his current speed of 45 mph and accelerates up to 70 in under 10 seconds toward Ano Vouves where the meet and delivery takes place.

Gorgons and company arrive at Ano Vouves while to the far rear of them set three luxury cruise ships docked side by side at Agia Marina, currently in the water but soon all three will set on custom made horse stilts, built for ships over 150 to 200+ feet in length. All four exit the SUV and take a walk around to get a good stretch from seating for such a long time, while a car is seen at a distance what looks like a used Land Rover with a peculiar man in the back-passenger seat.

Gorgon finishes his stretching exercise when notices this vehicle approaching very quickly before it comes to stop just several feet from the Range Rover. And again, from a distance a fleet convey of 10 plus trucks one after the other and a bus carrying 15 to 20 men in total. The mayor steps out with brief case in a hand and a smile on his face walking toward Gorgon with his right hand extended for a long-awaited hand shake.

"Mr. Mathias welcome, we meet again at last and this time under more pleasant circumstances." He greets gorgon.

"Mayor Daisuke, your honor it a pleasure to see you again and may I introduce my business associates Mikhail Bahrain Khrichov and his Lt's, Vladimir 'Big Crunchy' Bulnor and Krasimir Rostislav." Gorgon says shaking the mayor hand.

"And your other associates, Mr. Mathias will they not join us this evening?" he asks sensing something very strange and out of place here.

"It's unfortunate Mayor Daisuke but they are handling some other urgent business and couldn't attend this evening so your dealing with us." Gorgon replies.

"Gentlemen it's an honor to meet you as well and welcome to the Island of Crete." He says shaking Mikhails hand and giving a wave to Vladimir and Krasimir in kind.

He positions the brief case in front of Gorgon, and opens it revealing the Manilla folder with the paperwork inside while the trucks are stopped getting closer or within a few miles distance.

"As we agreed Mr. Mathias I will need you signature at the bottom of all three, where you see the x circled?" he asks while Gorgon pulls out a pen and signs very carefully each document and dates it.

"And my shipment Mr. Mayor as we agreed, I see the vessels docked but no trucks present?" he asks showing incredible patience.

"May I direct your attention leftward Mr. Mathias, the convey you see there carrying your product is arriving as we speak and on schedule sir." Mayor responds with confidence.

"And the men I hired along with my machine Mayor?" asks Gorgon again.

"Yes, yes, the Maxxreach Pocket Telescopicconveyor system or MR3-25/80-24? Indeed it comes with the convey Mr. Mathias just as you instructed days ago when we spoke. And if you don't mind me asking how was the wedding sir?" he asks while placing the paperwork and manila folder safely back into the case closing it shut.

"Oh it's a beautiful thing Mayor Daisuke, watching your first born marry for the first time and knowing you could very soon become a grand dad? Oh what a feeling! I held back my tears and kept my composure for the sake of my house guests of course." Gorgon responds with eyes briefly closed in a moment of reflection.

"Very good sir and congratulations again." The mayor replies when the convey of trucks finally arrives just 15 feet from their location, they begin parking side by side one after the other.

"And as you requested Mr. Mathias your cargo ready to transfer sir, if you'd like I will stick around to help over see this load?" The Mayor asks while Gorgon gives a look to Mikhail, Vladimir, and Krasimir to prepare the machine quickly.

"Mayor Daisuke I see no reason why not, I only ask this keep your distance inside your vehicle, whereas my business partner and his associates can be very territorial when it comes to someone invading their space, if you don't mind?" Gorgon asks cordially without issuing a direct order.

"Yes, yes, I understand completely sir and I will keep me distance thank you very much." Mayor Daisuke replies.

With that said the bus carrying Gorgons labor party or men pull up just 10 feet from where the Mayors car is parked and the men quickly set up both MR3-25/80-24. Gorgon surveys the area while Mikhail, Vladimir and Krasimir look on as observers very anxious to see this high action machine go to work, and with minutes the labor crew takes it out the rear of the bus, and begin assembling it piece by piece. They position them just off the shore line of Ethniki Odos Chanion Kissamou but further inland away from the water while another group of guys uses an anchor chain attached to one of the trucks to pull the first luxury vessel Cronos inward to set on the custom made horse stilts.

A member of the crew hits a switch on a wench machine which pulls the cruise ship out the water and up into to the shoreline to dryland and eventually onto the horse stilts where it seats exposing the bottom hull and Rutter's. In the middle of the bottom hull are two huge compartments designed to house hundreds if not thousands of packets or blocks of opium. The machines are positioned at the first and second compartments where twelve guys have already climbed in now waiting for the second of 13 trucks to pull up parallel to the cruise ships. With the machines assembled and ready to start, Gorgon watches as another crew member work the controls and the opium is off loaded from the truck on the Maxxreach

Pocket Telescopicconveyor system deep within bottom hulls of these cruise ships.

Gorgon positions himself on top of the hood of Mikhail's Range Rover taking a hard look around before getting everyone's attention he clears his throat to yell out his orders while Mikhail, Vladimir and Krasimir look on in admiration.

"Gentlemen, gentleman, your attention please? Gentlemen give me your attention? Over here! I need all three vessels fully loaded within 2 hours or less and not one minute more people, let's get to work." He orders after slapping his hands together a few times and carefully climbs down from the hood with a little help from Vladimir, while the men quickly snatch the product from the trucks and as many at a time unload the drugs onto the conveyor belt system.

This Maxxreach Pocket Telescopicconveyor has 17 speeds and a remote control or dual remote console for multitasking jobs including but not limited too massive shipping and receiving goods of modest size. Gorgon decides out of curiosity he wants to see how this dynamic machine performs and invites Mikhail to accompany him at the first luxury vessel being loaded with his product. He keeps a comfortable distance while at the same time taking out one of his expensive cigars, lights it till it's cherry red and slowly puffs. Mikhail pulls out his small case of custom Russian cigarettes joining Gorgon for a smoke also.

The two closely analyze its loading system while simultaneously keeping a close eye on the guy working the remote control console, it starts out at 1st speed but that's not fast enough and he takes it up to 5 but it still seems like it isn't moving as quickly so he moves the lever or joy stick up a few mover levels to 9th speed, now the machine stretches out 7 feet as programmed with the cow leather belt measuring at 30 inches in width, 1inch wide and strong enough to carry up to 10 + pricks at a time every 10 to 20 seconds from the trucks to the bottom hulls of these ships.

At this speed the labors are forced to step up their game and hustle much faster which means grabbing, snatching bricks and handing them off from one person to another, maintaining that momentum until all 13 trucks are empty and the transfers completed. Now they watch this process continue again with trucks 1 and 2 having almost filled the first lower half and moving into the second deep compartments. While all this is happening it seems like no one has seen or even suspected a rather ominous figure watching all this from a comfortable distance waiting patiently, and calculating his next move with gun in hand and a AR-15 semi- Automatic Assault Rifle strapped around his shoulder with 6 full magazines ready.

Christen tries to keep himself hidden from sight behind the Range Rovers driver side now inland of Ano Sfiniari just 15 miles west of where the operations happening. He figures he will make his move once they've completed the transfer on vessel number three and truck 12 pulls off, if they don't force his hand in the meantime. And as expected Vladimir spots the Range Rover from a distance figuring Christen has been following them all this time and Gorgon must be alerted. He calmly steps to Gorgon and Mikhail with Krasimir looking on not saying a word until he's given an order for heads up.

"Sir afraid we have company, a very uninvited guest Mr. Mathias in the distance of Ano Sfiniari area." Vladimir tells him with his fists clinched and ready for battle. Gorgon pretends not to notice but notices Tisdales Range Rover and a familiar figure hiding at the driver side while cracking a sinister smile.

"Excellent Vladimir very good, keep a careful, discreet eye on him in the meantime while the men continue." Gorgon orders Vladimir.

Gorgon steps back over to Mikhail who's keeping a close eye on this amazing machine and it's incredible efficiency with the transfer speed. After truck 1 is finished the driver pulls away and his fellow labors quickly move truck 2 into position while the MR3-25/80-24 is put into neutral or sleep mode until truck 2 is positioned just right and the men prepare for another quick transfer. The belt extends into the truck where the guys start loading the reddish brown bricks in a small pile of 10 per six inches apart considering the load is 3 1/2 tons of opium in 13 trucks.

The men load up to 300 bricks while the machine remains in neutral then the same labor guy, starts it up again at 2nd speed this time giving the guys in the truck an opportunity to hustle and load as many more as possible. Now he warns 'he will kick it back up to 9 so move your assess' and the guys in the truck start snatching bricks 2 and 3 at the time for pile up on the belt. With great effort the men manage to clear half the 2nd truck in under 10 minutes but they understand time isn't on their side, although they continue the pace nonstop until they've finally emptied truck 2 in 11 minutes flat. Filling the first half of the deep hull of vessel 1 and so much more to go before getting to vessel 2.

After truck 2 is finished the belt is retracted back several feet until its clear for the driver to pull away and his fellow labors quickly move truck 3 into position while the MR3-25/80-24 is put into neutral or sleep mode again until truck 3 is ready or just right and the men prepare for another quick transfer. The belt extends again into the truck where the guys start loading more of the reddish brown bricks in a small pile. The men again load up to 400 bricks while the machine remains in neutral then the same labor guy, starts it up again at 2nd speed this time giving the guys in the truck an opportunity to hustle and load as many more as possible. With great effort the men manage to clear half the 2nd truck in about 09 minutes but they still aware that time isn't on their side, although they continue the pace nonstop until they've finally emptied truck 2 in 11 minutes. Filling the first half of the deep hull of vessel 1 and so much more to go before getting to vessel 2.

And again truck 2 is finished the driver pulls away and his fellow labors quickly move truck 3 into position while the MR3-25/80-24 is put into neutral or sleep mode until truck 3 is positioned just right and the men prepare for another quick transfer. The belt extends into the truck where the guys start loading more of the reddish brown bricks in a small pile. The men again load up to 300 bricks while the machine remains in neutral then the same labor guy, starts it up again at 2nd speed this time giving the guys in the truck an opportunity to hustle and load as many more as possible.

After truck 3 is finished the driver pulls away and his fellow labors quickly move truck 4 into position while the MR3-25/80-24 is put into neutral or sleep mode until truck 4 is positioned just right and the men prepare for another quick transfer. The belt extends into the truck where the guys start loading more of the reddish brown bricks in a small pile.

The men again load up to 300 bricks while the machine remains in neutral then the same labor guy, starts it up again at 2nd speed this time giving the guys in the truck an opportunity to hustle and load as many more as possible. After truck 4 is finished the driver pulls away and his fellow labors quickly move truck 5 into position while the MR3-25/80-24 is put into neutral or sleep mode until truck 5 is positioned just right and the men prepare for another quick transfer. The belt extends into the truck where the guys start loading more of the reddish brown bricks in a small pile. Now with the first, second and third deep compartments filled in Vessel 1, the operator uses the wench again but this time he applies the leverage from the machine lowering vessel 1 back into the water from the shoreline.

The men once again load up this time 375 bricks while the machine remains in neutral then the same labor guy, starts it up again at 2nd speed this time giving the guys in the truck an opportunity to hustle and load as many more as possible. After truck 5 is finished the driver pulls away and his fellow labors quickly move truck 6 into position while the MR3-25/80-24 is put into neutral or sleep mode until truck 6 is positioned just right and the men prepare for another quick transfer. The belt extends into the truck where the guys start loading more of the reddish brown bricks in a small pile.

The men this time load up to 450 bricks while the machine remains in neutral then the same labor guy, starts it up again at 2nd speed this time giving the guys in the truck an opportunity to hustle and load as many more as possible. After truck 6 is finished the driver pulls away and his fellow labors quickly move truck 7 into position while the MR3-25/80-24 is put into neutral or sleep mode until truck 7 is positioned just right and the men prepare for another quick transfer. The belt extends into the truck where the guys start loading more of the reddish brown bricks in a small pile.

The men again load up to 500 bricks while the machine remains in neutral then the same labor guy, starts it up again at 2nd speed this time giving the guys in the truck an opportunity to hustle and load as many more as possible. After truck 7 is finished the driver pulls away and his fellow labors quickly move truck 8 into position while the MR3-25/80-24 is put into neutral or sleep mode until truck 8 is positioned just right and the men prepare for another quick transfer. The belt extends into the truck where the guys start loading more of the reddish brown bricks in a small pile.

The men again load up to 300 bricks while the machine remains in neutral then the same labor guy, starts it up again at 2nd speed this time giving the guys in the truck an opportunity to hustle and load as many more as possible. After truck 8 is finished the driver pulls away and his fellow labors quickly move truck 9 into position while the MR3-25/80-24 is put into neutral or sleep mode until truck 9 is positioned just right and the men prepare for another quick transfer. The belt extends into the truck where the guys start loading more of the reddish brown bricks in a small pile. Now with the first, second and third deep compartments filled in Vessel 2 Hyperion, the operator uses the wench again but this time he applies the leverage from the machine lowering vessel 2 back into the water from the shoreline.

The men again load up to 300 bricks while the machine remains in neutral then the same labor guy, starts it up again at 2nd speed this time giving the guys in the truck an opportunity to hustle and load as many more as possible. After truck 9 is finished the driver pulls away and his fellow labors quickly move truck 10 into position while the MR3-25/80-24 is put into neutral or sleep mode until truck 10 is positioned just right and the men prepare for another quick transfer. The belt extends into the truck where the guys start loading more of the reddish brown bricks in a small pile.

The men again load up to 475 bricks while the machine remains in neutral then the same labor guy, starts it up again at 2nd speed this time giving the guys in the truck an opportunity to hustle and load as many more as possible. After truck 10 is finished the driver pulls away and his fellow labors quickly move truck 11 into position while the MR3-25/80-24 is put into neutral or sleep mode until truck 11 is positioned just right and the men prepare for another quick transfer. The belt extends into the truck where the guys start loading more of the reddish brown bricks in a small pile.

The men again load up to 490 bricks while the machine remains in neutral then the same labor guy, starts it up again at 2nd speed this time giving the guys in the truck an opportunity to hustle and load as many more as possible. After truck 11 is finished the driver pulls away and his fellow labors quickly move truck 12 into position while the MR3-25/80-24 is put into neutral or sleep mode until truck 12 is positioned just right and the men prepare for another quick transfer. The belt extends into the truck where the guys start loading more of the reddish brown bricks in a small pile.

The men again load up to 300 bricks while the machine remains in neutral then the same labor guy, starts it up again at 2nd speed this time giving the guys in the truck an opportunity to hustle and load as many more as possible. After truck 12 is finished the driver pulls away and his fellow labors quickly and finally move truck 13 into position at last while the MR3-25/80-24 is put into neutral or sleep mode until truck 13 is positioned just right and the men prepare for another quick transfer. The belt extends into the truck where the guys start loading more of the reddish brown bricks in a small pile.

The men again load up to 300 bricks while the machine remains in neutral then the same labor guy, starts it up again at 2nd speed this time giving the guys in the truck an opportunity to hustle and load as many more as possible. Now with the first, second and third deep compartments completely filled in Vessel 3 Oceanus, the operator uses the wench again but this time he applies the leverage from the machine lowering vessel 3 back into the water from the shoreline.

The operator working MR3-25/80-24 uses the remote control console to retract the conveyor belt into the machine, and back to its original size before he gets help reloading it back into truck 13. The operator rides back with truck 13 following the truck convey to the other side of Crete.

After witnessing this successful transfer done in under two hours Gorgons cracks a smile while at the same time shaking hands with Mikhail, and giving a nod to Vladimir at his left and Krasimir at his right both keeping a sharp eye out from James Christen. Gorgons looks at the limo carrying the Mayor and gives him a wave or sign to come out the coast is clear, job is done you can now step out of the car.

"I confess Mr. Mathias I've never seen so much opium of that volume transferred so fast and with so much efficiency and one last thing?" asks the mayor before he leaves.

But Gorgon already knows what he's about to ask, he reaches into his right jacket pocket pulling out an envelope with a cashier's check in it containing payment to the mayor and his crew for an amount in the low six figures, something in the range of $Two hundred and eighty five thousand dollars to be made out in euros.

"As we agreed Mayor Daisuke, I'm a man of my word and very few men can make that claim sir, very few men." replies Gorgon with absolute certainty. Mayor Daisuke takes the check out to analyze the bank and account numbers before he places it back in the envelope, slipping it in his suit pocket.

"But how do I know?" he asks and gorgons quickly interrupts him.

"The moneys in the account and that check will clear in a matter of 2 hours or less, just call the number to that bank for verification and you will have your money paid in full, so are we done here Mr. Mayor?" Gorgons ask again running out of patience and folding his arms across his chest.

"Yes, yes, our business has concluded for now, and you will hear from me very soon Mr. Mathias, good evening sir." He says walking back to the limo when he reenters its takes off.

"And good evening to you Daisuke, till we speak next time sir." Gorgons says taking one last puff of his cigar which seems to have gone cold or out.

Chapter 8

SHOWDOWN ON ISLE OF CRETE

Christen remains in the same spot waiting patiently to make his move after witnessing the complete transfer to the three vessels, the 13 truck convey leaving with the mayor following close behind, he figures his time to strike it's now or never. Christen opens the trunk again and to his surprise finds in the right corner behind the passenger seat 11 feet of rope, he's plan is formulating now. He reenters the Range Rover driver side, turns over the engine when he slips the keys into the ignition, puts it in drive so this time he accelerates toward Ano Vouves from 16 miles out.

Within 10 miles he uses the rope to rig the accelerator pad to the floor with one Magazine knowing the Range Rover will hit 80 mph in no time. He also uses the same length of rope for the steering wheel keeping it straight and tight so it doesn't turn very much than he jumps out in tuck and roll fashion still holding the Bushmaker AR-47 Assault Rifle. He seats stationary on the ground watching the Range Rover pick speed before they notice and take immediate action. Its Vladimir who hears and notices this vehicle speeding toward them from 6 miles away, but without causing any panic or alert, he calmly and quickly moves to their vehicles trunk and whips out his own Assault rifle.

He checks the magazine first and its loaded full, slides it into a AK-107-GP-25 Grenade Launcher, he gets down on one knee while Gorgons yelling, screaming in his ear, shoot, shoot, dammit, shoot. Vladimir pulls back the fighting stick and aims toward the Range Rovers tires, while Christen at the same time takes full advantage of this diversion, he makes every effort possible cutting across and around Ano Vouves while Vladimir manages to blast the hell out of the Range Rover, filling it with some 40 holes and takes out the two front tires causing it to flip over from hitting tree stump. While Christen gets close Krasimir has eyes on him at the same time Gorgon and Mikhail prepare to board vessel one docked a few feet in the shoreline with a ladder step on the side just long enough for them to reach and pull themselves up.

With the rover flipped over on its side Christen takes cover behind a tree thick enough to shield him from any fire, now having to contend with both Vladimir and Krasimir pining him down with constant fire then they stop. Vladimir motions to Krasimir move in closer but Christen spots his move, countering with shoots of his own, driving him back and making his own calculation to separate the two and gain an advantage. Christen pulls out his P29 smith and Wesson attaching his specialized four inch silencer or suppressor courtesy of P Department, he carefully stoops down on one knee just three feet from the tree peering at both sides, he spots Krasimir reloading on his right, and fires catching him in the left shoulder.

A lucky shoot maybe or just hard core training on his part when Krasimir hits the ground attempting to nurse his wound. Christen thinks about stepping out but Vladimir has him in his sights and he thinks better of it. Vladimir opens fire again at Christen but at this time at his far right when Christen fires catching him in his arm or bicep muscle and it's a clean exit wound. Krasimir pops his head up and takes one right between the eyes he's done, the shoots blows a four inch hole out the back of his head. Vlad sees this out of frustration and opens fire again on Christen who hits the ground rolling to avoid the shoots and Vlads magazine is empty. Now the two of them are seven to eight feet apart when Vlad throws away his AK- 107-GP-25 with Grenade Launcher and challenges Christen, to hand to hand combat, mano a mano with both hands up.

"You and me straight up, no guns? Are you coward?" he challenges James with his left bicep wounded.

Christen happily gives Vlad a nod while cracking a smirk and drops his pistol and takes off the Bushmaker AR-47 assault rifle placing it on the ground. Now they begin to circle one another, sizing each other up like competitors in a UFC bout and Christen is clearly out matched but none of that really matters now, this is a classic case of brains over brawn. Christen doesn't make the first move in fact he fakes a few times like he's going to throw a punch but never does and then gets caught with a stiff left jab to the nose by Vladimir, and it's a solid hit.

Chapter 9

MONO E MONO CHRISTEN VS VLAD

ow Christen must decide which offensive or defensive tactic he wants employ on Vladimir, but will it even matter? There's a little blood trickling from his nose but no matter, this time he draws Vlad in closer and parries with a left faint cross jab to Vladimir's right chin but as Vladimir braces himself for the blow, Christen catches him with a shot to his solar plex and right side ribs but it's nothing, almost like he was being poked or tickled. Christen now follows this with a combination of straight body shots to Vlads midsection and attempts a right and left cross to his face but Vlad moves back his head in anticipation, not giving him any chance to connect. Now Christen doesn't really know any hardcore close quarter combat nor will he try a right or left side kick and a fancy, speedy reverse round house kick only to have his feet and legs caught by Vlad and possibly broken or twisted on contact.

He sees this as the problem with fighting a real underground MMA street fighter like Vlad, you can over plan what you want to do in your mind a thousand times over however, but executing it is something else entirely. Vlad has fought so many different opponents in Ukraine and Russia there's nothing he hasn't seen, no technique he hasn't countered, almost no counter move he hasn't dealt with unless by chance Christen surprises him with something out of the ordinary, so now Christen is finding out fast this man is built solid all around, so any attempt to catch him off guard or surprise him in anyway?

Totally futile! Vladimir just cracks a sinister smile knowing this man has no idea who he is or what he's up against? Now here comes the small talk again.

"You wanna know why crowds call me 'Big Crunchy'? How I acquired that name?" Vlad asks him almost licking his lips. And now James is thinking really? Are we really about to have this conversation right now? Then replies… "Do I look like I give a shit fuck face? But since you in such a jovial mood, due share Vlad." Christen says out of frustration.

Vladimir folds his fingers together while he studies Christen before telling or revealing how he became known as 'Big Crunchy'.

"I used to compete in MMA let's say several years ago light heavy division in Moscow, anyhow one of my finishing holds was a what I called dragon swipe slam. I would hoist my opponent in the air while he had his legs wrapped around my neck and shoulders then slam him hard to the mat several times." Vladimir says with glee as he told this same story to Gregory just days ago on the Motel street corner of Athens, Greece.

Now again thinking of the pain and punishment he dealt out to his opponents inside the UFC octagon. And he continues!

"Then once I'd get in real close quarters I snatch him by the waist and twirl his body in midair dropping him directly across my right knee or sometimes left knee until I heard crunch sound of his lower back or vertebrate listening to the sound of his spine upon impact. That beautiful crunch sound of my knee connecting with the lower spinal cord." Vladimir replies and Christen has heard enough and when Vlad wasn't looking or aware Christen has possession of his P229 Smith and Wesson hand gun hidden in his pants.

So Vladimir continues, "So fans start to chant "Crunchy", "Crunchy", "Crunchy". And this feel me with such pride when I hear this from crowd, "I am "Big Crunchy". So with this Christen is thinking to himself, you will never get the chance to apply that hold on me, that I can assure you Vlad.

Vladimir throws his hands in the air inviting Christen to come on in, give me your best shot, you can't hurt me no matter what you try, or whatever your thinking will fail miserably so, let's get this over with now. But Christen lounges in with a combination of jabs and straight punches to Vladimir's midsection and chest while at the same time catching him with a unexpected upper cut to his left jaw. Which stuns him but doesn't really have a shocking effect or potential knock out, it just pisses him off even more while Christen begins to realize he must try something else, something more dramatic and dangerous or this guy with the MMA underground background from Russia will try to hurt him bad or at least cripple him.

Christen glances over at the first luxury cruise yacht gradually floating back into Chania Bay several miles from Creten/Mediterranean Sea noticing Gorgon and Mikhail had just boarded it while he and Vladimir circle each other again only this time Christen rushes in like Mike Tyson aiming for his midsection again but catches him with a stiff right cross jab to the left side of his neck. And there isn't even a crunch sound not even a bruise like damn, is this guy even human or he has such a high threshold of pain it doesn't matter how hard you hit him, or stab him depending on where you stab him, he seems almost impervious to pain. But Christen won't give up under any circumstances and attempts a delta whirl slam wrestling move on Vladimir after executing the stiff right cross jab to his neck, he grabs his midsection or waist and manages to hoist his body off the ground and in midair for a slam but Vladimir has this technique scouted or he's already seen it used and skillfully executed on many of opponents, he counters with a leg scissors around Christens head throwing him hard to the ground.

Christen attempts to get vertical and regain his footing but Vladimir won't have any of it, he now has Christen in an arm bar with legs scissor around his head again. And with this arm bar it's very uncomfortable so when Christen attempts to pull himself loose or maneuver his body in a way that will counter this painful grappling hold, Vladimir twists his arm/elbow or uses joint manipulation forcing Christen to reverse the position of his body regaining a little release before Vladimir quickly counters him again. Only this time Christen finds himself on top of Vladimir but his head still in a scissor lock with arm bar.

But for him the very idea of lifting this tall, rock solid Alpha male off the ground seems nearly impossible, with one arm and hand free, his right clinched fist he targets Vladimir's stomach and ribs with a series of body shots, 3 in 5 shot sequences, one-two-three-four-five, then he takes some deep breaths before Vladimir can recover and again, one-two-three-four-five, Vladimir tries to incapacitate Christen arm but the body shots are taking their toll on him and Christen goes in again on him, one-two-three-four-five this time on the ribs and Vladimir lets go of the arm and neck scissor finally rolling backward and putting space between he and Christen but James won't have it. Vlad tries to cover his ribs when he finds himself under heavy assault by Christen carrying his P29 Smith and Wesson behind his side hidden from sight.

Vlad notices Christens hiding something and catches him off guard with a swift kick to his chest and neck which almost incapacitates James again but he never releases his grip, at this point Christen finds himself on his knees when Vlad moves for his left arm to apply an aikido style waist control called Yonkyo. This leaves Christens right hand free carrying his pistol when he moves it toward Vlad's neck and his face with Vlad realizing he has a muzzle two inches from his nose and in panic he attempts a counter roll over, Christen pulls the trigger, it fires but misses, he pulls the trigger again toward the face of a desperate and horrified Vlad sensing this is it for him, this bastard could get lucky and shoot him in the face?

Yes, yes, the second time Christen fires and the shoot blows off part of Vlad's left ear, but he's still attempting this waist joint control technique on Christen who turns the muzzle another three degrees and fires into Vlad's face via his nose and it's over he too has Vlad's blood spewed in his face. He breaks Vlad's grip while rolling away at the same time staring down at his ultra tough but fallen adversary. Damn, damn, his mind is spinning like a top wow, this man literally put him through hell and after all this, the close quarter combat for which he really has no experience considering, he actually held his own against a beast of a man and totally rugged at that.

Now he understands time, time has escaped him and the truck convey has disappeared leaving the three luxury yachts with Gorgon and Mikhail having witnessed the eventual demise of a man both thought would destroy James Christen with absolute ease. Clearly they underestimated this man who may or may not have recovered from the Truth Serum or Sodium Pentothal they had him injected with just hours before. Christen slowly regains his footing while his left arm feels almost useless from the beating and twisting it took from Vladimir, so now he's standing straight up, this time staring out at the rear deck of this luxury yacht as Gorgon and Mikhail stare back at him, knowing it's only a matter of time for them.

He's pondering or thinking my body was beaten to shit, and these two assholes can't get away after all this. Hell, fuck no! While Gorgon watches Christen from the rear of the lower deck he makes a call to 'The Kraken' for a update on Perseus and Capt. Juden still waiting at Paleohora and Ayla Roumeli for that all important contact from Gorgon. Juden sits in his favorite seat at the yachts command center while Persues and Melissa have already gotten dressed when that call comes in, he lets the phone several times before he picks up.

"Gorgon? Yes sir, what's your status sir?" He answers trying not to sound too over inquisitive.

"Where are you now Captain?" Gorgon asks while trying to keep a watchful eye on James Christen.

"We are just a few kilometers from Paleohora." Juden replies when Perseus finally renters the yacht command center with Melissa at his side holding his hand.

"Good get over here ASAP! We have a situation that I can't get into over the phone but make it quick Captain." Gorgon orders him before clicks off.

"We are in route Mr. Mathias, right away sir!" replies Juden before hangs up.

Now Perseus gives him this look of bewilderment as Melissa stares back and forth at both men but not saying anything.

"That's was your father again Perse." He tells him while me moves to the wheel and grabs lever and pushes it few degrees upward the yacht jolts forward picking up speed.

"What the hell is happening now, what's the emergency?"
Perse asks concerned.

"He didn't say but we're going to meet at Ano Vouves now, The north east part of Crete. Juden continues to steer and Navigate the yacht to Ano Vouves as fast as possible with the sails wrenched tight, the sea winds give the yacht added push. Perse and Melissa keep a short distance from Capt. Juden while he drives the yacht from Palephora over to Cap Krios while making a wide bank toward Ano Vouves sailing past Ag Artemis, Ano Elafonissi, Ano Hrissoskalitissa, Akr.Mavros, Akr.Karavoutas, and Ano

Sfinari the very port where Christens Ferry was earlier docked and left soon after.

While the Kraken continues sail Christen pursues Gorgon and Mikhail from land to water Chania Bay, oh yes he realizes he has to do a little swimming but not much, just 23 feet from the shoreline to the side deck stairs where Gorgon and Mikhail used to board this yacht. He walks out into the water just enough unless it reaches his waist then as he moves deeper while it comes up to his chest, now it seems he's losing his footing and decides to take the dive in without taking a brief deep breathe.

He starts working those arms and legs muscles again but this time against the underwater current, once again it all starts coming back those months of swimming lessons many, many years ago at the Cape Town Athletic Sports Academy in Cape Town, South Africa. He comes up for air after managing to swim at least 6 to 9 feet under water before he goes into his swim sequence again, left side, arms and legs, right side, arms and legs, pulling himself through the water ever closer to the side deck stairs. Now he finds himself at 10 feet, just within range of reaching up for the base stair. He takes a few more strokes till his hands hits the base and he pulls himself up, taking the stairs two at a time till he reaches the lower deck level and he's met gun shoots coming from Mikhail. Christen ducks out of sight or takes cover not willing to expand any of his ammo while he finds a spot on the lower deck to stay hidden.

That strategy fails miserably in fact there really isn't a place on this luxury for him to hide whether it's the lower, middle or upper deck. He takes a different strategy this time while he can hear foot steps either around him or one other conclusion, he's about to be confronted by Gorgon, and or Mikhail. Well surprise, surprise it's the Yachts Captain with his hands up yelling, "Don't shoot, don't shoot please. Who are you and how'd you get on this yacht?" the captain asks while Christen looks around for a surprise attack.

"It's a long story, and one that I can't get into right Now, so with that said, I will ask you a question? You have two passengers on this deck and I'm looking for them, you don't have to say anything just point me in the right direction." Christen asks when without warning he takes a blow to the back of his head and drops like a sack of 50Lb potatoes. It was Gorgon using the Yachts Captain as a tool of distraction while he tries to incapacitate Christen. Here we go again, here we go again, he keeps thinking to himself why, why, why, he thought he gained the upper hand, he thought after he took down big, bad Vladimir, all he had to was find a way to stop these yachts from leaving Crete and figuring out a winning exit plan which included blowing these vessels straight to hell and the 3 ½ tons of opium with it. His mind is spinning again only he can feel his dead weight being moved to another part of the yacht to another.

This Captain or maybe it was Gorgon and Mikhail put his limp body inside midsize cabin on the lower deck while, they race up to the mid deck looking out for the 'Kraken' which speeds just 8 miles from their location. Mikhail paces back and forth on the mid deck while the 'kraken' sails fast into Kolpos Kissamou just under 3 miles from Ano Vouves, Mikhail turns his attention to Gorgon while he makes his final call to Capt. Juden.

"Captain how far are you, are you close or what?" he asks turning toward the sea as the 'Kraken' makes its approach.

"Yes, Gorgon I can see you on the mid desk from a short distance, we will arrive in under 10 mins' time." He replies. Hanging up the phone at the command center while Perse and Melissa look on at the luxury yachts docked one after another.

"I see my dad and Mikhail on the mid deck, looks like that shipment transfer was completed on time." Perse comments to Capt.Juden while Melissa grasps his right hand very tight.

"So what's the plan now Captain Juden?" Perse asks him.

"Only your father can answer that question son, I'm just your personal transport." Juden says.

Perse moves to the west side of the Command Center with Melissa following close behind him, attempting to get a closer view of what looks like bodies on the ground from a distance. And he suspects what might have happened but stays silent and won't acknowledge it. Gorgon begins waking his hands from the mid deck as the 'Kraken' begins slowing down to a crawl just 45 feet from the shoreline of Ano Vouves. 'The Kraken' pulls in ever so close until its nose to nose with the first yacht but there's still several feet between decks for someone to climb aboard vessel to vessel. Gorgon moves around to mid deck while the 'Kraken' continues lining up then comes to a stop, now all four are completely parallel to each other. Gorgon climbs up the med deck rail of Cronos and jumps onto the

'Krakens' deck where he's met by Perse and Melissa who both give him big hug while Capt. Juden brings the vessel to a complete stop.

"So, newlyweds how's the honeymoon going between you two and Melissa are you enjoying yourself on the 'Kraken'?" he directs the question to her while Perseus ponders what he saw past the shoreline.

"OMG! Mr. Mathias this yacht is incredible, I mean it's like living in a Condo on the water and it has everything you could possibly want, 5 cabins, -single and triple, 2 quest staterooms, and 1 staff cabin, yes, I enjoyed it very much thank you." She replies with a smile while Gorgon claps his hands together showing his gratitude.

"Wonderful, wonderful now I have a request for you no strike that there's been a change in plans." He firmly orders then adds.

"Your continuing your honeymoon on Cronos and I will inform Capt. Juden of this new development and have your luggage transferred there ASAP!" he says before giving Melissa a kiss on the cheek and pulling Perseus in for another hug when he leaves them and heads toward the Command Center.

Noises and voices, the sounds of footsteps and conversations swimming around in the subconscious of James Christen, slowly coming out of the semi concussion he suffered from that unexpected blow to his head. Laying on his side he turns over on his back attempting to regain his equilibrium while at the same time plotting his next move. He still suspects Gorgon and Mikhail haven't left the vessel but nevertheless he knows he must move swiftly and fast if he's effort to shut down this operation is successful.

In the meantime Christen moves around the tiny midsized cabin slowly regaining his senses again this he puts his head to the door, listening for any footsteps or possibly someone guarding his door. He slowly cracks it open taking a cautious peek but theirs no one in the dense hallway on either side, and this is good for him. He moves back up to the lower desk but this time on the east side rail to get a look at the Kraken from a different angle where he sees Perseus and Melissa holding hands, and doesn't realize he's been spotted by Mikhail at the opposite end making a call to Gorgon. Christen swiftly ducks down and moves fast toward Mikhail but down the west side of the lower deck where he is met or almost caught with a backhand hammer fist to the face and he blocks it or parries before Mikhail has an opportunity to connect.

These two are almost face to face when Mikhail attempts a left knee to Christens midsection but this move is somewhat anticipated by James, who blocks Mikhail knee with his right foot while preparing for a MMA style scoop slam. Christen maneuvers under Mikhail just enough to get his hands on grab his inner thigh and waist for a quick hoist and lift like delta/whirl and he's on his back. But he can sense something or someone watching and ducks down from barely getting hit with bullets. He hears several shots over his head while he stays down on the floor of the lower deck rail, after a few minutes goes by he's back on his feet and on the move over to the 'Kraken' for a finally confrontation.

The newlyweds wait back in their cabin before Capt. Juden has a chance to transport their luggage to the 'Cronos', but it doesn't look like that's about to happen anytime soon when Christen climbs over the deck rail from Cronos to the 'Kraken'.

Christen looks around with extreme caution everywhere on the lower deck but sees, and hears nothing around him until he continues to move down the east hall to some stairs going up to the middle deck. When he reaches the top oh what a surprise is waiting for him, before both his feet touch the stairs he's hit in the right chin with something solid, like a 16inch baton.

He falls to his hands and rolls over and continues to roll while he starts taking kicks to his stomach and rips also. Yes he's now feeling the wrath of Gorgon while Capt. Juden watches from the Command Center with a smile on his face enjoying every moment of this. But Christen won't tolerate any more of this he blocks Gorgons right ankle with his left hand and manages to kick him in the groin with his right foot, sending the man to the floor himself reeling from the sudden shock of pain after getting hit in the family jewels. Christen again regains his composure while holding his midsection and moves toward the Command Center to face Capt. Juden but doesn't notice a fallen Gorgon raises again and follows Christen in hot pursuit.

Perseus and Melissa over hear what sounds like a lot of rumbling and hasty footsteps on the middle level and leave their cabin to investigate. Perseus doesn't know this but his wife has been working deep undercover with Greek intelligence to bring down Gorgons organization, and with Christen disrupting everything, he's the gift that just keeps giving! He may accomplish what's taken her years to pull off. Christen reaches the Command post and finds Capt. Juden looking for a weapon of some sort no it's a pocket knife, not a good move for him.

"Look I'm just the Capt. of this yacht, I have no quarrel with you mister." Juden says before he flicks the pocket knife open.

"Really? Your guilty by association Capt. think about this, it's not worth a permanent headache." Christen warns him in advance but it doesn't matter.

He makes a lunge for James which seems very academic considering Christen is only 4 feet away and get caught with a stiff right jab between his eyes after Christen side steps him. He falls to his knees and Christen follows up with his own knee to the Capt.'s forehead and watches him drop.

But he when turns to cover his back theirs no Gorgon, in fact Gorgon that sneaky bastard went to warn the bride and groom of trouble abroad the 'Kraken' in the form of a battered and very bruised James Christen. So James decides to make his presence known.

"Newlyweds, newlyweds looks like the honeymoon is over, and Gorgon? Why don't you come out and let's finish this? Perseus, Melissa, decide?" he belts out a forceful yell while Perseus looks around for a fire arm or any weapon he can find to help his father.

Christen leaves the command center after putting down Capt. Juden and still dealing with a lingering side effects of the truth serum, he almost stumbles down the stairway going into the lower lever deck just several feet from the newly weds private cabin. It's very quite like dead calm and he figuring somethings way, way, off also before he confronted Capt. Juden Gorgon was right behind him, now he's thinking where the hell are these people and what the fuck is happening right now. He wants to knock on the door but he keeps thinking to himself is he attention is off by just a few seconds and not even a minute, he's done. He looks back and forth but hears nothing then decides well to hell with this, he grabs he knob to the cabin and twists, the door is open.

So now is time to do some investigating while he figures out where's the newlyweds and now he's new nemesis Gorgon! He moves around the cabin looking for a weapon, but remembers he still has his shoulder holster on with his signature weapon but there's chance Gorgon or Perseus could get lucky, hell maybe even Melissa and get the drop on him. He checks under the bed, nothing, the small closet and nothing, the drawers, one after the other and nothing, no weapons found. Ok, as he bad luck goes before he can leave the cabin he's confronted by Gorgon and

Perseus all at once, with Gorgon forcing into him with a fist push to his chest and followed by a left cross jab to his chin and it connects. So when Christen attempts to recover he's pressed hard by Perseus who comes on real strong with crazy swings of his own and he tries a kick to Christen midsection which comes up way short. Christen grabs Gorgon and throws him hard into the small closet but doesn't anticipate Perseus grabbing for his gun right out the shoulder, now that's some bold, slick shit right there.

Perseus manages to snatch it out but never gets a shot off when Christen grabs the gun and places his right index finger inside the trigger while at the same time switching the pistol safety to unarmed, very smooth! But this is far confrontation is far from over, Christen catches Perseus with a quick right cross to his left temple and a left hook to his ribs, he hits the ground doubling over in a fetal position, and now Gorgon after watching this lets out an angry howl.

"My son, my son, you son of bitch, it's over for you, your done! Says a furious Gorgon before he rushes toward Christen.

Bad move, Christen has all the time he needs seconds, just seconds to grab his pistol, flick the switch back to armed and get off a shot first in Gorgons chest, then another one into this throat and its over he's done. He hits the floor with blood gushing out of his Addams apple like a geyser of water all the while Melissa witnesses everything from the door. She doesn't know if she wants to cry or what? The woman is totally conflicted, and she's carrying a gun of her own hidden behind her back from Christen and Perseus when he finally get to his knees seeing his father laying on his back dead from multiple gun shots he tries to fight back to tears but the sight is just too overwhelming for him.

"Dad, dad, dad, no, no, no, not like this, not like this." says Perseus with tears streaming down his face. Then turns his gaze on Christen with fire in his eyes and vengeance in his heart when he notices Melissa standing in the door way motionless.

"Melissa, Melissa, shot him, shot him dammit, don't just stand there kill him mm. Woman pull the fuckin trigger please!" Perseus begs her but she can't do it, she just can't bring herself to shoot Christen.

"Perseus, honey, baby, I, I, can't, it's just so hard for me, don't make me an accessory to murder please." She says slowly revealing the small caliber gun she holding and very reluctant to shot when she finally points the gun at Perseus, while her hands shake hysterically.

"Melissa, Melissa, what the hell are you doing, what the fuck, you insane, crazy bitch." He yells at her out of shear frustration.

"I'm so, so, so sorry baby but I have to do this, it has to be done." She says slowly squashing the trigger.

"What the hell are you talking about damn you?" a frustrated Perseus askes.

"This is for my father goodbye, my love." She replies before firing a shot into his chest, he puts his right hand on it while looking at his bride in absolute shock and horror when she fires another one right between his eyes and he's done. She now looks at Christen who slowly and cautiously approaches her taking the gun from her hand.

"What's next James?" she asks Christen still shaking, regaining her composure and coming down from her adrenaline rush.

"These bodies have, we to move these bodies Melissa at lay them on the bad, one top of one other." He suggests to her

"I'm not touching any dead corpses, no hell no!" she replies with a look of did you hear what I said?

"Well it guess it's up to me then? I'll do it, I mean who else will? Considering I've practically took down an entire Greek/Russian opium ring alone, and all you did was get married very good for undercover work." He says very sarcastically.

Now she gives him this wicked stare like who the hell do you think you're talking too? Before he sizes up Perseus, he looks around for bath towels and finds at least six of them in sky blue color, all folded up neatly stacked, nice and wide inside a compact cabinet above the bed. Yes, yes, he's thinking this is good, very good first he grabs one, and he's snatching it open and out it unfolds in the air like a damn cape. He places the towel at the head of the bed all stretched out neatly, and quickly grabs another one doing the same thing but at midpoint this time.

He reaches for the third towel unfolds it out and with the snatch open places it below midpoint so now he's ready to start moving these two one at a time. He sizes up Perseus head to toe before making any attempt to actually move him.

The man stood 6 feet and 2 inches tall and may have weigh in excess of 200 pounds maybe more. He's laying just 3 feet from his dead father, his legs draped over Gorgons knees, when Christen kneels down to grab him under his arms, he lifts the dead weight straight up, until he in a standing position, next step, he takes another kneel, grabs Perseus dead body around both legs and carries him a few feet for a dump on the bed. And during all this is, this lazy, inapt, incompetent winch just watches this man again, over extending himself.

And with that task on to the next, it's Gorgons turn but this time he's in seating position in the closet but dead weight. Again applying the same technique with Gorgon but this time positioned himself, head to chest for a lift at his arms again, he pulls gorgons body up and out the closet, on to his shoulders and gives him a dump on the bed on this time opposite of Perseus. Kind of like in a six-nine position only now they both lay flat one on top of the other.

And after all this, dumping two dead bodies on a bed while she watches, and the executive cabin begins giving off a horrible stench. He now gives her a peculiar stare before he opens his mouth for a question and she just looks at him with both arms crossed like she knows it coming but what the hell bring it.

"First of all what happened to you? Where in the hell did that come from?" He asks her totally perplexed at what he just witnessed.

"I'm an agent with Interpol working undercover for Greek intelligence." She replies shaking her head in disgust after months, years being undercover. After hearing this Christen shakes his head in absolute disbelief like wow, sounds like a lengthy operation? But he can't resist the urge to ask that most unpopular question.

"Tell me Melissa, when were you planning to make your move after he got you pregnant." He says when she tries to slap him with her right hand and he catches it before she connects.

"Why you piece of shit, how dare you, how dare you? You have no idea what my life has been like these few years." she tells him but he isn't fazed by any of this.

"Don't do that, don't do that, your projecting that frustration on the wrong person, and he's dead now so your long nightmare is officially over." Christen says trying to relieve her of any guilt she has from pulling that trigger.

"So again, what now, what's our next move?" she asks again handing him the gun from her shaking hand.

"Well we find the shipping manifest or Captains itinerary for any details on where these vessels are going." Christen replies before leaving the cabin with Melissa following close behind him.

He figures all the information on where these vessels are traveling, he will find on those manifests in the Captains office on the 'Kraken' or aboard the 'Cronos', so either way those ships will never leave Crete. He reaches the command center again making his past the Captain's chair and into the small office when he focuses he's gaze some paperwork inside a folder on the desk which as it turns out happens to be the shipping route and schedule itinerary all faxed to Capt. Juden by Gorgon just days before.

What they don't know is next to the door of this office is hidden compartment of weapons and munitions, housing 3 AR 15's, 2 IA2 5.56 mm Carbine rifles and 1 HK G3 Pistol with dozens of boxes in the bottom shelf or drawer carrying various caliber bullets matching the rifles. Christen takes a seat while opening the folder, and begins analyzing the paperwork one sheet at a time. The first one being luxury yacht 'Cronos', the second 'Hyperion,' and the third and last one 'Oceanus'.

Melissa comes in close to him and snatches the first batch of paperwork for 'Cronos' in the folder, three to six pages everything stapled together, and detailing everything from water routes to ship yacht size, including shipment specs and departure from Crete and arrive in Beijing, China first, then finally, Taiwan last.

"Christen, if I'm reading this correctly these luxury yachts are scheduled to arrive in Beijing, China in several days from now." She says studying the other paperwork in the folder.

"These yachts will never make the trip Melissa, and you can bank on that one." Christen says with defiant tone in his voice.

Melissa studies the other documents for 'Hyperion' and 'Oceanus' all detailing the same information including shipment Specs.

"James we have no way of getting rid of these vessels, they're just docked here, how do we destroy this shipment?" she asks very concerned. But Christen cracks a smile and gives off a sigh and then a brief chuckle.

"Melissa back on that shoreline there's a shot up, banged up Range Rover with assault rifles, ammunition and a case of plastic explosives included with six cubes and detonation sticks." He tells her while he grabs all the paperwork and places it back in the folder.

He leaves the Capt. office with her trailing close behind him, and never stops until he reaches the lower deck on the east side of the yacht where the side stairs go down to the base or bottom just several feet from the shallow water.

"Melissa stay on the 'Kraken' until I return, I have to move quickly and swiftly in the next 45 minutes to an hour and half." He commands of her and she complies willingly.

"James I won't leave the Command Center, go and be careful, god speed. I will contact Andromeda in the meantime. She has to be told about what has transpired here." Melissa says concerned Annie with become hysterical and possibly seek revenge on Christen once she learns what's happened. Christen leaves the Command post existing back to the lower deck on the east side of the yacht where the stairs are while his head starts spinning again and his heart pumps faster from the adrenaline rush. Damn, that blasted truth serum, and I haven't drop dead yet? He thinks to himself, maybe just maybe that advice he got from Winston actually, paid off or he was just trying to buy Christen some time? This isn't the moment to start second guessing himself especially when he's so close to shutting this operation down completely.

The 'Kraken' pull in closer to the shoreline so the sand is just 7 feet from the front hull leaving Christen more solid ground to walk on this time as oppose to stepping into 2 to 4 feet of water again. When he reaches the bottom base of the stairs and steps off he picks up his pace faster this time in a straight line toward the banged-up, shot-up Range Rover and dead bodies he left behind. Those same tracks remain of that super machine they used to transfer all that reddish-brown brick from those tractor trailers to the luxury yachts, and he never got the chance to stop then but this time he feels he can redeem himself and blow the whole operation straight to hell.

After he walks over the bodies of Vlad and Krasimir before he reaches the shot-up, banged-up Range Rover and who would've guessed it but the guns and plastic explosives are still intact. Buried on its left side just a few feet in the sand from the shooting impact were the assault rifles and c-4 case with detonation pack laying on a glass window. Christen carefully grabs the case out the rear of the Range Rover leaving everything else, he places the case strap around his shoulder and makes a mad dash back to the shoreline. Now seeing that all three yachts are so closely docked together, he doesn't have to wonder how he will get from one point to another.

He can simply hop or jump from one deck to the other provided they are within 3 to 4 feet or at least 16 to 32 inches in width, apart. He approaches the shoreline again carrying this pack around his shoulders, starts back up the base to the top stairs of the 'Kraken's east side. But doesn't stop once he reaches the lower deck, he races around the yacht to the west side where it's parallel to 'Cronos' and makes the jump deck to deck. But he doesn't stop there, he continues the same pattern with 'Hyperion' until he finally reaches 'Oceanus' lower deck which for him is somewhat further but he manages to clear the jump with no problems and quickly finds the engine room with stairs just under the command post.

On almost every luxury yacht located at the east side corner hull is the boat fuel system, mostly built different but many having same function and varying in size and design. He sees what looks like a box with lines or hoses making connections throw a wall outside, so he figures that must be where the vessel is fueled nevertheless it's time to plant the explosive. Christen opens the case, takes out a stick or cube of c-4/timer with some sticking adhesive on the back, he places it on the side of the box now begins taking the wires and detonation sticks out. He places the sticks in the c-4 and the wire attached to the timer set for 10 minutes, so there it is and now he must complete this with the other two vessels and get himself and Melissa clear of the blast within 10 minutes' time.

While Christen leaves the engine room and ascends to the Command post via the stairs and out to the lower deck for his next move to the 3rd luxury yacht 'Hyperion' Melissa gets herself ready to infuriate Andromeda with the unexpected news of her father and brothers demise at the hands of James Christen. Melissa makes the call to Andromeda still at home at dad's manse with no idea of what's transpired in the last hour or so. The phone rings and she gets a continual dial tone until finally Andromeda picks up wondering how the honeymoon is going?

"Melissa, are you and my brother still on the yacht and how's honeymoon? I feel so alone here by myself with no one to keep me company Melissa. I only wish James was here with me right now, I could have him all to myself." Annie confesses to Melissa.

But while Melissa listens intently to Andromeda she knows once this unfortunate information is dropped the tone of this conversation will change dramatically. And she takes a deep breathe herself before reveals what's happened over the last two hours.

"Annie are you sitting down or standing up?" she asks pacing back and forth in the command post trying to find an easy way to say it, but there's no easy and so she sucks it up, and prepares for whatever comes.

"Annie, Annie, are you still there, Annie, say something please." She asks almost pleading.

"What kind of question is that Melissa? Why would you ask me such a thing? What the hell is happening? Was there an accident or something? Tell me my brother is ok, TELL ME MY BROTHER IS IN GOOD HEALTH MELISSA?" she says screaming hysterically at the top of her lungs.

Now Melissa sits back in the Captains' chair and folds her legs together, relaxing her body, doing everything she possibly can to keep and hold her composure.

"Annie theirs no easy way to say this so here goes, they're all dead, all of them. Gorgon, his partners and the body guards and or henchmen, including your brother, my husband, they are all gone, everyone forever!" she tells her bracing for what's to come next.

But none of this registers with Andromeda, in fact she thinks all this might be a sick joke that Melissa is playing on her sister in law and starts laughing at the mere thought of it. Just the idea alone for her seems incomprehensible, there's no way in bloody hell any of this is true, no fucking way!

"Ha, ha, ha, ha, ha, ha, ha, ha, ha, ha, ha, ha, ha, ha, you got me with that one, my sense of humor is dry but this is a little over the top for me and I'm really in no mood right now for dark humor, sister in law so put my father and brother on the bloody phone this second." Annie demands now standing up straight.

All while this is happening Christen makes his way back to the 'Kraken' after having successfully set the explosives on all three luxury yachts with the engines set on full neutral meaning the yachts aren't moving but all the lights are on and the vessels are running but aren't going anywhere. Christen lands on the lower west deck and races to the Command post to find Melissa on the phone with Andromeda. He reaches the panel where the yachts steering wheel, gear shifts and ignition switch are present while observing Melissa's tone and expression, she gives a look of you want to talk to her? He takes the phone and lays it's out.

"Melissa while I talk to Annie, you take the wheel and get us the hell out of here." He pleads to Melissa.

She hands him the phone while at the same time manning the wheel and monitoring both sides of the yacht. She grabs the gear and moves it to reverse at full throttle knowing they are on the clock and its ticketing down fast.

"Annie, I have you on speaker, everything Melissa just told you is true." He says and in a somber but calm voice.

"James what is she talking about? My father and brother Are dead? The whole operation is over? This is madness and I don't except this! So you explain it to me right now." she's tells him.

And while this continues Melissa skillfully guides the yacht backward always watching the space to her left in regards to 'Cronos'. The yacht now has pulled away at least 12 to 25 feet when she shifts gears full throttle, making a sharp U-turn back toward Paleohora just beyond Ano Elafonissi.

"Annie, one of your fathers partners Tisdale had his goons Roman and Gregory shoot me up with Sodium Pentothal at a warehouse in Vouliagmeni near Port of Piraeus. And tried torture afterward but thought otherwise, so let's say the brothers weren't on the same page. They're gone forever including Vladimir and Krasimir so what you heard was true, as difficult as that may sound it's over." Christen says with a calm voice.

But Andromeda still isn't convinced of the shocking news she's had to listen too, in fact in the back of her mind she thinking this is all bullshit and she's intends to call her father, hoping, praying that what Christen and Melissa told her? Are outright lies, but then again, what if, just what if he did manage to slow down, or kill Gorgon, his partners and their body guards or Lt's? It seems inconceivable to her given that she's met these men before but under different circumstances, so the idea that Christen killed them all seems a bit incredulous to her.

And the timer ticks past 7 minutes on almost all three yachts while Melissa steers the 'Kraken' back in the same path for which it traveled. With Perse still conversing with Andromeda at the same time watching Melissa steer the yacht.

"How are we doing Melissa, are you ok? Can you handle this monster?" Christen asks while he still has Annie on the line.

"I think you should worry about Annie, James, when she realizes the truth, the real truth, 'hell hath no fury'!" Melissa says looking back indirectly at Christen.

"Annie, Annie are you still there." He asks before she comes back on fire.

"Damn you, damn you James, he won't answer his phone and I can't reach my brother. You, you, bastard, whatever you do, don't return to Athens, I swore on my father and brothers eternal soul, I'll find a way to avenge them and kill you." She says out of sheer pain and anguish.

"Annie I'm coming back to get my luggage and I'm leaving afterward, at that point whatever happens I'll deal with it some other time." He replies staring out the window of the command post.

"And Melissa, Melissa you bitch, my brother loved you, he made sacrifices for you and this is how you repay him?" she asks with growing frustration.

"Annie, sweet little sheltered Annie, you come from a family of thieves, lairs and killers, only your dad was smart enough to surround himself with men who didn't mind getting their hands dirty while he schemed and plotted." She answers back.

And by this time the clocks on those yachts reaches 4 minutes continuing the count down while this time Christen takes the wheel and Melissa begins her final conversation with Andromeda while she looks at the clock on the panel, thinking The blast is getting close.

"Annie for what it's worth I enjoyed spending time with you, your father and brother. I always thought Gorgon had a morbid but dark sense of humor, and being around him was never boring, he always kept you laughing." She tells Annie while Christen steers the yacht.

And now the clock continues to count down 3 minutes and 53 seconds but they still haven't reach a clear point from the possible blast wave.

"Melissa it doesn't matter what you say right now, the only thing of importance to me, is confirming that my father and brother are dead, nothing else." She says with determination in her voice.

All the while Christen keeps his eyes on the vessels docked at Ano Vouves the 360 monitor one the panel inches from the wheel and gear lever. The clock continues ticking down to 2 minutes and 45 seconds while Christen observes the evening night sky has a half moon. Its seems like the conversation with Andromeda has ended but she's still on the phone with Melissa grinding out the female bonding scenario all the while Christen steers the 'Kraken' further away from the blast area.

"Tell Christen I'm packing all his luggage and leaving it all outside the manse by the curb, so he doesn't have to reenter the house. I think it better this way for everyone involved Melissa you especially." She says still pacing back and forth in her room.

"No worries Annie, you do what you have to do ok? Just remember this any thoughts about revenge or avenging what happened with be met with swift retaliation, plain and simple." Warns Melissa hanging up the phone and pushes Christen out the way so she takes control of the steering wheel again.

"Oh sounds like it went really well, Melissa?" Christen says being sarcastic as hell but the look on Melissa face tells a different story.

"She's still in shock Christen after the untimely news of her father and brothers demise. Oh yeah, she's leaving all your luggage at the curb outside the Mathias mansion." She repeats the order.

"Yeah, I overheard that one too, so it works out for me once we return to Port of Piraeus and I retrieve my luggage from the mansion I head back to Pillisworth, so much for weddings.

And how about you Melissa?" Christen asks her while he folds his arms across his chest seating in the Captain's chair.

"I report back to my contact with Greek Intelligence and take a flight home to Bucharest, Romania." She says while guiding the yacht in a straight path toward Port of Piraeus, downtown Athens, Greece.

The detonators get closer to 1 minute now and the real count down begins with Christen keeping his eye on the 360 peripheral scope on the panel watching the Luxury yachts from a clear distance. 58, 57, 56, 55, 54, 53, 52, 51, 50. Christen steps off the chair and straight to the panel placing his left hand on Melissa shoulder and she slows down raising the gear lever back up to Neutral.

"What's wrong James we are so close to escaping, we can't stop now?" she says worried but he wants to be sure.

"Hmm, umm, I need to know Melissa, I want to see the blast from this distance." He says giving her a indirect glance while he stares out the window and at the 360 peripheral scope, giving them a incredible view of the rear top side of the 'Kraken.'

"How do you even know this will work Christen? What makes you so sure the explosive you planted will do the job?" she asks still very doubtful.

"Every yacht has an engine room where the fuel line is located and very vulnerable to explosive charges, with the C-4 I planted on all three Yachts, I'm absolutely certain it will create beautiful a mess of things. And I want to see it from a distance, I want to witness all that opium, all 3 and half tons of it blown straight to hell." He says with much drama in his voice.

So she steps back from the steering wheel and sets back in the chair reserved for the Captain, patiently waiting with Christen with her arms folded across her chest.

"Ok, you've sold me Christen, but it must be getting close to detonation by now right?" she asks again keeping a keen eye on the 360 peripheral scope and the clock hits 39, 38, 37, 36, 35, 34, 32, 31, 30, 29, 28, 27, 26, 25, 24, 23, 22, 21, 20 seconds and Christen gives a Melissa a grin of total satisfaction like he's anticipating something marvelous about to happen. 19, 18, 17, 16, 15, 14, 13, 12, 11, 10.

"You really enjoying this aren't you James?" she asks him as time tacks away.

"Considering what I had to endure the last couple of hours? For me Melissa, this is icing on the cake." He says rocking his head back, this time staring at the ceiling 09, 08, 07, 06, 05, the detonator finally hits 04, 03, 02, 01, and 00.

Suddenly they hear the sound of a thunderous blast creating a concussion wave from the impact, the explosion from the fuel line in makes contact with the tank housing the yachts fuel, this creates an chemical wave of fire from the engine room, causing all walls and pipes to buckle from the blast. From the engine room to the upper lower deck, floor by floor, to finally the whole yacht cracks in half. Melissa watches as Cronos goes up first expending in flames and debris flying everywhere and then a few seconds later, Hyperion explodes into a massive fireball followed by Oceanus all in one beautiful sequence, incinerating every brownish red brick of opium stored in those button middle hulls.

The massive fireball of three yachts lights up the evening night sky from the shoreline of Ano Vouves North east section of Crete. It almost resembles a Nordic Viking funeral pyre, from the view of the command post, all three yachts begin their fiery ascent into the Mediterranean sea while Christen and Melissa look on absolutely amazement from the Kraken.

"I know nothing about explosives or anything like that only what I've seen on TV and movies but after witnessing it from this vantage point, James I'm a believer." She says.

This time stepping off the chair again and back to the panel ready to grab the wheel and dropping the lever back down to 1st gear. The yacht jolts forward after having been rocking side to side and up and down from the choppy waters. She turns sharp right while dropping the lever into 2nd gear when the motor picks up speed pushing the yacht up some 26 knots or 32 miles per hour on water. She follows the same path pulling away from Kolpos Hanion, dropping the lever to 3rd gear, this time the yacht picks up 52 knots or 67 miles per hour, with Melissa handling the wheel like a pro yachtsmen.

"I presume you know the exact route via Port of Piraeus." He asks her while relaxing in the chair with his legs crossed.

"Yes, I got a good look at the map on Judens' desk while you were examining the shipping paperwork." She replies.

"We should pull into Port in under 1 hour or less, any other questions you have." She asks with a smirk on her face.

"Oh, no, no, ummm enjoying the ride, and for the record, you really look like you know what your doing behind that wheel Melissa." He says smiling back at her.

"It's all relative Christen, my dad once owned a 38 foot sail boat many years ago when I was only a teenager, he let me steer it and why not? There's no heavy traffic on water, nothing but open sea, not traffic lights or stops signs, people suddenly crossing the street or bicycles cutting around your blind spots, just open sea." She replies guiding the yacht on a straight path.

Christen kept his eyes on the 360 peripheral on the panel watching the last yacht Oceanus descend into the Mediterranean Sea with the back deck going down last, followed in the floating wreckage at the surface surrounded by fire and melted packs of Reddish brown opium. Now he folds his arms again while focusing his gaze indirectly on Melissa and he can see the lights of gargantuan cruise ships around the Ports of Piraeus and cross port of Corinth. Royal Caribbean, The Royal Princes, Holland America line among others lined up parallel to each other with crowds of people boarding.

"Wow, I never realized how beautiful port of Piraeus looks from this vantage point Melissa. And those Cruise lines? Good god those ships are huge, I read once two years ago that some Cruise line executives were in talks to build even larger fleet of vessels to keep up with the demand?" he tells her while she continues steering the Kraken ever closer to port.

"Yeah, well when you have so many millionaires, billionaire celebs visiting this part of the world from all over the globe, then yes, like most typical filthy rich capitalists they like to throw money around. They have these insane parties for business guests and weddings so they don't mind throwing it away on cruises." She replies again.

And while she continues this stimulating conversation with Christen she looks for a secured spot to dock the yacht considering she's now within three miles of Piraeus, and finding a safe spot or area is proving very challenging for her.

"James be a dear and find the LED emergency light switch for me on the panel while I navigate this yacht to a unsecured dock." She asks him

"OK, for the sake of being ignorant, it wouldn't happen to be a red button instead of a switch? But it marked lights?" he says very unsure but he flicks it anyway and shazaam four very bright lights out side on the top deck come on.

"Yes, very good, very good, your making yourself useful Christen and I think I've found my spot so hanging on. This might seem like a squeeze from a distance but I think we can fit it." she tells him again while skillfully navigating the Kraken between two mammoth Royal Caribbean Cruise liners with five to six feet of room on both sides.

Christen steps out the command post to the outside deck to get an idea of how well she's guiding this yacht through the Piraeus port while watching out for fishing boats, and other obstructions in the water.

"James how close I'm I to docking, give me clue, a hint something? I'm ready to park this damn thing" she asks christen.

"So far, so good Melissa, just a few feet more and it's done." He tells her.

He waving his hand right hand, signaling closer, closer almost there when the Kraken stops inside The Ariston Marina just one mile from Port of Piraeus, dozens of similar looking yachts. He looks back at her through the window and waves both hands to stop, at this she raises the lever back up to park, when the engine rotors stop. By this time she leaves the command center of the yacht and returns to the executive cabin for a brief moment to retrieve her luggage, she snatches a towel from the cabinet above the bed in the cabin using it to cover her nose and mouth.

She reaches down at the base of the bed where her specialized travel pro case seats, half zipped up, and carrying most of her clothes and shoes still packed. Before she has to time check everything she's met by Christen in the hall coming back in from outside on the front lower deck.

"So you have everything you need all packed and ready? He asks her.

But she gives him a peculiar look again top to bottom wondering out loud…

"You aren't thinking of leaving here looking like that are you? I mean don't you want to at least change into some clean clothes?" she asks him again.

"What? You expect me to look through his clothes for something that fits." He replies.

"Well you two are about the same size, your only two inches shorter, and I'm sure you both wore the same size shoe or close to it?" she says.

After shrugging her shoulders she grabs the handle from case pulling it out the cabin to give Christen some room and time to look through Perseus clothes. Christen steps in and does a quick look through the small closet, and fortunately for him there's no blood of the clothes, or shirts for that matter. He sees several different pair of beige and light blue khaki shorts, three sports jackets, all matching the khakis, five short sleeve shirts matching the beige and blue khakis, and three pairs of regular name brand sneakers and a pair of brown slip on shoes. Turns out Perseus wore a size 12 while Christens shoe size is of 11, well just one inch off, not bad considering. There are other items as well cute brown, olive green, and royal blue Hanes under wear for men.

Now he quickly grabs out the small closet the beige khakis shorts with a blue short sleeve shirt to wear, placing them on top the corpses and begins changing clothes, while Melissa patiently waits outside with her back to him. Knowing he only has a few seconds if not minutes to get himself dressed, he does a superman routine, quickly slips off the shoulder holster with his gun still housed, shoes, pants and wet socks, snatches off his dress and muscle shirt, than starts slipping on the khakis first with a quick zip, and button then applies the blue shirt sleeve shirt around his upper body. He reaches into his right pants pocket for his keys and wallet which they never took from him knowing his passport remains back at the Mathias mansion with his luggage.

One last item, he sees the sneakers on the floor he wants to wear while at the same time he spots a towel in small the cabinet above the bed and uses it to completely wipe his face clean even though its dry while she turns back around to observe him shaking her head in total amusement. He bends down on one knee first to slip his right foot into the first sneaker, and does the same with his left while she continues her stare at him.

"Aren't you going to at least get a wet towel to properly wash the blood off your face?" she asks folding her arms across her chest.

"Wait there Christen and give just me under five minutes don't move." She says.

She leaves her luggage in the narrow hall races into a nearby bathroom the size of a half studio apartment, and she find face towels hanging from tiny racks, well all in one motion she hits the knob for both hot and cold water on the sink, rinsing the towel until its soaking wet. She doesn't completely rang it dry but keeps it moist at the same time she makes a mad rush a few paces back to the executive cabin before she hands it to Christen.

"Thank you". He says to her. Before he applies the towel all over his face, neck and chest.

"Now wasn't that easier Christen, didn't that seem more obvious to you?" She asks sarcastically.

"Right about now, Melissa I really don't give a shit but thanks you for that." He tells her.

She shakes her head again giving him a smile of pity but at the same time she has hidden admiration towards him considering what he was up against and managed to overcome the odds with insane determination.

"So are we finally ready to get the hell off his yacht

Christen its approaching almost midnight?" she asks him anxious to leave and fly back home for debrief.

"No problem just one last item and we're out. We're gone madam." He tells her.

Grabbing the beige jacket he puts it on and its looks rather nice around his slightly ripped light caramel upper body. Now that the jacket fits, Christen quickly inspects his gun, pulling it out the holster pocket, he flicks the mag release button and the clip drops, funny he never took it off or unscrewed the Silencer from the muzzle back at the warehouse after he emptied

It into all three thugs Tisdale, Alexandr, and Krasimir while Never thinking to detach the silencer and place it back in its Gun pocket compartment.

It's not totally empty; in fact it still carries 5 bullets in the clip so now he slips it back in hearing a click sound before he pulls back the slide now there's one in the chamber again. He turns back around to find her still there staring back at him and throwing her hands in the air like are you ready not?

"Alright, alright Melissa lets go, you've waited for me long enough." He says.

Leaving the cabin he closes the door behind him shut and proceeds to follow her down the hall to the right exit door leading them both upstairs to the lower top deck where's there's close space for them to step off to the marina crosswalk. She allows him to takes the first step off the yacht, he then reaches back to grab her luggage and her hand assisting her in stepping off to the painted wood pavement. The moment her feet touches the ground he hands the snatch handle back to her and they start their journey through the front of Ariston Marina leaving the emergency lights on the Kraken without a care in the world.

Like who's going to asks questions? Who's going to snoop around, who's looking for this yacht, beside the fact the explosion took place some 30 plus miles away on a part of the

Island where hardly anyone goes and it less populated, which in part explains why Gorgon and his partners chose that spot. Knowing full well they could get away with the operation and cast off in the dead of night well into the morning hours without being stopped by the international police or checked for contraband. The Greek police have no jurisdiction beyond Crete, however they can alert other governments to the vessel sailing through and check on board for contraband but then it sails where ever it wants, at its own risk.

They are spotted by a young man at the front desk after they've follow a visitor and tourist path around the Ariston Marina office. One the grounds are tiny poplar bushes and some Cypress trees are planted along the path from the Marina going out to the parking lot. The young man working gives them a brief look and nods his for acknowledgement but never approaches them from the office or even makes a call. From a vantage point of the TV screen in the lobby it appears he's watching his favorite program and doesn't really care about bothering these two or asking any questions like who are you and where did you come from?

Chapter 10

BACK TO PILLISWORTH

To their right further down the street were Athens Shuttle buses and some tourists standing in line single file, moving at gradual pace to board the ferries waiting for them at the pier. But parked closer to the Ariston marina were Athens taxi cabs with the national symbol of the Greek flag waving on the top hood of all the cars. The walk to the taxis wasn't very far in fact considering the whole area was so compact meaning everything was very close or within walking distance. They didn't hold hands or barely even look at each other just keep their pace with Melissa dragging her luggage from behind and Christen keeping his hands in his pockets. Not they were just 4 feet from the last taxi when Christen waves his right hand to get the drivers attention, while the guy smokes his cigar standing beside the car door looking out potential passengers.

"Are you in service or no?" Christen asks pointing to the Cabs trunk.

"Yes, just taking a cigar break, and enjoying the evening Breeze." He tells them.

The driver walks around to the trunk, pulls his keys out his right pocket and quickly sticks it in the latch with a twist of his hand, it pops open. Christen grabs Melissa's luggage and gently but quickly slides it down in the bottom while allowing the driver to close it shut. He opens the left passenger door for her and watches her step in and crawl over the seat to the other side and gets in closing it behind him. The driver jumps in his seat, shuts his door, throws the gear in drive and pulls away from the curb.

"Where we going people, where's our destination?" he asks Peeking through the rear view mirror to the back seat.

Melissa now studies Christens expression wondering which one of them will give him an answer. But he just folds his arms across his chest and looks at her then nods to the driver.

"Sir we're going to the Lycurgus District, Mathias mansion at…" she says and he interrupts before she can get it out her mouth.

"I, I, know where that is thank you." Replies swerving around traffic from the pier while rapidly cutting throw downtown Athens back into the city limits.

So now Christen gives her a sly smirk and relaxes his head against seat rest while Melissa gives off this frown and stares at the driver who ignores her.

"You think this is funny don't you? Does this amuse you

James, and Mr. Cab driver? Your customer service skills really suck ass." She screams out.

But he continues to ignore her, eyes forward, concentrating on the road in front, he merges unto Dim Gounari, taking it around to Alipedou Blvd, which stretches some 3 miles with developments of malls, shopping centers, a Greek Orthodox Church where Archbishop Ausgustine Sinilos, the former assassin turned holy man holds his Sermons. Alipedou Blvd merges into Loef. Athinon Pireos pkwy when they come to an intersection, and left west at Leof Kifisou Dr. which runs straight into the Lycurgus District just 2 miles ahead. She recognizes this area from a few years back when Perseus would take her to see off Broadway plays at the St. Makrigianni theater. The Cabby drove very fast but careful, zig zagging around cars and buses until he finally reached the Lycurgus district and closing in on the Mathias mansion. Melissa gives Christen a look of almost there while pointing out the homes of the wealthy and super rich of that district. Judging by the area and neighborhood they were within few city blocks of the Mathias mansion right in the middle of Magnolis Dr. home to many of Athens cultural elite and notorious residents.

The cab driver begin slowing down within 8 feet of Magnolis Dr. and made his right turn there was a mammoth sign on the residential gate facing the street a 4 foot M with a weird gothic circle around it. Entering the private they passed five large estates before pulling up to the Gate of Mathias Mansion and the gate is closed. Melissa orders the cab driver,

"Give me a just few minutes ill handle this" she says before she exits the car.

And walks up the touch key panel controlling the gates entry and hits a series of numbers or codes and it swings open. She quickly renters the taxi cab and the driver pulls in fast up the drive way and around to the front of the house.

And seating outside on the curb is the luggage, waiting for Christen to take it and leave Greece courtesy of Andromeda, with both front doors closed and the area completely quit. Christen exits his side, races around the grabs his bags while the taxi drive pops the trunk from an knob on the floor inches from the brake pedal. He looks up at the windows and sees nothing as if no one's home, and he figures this woman is mentally destruct and full of vengeance but he wasn't waiting around for any pointless discussion with her and throws his luggage in the trunk besides Melissa's and slams it shut.

He renters the car and the taxi pulls off just as he's closing door, makes another quick drive around the circular driveway, throw the gate and back out into the street, speeding towards Leof. Kifisou Drive again. Now the driver looking both ways makes that left turn back down Leof. Kifisou Drive and continues to merge on Loef. Lavriou Pkwy, connecting with Spirou Davari which runs directly to Athens, Greece International Airport.

"So what's next for you Melissa? A different mission, another assignment perhaps?" he asks her leaning back against seat real close to the door.

She rolls her eyes and breathes a sigh of relief, shakes her head in disgust but not at his question but reflecting back several years, ago when she took this assignment from Greek Intelligence. Thinking about what happened to her father so many years ago, and the double cross at hands of Gorgon, she waited so long for the opportunity, the right time to seek vengeance but it never presented itself, and then who comes to visit for the wedding? The very man whom unsuccessfully disrupted his pipeline in Turkey only to destroy it some weeks later the Island of Crete, this was delicious irony for her now thinking about how She's going to answer his question and whether it's the answer he's looking for?

"I have to report back to my superiors as soon as possible Christen and I presume you do too?" she asks him while staring out the window allowing the breeze to hit her face until she turns to face him.

Christen nods his head in agreement and suspects the information from that surveillance photo he sent back to headquarters in Pillisworth, South Africa was already extracted from the photo-scanograph. That state of the art computer linked to practically every intelligence agency on this planet.

"So, are you staying in Athens or? Where are you going from here?" he asks her while the taxi approaches the outer parking lot of after traveling down Leof.Lavriou to Athens, Greece International Airport.

"I'm going back home to Prague, Czech and reassess my life, my future in the intelligence community. I'm tired Christen, I've given so much of life to these people and now it's time for me again." She tells him.

"Yes, going into the field can be taxing and very stressful, It's not for everyone. It takes a special kind of person do to This job and keep ones sanity." He replies.

"People we're approaching the airport now, where should I let your off?" he asks turning into a crowded but very quiet parking lot.

Oh, yes Virgin Atlantic Terminal 6 thank you." He tells the driver.

The taxi takes a loop around the east end of the airport where the signs posted east Terminals 1-6 in exotic colors red, orange, yellow, green, purple and sky blue. Terminal 1 Grand Flyer Airlines with red dot, Terminal 2 Europa Airlines with orange dot, Terminal 3 Superior Airlines with yellow dot, Terminal 4 Sky Arch airlines with green dot, Terminal 5 Regency Airlines with purple dot and finally Terminal 6 Virgin Atlantic airlines with sky blue dot. The taxi pulls up to the curb of Terminal 6 after a van pulls off and parks. He pops the back trunk and exits the driver side while James and Melissa both exit and meet at the back trunk for their luggage.

Christen reaches into his pocket wallet and pulls $150 euros Cash handing it to the driver and they shakes hands. Melissa grabs her luggage out along with Christen snatching his

After hers and they leave enter the terminal together while the drive shuts the trunk closed, enters he's taxi and pulls away from the curb, speeding around the west loop back toward Leof. Lavriou and back into the city limits. Christen and Melissa look around Terminal 6 and to their direct left are boarding stations and the agents waiting for business and more passengers to check in. Melissa steps over to the first one followed by Christen approaching station 2. She places her luggage on the Scale while taking out her women's wallet, she pulls out a euro American express platinum credit card, handing it to the guy behind the counter. Christen does the same and his luggage weighs just under 90 pounds per bag, so it gets charged extra for being heavyweight but he gladly pays it pulling out his credit card from his wallet and his passport for identification purposes.

"I want to book a flight first class one way to Pillisworth, South Africa." He tells the guy. At this moment he watches the clerks fingers work the key broad like a master typist.

"We have a flight going out scheduled in 45 mins for Pillisworth, South Africa and your in luck there's no connecting Flights so it a straight shoot for you." The agent says waiting The tickets to print.

He keeps his light bag and checks his watch he time was 11:05 pm in the evening and within less than 2 minutes his tickets come popping out this machine like a sausage maker, and placed in an envelope, while over at station 2 Melissa has received her tickets in envelopes also. All luggage are taken to different destinations her to Prague, Czech, Republic and his going to Pillisworth, South Africa. They meet each other again at the screening area where both have to stand in open spot while machine scans them top to bottom and they're allowed to walk through for security purposes of course.

"So I guess this is where we part ways James, you should visit Prague sometime, I think you'd enjoy it?" she asks him before turning toward the seating area for Europa airlines in Terminal 6.

"Well what airline are you taking to Czech Republic, and if I'm ever in town I'll look you up Melissa." He tells her before she leaves him.

"Europa, James via Athens, Greece one way. No connecting flight." she says walking away while turning, staring back at him.

"Well for what's worth you're a half way descent field agent Melissa, and don't take that personal or literally. Consider it a compliment from field agent to another." He says with a grin on his face and shrugs his shoulders.

"I won't Christen and watch your back with you know who? I know she's seething over what happened with her father and brother, you know the old saying 'hell hath no fury, like a woman scorned?' just try and stay off the radar Christen please?" she says getting further and further away.

"I'll keep that under advisement Melissa, thank you." He tells her again.

"Christen, I'm serious don't underestimate her, she will Inherit her fathers business, all his international contacts, and his business allies from others countries. Take heed! Please?" she begs him.

Now he thinking where have I heard all this before, I'm suddenly getting a case of da'ja'vu all over again. But he just nods in agreement with her and gives this wave like don't miss your flight.

"Melissa take care, travel safe and god speed." He tells her finally bidding her farewell.

So now she turns back around and begins her stride toward the seating area of Europa airlines connection at Terminal 6.

After everything she said but Gorgon, he's heard this all before from Tarken and took it with a grain of salt although he's thinking now by some chance of fate she aligns herself with his long time enemy Durant Lucern Craven, that could be something to worry about. That would give him serious consternation and much personal concern. He now starts down the opposite corridor toward Virgin Airlines seating area, and spots a few seats filled with late even passengers taking his flight or not. The seating arrangement almost resembles a miniature maze but not as complicated, he finds three seats unoccupied and takes one facing the outer run way where the planes come to take boarding passengers.

He places his light bag on the chair next to him and checks his watch which has exactly 45 minutes before midnight. The monitor for arrivals and departures shows a list of flights top to bottom, some on time and others coming behind schedule. His flight number was #8564 one way Athens, Greece to Pillisworth, South Africa. While waiting on his flight it suddenly occurred to him maybe he should have stayed in Geneva, Switzerland, but the idea of attending a wedding seemed reasonable at the time, and what are the odds that he's abrupt encounter in Turkey would bring him in contact with these brutes.

The official report he received from Admiral Manning was proceed with caution, the situations potentially dangerous. He always followed orders but in this case there was counter surveillance happening on both ends and he barely made it out of the blast alive. He keeps thinking it's interesting how he can reflect on all this now seating in an lounge in Athens, Greece, International Airport after getting shoot up with truth serum or Sodium Pentothal and half beaten to death by twin Ukrainian thugs and went head to head with a former Russian MMA fighter called 'Big Crunchy'.

It's an absolute miracle he hasn't completely suffered any brain damage from the side effects but once he returns to Head

Quarters they will insist he under goes an evaluation, and a battery of tests to determine his mental state, then on to the next assignment. The time is now 11:35pm, yes time just seems to tick away slowly or fast depending ones perspective when your seated alone in airport terminal waiting, and waiting for the plane to arrive. At that point he looks over to the boarding exit and two agents are now behind the podium preparing to announce his flight.

"Ladies and Gentleman your flight for Pillisworth, South Africa will arrive in 5 minutes." One of the agents calls out.

Christen keeps his eyes on the outside, although its dark, well actually pitch black, those aviation lights are everywhere, and the run ways lit up like a scene out of Star Trek. Christen grabs his light bag from the empty chair and makes his way over to the line forming in front of the agent preparing to scan the tickets. Two minutes have flown by just that fast, while observing the 9 others passengers standing in line of head of him, they all notice the 747 plane pulling up to the jet bridge and it parks.

By this time he almost hear footsteps coming up the ramp but it seems premature for that, or he's so anxious to get on this plane and get back to Pillisworth, while some people are nervous about flying he actually enjoys it. The feel of those turbine engines firing up and that sudden jolt forward when the plane picks up speed and ascends hundreds and hundreds of feet into the sky within mere seconds, and the ground completely disappears from sight. Time keeps ticking away while they wait patiently until one person comes walking out followed by more people, two a time, three at a time, four to five at time until finally after several minutes the front, middle, end of the plane passengers have left.

Now the agent signals for everyone to step forward and have the tickets out. This line's starting to move relatively fast he thinking to himself, the first six have already been scanned, and rushing toward the plane, now the next three, and his ticket and passport are scanned and reviewed, his given the green light and follows the others through the jet bridge and turns the corner to his left theirs a Mulatto or biracial flight attendant standing at the door greeting everyone before they take the assigned seats. Christen is greeted at the door and to his right it's two long isles, to the windows are one row of three seats, the middle are two seats, and the far side three seats. Christens ticket has him seating almost near the rear of the plane cabin but he's closer to the middle. His seat 11A at the isle and how convenient for him, it must be the law of averages in his case where as he's always seated near the isle.

He continues moving down until he finds his seat and takes it making himself comfortable while his fellow passengers continue coming aboard and finding their seat. 11:46pm the last passengers arrive and it's a couple taking their seat near the front very close to a screen in the middle wall of the cabin facing both isles. The flight attendant slammed the door shut and prepares to give everyone instructions on flight safety while pilot starts speaking over the planes intercom system.

"Ladies and gentleman, I'm your pilot Capt. Hamed Iziz for this evenings flight to Pillisworth, South Africa, our flight will be 11 hours and 10m so our official eta will be 12 hours' time." He says over the intercom

Now everyone gets the pre-flight safety demonstration from the flight attendants before takeoff.

"I will direct your attention to the attendants in the isle, international aviation rules specify that our flight attendants inform you the oxygen masks in the above compartments, also in the event the cabin depressurizes, keep your head down close to your legs while wearing the masks." He continues.

"Welcome aboard and thank you for flying Virgin Airlines our flight will begin shortly." He ends his speak.

Now he can hear the plane engines begin turning over and that incredible humming sound coming from the planes turbines. He straps on his seat belt and pulls a Virgin flight tourist magazine from back seat pouch, and begins flipping pages front to back. Analyzing the different advertisements, and paid commercial venders in this fancy, swanky magazine published by Sir Richards Branson's brand or label Virgin

Enterprises. Before he reaches the last page and actually reads through the commercial articles with the pricey trips and upscale restaurants.

At the very moment he flips the lid up half way covering the window to reveal the outside terminal, now the planes starts moving in reverse but the engine sounds very quite. The plane pulls away from the Jet Bridge, continuing to move in reverse until it 20 to 30 feet from terminal and makes a right turn toward the runway. The plane now faces the runway lights, sets still a few seconds then begins moving forward, this time five to ten miles and gradually begins picking up speed.

Now ten miles an hour becomes thirty five to forty miles an hour and finally the plane goes into full throttle and there's no more lights when it begins its ascent into the night sky. From a height of 1000 feet Athens, Greece, International looks like a futuristic space port from the sky. Christen closes the magazine and places it back in the seat pouch while adjusting his seat back few degrees, rests his head back, closes his eyes and enjoys the flight. This a could be the perfect opportunity for him to fall into a deep sleep and let his body relax, but he can't, his inner self won't allow him to forget the ordeal he's just experienced the last few hours, and he maybe still have the truth serum in his system.

It's amazing, absolutely amazing he's still functioning and seemingly healthy for a man who was shot up with large doses of Sodium Pentothal and hasn't completely lost his mind. Also for the record he's heard stories in the intelligence community of field agents who've used this as a means of extracting information from people or would be terrorists, but the bad guys used it too. They have their own intelligence apparatus/counter intel or criminal networks they deal with, so for Christen having been many places and seen a lot of strange things as a field agent, sometimes you hear these stories or rumors and think of them as merely urban legend. The fact remains though or at least from what he's heard over a period of time the side effects of Truth Serum results in brain damage, after the brain is relaxed from the chemical it attacks the neurons destroying them on contact like a cancer spreading across both Left and Right lobes until it hits the central nervous system.

When this happens an individual loses his or her auditory skills, causing reduction in one's attention span like Attention Deficit disorder but he seems to be functioning and well intact? At least once he returns to headquarters and get evaluated from being in the field, gets his blood work done, blood pressure taken, and a some other field related tests then they determine whether he suitable for field work again. He opens his eyes and looks down at his watch which has the time 3:45 am he peers down the isles back and front, but sees no one until a flight attendant steps out from the cabin kitchen curtain and spots him waving his hand. Before he realizes he can actually hit a button and get these people's attention, she comes out from behind the curtain, the Mulatto or biracial attendant with short red hair go figure? She moves quickly to the mid plane cabin and cuts across till she just 5 rows from Christen, and they are almost face to face.

"May I be of service Sir, and thanks for flying Virgin Airlines." She asks with a customer service smile.

"Yes well, if I may ask? Do you serve spirits on this flight, well alcohol?" he inquires with a smile of his own.

"Yes, yes, we have gin, vodka, brandy, whiskey, and beer. which would you like sir?" she asks him again.

"Ok, would you happen to have any Schnapps stocked back there? I have a taste for Schnapps Mint Cinnamon on the rocks." He continues to ask her.

"Well I can check but I'm sure all we have is Gin, Vodka, Brandy, and Whiskey." She replies again firmly.

"I'll return shortly if I find any of that in stock thank you." She says again before leaving.

"And thank you madam, I very much look forward to that." Christen says watching her turn and walk away.

He's thinking to himself omg, omg, that beautiful round ass, those delicious feet and toes, he sighs and cracks a smile shaking his head thinking again some women are created absolutely flawless and then some just lack any sex appeal at all. And he managed to get her name from the tag she's wearing on her shirt, Maggie, isn't that something? Christen looks out the near window to his left and sees nothing but a dark sky and some stars in the horizon with a crescent moon glimmering at the earth. He keeps his glance indirectly at the kitchen and it seems as though she has found 5, 4 ounce bottles of Peppermint Schnapps, now she looking for some cinnamon to sprinkle in the bottom of the glass.

She flipping through tiny cabinets in the kitchen finds glasses in the shape of 3 * 4 inches with napkins packed inside of each stacked in fives on top in rows of three, 15 glasses in all. With that she takes out a 32 oz stainless steel cocktail shaker placing everything on the counter and removes the top of the lid from the shaker. Now she takes a spoon and applies several drops of cinnamon inside the middle pocket till it's a tiny pile and drops it in the bottom of the shaker, with three cubes of ice, and now here comes the Peppermint Schnapps, she unscrews the cap off one bottle and hears this crack sound, begins emptying the beverage into the shaker, then repeats this again with the other 4 bottles till it's near the top, applies the lid and shakes it for a full 2 minutes until the cinnamon and peppermint Schnapps have bonded together and cold from the ice. She now removes the lid and pours the mix into the glass till its half full, grabs the napkin from the counter, wraps it around the full glass handling it with much care while she leaves the kitchen and moves back down the isle toward Christen.

He looks up at the flight attendant coming to his seat carefully holding the glass until she's at his seat and hands it to him with a surprised smile on her face.

"You're in luck I found several bottles and that cinnamon you requested now enjoy your beverage." She says.

"Thank you very much." He tells her taking a sip while she walks away.

He's been longing for the taste for days now and it seems most joy able to him when he's on a long distant flight. Schnapps Mint Cinnamon a drink he was introduced too while visiting an old friend in Hamburg, Germany. They went to a pub in Hamburg Neustadt at 3am in the morning, and the place was surprisingly kind of crowded at 3am, like these people don't sleep? He thought to himself taking small gulps of the beverage while staring out the window. The man's name was Danny Cicero, yes very weird a field operative with Interpol working undercover in the Excalibur origination. Cicero's preferred drink was Schnapps Mint Cinnamon stirred and not shaken, a differing reference to James Bond 007, which Christen though was very comical poke at Mi6 favorite spy. While at the bar he ordered two from the bartender, one for himself and another for Christen, and before taking a drink they both touched glass saying cheers mate.

The alcohol was very strong for his palette but he drink it down every last drop of it, and Cicero ordered more rounds and this time two shots of German Whiskey, Hohlor, Whessky, Bourbon Style. Not being a heavy drinker Christen almost relented but thought to himself what the hell? Why not. They both lifted the shot glasses first, bottoms up, one full gulp, slammed them down then took sips of the Mint Cinnamon Schnapps, now Christen had reached his limit and lucky for him neither of them was driving back to the hotel. The more he thought of that he closed his eyes and cracked a smile, taking his last full gulp of the drink and placing the glass in a holder next to him between seats. He checked his watch and the time was almost 5 am in the morning, another 9 hours to go but the alcohol starts kicking in when he closes his eyes one last time and drifts into a deep sleep.

He's totally unaware of it but every time his on a flight and consumes a glass, minutes later he starts snoring and its publically embarrassing and no one says anything to him, or maybe they don't want to disrupt his rest time, for some people waking up a person when their snoring or sleeping too loud, can be seen as very disrespectful. In his subconscious he can feel someone or something tugging or pulling at his hand or maybe tapping his shoulder but his bodies so relaxed, he drifts into this dream state of extreme torture again where he's lying face down on bed in some strange room with his hands tied to the bed frame and he's nude top and bottom.

However he isn't gagged or anything in his mouth but their a tiny mirror on the bed frame facing him, and he notices a small group of people standing around the bed, all wearing strange masks to disguise to they're faces. Ok, ok he's thinking to himself I'm about to become the victim of some sick sado masochism. And his mind starts racing again, how in the hell did he find himself in this scenario and why? He struggles to move or free himself from the bonds when finally a trio women enters the wearing different color leather customs and carrying various whips with blades on the endings.

One climbs on the bed pulling out a Patton and strikes him in the lower back hard, watching him reel in pain, crying out. She steps off and another dominatrix climbs on the bed this time with a rather long aluminum dildo in her hand, measuring some 7 to 12 inches, and he sees this through the tiny mirror and starts thinking oh my god, oh my god, no, no, no, don't you dare try to stick that up my ass. But it's coming when she spreads his butt cheeks starts to ramming it hard, he gives off this howl like a wounded animal in excoriating pain.

But it's doesn't stop there, no, no, she rams it in again, twisting and twisting, and twisting and gives off a scream of her own like yes I've the supreme conquer look at me. And she finally claims off the bed for the last one to start, and this one has those whips with the blades on the end very similar to the ones that Roman soldiers used to torture Jesus Christ. She stands up on the bed this time right and takes a wild swing for a few seconds then bring it down cross his back.

The blades make contact with his flesh and cause slight Lacerations, but then she really gets into it, bringing it down Hard, ripping into his flesh like she filleting a fish. Christen can't hold back the sudden pain of his back from the blades but he keeps thinking and asking himself is this real? This can't be happening to me right now? Or maybe just maybe the side effects of that truth serum is finally wearing off? Sweat pours from his body like someone poked holes from a water filled balloon, and he's breathing heavy from the pain of those blades but it's not real? His ass is on fire from the dildo and his back is bloody mess but he keeps wondering is this a dream? I'm I imagining all this, but he feels someone tapping him on the shoulder again and it's the mulatto airline attendant and this time she manages to get his attention.

"Is there a problem?" he asks her.

"No, you're just snoring really loud and its effecting the other passengers in this cabin so I've brought you some magazines to read or look through while we're still in flight." She tells him placing the magazines on his lap.

"My apologies for that, I guess it the side effects of that Schnapps Mint Cinnamon?" he replies again.

"Ok well maybe you might consider a new drink or cocktail instead of this? Just a suggestion not an order." She says. And he nods his head in agreement.

"Of course, everything in moderation. Thanks for the magazines." He tells her before she walks away. He looks through them and its Home and Garden, Esquire Magazine, Time, and last but not least Men's Fitness Magazine, now he finds this particularly funny. The body building magazine for men and women but mostly men, he looks through the pages from the back to the left, then front to back and it's all very familiar to him from celebs, to pro athletes from Europe and the United States.

Advertisements for supplements, vitamins, some of which he's bought before through underground herbal markets in Pillisworth. And pictures or photos of a list actors and some singers working out or performing they're favorite work out techniques. Side curl reps, lateral presses, upside down pushups which are very hard unless one has strong upper body strength. He looks at his watch and the time is 10 mins after 7 am in the morning, that dark dream he had was so real during those few hours he actually thought he was getting sexually violated. He lifts up the window slot just half way and the view is beautiful, the plane cruising at 45,000+ feet above the clouds, as far he knows they are flying Cairo, Egypt, either way sometime between 2pm and 3pm in the afternoon this plane will land at Pillisworth International Airport just 15 miles from Cape Town, South Africa. He closes The Man's Fitness magazine and places it at the bottom of the pile, then picks up Home and Garden, yes Home and Garden. Opens up to the first page and finds pictures of cookies and pastries, and list of deserts for this 92 year edition.

He doesn't really read every article in the magazine only scans through the first 12 pages till he spots an peculiar advertisement for cannabis oil? Cannabis oil, advertised in Home and Garden? Could this be a typo or some sort of mistake by the magazine vendors? He seriously doubts that and in any case money talks, these magazines make the bulk of their money or profit from advertising vendors. The company that bought the ad sells 15 different blends of Cannabis oil and their located in Vancouver, British Columbia, wow what a coincidence but Christen doesn't think so at all. Vancouver, BC is located in the Western part of Canada above Washington State and very liberal with their drug laws unlike the US.

The following pages dealt with various gardening designs from around the world, China, Japan, Russia, South America, North America, Eastern and Western Europe, the United Kingdom, Scotland, Ireland, New Zealand, Mexico, and Australia just to name a few. Many of these designs were some of the most creative and the most bizarre he ever seen published in Home and Garden, like they're was some global competition to see who could come up with the weirdest design?

Now his boredom started to set in from reading these damn magazines won't keep him at all preoccupied the next couple for hours, so he reflects on his brief meeting with Euro Asian cryptographer and SIA intelligence analyst Pavel Sing. He and Christen were to develop a new counter terrorists program for South African Intelligence before Christen went off to Ankara, Turkey and Pavel left Pillisworth for Beijing, China and they've lost contact with each other for weeks afterward.

The counter terrorists software would rival that of CIA, Mi6, Israeli Intelligence, People Republics of China, Interpol and practically every other intelligence agency on this planet. The little known fact was Pavel Sing was a wizard at cracking passwords, and hacking into the most secured computer networks which is how he wound up on radar of South Africa Intelligence in the first place. Rumor has it, Pavel was 19 credits shy of getting his undergraduate degree from the University of Hamburg in Germany before South African Secret Service the former name of South African Intelligence, recruited him, after he hacked into the Cape Town, South African defense department using nothing but a Optima Lap top with 985 MHz and a flobby disk, just years before the flash drive was created. They give him his own office and soon he was managing his own intel division, until he was assign to some jobs in South East Asia, Japan, Taiwan, and South Korea.

He returned to headquarters 3 months ago for debriefing on his field work and hacking operations before he was sent to Beijing for an informal investigation of industrial espionage. Christen looks up the screen in the middle of the cabin broadcasting the latest weather patterns on the continent of Africa from Cairo, Egypt going down into Cape Town, South Africa. Now he hears a beep sound coming from the planes intercom system and it's the Capt. Speaking.

"Ladies and gentlemen we are approaching Pillisworth, International Airport earlier than expected, judging our current fight path the eta will be less than 15 mins." He announces and hangs up the phone mic.

Christen already anticipates a luck warm reception when he enters headquarters has to face a battery of questions, than the ever adorable and quirky Nickel Currency, peppering him with all sorts question about the wedding cake, the reception, the guests, was there a band, what kind of Champaign was served? What type of food was served with the

Champaign? But one of the most important questions of all, did I enjoy myself while I was visiting? And he'll wonder were those same questions asked of Tarken when I returned or because our situation is slightly different, he gets an immediate pass while Christen is grilled on general principle but it's the price one pays for being the go to guy or field agent for a regional government intelligence agency and super power.

He carefully places the magazines one by one inside the back chair Pouch or pocket and uses the other pocket for the remaining magazines. His watch reads 1:35pm South African Standard Time(SAST),but the clock on the screen in the middle cabin has several time zones shown simultaneously. He can feel and hear the wing flaps on both sides adjusting according to wind speed pattern, and the pilots preparing to land the plane. Christen lifts up the window slot ¾ to get a view of the outside and the plane descending to Pillisworth, International Airport. from his point of view.

Amazing, absolutely amazing one minute they were at a cruise altitude of 43,000 feet and the next just above 2500 in under 20 minutes. The plane begins descending even faster while now he can almost see the run way from the side of his window but it's the shared runways of other airplanes docked at the terminal. Seconds go by and then theirs a thump sound of the wheels making contact with the ground runway, and the Capt. Iziz makes his final announcement.

"Ladies and Gentlemen we have arrived at Pillisworth, International Airport ahead of schedule and will be docking any moment now, I ask that you remain seated until we come to a complete stop, I hope you enjoyed your flight and thank you for flying Virgin Airlines." He finishes his announcement. Upon hearing his Christen observes his follow passengers making preparations to leave, some grabbing jackets from the top compartments above their seats. The front and middle row passengers all start moving in a frenzy as quick as they can before the plane pulls up to the passenger boarding bridge at Virgin Terminal. The plane moves closer and closer to the passenger boarding bridge until it's perfectly aligned, then comes to a complete stop, while now the passengers are ready to finally leave.

The Mulatto flight attendant prepares first door in the front cabin for release, while the passengers form a line at both rows very eager to leave this jet. Christen doesn't even bother raising up from his seat, no he just relaxes knowing once that door opens there will be a mad dash for it. With the boarding bridge finally aligned the flight attendant opens the door signaling to the passengers it's time to depart from the plane, Christen from his view watches the first row file out the door, followed by the middle row of passengers and he's almost the last one until he quickly raises up, grabs his jacket and bag from the above compartment and follows the line out. While he's walking he slips the jacket on and gives the attendants a wave good bye as he walks through the door and down the path into the Pillisworth terminal lobby.

Right away he starts looking for a public phone so he can call a taxi for a ride back to his apartment, unpack his things, and get a few hours rest before he returns to HQ for his meeting and debrief with the Director of Intelligence Manning, Minister of Defense Crowder Forkhold, and the Chief of Staff Yusaf Tarken. Tarken might express absolute shock seeing Christen alive and well but he'll deal with that scenario when it happens, he thinks to him with a grin of slight self-confidence. Christen finds digital monitor facing him in the middle of terminal seating area with a map of the airport showing where almost everything's located including phone booths.

The monitor shows Pillisworth International Airport terminal in 3D with 2 stories or two levels and a legend of the side detailing the different terminals, shops, and restaurants, restrooms in various colors or dots. The airplane Christen arrived in Virgin Atlantic parked at Pillisworth International Airports Northwest terminal, whereas the Airport terminal has four main terminals, North, South, East and West. The Northwest Terminal has Virgin Airlines and or Virgin Atlantic Airlines which means it was built to accommodate both if need be. On the monitor the bag claim area is located down stairs or on the lower level where there are several phone booths within walking distance of each other. He spots an escalator to the lower level just 11 feet from where he's standing, and moves quickly in that direction, planning and plotting again his next move before he leaves the airport and makes it back to his apartment in Midtown Pillisworth, South Africa.

He reaches the base of the escalator deciding go to baggage claim first then call a taxi, and not the other way around. Looking straight ahead he notices three different baggage claims on his left one after the other and on his right smoke shops, restaurants, a few wine and beer bars, and two shoe stores all this on the lower level of an airport terminal. Now his thinking how in the hell did I miss this before or the last time he was there he didn't stick around to notice anything, he was too preoccupied at the task at hand, so observing his surrounding didn't mean very much to him. Now after passing the first baggage claim, he finally approaches Virgin Atlantic and he's joined by 18 other people standing around the revolving carousel, waiting for the bags and luggage to come out from behind the plastic doors.

He check his watch, which reads 2:46pm South Africa time and yes 45mins flow by just that fast, now the carousel starts moving slow then after a few minutes its picks up speed, now a stream of different luggage comes flowing out, followed by more bags while he doesn't see his, the follow passengers around him form a circle around the carousel as more luggage comes streaming out, now they start the grabbing process. 6 people out of 18 have their luggage with a few more showing up and finding their places for that specific grab. Christen spots something very familiar coming out resembling his luggage while he stands behind a couple waiting for theirs to come around. He moves pass them while spotting his from 6 feet away, and positions himself at the just the right time when he finds an empty spot where no one standing.

Perfect, perfect the timing and opportunity has come, when the couple snatches their luggage from the pile, he sees his and makes his move like a cobra snake on the hunt. He kneels down to extend his hands and makes the grab for both, the snatch is successful, now he can call that taxi and finally get home. He walks away very pleased with himself carrying one bag over his shoulder while he has the other case luggage handle by hand with wheels in tow. Straight ahead he sees the numerous doors leading out to the lobby curb and parking lot but there are few phone booths on both sides positioned outside the ships and baggage claim areas.

The first phone booth he spots he makes that call to operator who directs or connects him with a commercial cab service that's makes runs to this terminal very often during the week.

"Good afternoon, Operator, can you connect me with Pillisworth car service please?" he tells the dispatcher.

"No problem, that will be a charge of 2.50, are we using visa or Master card today sir?" she asks him while he reaches into his wallet his government ID.

"I'm an employee with South African Intelligence and here's my ID # 7869-2386-fin*." He almost orders over the phone.

"Ok, just one moment sir while I run this through our database files." She replies typing in the numbers and letters from his SAI ID card.

"Ok, sir your credentials appear valid and I will connect you with Pillisworth car service dispatch stand by." She says punching some buttons and the call is redirected to the taxi service.

"Pillisworth Car service, how may we help you this Afternoon?" dispatch says over the phone.

"I need a taxi for pick up at Pillisworth International Airport asap!? How soon can you get here?" he asks again

"Give me about 10 minutes to notify a driver in your area and he or she will be there very soon." Dispatch says.

"Outstanding, I'll be waiting outside at the curb wearing blue and beige, thank you." Christen replies again.

"No problem, eta 10 minutes or less sir good bye." Says dispatch before hanging up the phone.

So now he finds himself waiting again, oh the inconvenience of waiting for a taxi, when his car that silver two door BMW sets in a garage underneath his apartment, with a full tank of gas, just waiting for its owner to get back behind the wheel and blow it out again on the open road. 6 minutes have already gone by and still no taxi in sight, maybe the cabs caught up in traffic or god forbid he had an accident in traffic via the airport. No, no, no, Christen think positive, think positive, think positive, 5 minutes, 47 seconds and counting. A few taxis pull up to the curb but not the one he called for while he watches car after car picking up passengers one after the other until finally when he least expects a taxi parks directly in front of him and pops the trunk open.

Christen quickly dumps his bag and luggage in the trunk and slams it shut before entering the back passenger seat from the right door, and the taxi pulls off.

"Where too sir, and let's be clear I charge by the minute." The driver says punching a button on his fare clock.

"Not a problem and we're going to Midtown Pillisworth, Botha District, I have an apartment flat there, I plan to unpack my things, lay down in my bed and sleep for a week." Christen tells the driver while they leaving the parking lot area of the airport.

"Well I know where that part of town is so relax and enjoy the ride, and I'll have you home in under 25 minutes." The taxi driver says

Now this man has Christens attention while he seats back and enjoys the scenery from the outside of the airport parking lot to the driver merging unto Crestier expressway going into midtown Pillisworth. There are three different routes converging into the Botha District but the shortest one, the one all the taxi seem to like taking was Masekela pkwy North named after legendary South African trumpeter Hugh Ramopolo Masekela. The street slices through a five mile block of former hostile gang territory once controlled the Pan-African syndicate, now it's filled with private schools, an upscale Sam's club connected WallMart shopping center. Yes, Wall Mart saw an opportunity to snatch up 6 acres of land and offered the local people here deal they couldn't refuse. Masekela Pkwy North runs directly into the Botha District and Cramdone Place, where Christens apartment located among the Vorster Condos in the same area.

The taxi approaches Cramdone Place and looks to Christen in his rear view mirror about which way to turn left or right? But Christen signals to the arrows pointing right so Cramdone Place, it's a one way street going east and not west. The taxi makes his right turn and at Christens direction after driving past 5 buildings stops in front of a red brick two story apartment with what looks like three chimneys on the roof. And his two car garage underneath where his early 90's silver two door BMW waits to be driven again.

"This is where I get out, thanks." Christen says while the driver pops open the trunk again.

"You owe me $75 rand." the driver says.

Christen exits the car to grab his bag and luggage out the Trunk, he reaches in with both hands and snatches both out simultaneously placing the luggage on the ground while closing the trunk afterward. He moves to the driver's window and pulls out $100 euro bill.

"How's this instead, it has to be worth more than South African rand?" Christen says placing it in the drivers right hand.

"Yes, yes I can always go to my bank and convert this for more money thank you." The driver says before he's about to pull off.

"Thanks and drive safe." Christen tells the driver tapping the hood and he pulls off down the street.

Now he grabs the luggage handle rushes to his front door to punch in the access key code for entry. Yes not all field agents have to use an actual key to enter their homes, he pushes the door open to the inner hallway of his apartment and midsized living room, with all the amenities of most apartments. A screen TV facing a rust colored couch and matching colored sofas with a table in the middle. His kitchen to the left with a door leading to his private back yard and another door inside the kitchen going straight to his multi car garage. On right side of the apartment his bedroom adjacent to full bathroom with fancy designed shower and midsize walk in closet.

He checks his cordless phone seating on the table for any messages and only finds 7 mostly from Switzerland and two from Head Quarters now he places the cordless back on the stand by charger and drops both the bag and his luggage in the couch and takes off the borrowed beige jacket, then slips off his shoulder holster with pistol and silencer intact, tossing both this time on the left sofa seat. Now its straight bee line for the bedroom, takes off his wallet and places it on a miniature drawer to the right side of his bed, where his car keys are, he now kicks off his slip on shoes and jumps on the king size bed, his body makes contact with the mattress while he feels like he's about to sink into a pool of quick sand, his body lays flat with arms and legs spread apart.

Christens body rocks up and down or back and forth until he finds himself staring up at his ceiling and his eyes slowly close shut. It's now after 3pm South African time and another call comes in, and this one is Manning the Director of SAI leaving a very short message under minute.

"Christen, this is Director Manning, I will assume your heading back on Pillisworth, and in case you aren't aware of certain developments in Crete and Athens we'll discuss those when you return, god speed." The message says then goes off.

And he doesn't even hear it, just tunes out all noises and sounds, everything inside the apartment except for the outside. The sounds of bird chirping, winds blowing, and every so many minutes cars driving by from others blocks away, his mind still very much aware of what's around him, but his body finally enjoys the rest it's been screaming and pleading for but it seemed like he was ignoring it. After all duty calls even in the face of fatigue and exhaustion from on the job stress, and extreme multitasking. That deep sleep begins taking over and he drifts this time into one of his insane, crazy dreams of supernatural sado-masochism like his sub-conscious mind can't escape this psychological torture. Or maybe, just maybe it's the final side effects of that damn truth serum wearing off and causing some temporary brain damage or sorts.

Either way, he figures after at least 6 to 8 hours of sound sleep, he'll shower, get dressed, fix himself some lunch or perhaps order it from a deli or restaurant close to Head Quarters in his uptown office. Until that time his body continues to recharge and he keeps trying to fight off this continual dream site as if it's a time loop or someone playing an irritating song over and over again. No, no, no it's more like a bad movie, or film you don't like watching but you click and turn the damn channel, and there it is broadcast on a different station, over and over again. And you start thinking to yourself why I'm I having this continual dream or I'm I really just psychologically fucked up? No, no, no that's not the answer Christen, no this is the result of the chemical effects wearing off and your brains attempt to fight through it by repeating it, over and over again, trying to make sense of it, but it makes no sense at all. It's just something that refuses to stop no matter how hard he tries to relax his mind, and reset or reboot, it starts over on the same damn thing, every second, of every minute, and so on, and so on! 3 hours have gone by and his rolling over on his left side now, switching positions in his bed, and still can't shake this nightmarish thing flowing around in his head. Now the left side position doesn't work for him and change to his right side, resting his head on his arms bicep, this position serves him well for another 4 and ½ hours until his bed clock says 10pm and he's somewhat well rested.

Now's time to unpack his bag and luggage and take a trip to Headquarters for some intelligence research of his own, he leaves his bedroom and makes a another quick dash back to the living room area for his luggage and bag containing his bloody clothes. Now he could have left this on that luxury yacht and yet he decides to carry it back with him, that's so there will be no trace of him for any investigators to find. It's likely the blaze wouldn't destroy everything and news will travel fast regarding the demise of this triad of Cerberus a group he never knew existed until getting that damn wedding invite from Tarken.

He grabs the luggage first carrying it back to the bedroom and begins to unzip and unpack, and it's very systematic with the pants going into his closet first on the right side of his room directly facing the bed, with just enough walk in space of about 6 feet in length and a width of 6 feet or at least 72 cubic inches in width. He hangs up the pants first one after the other, then grabs the shirts applying the same quick system with the pants and they're all separated from each other but keeps his boxer briefs on the bed with one pair of black slacks out with midnight blue suit, brown belt with a sky blue dress shirt and dark blue socks to match, including his stylish watch. The rest he leaves in the luggage case for the following morning, now it's time for a quick shower and he's back behind the seat of his new sleek, beautiful 2 door silver mid 90's BMW.

He undresses or takes everything off his body before entering the bathroom, turns on both shower dials to Luke warm and climbs in under the water streaming down over his naked body. He snatches a used bar of soap from a net bag hanging off his shower spout and begins applying the soap all over his top torso and mind section, then applies it between his legs, genitals and his behind. At this point his whole body is well lathered, from top to mid bottom with this sweet smelling soap courtesy of South African intelligence men's hygiene and beauty service, and yes they sell cologne and women's perfume too. He places his head under the shower stream and lets the Luke warm water rinse him clean. The soap goes back in the net and the shower dials are turn off while at the same time he uses his hand and fingers to clear the water from his eyes, and grabs a midsize towel from a rack above his toilet to dry off his body.

Afterward the towel goes back on the rack while he opens his mirror cabinet finding a full bottle of unused body spray, for which he applies rather liberally to his chest, under arms and neck. It goes back in the cabinet, now time for the bottle of cinnamon mint mouth wash, oh yeah! In the lower shelf it seats just there 17 ½ ounces, he grabs this bottle, unscrews the cap and take a swig but doesn't swallow. No, no, no he lets the liquid settle in a his mouth for up to 15 seconds before he gurgles it all around and lets it burn his taste buds just little before he spits it out. After that no need for another, his mouth and tongue are already hot from the chemical in the mouth wash, not the bottle goes back in the cabinet, and time to get dressed. Christen changes the bathroom light to a slightly darker shade but well light enough that he can still see very well.

Exiting the bathroom and back into his bedroom, he throws on his black boxer briefs first, then the muscle shirt and socks, followed by the pants slacks, shirt and belt slipped around his pants waist. He buttons up the shirt to his collar and wrist buttons tucked into his pants, then zipped and button up around his waist. The slip on shoes go on now followed by finally his suit but not until he puts back on his shoulder holster with that P227 Smith and Wesson pistol with hidden compartment for a 5 inch silencer intact. He grabs his wallet, car keys with remote lock attached, watch and suit before leaving the bedroom and into the kitchen where it still looks the same way it did before he left it almost 2 month ago before the incident in Anakara, Turkey. He reaches for the refrigerator handle and yanks it open but its almost bare with the exception a bottle of grape juice just under half full.

So now he checks the expiration date on it and it's only three weeks old no, no, grape juice for him. He takes the bottle unscrews it and pours the rest down the sink, capping the bottle for a toss in the nearby garbage can. It's a straight hit and it falls in the garbage completely like a perfect 2 or 3 point shot. He looks at his watch again and it's now 11:15 pm South African time, and he realizes he's still in his apartment now it hits him quick, fast and in a hurry to get over to headquarters. He closes the frig and makes a mad dash in the living room to The left sofa where his shoulder holster waits in the seat, he grabs it with both hands.

And doing this slides the holster over his shoulders with the gun and silencer intact, he checks the clip from the pistol which is full slides it back in the chamber till he a click sound and pulls back the slide, click, snap, the bullets in the chamber and ready. Now he finally puts on the suit jacket, grabs the bag with his bloody clothes getting it ready for his mini-incinerator located in his underground garage facing the 94 2 door Silver BMW. This time makes a bee line for the underground garage just across the hall from his kitchen, he never locks the door to the garage knowing no one will to break into his apartment? The only entry to the outside door is coded via key pad, or his employee pass whenever he decides to uses it and he keeps that either in his cars dash board compartment or in the desk drawer of his office at headquarters. Before he opens the door, his hits a garage light switch on the wall and the door takes him to 6 stairs leading down to the garage which isn't very large or small but holds enough space for a small office 20+ people.

The car is parked just 5 feet from the stairs with a few boxes stacked against the walls in both sides, and various cabinets, and selves on the side near the door leading to his kitchen but on the opposite side miniature office with a desk, pc screen, key pad and mouse, and the tower on the floor underneath. One both sides are reference tools, books, maps and munitions or guns for the very dedicated field agent who's always looking to upgrade his weaponry or tinker with it after its assigned from P-Department at HQ. Before he reaches the garage floor he hits a button on the remote, there's beep sound and the cars front and back lights flick on and off. Now its unlocked and unarmed, yes this silver beauty comes with some very interesting yet lethal surprises under its hood, the back trunk, and within the tire rims, all courtesy of P-Department.

He places the bag carrying his bloody clothes on the BMWs hood then opens the driver side door to throw his suit in the passenger seat. After closing the door its time inspect his incinerator before he burns the bloody garbs, now this machine stands about 5 feet 6 inches and weighs an excess of 500lbs or more and he didn't have to move into the garage after he ordered it. It has two dials and a power button, one for the heat and the other for the time also the 2inch thick glass doors have two features, they can open and close or slide open and slide close. The dial for the heat goes up to 1000 degrees Fahrenheit but he's never tried it that high before however this evening maybe different. The inside has a steel rack separating top and button with numerous holes, or vents in its button all connected to two controlled 6 feet hoses, one pumping natural gas or propane into an attached 3 foot, 14 inch round tank and other releasing its steam or heat outside a vent in the garage wall sort of like a chimney only coming out of a wall and not a roof.

He pushes the power button, it turns red and grabs the handle to slide the door open, then he grabs the bag and unzips it inside the machine, emptying its contents, shirts, pants, and socks all covered in blood, inside the incinerator and slides the door shut while turning knob a few degrees counter clock wise to lock it. Christen turns up the dial to 175 degrees

Fahrenheit while he watches the flames shoot out of the tiny vents, and the cloths catch fire and he turns the dial up some degrees more to 245, he also knows its programed or timed to shut off once the garments have been completely burned or turned to ashes. With the bag emptied now it's back to the car so he climbs into the driver's seat and tosses the bag behind him while he shuts the door and starts the engine or turns it over.

Directly above his rear view mirror is his trusty remote control for the garage door so before he puts the gear in reverse, his presses the button and the garage door immediately opens up and without missing a beat, he puts the gear in reverse while keeping the steering wheel straight and applies just a little pressure to the accelerator and the car jolts backwards but doesn't hit anything. It clears the garage opening then the side walk, the street curb, then Christen finally turns the steering wheel and the BMW makes a left reverse turn into the street and with no oncoming cars or traffic.

He puts the gear in drive, this time pulling off down Cramdon Place doing a speed of 0 to 45 mph in under 11 seconds for three straight blocks before coming to a stop sign. Until he merges into Masekela Pkwy South connecting him back to Crestier Freeway just several miles into the heart of Midtown Pillisworth. He hits the power button on his cars stereo which also has a direct link South African Intel's radio frequency and direct contact to the Directors home and his office headquarters. Christen pushes channel 1 and keeps it in until he sees Station 589 Am on the international frequency, then hits a automatic button for Morse code, this lets everyone know his mission or Operation whatever was completed successfully and his in route back to Headquarters. But he doesn't check any international news like CNN or BBC for what might be going on in western or eastern Europe, not even Greece or Turkey, for he suspects he'll have to report on everything the moment he's in a room with the Director of Intelligence, Winston Pinkheart of P- Department and the new Minister of Defense Crowder Forkhold, and The Chief of Staff Yusaf Tarken.

He lets this frequency broadcast for a few more minutes before he terminates it knowing other organizations lawful and criminal might decide to try and decode it, or even listen in. He sees a sign ahead that reads Crestier Freeway exit ¾ of a mile and famous street sign and symbol for SAI headquarters in South African colors Black, yellow, and green. He merges again toward Crestier from left lane to far right lane, and take a

360 degree loop around until he's on the Crestier Freeway now with only another 5 miles to go before he reaches Headquarters.

Now that he's off this station he switches to FM and finds some stations playing Jazz music which he finds very relaxing while he drives. While driving the legal speed limit of 80 mph he can see the headquarters of Daverqius Exports the covert name of South African Intelligence, while he keeps his car in the middle lane with very little traffic to deal with. The evening night sky presents a crescent moon with stars forming various shapes of the constellations if you can identify them earth, or sometimes they will tell which direction your traveling in provided you use a reliable compos. Christen begins hearing what sounds like a helicopter hovering hundreds of feet overhead, now he sees lights flickering on and off but the helicopter practically invisible from the ground.

Could this be the director meeting him from his private resident or perhaps the Minister of Defense and the Director of Intelligence traveling in the same copter. Christen sees his exit and quickly takes it now that he's within minutes from Headquarters now driving down Mandela pkwy and every two streets or blocks there's yellow and red lights unlike in those in North America. And those same streets named after a former member of the ANC with a mural or bust dedicated to that's person. There are 8 buildings on both sides of the street, each one standing or towering 24 floors or stories but coming up on his right, we have building 4 and finally his arrived at Headquarters.

He makes a right turn into the 4 level underground parking lot but stops first at the ticket booth, and a yellow and black striped arm comes down acting as an obstruction, he sticks out his left hand, hits a few buttons for his secret access entry code and the machine spits out a ticket out. He places it in on his dash board near his vehicle registration and the arm goes up and stays few seconds when the car jolts forward. He takes it to level 2 where he has a reserved parking spot in the middle of Nickel Currency and Winston Pinkheart. When he arrives on 2 level both spots are open including his but he suspect not for long when they discover he's back for another assignment and or mission. The underground parking levels at headquarters are designed with an elevator in the middle of four quadrants north/ south, east/west. Parking levels 1-4, he pulls the car inside his little space in north quadrant and parks it, then grabs his suit out the back seat but leaves the bag underneath. Before He shuts the driver side door he pops open the rear trunk for his business case/ bag, then closes the door shut. He plays with the remote again now the car is armed and locked, he makes his way to the elevator, hit the button with arrow marked down. He can hear the car descending to level 2 but also sees the elevator numbers above the sliding door going down.

As he now recalls headquarters covers all floors 1-7 and 8-11 on the east side offices and 2-13 on the west primarily for Research and development or design for P-Department. This can be anything from the development of new weapons technology, miniaturized explosives, to nanotech smart bombs, etc. the list is endless. The elevator door stops at parking level 2 and the doors slide open, so he walks in and hits the button for 5th floor which is where his office is located on the east side of the building opposite the Directors office. The car begins its ascent to parking lot 1 then floors 1, 2, 3, 4, and then 5, the door stops, slide opens and he steps out, walking to his left down the hall to room 508 his office near the far side. After walking pass rooms 501 to 507 he pulls out his wallet and rubs it on this security pad for entry and hear his loud click sound. He twisted knobs and the glass door is opened. His office is set up very similar to his living room, theirs a table in the middle but this time only one couch with his desk and PC, tower, with mouse and key board.

From wall to wall he has about 7 and ½ feet of space, with the ceiling at 9 feet in height, so it can fit up to 14 people if need be but he enjoys his privacy. His office has two walk on rugs, one just several feet from the door, and another directly under his office desk and chair. His private restroom seats behind a door parallel his office couch, while the walls of his office have a distinct sky blue color and there are various pictures of him in different locals around the world of missions he's been on. Some photos of him with certain foreign field agents of various global agencies in the fight against terrorists or enemies of the state.

Sitting directly across from his desk is a small wet bar, yes he has his own wet but he doesn't always keep it fully stocked with beer on alcohol, that would be against company policy which he's been known to break from time to time. Christen grabs a glass out of his wet bar cabinet and some cubes of ice, dropping them in while he looks for 1/2 bottle of Grey Goose vodka and finds it twisting off the cap and pouring it in till it's 1/3 full, not even half a glass. He takes it over to his desk and hits the power button on his pc tower while he takes a sip laying it just inches from the key board. The monitor goes from a black screen to a light screen showing Windows 96 and then South African Intelligence screen asking for the User ID and password. He types in the user name which is Christen-J, and the password being SAI-CJ, while he hears footsteps from down the hall getting closer and closer to his office. The system continues to boot up and finally South African Intelligence screen comes into full view, with various links to all departments in Headquarters including information on confirmed kills or deceased targets.

He looks up at the door seeing a man about to knock and he seemly ignores him, but he wants to see whether this person will identify himself first, before he's invited in. bom, boom, boom, goes the knock on the door then comes the intro of "James it's Pinkheart! When did you get back?" he asks him very surprised of not shocked.

"Oh come in Winston, the doors not locked, I'm just checking my unread directive for the last couple of weeks, and catching up on some intel of my own." He says while working the keys on the board with his fingers.

"I arrived at Pillisworth Airport this afternoon and decided to get some rest first before I returned to Headquarters tonight." Christen replies.

"Your all over the news Christen, that explosion on the Island of Crete made the international press, and people are talking about a cargo of 3 ½ tons of opium destroyed, part of a joint Euro-Grecian-Russian-Asian multibillion operation or pipeline disrupted." He says with some files in hand. He places the file on Christen desk and takes a seat noticing or picking up the scent of vodka from Christens glass.

"You mind if I have a glass of that?" he asks licking his lips at the idea of getting a sip.

"Grey Goose? Sure not a problem, I'll get you a glass and then go over this file." He says to him raising from his seat.

He moves over to the mini wet bar again grabbing a tiny glass from the cabinet and pours some vodka in it just enough for a few sips, while at the same time slipping the bottle back in the cabinet with the cap still off. He places it on the desk in front of Winston and seats back down to go over the file with a black ribbon placed around it marked Top Secret (Operation Cerberus).

"Director Manning plans a debriefing with you either after midnight or he'll wait until tomorrow morning with everyone present except Nickel Currency." Winston says before he takes a sip and savors the taste of this Vodka.

"Any new developments from P-Department Winston? You were experimenting on some new weaponry before I left, anything fun and exciting I should know about a head of time?" he asks while him reading his unread online directives.

"Everything's in the file Christen, every things in the file, and when your done reviewing it, you know where to return it?" Winston asks finishing off the last drop of vodka.

"Of course Winston, and leave the door unlocked your way out thanks." He tells him while he multi tasks reading the file and going over his emails.

Christen finishes off his Grey Goose vodka and continues reading one last email before opening this file marked top secret. Interesting he wasn't privy to this information about the triad of Cerberus before in fact he was given very limited intelligence on this group at the beginning, hours and days before that clandestine meeting in Ankara, Turkey went completely to shit. Now after almost a week plus and still recovering from that dreaded Sodium Pentothal he gets this thrown at him. Or maybe he wasn't meant to know about this operation, it could be that all this was a test of his resolve and he passed or it was just about will he survive this or not?

All those questions will be answered once he's in a room with Director Manning, The new Minister of Defense, and the Chief of Staff. He continues looking through the files, studying the photos, intelligence clippings, and there's 2 USB flash drives marked in colors green and black. Perhaps audio surveillance files, or actually incriminating video footage from the intelligence community. Christen looks at the clock on his screen and it reads 12:51am South African time, he decides to close up the files on his desk, and relax on his office couch, hell take a nap and sleep off that Grey Goose Vodka at least for the next couple of hours until he's called in for his debriefing in the Directors office which could be sometime between 6 and 7am in the morning. He closes his eyes and his subconscious mind drifts back to the moment he squares off against 'Big Crunchy' Vladimir Bulnor on the Island of Crete. This guy had a reputation for being one of the most feared and brutal underground MMA fighters in Moscow or maybe even Ukraine and Christen took it to him.

Considering he could've gotten his head taken off and the rest of his body mauled, even mangled and he never backed down, even in the face of sudden defeat. But the breaking point for him was just before that incident happened when he gets the escort to that warehouse near port of Pireaus, in downtown Athens at Vouliagmeni, at the bogus request of Gorgon to trouble shot a pc for him and with his attention elsewhere, one of those Ukrainian thugs almost broke his neck with a sleeper hold. But he was doing so under orders or instructions by the late Master mind Gorgon Mathias. He feels a slight breeze in his office and voices in the back ground, but now this annoying poking sensation in his ribs and right shoulder blade.

Yes, it's Tarken trying to wake him up from a deep sleep and Director Manning in the back ground with a smile of amusement on his face while this is happening.

"Christen, James Christen, wake up James, wake up, wake up, wake up, wake up!" he keeps repeating this until Christen finally turns over on the couch and opens his eyes.

"There you are, he's awake and conscious Director." Says Tarken cracking a smile and folding his arms across his chest and this time he seats on the couch facing Christen directly.

"What time is it?" he asks? Wiping crusts from his eyes while he seats up straight, gathering himself.

"7am Christen, and you were snoring, very loud. We could hear you from down the hall, luckily for you the rest of the employees on this floor don't clock in till 9:30." Tarken replies again.

"7am? My god, I just laid down fifteen minutes before midnight and it's already 7am in the morning?" he asks just realizing how tired his body was or that Grey Goose Vodka acts like a sedative for him the 8 % alcohol knocked him out cold.

"Agent Christen are you're sure, you're ready for the briefing or do you need time to sober up?" The Director asks moving toward the office door.

"No, no, no, no I'm ready gentlemen, let's do this, just give me another 5 minutes to throw some water on my face and a tie around my neck. I'll join you both in your office Director shortly thanks." He says but before he rushes into his restroom while they exit his office, he grabs a black silk tie from his suite jacket pocket applying it to his shirt collar neck.

His bathroom doors already slight opened, but he pushes it wide open, hits the light switch on and twists the knobs on his sink hot, and cold to Luke warm, then colder letting the water stream out at least few seconds before he places both hands under it. His hands form a bowl filled with water and he applies it to his face a few times. To his eyes, nose and lips, over and over and over again until he finally feels refreshed and ready for those questions. While he stands in front of the mirror to begin his Winsor knot, he pulls the wide end on the right side and extends about 12 inches below the narrow end. He crosses the wide part of the tie over the narrow part. He pulls the wide end up through the opening at the neck, then down, Passing the wide end underneath and to the right of the narrow part with the wrong side facing out.

Cross the wide part over and to the left of the narrow part with the correct side facing out. Pull the wide end up through the opening at the neck now when bringing it down, he passes it through the loop at the front. Holding the dangling parts with one hand, Christen slides the knot carefully up toward the collar with the other hand until snug, then lower the collar quickly, it's done he's ready for the briefing now. Before he leaves the bathroom he switches the light off, grabs his suite jacket from the couch and the file from the desk he reviewed just hours ago.

He doesn't even dry his face while he leaves the office but figures the air will do it before he reaches Director Manning's quarters. He passes several offices before he reaches the elevators in the middle hall, hits the arrow pointing down while the elevator mark reads 7 letting him know they're already at the Directors office. He hears the car descending to his floor and the doors slide open once it level, he steps in to hit the 7 button, watches the door slide close. The car ascends quickly 2 floors up, stops and the door slide open again, he steps out with file in hand facing double doors marked Directors office. He knocks twice then opens one door and finds all three men in The room with Director Manning seated at his desk flanked by Tarken seated in on his right and the Minister of Defense to his left staring out the window while having a conversation on the directors cordless office phone.

"Agent Christen, welcome have you met the new Minister of Defense Crowder Folkhold?" he asks while Christen steps in front of his desk and takes a seat.

Christen raises again to give this man a formal hand shake before he seats back down.

"No I don't believe I've had the pleasure, Minister Folkhold sir good morning." He says before taking his seat again.

"Director Manning was filling me in on the details of your latest assignment Operation Cerberus. I presume it was a success and I understand you were invited to a wedding in Athens, Greece? The grooms father an old college classmate of The Chief of Staff? The plot thickens?" the minister asks him.

"Agent Christen aren't you curious as to why you weren't ordered back to headquarters while you were in Switzerland?" Manning asks him.

"The thought had occurred to me, I suppose you had your reasons sir?" christen replies.

"Yes, we identified the mystery man in that photo you sent via courier the moment your touched down in Athens, Greece. I was explaining to Minister Forkhold the ingenious of our photo-scanagraph. Minister we are connect to every intelligence agency in the world, Mr. Manolis Mathias ID came up red-flagged from Interpol's most wanted list." Says Manning.

"Agent Christen the International press reported an explosion of luxury yachts on the Island of Crete?" Manning asks him.

"Yes sir, they were planning to use these yachts as transport for 3 ½ tons of opium to South East Asia. They never made the trip sir, and I was helped by an undercover agent with Greek Intelligence, the grooms wife, imagine my surprise?" Christen replies.

"Yes, we were told she's been working undercover for years as Perseus girlfriend, until he decided to finally pop the question, she never found anything incriminating on Gorgon." Manning tells him.

"That's because Gorgons reputation was well earned sir, he's super secretive and only trusted his partners to an extent, so she was keep in the dark." Christen replies.

"And the status of his partners, their henchmen, his son and daughter Andromeda?" the minister asks

"All dead sir with exception to his daughter Andromeda, she will no doubt inherit her father's business empire, as far as his international connections I can't speak to that." Christen replies again.

"One last thing before your dismissed Agent Christen, Winston informed me about an injection you suffered of Sodium Pentothal? And you haven't experienced anything abnormal as a result?" Manning asks curiously.

"Yes sir, dreams of sadomasochism sir. But id very much like a physical before I leave the building...... sir." Christen replies again embarrassed.

"Oh without question Agent Christen, I'm sending you for a medical exam ASAP. Before you leave here's your new assignment." Manning tells him handing him a new file marked classified. And Tarken decides to lend his two cents in this discussion before Christen leaves the office.

"James I must say I'm surprised to see you and looking very well considering the circumstances?" Tarken tells him.

"I'm a survivor Tarken, survival of the fittest. I'm sure you've read Charles Darwin in college? Sir Winston brought this to my office last night and I'll leave it here with you, and I will go over this new assignment. Has anyone heard from Pavel? We lost contact with each other sometime ago?" Christen asks.

Now Manning and Minister Forkhold exchanges smiles and glances at each other and Christen without really saying anything but Manning can't resist the urge.

"That file contains all that information Agent Christen." Manning tells him before he walk out the door.

"Very good sir, gentlemen it's been interesting. Tarken." Christen says before leaving.

He opens the door to hall again and back to the elevator hitting arrow marked down but this time the door slides open again. He steps back inside the car, the door slide close and it descends back down to the 5 floor and stops, slides open and he steps out, making his left turn down the hall to his office. He passes the same offices again and finds maybe one is occupied Room 502 before he reenters his.

He places the file in his bag, turns off the power on his PC tower, monitor, and the lights in his office. It's time for him to get back to his apartment/condo but not before he stops by the medical office for treatment, it's been a taxing week for him.

www.ingramcontent.com/pod-product-compliance
Lightning Source LLC
Chambersburg PA
CBHW050351190726

48284CB00007BB/2233